VOICES IN THE FOG

A Novel By

Thomas J. Nichols

Cover Design by Chris Hieb

Authors' Publishing House
Midland, Texas

VOICES IN THE FOG

ISBN (10): 0-9788843-9-6   or
ISBN (13): 978-0-9788843-9-0

For more information, contact:

Authors' Publishing House
2908 Shanks Drive
Midland, Texas 79705

Or visit our website:

www.authorspublishinghouse.com

Other Works

By

Thomas J. Nichols

א

Color of the Prism

The Third Dawn

Noble Generation II – Memoir

Visit his website at:

www.thomasjnichols.com

About the Author

Chief Thomas J. Nichols' law enforcement career began in the Tucson, Arizona Police Department. He retired as Deputy Chief from that department to accept the leadership of the Lubbock, Texas Police Department. He later retired from municipal policing to accept the challenges of a rapidly changing society by establishing the Lubbock School District Police Department.

Thomas still holds that position, as well as numerous assignments on local and state boards and commissions that address the issue of crime and violence. He has published local, regional, state and national articles in journals on policing techniques and school safety, and has penned an award winning novel and short story.

A graduate of the University of Arizona, magna cum laude, the chief also graduated from the FBI National Academy, the FBI Executive Development Program, the Senior Management Institute for Police, and many other training programs on organized crime, narcotic and dangerous drug investigations, and executive protection.

His experience has ranged from being a rookie jailer to administering multi-agency covert narcotic and organized crime investigations, serving at the rank of Chief for over twenty-five years, then to executive protection for heads of state. He has testified numerous times before legislative bodies on issues of crime and punishment, and was acknowledged as a criminal justice expert witness at the District Court level.

His service to the community has ranged from serving as President of Hospice of Lubbock, President of the Rotary Club of Lubbock, and as a member of the Lubbock Symphony Board. He was awarded the Salpointe

High School Alumni Service Award for his service to the community, and is a Paul Harris Fellow.

Married and a father of two grown children, the author resides on the high plains of the Llano Estacado of Texas.

PREFACE

Christie Cole was ready to begin her career as a Special Agent for the Federal Bureau of Investigation. A new graduate of the FBI Academy in Quantico, Virginia, she eagerly awaited her first assignment.

She was to accept an undercover role in a branch of the FBI she never knew existed – a secret arm of the Bureau that reached into the inner core of governments worldwide. To conceal her true identity and to protect her life and her assignment, she would take on the persona of a newly created woman, Ann Marie Beaudet. Christie Cole would cease to exist on the face of the earth.

Her investigation into the private and professional life of a Justice of the U. S. Supreme Court would take her to the depths of international intrigue, and place her in harm's way from enemies of the United States. She would soon be at the center of an international conflict of disastrous proportions reaching the countdown to nuclear war.

Ann Marie Beaudet's harrowing experiences make Voices in the Fog a page turner from beginning to end.

Voices In The Fog

CHAPTER ONE

Situated amid some of the most prime real estate in the country, the FBI Academy stretches over four hundred acres of rolling tree-lined hills and lakes of Northern Virginia. Its massive classroom buildings, dormitories, laboratories, and auditoriums dominate the landscape. Here, aspiring agents learn the skills and the values of their chosen vocation. They will memorize them until they see them in their dreams, yet before the bell tower chimes the noon hour, one of the new agents will find her lessons of values and integrity shattered.

Two men parked their sedan in the parking lot amid hundreds of others who brought families to see their sons and daughters graduate from the FBI Academy. The nattily dressed men, however, didn't have a relative among the newly sworn Special Agents. Their mission was much more ominous. They would ensnare their target and forever change her life from the neat and organized profession she sought for so many years.

*****

The auditorium was three-quarters full. A few people still straggled in. The fifty members of the graduating class sat in the front center section. Behind them, friends and family members chatted and laughed, sharing congratulations and favorite stories about their graduate, but the new agents sat quietly, their eyes focused on the stage where several men in dark suits stoically faced the audience.

The two men came into the back of the auditorium and stood for a moment near the doors. The first man was older, but the cut of his tailored charcoal suit did not disguise his trim, muscular body. His thick brown hair was lightly salted with gray, and his eyes missed nothing as they scanned the new agents.

The younger man's gaze ranged over the auditorium until he found the young woman he sought. She sat tall in the seat, her dark hair braided and neatly coiled at the nape of her neck. He touched his companion's arm. "There she is," he whispered. "First row, second from the end."

The other man nodded. "I see her. Let's sit here in the back where we can keep track of her and see if she goes to the reception." The young man nodded and they took the first two seats off the aisle.

The older one whispered, "Hard to believe how easy it is to get in here; walk in like we own the place, and nobody says squat. The old tricks still work: dress like one of the FBI executives, behave like one, and no one pays any attention to you."

His companion grinned. "Drove right into the middle of the Marine Corps base and walked through the front door of the Bureau's holy of holies. Nobody said anything to us. Hell, if I just stay in your shadow, no one will even see me. You look like you own the place."

He flipped the pages of the program to the list of graduates and ran his finger down the page. He grinned. "Here we are," he said. He showed his companion the page, his finger touching one name. Christie Cole. His voice was hushed. "That's our lady. Just another hour or two, and she's ours."

*****

Christie's heart pounded like a sledgehammer in her chest; her entire body seemed to pulse. This was her

2

moment. The one she ached for as far back as she could remember. She checked her watch. In twenty minutes she would receive her diploma and become Special Agent Christie Cole, Federal Bureau of Investigation. She gazed around the auditorium. Her classmates talked quietly among themselves. Occasionally, she met eyes with one and exchanged congratulatory smiles and victory signs.

She tried to concentrate as the ceremony began, but quickly lost interest when the Vice President of the United States launched into his speech, reading from his prepared text in a slow monotone. "The outcome of the new Vienna accord will provide stabilized currency - - "

Christie squirmed in her seat and noted with some satisfaction that she wasn't the only one having trouble concentrating on the Vice President. Above the droning prattle, she heard the shuffling of feet and the whisper of clothing as people squirmed and shifted in their seats. If the Vice President sensed he already lost his audience, he gave no sign. Even though he held the second highest office in the land, he was on Bureau time, and when the Bureau gave him twenty-three minutes to speak, it didn't mean twenty-four, so he kept to the script. Christie took some comfort in knowing the speech would be brief. The FBI managed the clock better than any basketball coach she ever saw.

She gave up on the speech, and thought instead of her grandmother. "Granny, I hope you aren't too disappointed," she thought. "I just couldn't keep on teaching school after you were gone. I know you didn't want me to be in the Bureau because you were afraid something would happen to me. But I'll be careful. I promise. Please, wherever you are, be happy for me."

Her thoughts ranged over the years leading to this moment. It was thirty years since she lost her parents in the tornado. Her grandmother took her in and nurtured her from infancy to adolescence. She bathed her, washed her clothes, taught her moral values, and guided her with gentle and loving care. Over the years, they became each other's mutual support.

Granny was a no-nonsense woman who thought speaking her mind was the best way to deal with people, and Christie tended to do the same. But their words were born of love and both knew it. Only once did a determined Christie disagree with her grandmother enough to argue against her advice. When she started to college, she wanted to study criminal justice and become an FBI agent. Granny was horrified.

Christie still saw the shock on her grandmother's thin face and the way her blue eyes, so much like Christie's own, sparked hotly. Her steel gray hair threatened to tumble out of its bun because she shook her head so violently.

"What if something happened to you, Christie?" she demanded. "You're all I have since your folks died."

Christie scoffed. "Granny, most FBI agents are paper shufflers – analysts, accountants, technocrats, and computer nerds. Most of them never fire their gun after they finish the Academy."

"I don't care." Granny's chin quivered. "I'd worry about you every minute. Why," she exclaimed, "you might have to live in New York or California, for goodness sake. When would I get to see you?"

"You could come live with me. I'll always take care of you, wherever we go."

Granny's irritation escalated. "You mean leave my home? Leave this house where your grandfather brought me as a bride? I won't do that. Never!"

Voices In The Fog

Christie argued a little more, but in her heart she knew she couldn't do anything to bring grief to her grandmother. So she followed Granny's advice to enter a "woman's" profession after college; she became a schoolteacher. It was a far cry from what she wanted to do, but it was a real job with a real paycheck; she had good hours so she could spend time with her grandmother. All in all, it worked out fine.

As the years slipped away, Christie took on a greater responsibility not only for herself, but also for her grandmother: shopping; getting her to her doctor's appointment; washing her clothes; and finally, bathing and feeding her. As Granny aged and became more dependent on her, Christie surrendered more and more of her personal life and accepted her role of caregiver with a deep love that grew stronger over the years. Granny was her only family, and Christie couldn't bear the thought of life without her.

The cycles of life are inevitable, Christie thought. Granny Cole cared for her as an infant, but in the end, Christie cared for her as though this wonderful woman was her own child. It was with profound sadness that Christie held her hand and kissed her cheek when Granny breathed her last and surrendered her life to a higher being.

Alone then, Christie knew she wanted to do something else with her life. Not that there was anything wrong with teaching school and wiping runny noses, but there were new lands; new vistas beyond the horizon. She could do more, much more. She was assertive when she needed to be, and that time arrived. She could not imagine another time in which she would ever again feel so unrestrained, so free. Her only hesitation was self-inflicted. One side of her consciousness reminded her there was always a degree of safety in staying where she was; living in Granny's house, keeping the job, keeping her life the same. Another voice in her heart told her that, after seven years of teaching, the time was right for change. It would never be better. She loved Granny with all her heart, but now she was free to chase her dream, and she would do it.

She was ready for new challenges. It was not long after she buried her grandmother that she attended a job fair, applied to and was accepted by the FBI. It happened so fast she hardly believed it. It was like a whirlwind.

Christie was even more convinced she made the right choice when Granny's house sold only days after it went on the market. Once she set the wheels in motion, she did not turn back.

*****

Abruptly aware of movement on the stage, she glanced again at her watch. Precisely on time, Director Thomas Hamilton approached the podium. The graduating class stood, made a sharp right turn and filed to stage left. They practiced this maneuver earlier so much they could do it in their sleep. The directions were specific: when the announcer says your first name, step off with your left foot. Depending on your height, it should take thirteen to fifteen steps to reach the podium. Your left foot should be forward; shake the Director's hand with your right hand as you accept the diploma with your left. The camera is focused so the picture will be snapped just as you touch the diploma. The lens is aimed at the Director, and if you are where you are supposed to be, you will have a lifetime keepsake. If not, you will have a picture of the Director shaking hands with somebody and only you will know it's you.

Voices In The Fog

"Christie Cole," announced the voice over the loud speaker.

Christie caught herself when she stepped off on her right foot, did a quick stutter step and reached the Director on the thirteenth step.

"Congratulations, Special Agent Cole," he said.

A darting smile, a shake of her hand, and she exited stage right. Three steps further and the class counselor presented her with her badge and identification card. It was over. Christie Cole, former Special Education teacher for the Sunnyside School District, Sunnyside, Texas, was now Special Agent Cole, Federal Bureau of Investigation, Department of Justice.

*****

Christie joined the other members of the graduating class in a solemn procession that turned out to be a light-hearted combination of a bunny hop and rumba line from the auditorium to the dining room. She looked forward with mixed emotions to what would be their last time together. She will not see most of them again, although she might run into one or another of them occasionally when she went back to Quantico for a re-training session, or – an exceptionally rare event – she might even serve in a field office with one of them. But overall, when they went their separate ways today, they were finished as a cohesive group. Their careers would take them to the far reaches of the world. A few were assigned to rookie jobs in the major cities – New York, Chicago, Houston, and Los Angeles. Most would be going to posts in what were referred to as mid-size urban locales – Little Rock, Tucson and Salt Lake City; still others received what were kindly identified as "less populous stations," or what the classmates realistically called "hardship outposts:" Rapid City, Fargo, Anchorage, and a few lesser known and even more remote stations that housed Bureau offices.

Two graduates, the top overall achievers in the combined courses that included Constitutional Law; Search and Seizure; Bureau Policy and Procedures; countless study sessions, term papers, audio/visual presentations; and firearms and physical fitness, were given assignments for advanced training. Christie and her friend, Roberto Sanchez, took the honors in this class, and Roberto already knew he was going to the Federal Training Academy in Glynco, Georgia, for assignment to Embassy Duty in some far away place. Christie's assignment papers only listed her new position as "To Be Determined," which generally was understood to mean the Bureau had not yet decided what or where she would be going, only that it would be some sort of advanced training or specialized assignment that was not yet finalized.

The night before, Christie, her roommate, Dierdre O'Conner, Roberto and a few other classmates celebrated in the bar, or what the students called the "slop chute." Except for Dierdre, a teetotaler, they chugged beer and shooters – back and forth between tequila and Jack Daniels until every syllable they uttered became hilariously funny. By the midnight closing time, only Christie and Roberto were left.

"Whaddya say?" Roberto said over the top of the foaming head of his beer. "I think they'll need some suave Chicano dude in Prague or Berlin, don't you?"

Christie lifted her sleepy eyes, brushed her long, dark hair back from her forehead and gave a soft laugh. "Roberto, *mi amigo,* if they're looking for some Latin lover to seduce a sleazy Czech spy into spilling her state secrets, something tells me they're not going to be searching you out."

She tilted her head and gazed at him with a puzzled expression in her blue eyes. "Roberto," she said, "I'm a little tipsy, or I wouldn't be saying this."

"S'okay. Go ahead."

"Do you realize that over all these months, you haven't screwed one woman in this whole class? Not one." She laughed and punched him on the biceps. "Hey, look, women keep track of that stuff, and you haven't tried to get one of us into your room, or bed us down in some sweet little motel room in Fredericksburg."

She took another swallow and looked at him intently. "You better be a damned good spy, 'cause you sure as hell aren't going to seduce some little whore over there and learn much about anything."

A sheepish grin crossed his face. "Hey, c'mon, you don't have to be so cruel. Besides, maybe they'll want me in Paris, where I'll have to spend all my time fighting off all those sexy French girls. Yeah, that'll be exactly what they have in mind for me. Poor me, but somebody has got to do it, so I'll sacrifice my body for my country." He drained his glass and eased it back down on the table. She reached over and wiped a smear of foam from his upper lip.

"Anyhow, what about you? Locker room buzz says you kept yourself pure for the Bureau, too." He gazed at her solemnly for a minute and spoke in a remarkably sober tone. "You know what I think? I think we're alike – we wanted more than anything to ace this program, and that meant we needed to block out everything but work."

Christie leaned forward on her elbows and gazed into his eyes. "Yeah. You got us both pegged. On the other hand, plenty of time for fooling around now. Interested?" She grinned.

Roberto laughed uproariously. "Yeah, sure. If I made a move on you, you'd be out of here in a flash, and I'd never catch up with you."

"You got that right." She lifted her final shot of tequila and shot it down in one gulp. "Shit, that burns. I've never drunk so much in my life, and now I know why."

Roberto slipped down in the booth and yawned. "I'm about to crap out, but before I do, you were going to tell me what you thought you'll be doing. If you're sober enough to think and talk at the same time." He grinned. "Are you multi-tasked, or can you only do one thing at a time?"

Christie leaned across the table and whispered. "I'm not that tipsy, so I can answer your question truthfully. Yes, I am multi-tasked. See, I'm breathing and talking, so there. I think I know what they're going to do with me. Maybe. I know they're short on class counselors, so they might keep me here for the next class. Or, maybe, they might send me to spook school and teach me how to get some Latin lover to spill his guts to me."

She laughed at her own humor, loud enough that the few remaining patrons turned to look at her. "Oops," she whispered. She straightened her shoulders, rearranged her skirt and blouse in a comic effort to restore her dignity. "Actually, I wonder if they'll send me to Headquarters in D.C. for some cool job. Maybe it will be communications analysis or organized crime. I guess I'll find out tomorrow after graduation."

"How so?" Roberto peered at her through silted eyes.

"I checked my mail before coming over here. There was a note from the Academy Director in my box."

Roberto, suddenly alert, sat up straight. "So what'd it say? Why didn't you tell me?"

She shrugged. "Nothing to tell. It just said to check with the office after the reception tomorrow and they would have some papers for me." She held her hands in front of his eyes and wiggled the fingers. "Ooooh, isn't that creepy? A secret assignment already!"

Roberto batted her hands away and shook his head. "You're some kind of woman."

"I prefer to think of myself as gifted," she said. "Anyway, I kinda like the suspense. It's like Christmas morning, and I can't wait to open my present, the biggest and best one under the tree."

She sat back, yawned and stretched out her arms over her head. "Anyhow, all I really know is that the bewitching hour is here, and at ten o'clock in the morning we're on stage with the man himself, so I think we need to call it a day."

Roberto stuffed a five-dollar tip under the empty pretzel dish and took her hand. "*Senorita*, may I walk you to your room?"

"*Si*. I am honored," she said as she tucked her hand inside his elbow. He walked her through the glass-walled tunnels to the library.

"Here is where we go different ways," he said philosophically. He kissed her cheek and said goodnight, then watched her go to her dorm. When she was out of sight, he smiled and turned toward his room. She was a hell of a great woman and he just now realized it. It was too late.

*****

Voices In The Fog

Christie looked around the dining room for Roberto and saw him standing with an older man and woman. The woman looked so much like Roberto that Christie knew it had to be his mother. He waved at her, and she started through the crush of merrymakers toward him.

She kept her eye on Roberto and his parents and strolled through the crowd of moms and dads, little brothers and sisters, aunts and uncles, all smiling and hugging the new graduates. It was a grand day for everyone. She had a sudden, sharp longing to have someone here to share this day with her, to be proud of her. Granny died almost two years ago, but Christie usually didn't mind being alone. Everybody's life was different, and hers was no exception. The unexpected pang vanished and she watched the people with an amused smile. She saw several children whose eyes lit up when they looked at their brother's or sister's shiny new badge. They couldn't wait until they were old enough to join the next generation of Special Agents.

She paused momentarily to let a little knot of well-wishers move their graduate toward one of the serving tables draped in red, white, and blue bunting. Her eyes rested on a man she didn't recognize. There was something funny about him, though. He was watching her. She was sure of it, but when she looked at him, he averted his eyes and scanned the opposite end of the room. She was positive she didn't know him. She would certainly remember if they ever met. She smiled to herself. He might be her type, if she had a type. Tall enough she could look up to him in her medium heels that took her to six feet. Slim, but not thin. A sharp nose except for a slight list toward the left. "Been broken a time or two," she thought. Thick, burnished, blond hair cut close in back, but with enough left that a woman could run her fingers through it, if one was so inclined. She shook her head mentally. During the seventeen weeks of the course, she didn't have the time or the inclination to think about men. The end of the course must've created a void that her subconscious thought needed to be filled, even with nonsense, if necessary. Casually, he turned and headed toward the door. She watched and smiled. Too bad she hadn't met him before. Something about him definitely caught her attention.

She found Roberto and his parents standing next to the punch bowl. "*Oye*, Roberto," she said. "Congratulations."

Roberto put his arm around her waist and kissed her cheek. "Mom, Dad, this is the lady I was telling you about. She tied me for top score, and," he grinned and squeezed her, "she can drink me under the table."

Christie felt heat rising in her neck. She gave Roberto a quick jab to the ribs. "Only on very special occasions," she told the elder Sanchez. "Occasions like graduating from the FBI Academy."

After visiting with Roberto and his parents for a few minutes, Christie took her leave and moved on to another group standing at the dessert table. She found her roommate, Dierdre, nibbling an éclair and sipping her latté. Christie took a plate and filled it with an éclair and some carrot cake, poured a cup of hot coffee, and edged in between Dierdre and some little kids.

"What about your mom and dad?" Christie asked.

"Well, you know what I told you." Dierdre looked down at her feet, swallowed hard and held back her tears, "about Mom's little drinking problem. Dad called my cell phone a few minutes ago and said she had gone on a binge last night and was in no condition to come."

A single tear trembled on her left eyelash, then slid down her cheek, leaving a trail like a narrow scar.

"I'm sorry," Christie said. She put an arm around Dierdre and hugged her. "I'm really sorry. So, what are you going to do?"

"I've got my car packed and ready, so I think I'll finish up here and head out. It's a long way to Fayetteville. I can get a couple hundred miles under my belt before I stop for the night."

Christie put her empty cup and saucer on the table. "C'mon, I'll walk you to your car."

"No, please," Dierdre whispered. "I just want to be alone, but thanks anyway." She wiped away more tears that were coursing down her cheeks. "Thanks for being such a good friend. You've helped me over some really rough spots."

Christie smiled. "That works both ways. I'm glad they put us together." She shook her head. "Seventeen weeks, and every time we thought we'd have a free minute, they threw another project at us. I can't believe how the time got away. Now, suddenly, it's over. It's amazing." She laid her hand on Dierdre's shoulder. "Maybe we'll run into each other from time to time. We can e-mail each other and stay in touch that way."

The two new federal agents hugged, looked down at the éclairs, and each scooped up one. "For the road," Dierdre said before she stuffed it into her mouth. They faced each other silently, and Christie's eyes suddenly began to burn.

"Special Agents don't cry," she said aloud. "Goodbye, Dierdre."

"So long, Christie. See you around."

Voices In The Fog

Christie watched Dierdre work her way through the crowd, and in a few seconds she was out of sight. Christie eased herself around the tables and chairs, grabbed a carrot stick and nibbled it as she moved in the direction of the door. She reached it, paused for a moment, but did not look back. Everyone's life was different, but in some ways they were the same. Dierdre would survive, and so would she. They were strong women. They could manage alone.

CHAPTER TWO

Now it was time to find the Academy Director as instructed in the note she received the day before. She took only a few steps down the corridor when she felt a hand on her shoulder. She jumped with a start, not having heard the footsteps behind her. Her heart pounded as she whirled and found herself facing the tall man she noticed earlier in the dining room. "Who are you? What do you want?"

"Relax, Agent Cole. I didn't mean to startle you." His smile was electric, lighting up his smoke gray eyes with enough power to illuminate all of Quantico. "You got away from the reception before I could find you, and I need to visit with you for a minute."

She quickly sized him up. Navy blue suit, crisp white shirt, and red and blue striped tie. A poster boy for patriotism. "Have we met?" she asked.

"No, we haven't. I'm Rod McCarren." He extended his hand and she gripped it firmly.

"Nice to meet you, Mr. McCarren. Are you with the Bureau?"

"Not exactly." He gave her an 'aw-shucks' grin. "But the Director sent me to get you. There's someone he wants you to meet." McCarren stepped past her and started down a long hall with a series of doors on either side. "Follow me, please, Agent Cole," he commanded. He stepped out at a brisk pace, his gleaming black wingtips echoing on the tile floor. Christie hesitated a moment. It seemed so strange. This was a man she never met. Nevertheless, she recalled the note ordering her to get her duty assignment after the graduation exercise. She still did not take a step. "Is this about my assignment?" she asked.

Voices In The Fog

McCarren turned back to her and nodded. "Come along, please. He's waiting." He walked swiftly through the revolving doors, leaving her to pause and catch the next swing. By the time she got through, McCarren was already going past the counter and the information clerk's desk, then into the hallway to the administration offices.

"Excuse me, but where exactly are we going?" she demanded. She hurried and grabbed McCarren by his shoulder. He glanced back at her without the brilliant smile he flashed only moments before, and gave her a curt look. "You'll see, Agent Cole."

Wondering if she was suckered by a pair of broad shoulders and a million dollar smile, she followed him down the hall, suddenly aware that all of the offices were closed and the staff left the building. The building was eerily quiet. No secretaries or clerks; most of the lights off. No clicking typewriters or computer keyboards. Only a deadly quiet suite of administrative offices, closed for the weekend. Christie stopped in her tracks. She wasn't afraid. She was in the heart of a Marine Corps base and in the middle of the FBI Academy. What could happen to her here?

She heard the gong of the bell toll the noon hour as it echoed throughout the empty building. Apprehension grasped her heart like an iron fist.

"Just a damn minute. Who are you and where are you taking me?" she yelled. "What the hell are you up to? You try anything funny with me and I'll rip your balls off and feed them to you for dinner. Do you understand me?" She pointed her finger at the back of his head, but he ignored her and continued along the corridor. He stopped and turned to her at the last door on her right.

"Here is where I leave you, Agent Cole." He opened the door and stepped aside. "He's waiting for you." He brushed past her without another word.

Christie stood in the quiet hall, listening, and half turned to watch him stride down the hall. She took a deep breath and, slowly, put one foot in front of the other, pausing to listen for any sound other than her own heartbeat, but there was nothing. She reached the open door and inched her head inside, not knowing what to expect. Maybe it was the Director. Maybe it was the President himself. Who knew? Or, maybe nothing but one last practical joke concocted by her trainee buddies.

"Come in, Miss Cole." The voice was soft, but she sensed an underlying layer of steel beneath his words.

She stepped forward, quickly taking in the surroundings. A spartan office. Not as big as her dorm room and not furnished any better, either. An inexpensive oak desk, a couple of chairs, and a stack of boxes in the corner. A fire exit door on the opposite side of the room and that was it. Nothing else. The man seated behind the desk was dressed in a charcoal suit that could have been fashioned by the same tailor as the one Rod McCarren wore. Christie judged him to be in his late fifties or early sixties. Brown hair sprinkled with gray, styled, not cut. Manicured nails. A late-in-life James Bond, she thought, as she stopped in front of the desk.

"Be seated, please," he said, gesturing to a chair.

"You're not the Director," she accused.

"Quite right, Special Agent Cole. We have not met formally, although I know a great deal about you." He smiled benignly and leaned back in his chair, poking an unlit pipe between his teeth. "Government buildings are all the same. No smoking." He paused and looked into her eyes, a piercing gaze that made her uncomfortable.

She didn't know what was going on, and her first instinct was to turn around and march out that door. She thought again about the note. "Excuse me, sir," she said. "But I'd really like to know who you are and why we're here."

"Simple enough," he replied. He leaned forward, clasped his hands and propped his elbows on the desk. "Please sit down. This may take a little time." She eased herself into the chair and smoothed the navy skirt over her thighs.

"We think you have too much talent to be a run-of-the-mill FBI agent. I'm here to offer you something better. Much better."

Christie shook her head. "No way. I've worked too hard to get here, and I'm not giving it up now."

"We're not asking you to give up anything. We're asking you to be more than you ever thought you could be. It is precisely because of your hard work that we're offering you this special assignment."

She gazed at him sternly. "I don't know who you are or what you do."

"My name is Alfred Williams." He sat back in his chair, thoughtfully examined his cold pipe, then continued without looking at her. "The assignment I am offering will enable you to provide a service greater than any ever offered by the Bureau or any other agency. Very few people who wear the badge will ever have the opportunity we are extending to you at this very moment. Not the Secret Service, the CIA, NSA, or any of the other agencies with all those different names and initials."

She shook her head again. "I don't understand."

"Patience, please. I'll explain." He hesitated for a moment. "You're aware of how the Bureau has been re-organized: The Counter-Terrorism Division is taking in the National Joint Terrorism Task Force; the Bureau has a new Office of Intelligence that was the bailiwick of the CIA, a new Cyber Division; now there is a split in the Laboratory Division, into a new Investigative Technology Division, and an updated Laboratory Division. The tight bureaucratic reins are being loosened, but none of that really affects us. We have always been different, and will continue to do so. Of course, we want you to be with us."

"Us?" She echoed. "Who's us? And why me?

"I'll get to that presently." He paused to give it a second to sink in, then continued. "Not more than one in a thousand agents will ever have the opportunity I'm giving you now. You will be paid nearly double what a Special Agent receives; you will retire at seventy-five percent salary after twenty years. And," his face suddenly became cold, his brow furrowed, his eyes pierced her like a dagger, "you will see a world you never thought existed."

Christie sat, transfixed. A shiver ran down her spine. She sucked in a deep breath to quiet her racing heartbeat. "Who are you? Who do you work for?" She looked around the room and gathered her thoughts. "Mr. Williams, if that's your name, you scare the hell out of me. Are you the Bureau?"

"Not exactly. Not the Bureau as you know it to be, and not as most people know it to be. As far as anyone is concerned, we do not exist." Williams slowly scooted his chair back from the desk, got up, and walked to the bookshelf.

She hadn't noticed it. He took an Ipod from the shelf, returned to his chair, and handed it to her. "Put the earphones on and listen for a minute. Tell me what you hear."

Christie fitted the earphones into her ears, sat back, and listened. It was soothing.

"Okay," Williams commented. "What is it?"

"Surf, I know that sound from where I grew up on the coast."

"Indeed. But listen some more. Tell me what you hear."

She leaned back, crossed her arms over her chest, and closed her eyes. Voices in the background. She couldn't make them out, but voices – several of them - perhaps men - maybe a woman, too.

"Tell me about it now," Williams said.

She pulled the Ipod free, placed it on his desk, and offered an innocent smile. "Hmm, people talking, but I'm not sure how many of them. It's too mixed up, and too much of the surf to really make it out clearly."

"Kind of like hearing voices in the fog, isn't it? You hear them, but it's unclear which direction they're coming from, or even what they're saying, right?"

She nodded in agreement. "Sort of."

"You lived along the coast and have seen that heavy fog roll in, haven't you?"

"Sure," she replied.

"You might even have been in your own neighborhood, but couldn't see your house even though you knew it was there." He leaned forward across his desk and continued. "You may have heard someone calling you, but couldn't tell where they were. The fog was the master of deceit. It blanketed everything. What you knew was there disappeared. Sounds and voices got lost somewhere in it. Things were mixed up."

Voices In The Fog

"I never really thought of it that way," she nodded, "but, yes. A heavy fog can put a blanket over the city. It's like a ghost town. You can't see anything, as you say, even if you know they are there."

"Exactly, and that is where we come in. What we see in public often is much different than what transpires behind closed doors. Sometimes it's legitimate, sometimes not. I can tell you only this much. Come to work for us, and in no time you will know more than you ever wanted to know. Come with us and sort out the voices in the fog. Help us find the truth. Help us cut through the deceit."

Christie felt like she was in a tomb. The room was deathly quiet. Not a sound from anywhere penetrated it. This wasn't a game; not some dirty trick from her friends. This was real, and it verged on being frightening. It was exhilarating, too, she thought. The only sound was the soft roar of the surf when she picked up the Ipod and held it to her ears. She listened, mesmerized as the sound softened, and then stopped.

Williams took it from her and returned it to the shelf. He gave a half-hearted laugh as he returned to his desk. "Fog along the coastline can be a beautiful act of nature, but when it's manmade in an attempt to conceal an action against our government or that of our allies, we," he pointed to her and then back to himself, "we have to navigate through it and bring the clear picture, the clear voices, back to our legally instituted government. Then we can respond appropriately.

"With our help, democracy can flourish. People can have the rights and privileges of a free world. They can prosper. They can live together in harmony. Democracy means freedom; people are free to do what they want." He paused for a second, then continued. "But, there are people in our country, and other countries, who keep trying to lay a blanket of fog over the world so things will fall their way to the detriment of others."

He sat again in his chair and leaned back. "It's been going on for generations: farther back than we have records. Everybody is trying to do their own thing, to get things their way, and that's where we come in. To see that it doesn't happen. At least, not every time."

He smiled when she sat back, crossed her legs, and adjusted her shirt. He had her interest. "We find things getting out of kilter – whether it's because of a nation or some political powerhouse, or maybe some private strongman. It might be anyone, anywhere. Might be a Jew or a Muslim; might be the Pope himself. Could be anybody, from any walk of life. They come in all sizes and shapes. Our job is to try to figure out why or how they got to the point where they want to upset the balance of power, and then we fix it. Sounds pretty damn simple, but it's not. In fact, sometimes it seems nearly impossible, but we hang in there 'til we get the job done.

"We won't ask you to torture or murder somebody. That'll not be your job. Your job will be to learn their secrets. Then others among us will deal with them."

"If you're not the Bureau, and not the CIA, who are you?"

"I didn't say we aren't the Bureau. I just said we aren't the Bureau as you know it to be." He smiled and cocked his head. "We're a different animal. We don't have a name. Names are troublesome. They get you identified. They get you highlighted. They bring attention."

Williams bit on the stem of his pipe. "No name, no printed budget. Nothing but quiet, efficient, and effective work to keep this little planet spinning as nature intended it to do."

Christie focused on the man across the desk from her; mature, but not old mentally or physically; slow and deliberate speech; a hint of a Texas accent, albeit a long time since he had been immersed in it; a man on a mission. She narrowed her mind's eye on him. He was analytical, thoughtful, careful and precise. He was a mystery: he knew it, and played the role well.

"Frankly, sir, I don't understand you. The Academy never taught anything about this. Or for that matter, they didn't teach anything about anybody like you." She took a deep breath and mustered up her courage. "I'm not sure I trust you, Mr. Williams. Is this some bizarre joke? You're losing me. I can't figure out what you're up to. If we're going anywhere with this, you owe me a better explanation."

"No joke," Williams said softly. "Only a sad truth about what people do to get what they want. It's a huge theater of the absurd. And your job, Miss Cole," he said as he again leaned forward, hands flat on the desk, "is to help us keep the world balanced. Help us keep things the way they were meant to be."

Christie shook her head in disbelief. "You're assigning a new agent, a greenhorn, to a situation of this magnitude? Why?"

Williams leaned back in his chair. His eyes pierced her like daggers thrust into her heart. "Many reasons. Your intelligence and your diligence. Your commitment to your country was another factor. Everything we know about you tells us you belong with us."

Christie didn't think she was in danger of dying, at least not at that moment, but her entire life flashed before her eyes. Everything? They knew everything about her? "Just exactly what do you know about me?" she demanded.

He looked at her, gave a slow, deep exhale, pulled the middle desk drawer open, and took a manila folder from it. He opened the folder and studied it for a minute. He looked at her; sympathy was evident in his gaze. "We know a tornado struck your home when you were three years old. Both of your parents were killed. A volunteer rescue worker found you under a pile of debris."

Christie nodded and smiled involuntarily. "Yes. Granny told me the man who rescued me was an FBI agent who worked in Galveston." She looked earnestly at Williams. "When I was older, I tried everything I knew to find and thank him. I didn't have a name and the FBI couldn't give me any information about any agents who might have been posted in that area, but that started my interest in the Bureau. I owe my life to that man. To me, he has always been the greatest person on earth. I've never been able to thank him for saving my life."

Williams nodded his understanding. "You can, Christie. That's what I'm telling you. You won't have to give up your ideals or your goals. You'll just be redirecting them."

Uncertain, she gestured to the open folder on the desk. "The information about my parents was included in my background check when I applied to the Academy. It's no deep, dark secret. So what else do you know about me?"

Williams glanced down at the folder again. "After your parents' death, you went to live with your widowed grandmother who lived on land that was occupied by your grandfather's family for generations. It was near Sunnyside, east of Houston." He glanced up at her, then back to the folder. "Your grandmother guided you as you developed a strong traditional culture and education. When you were in middle school, you played clarinet in the orchestra. You were a member of the marching band for the Sunnyside Hurricanes in high school."

She saw herself as a scrawny, gangly junior high student, taller than her classmates and so uncoordinated she embarrassed herself numerous times, stumbling over her feet, bumping the edges of tables in the cafeteria, dropping her book bag. She'd wondered if she would ever get through that stage – in fact, she was afraid she never would, that she was destined to be a klutz for life. Thankfully, it didn't work out that way.

"You loved athletics and made first string soccer and basketball teams. You were named to the Regional All-Academic Girls Varsity Team in high school."

Christie grinned. "All in my resume."

"You were awarded a full scholarship to Texas A & M, where you received a degree in Elementary Education, with a minor in Government. You continued playing clarinet in the college orchestra."

Her heart flew into her throat and she ducked her head. Oh, no. How much did he really know about her college years? When she raised her head, she was suddenly aware that Williams was gazing at her, reciting the facts of her life without looking at the folder.

"After graduation from A & M, you taught Special Needs Students in the Sunnyside school system where you were named Teacher of the Year after your first year. By your fifth year, because of your professional demeanor and ability to communicate with persons of every walk of life, and to parent and civic groups, you were testifying to committees of the State Legislature on issues ranging from unfunded mandates to the personnel evaluation system."

Christie waved her hand. "Again, résumé. It's all there."

"Not quite." Williams paused, then pulled a picture from the file and slid it across the desk to her.

She froze, then slowly reached for the picture. She cupped it in her hands. A little boy in a soccer uniform, smiling at the camera. Dark hair spilled across his eyebrows. He was missing a front tooth, but the smile that stretched from ear to ear was open and happy and totally uninhibited. It was exactly like her smile. Her entire body quivered. She gasped to catch her breath.

"Jason Christopher," Williams said. "Nine years old. Father, Dalton Quigby, a bassoonist in the orchestra at Texas A & M. Mother, Christie Cole. You had your baby when you were twenty-one. He was born at the Boerne Home for unwed mothers, just outside of San Antonio."

She fought to speak past the constriction in her chest, but he shook his head. "Don't even ask. I won't tell you where he is or who his parents are. You gave him up knowing you would never see him again." He came around the desk and sat on the edge. "He's happy. He's got a brother and sister, and parents who love him dearly. You have to be satisfied with that."

Christie's vision blurred. She tried to speak, but her throat was too tight. She fumbled in her purse, found some mints and hurriedly popped two of them in her mouth.

"You're not going to hurt him!" she raged when she could speak. "Is this how you operate? Blackmail? Threats?"

"Sometimes. But not this time. Not with you, Miss Cole. The truth is, we all have secrets. You and I, and everyone else. The only reason I showed you this picture of your son was to remind you of that fact. Everyone. Some worse than others, that's all. But, some people's secrets are so bad they ruin their own lives and the lives of other people; in some cases, millions of other people. There are ways, though, of discovering those secrets and using them to correct injustice and greed, to keep power out of the hands of those who would ruin us all.

"You? Yes, you have a secret. But it's not a tragedy and it isn't dangerous to anyone. You're a wonderful woman who had a baby when you were an unmarried co-ed. Your life and his went on very well."

"Very well?" she thought. "I was terrified at having to tell Granny. I thought my heart would break when that son-of-a-bitch denied his child. I cried myself to sleep every night in the Boerne Home, knowing that each new day brought me closer to losing my baby forever. Even now, not a day passes that I don't think of him, wonder about him, long for him. And we both have done very well?"

As if sensing her thoughts, Williams stepped around the desk, sat on the edge, and patted her knee. His voice softened. "I know it hasn't been easy for you, but throughout your life, including the loss of your son, you have shown the strength and character we prize in our people. So now, I'm making you a once in a lifetime offer. We looked at how you did in college, how well you performed as a teacher, how you handled the academy – everything. You're an amazing woman. You don't merely do well. You excel at everything you touch. Your academics are top notch; you're assertive but not aggressive; you handle stress better then most; you're flexible, athletic, and, an additional asset, you're beautiful." He allowed himself a small, teasing smile. "That always helps when you're trying to get information from men who don't want to give it up. You have that open face, All-

American Girl Scout appearance. You're like a young colt ready to be trained to run in the Kentucky Derby. You're perfect for what we do. Trust me. Come with us today."

"And how would I do that, if I don't have to kill anyone, which I won't. And I won't torture anyone either, so how would I help?"

"Everybody has one or two deep, dark secrets. All we have to do is find the ones they consider sensitive. That's all. Nothing more. Then we simply help that person or group or whoever else it is, to see the real truth. And when they understand the truth, we help them do whatever it is they need to do to get things balanced the way it's supposed to be. Nothing more," he said.

She saw her opening when Williams returned to his chair, leaned back, and laid his pipe on a notepad. The ball was in her court. She took a deep breath to steel her courage, grabbed her purse from the floor and started to get up. "I'm outa . . ."

"Just hold it right there, Agent Cole!" The tenor of his voice cracked her resolve like a slap in the face. He bolted from his chair and glared at her. "Hold it right there. We're not against the world, but we're fighting a hell of a dirty war to keep this country we love in the place we all want it to be, and that's not bad. Just different." His voice softened. "Just different."

She stared at him in bewilderment. This was totally unacceptable. She needed more time, more information. She couldn't just walk away from the FBI. Not after all that work. "Now? Right this minute? I have to make a choice that will change my life forever?"

"Today, or never. Five minutes after you leave this office it'll be the janitor's storeroom again. I was never here, and neither were you. Walk out the front door and go be another FBI agent. Or," he said with a gesture toward the fire exit, "go out that door to a new life. A life you never dreamed existed."

He waited and watched her, seeing that her mind was racing, overwhelmed with questions. She was trying to get a clear picture of what he was talking about; her uncertainty showed in her entire body. Her breast heaved as she breathed. Perspiration dotted her brow.

He knew she wanted to do the right thing, but nothing could have prepared her for what he threw at her.

"You should know something else," he said. "Come with us today, and Christie Cole will disappear from the face of the earth."

"What?" she exclaimed.

"You heard me. Christie Cole will fade away to a distant memory."

She took a deep breath. Sweat ran down her back. "I would never see Roberto again? Or Dierdre? Or any of my other classmates or anyone else I know?"

He shook his head, his dark eyes piercing into her very core. "No."

"I don't know," she murmured.

"There are others who will stop at nothing to achieve their ends," he answered. "Nothing. You see, my dear, Christie Cole has records all over the place. Work, school, everywhere. She can be found out, and if you're found out, you jeopardize our entire organization." He smiled grimly. "You could even be killed. In fact, if you were discovered, you undoubtedly would be killed."

He shook his head and continued. "We can't have that, so you have to start fresh, and we can take care of that for you. Everything new. You'll become a whole new person. Within a week, every computerized record of

Voices In The Fog

Christie Cole will be gone from the face of the earth. Everything – credit cards, drivers license, birth certificate – everything. For all intents and purposes, she never existed."

Christie sat back in her chair, numb. It was too much. She'd heard of rogue groups with loose affiliations within the government, but thought they were the figment of too active imaginations. Surely, Alfred Williams wasn't asking her to join such a group. She adjusted her skirt again and wiped her brow with the back of her hand. She shook her head in disbelief. "I'm overwhelmed. I don't know. I need time to think it over, please. I just can't tell you now what I want to do. I can't go this fast. I can't make such a decision right this minute."

"There is no time, Miss Cole. It's now or never. We'll give you a career beyond your wildest dreams. More money than you ever imagined making. And you will serve your country with honor and dignity. You may be assured of that." He offered a hard smile and continued, "But you'll never get a plaque or your picture in the paper. Nothing like that. What we do, we do for the service of our country. Nothing more. Miss Cole, will you join us?"

Christie slowly got up from her chair, conscious that her body language manifested her doubt. She looked down a dusty old globe that sat on the edge of his desk, gave it a delicate twirl, and watched it go around. "That's how it's supposed to be, isn't it Mr. Williams?"

"Precisely. Will you come with us and help us keep it that way?"

"I can't. I just can't," she whispered. She moistened her dry lips. "I've wanted this job for years, and you're asking me to give it up, just like that." She shook her head. "I can't turn my back on the Bureau. I'm sorry Mr. Williams, but the answer is no. I had a skeleton in my

31

closet and you've exposed it for no reason. So why should I trust you?"

"Because you're a patriot." He smiled, reached out, and took her hands in his. "And, your skeleton knows how to dance, so no, you're not ruined. You're just like the rest of us – human! Not perfect, but you'll serve your country because you have been approved by the highest office in the land."

Christie stepped away and turned to face him head-on. "The highest office? You mean. . .?"

"Yes, Agent Cole, I do mean."

She pulled up her chair and sat down again. Her subconscious reached out and tapped her on her shoulder. Her fingers trembled; her heart pounded. "The President?"

Williams nodded. "Will you go with us? Now. Not an hour from now. Not tomorrow. I mean this very moment – or never."

"People will miss me. My friends will wonder where I am. Roberto? Dierdre? What about them? All my classmates know me. At some point, someone will ask about me, and you can't just say I never existed. They know me. They'll ask questions."

"It's a pretty simple equation, actually. Time plus distance equals a lessening of friendships. You'll be surprised how fast the memory fades. Of course, there is always a little more. You know, computer failures; lost files; people quit; some die. Believe me, Miss Cole, in two years most of the people you know today will not have more than a casual thought about you. I know that sounds heartless, but it's a fact of life. Not one that I or the Bureau invented, just a simple cold fact of life."

Could she do it? Give up her identity? Could the woman who was Christie Cole cease to exist? She took a breath and held it a long moment. Williams couldn't force her to join him, but she knew if she rejected this job, she would forever wonder where it would have taken her. Perhaps forever regret it. "What about my car and my stuff?" Her voice was weak, a reflection of her lessening resolve.

Williams smiled and pointed at the stack of boxes in the corner. "Those are yours right there. We had your things packed while you were in the auditorium." He paused and smiled at her. "We know you well. We knew you'd come with us. You'll never regret it.

"You'll be going to a special place for training. Your personal possessions will go with you. We'll handle it, and take care of your car." He opened the desk drawer again, removed another envelope, and slipped it across the desk to her. "Twenty one-hundred dollar bills. Not bad for a worn out Honda with over 150,000 miles on it. I believe you've been talking about getting a new car, haven't you? This is more than you would ever get on trade-in."

Special Agent Christie Cole looked at Mr. Williams. Tears flowed gently from her eyes and ran down her cheek. "I won't be an agent anymore, will I?"

Williams looked at his watch: not quite two hours since the graduation exercise began. "I'm afraid not, Miss Cole. In fact, there's no record of you ever having been with the Bureau."

CHAPTER THREE

Christie walked through the fire exit, her purse slung over her shoulder, gripping a sealed envelope Williams gave her. She shut the door gently behind her and started down the staircase. The click of her heels echoed off the walls. A flickering florescent light bounced its rays over the landing where she came to a heavy metal fire door. She stopped for a second, took a deep breath, then opened it and went into the sally port.

Everything was as Williams described. It was a well-lighted garage. A floral delivery truck was parked there. EVERGREEN FLOWERS TRIANGLE, VIRGINIA was emblazoned with green, floral shaped letters on the side of the van. An elderly man wearing a white jumpsuit hopped down from the driver's seat as she went down the steps.

"G'day miss. At your service," he said with an Irish brogue. He opened the sliding door and showed her to a bench in the back of the truck. He flicked on an overhead light so she could see in the dark confines of the truck. He held out his hand to her when she sat down. "And the envelope, please," he said with flourish. She gave him the envelope which he tucked into his pocket as he slid the door shut.

She couldn't see him, but heard him clomping up the stairs. The door slammed shut. She sat alone in the shadows of the dim overhead lights, her mind searching for what lay ahead. Long, quite minutes slipped away. Suddenly, the silence was broken by the cockney Irish brogue of her custodian.

"Didn't forget ya, Miss," the voice called from atop the stairwell.

Voices In The Fog

The thumping and clunking of a dolly being guided down the stairs filled the garage. Moments later, the van door slid open. "Here you go, madam, all your things right here."

Christie scooted aside as the kindly gentleman loaded three pieces of luggage and six cardboard boxes into the truck. It was everything she brought with her to Quantico, including all the things she packed last night and this morning. A cold chill ran down her back. She fingered the tape on the box, knowing what was inside. Photographs of her parents and grandparents, as well as a few letters from friends back in Texas. She thought of Amos, the dilapidated brown bear that her grandmother gave her right after her parents died. She left the bear in Texas in storage with everything else she saved when she sold Granny's house. Now she wished for him. Would she ever see him again? Would everything she owned vanish from the face of the earth with Christie Cole?

Her guardian, at least for the moment, ran around the front of the van and slipped into the driver's seat. He hit the garage door opener, started the engine and drove away, leaving behind the final vestiges of Special Agent Christie Cole.

*****

The van was windowless except for the two front side windows and the windshield. She leaned forward and gazed out as they drove along the main road of the academy, a road she traveled so many times in the past seventeen weeks. Memories flooded her. A solitary tear flowed slowly down her cheek. They drove slowly past the buildings and trees, the lake, the Marine barracks, and

35

dozens of other little reminders that now were drowning her with their importance. This was where she wanted to be. She loved the gentle countryside. It was so different from her Texas home.

In the distance, she saw a platoon of Marine officer candidates jogging across the field. Things that passed through her life so smoothly now tugged at her heart not to be left behind. They were, in all likelihood, never to be seen again.

She glimpsed a dying tree, one she watched surrender its life in the few short months she spent at the Academy. Life goes on, she thought. So does mine. She leaned forward and tapped the driver on his shoulder.

"Excuse me, sir," she asked. "But where are we going?"

"Sorry, miss, can't tell you" he replied as his eyes met hers in the rearview mirror. "You know the rules," he said with a grin and his pleasant accent. "Promise you though, I'll get you there quickly. Now just sit back and relax."

The van left the academy grounds and swung onto Interstate 95, northbound toward Washington, D.C. Christie relaxed a little, kicked off her shoes and shifted about to find a place where she could lean back, yet still see out the front window. She watched as familiar landmarks zipped by, and from time to time she looked over the driver's shoulder to see the speedometer. He evidently intended to keep his promise to get her there quickly, wherever there was, settling in between seventy and seventy-five miles per hour, weaving effortlessly through the Saturday afternoon traffic. Through Woodbridge, on to Arlington, then following the signs to Ronald Reagan Washington National Airport. She watched closely as they avoided the passenger loading and unloading area, passed the airfreight gates and on to the private air service terminal. The driver pulled up to the gate, waved to the uniformed security guard, and eased the van onto the tarmac.

"Here you go, miss." He looked over his shoulder and smiled, bringing the van to a halt alongside a small jet. Christie stretched her legs and stepped out, blinded for a moment by the mid-afternoon sun. Suddenly overwhelmed with doubt, she stepped back. Her hand was still on the van's door.

The side door of the jet opened, and Rod McCarren came down the steps.

"I didn't expect to see you," She said, her voice cool.

"Hello, again. I'm your tour guide for this part of your trip." He gestured toward the plane. "Please, come with me."

Christie threw a quick glance at the plane, then back to McCarren. "C'mon and see your transportation. Not everyone gets to travel in her own private jet," McCarren said.

She tentatively put her foot on the first step. The driver got out of the van, leaving the engine running, and trotted toward them. He handed McCarren the envelope she gave him earlier. He gave her a smile and a nod of his head.

"I'll get your things," he said.

She watched as the driver, with practiced and efficient movements she thought were evidence he did this many other times, transferred her possessions from the truck to the cargo bay of the plane.

"Enjoy your trip. Glad to have you on board with us," he quipped. As quickly as he came, he darted like a little gremlin back to the truck and zipped out the gate into the weekend traffic.

Voices In The Fog

She climbed up the steps and stood on the top one a moment before going into the passenger compartment. She glanced around and noticed the lettering on the tail: NASA, and a couple of numbers. She didn't catch them in her hurried glance: 705, 205, or something like that. Nevertheless, it put her at ease to be able to gather at least a little bit of information on her

own. "Lear" was embossed on the hatch, so if nothing else, at least she knew she was in a government Lear Jet. It may not be a lot, but at least she knew something. NASA. Was that her new employer? No. Not much likelihood of that, she thought. Probably just an effort by whomever she worked for to keep their identity quiet and, at the same time, to make some effort to pool resources with another agency. All part of the government's effort to be more responsible stewards of the taxpayer's money. At least, that was what she was told at the Academy.

She looked around the dim cabin. It was filled along the bulkheads with electronic equipment, dials, gauges and different kinds and shapes of radar or some other kinds of monitoring screens, and the most valuable of all inventions, microwave oven. From the rear section, Rod unfolded two Coleet seats that were recessed into the wall and locked them down. He invited her to take one and waited until she was perched on its edge before taking the other one.

"Where are we going?" she asked anxiously.

"Here are your orders." McCarren broke the seal open, removed the single piece of paper, and handed it to her without looking at it. "We have a fairly long flight and there's a great deal we have to do, beginning with this – your new identity. Memorize everything here. It's the new you. The new person. I'll be briefing you, as well: testing you, as it were, so you'll be thoroughly familiar with your new identity by the time we get to our destination"

She unfolded the legal size paper and examined it dubiously. "Not much here."

McCarren grinned. "It's enough. First, we need to talk. We'll be in the air in a few minutes, and there are some things you need to know, so listen to me."

She heard the whine as one engine and then the other came to life.

"We'll be on this plane for a few hours. We'll stop for fuel once, but you can't get off to stretch your legs or anything. The pilot and navigator won't come back to visit or speak to us at all. They don't know you, and you won't know them. I'm sorry, Christie, but that's the way we work. Secrecy is our byword. That way none of us can ever slip and give up anything or anybody."

It was suddenly too much for her. It was too much secrecy, too much change. There was too much she needed to know.

As if sensing her discomfort, Rod paused for a second. "Don't be afraid. You'll see. It works very well in the long run. Although at times, I must admit, we all get a little lonesome to visit with somebody about work, but you'll more or less get used to it. Anyway, it'll be dark by the time we reach our destination. Then we'll transfer to a helicopter for a quick trip to your first assignment." He gave a short laugh. "And you thought you were out of school. Well, you're back in again for a few weeks."

"Can you tell me what kind of school or where I'm heading?"

"I'm going to tell you as much as I can. It'll take a while. But we have the time."

She adjusted herself to get more comfortable. "Shoot."

Voices In The Fog

"You'll be in school with several other students; some men, some women. Some will be farther along in the course than you; others will come in behind you. This isn't a regular school with standard classrooms and teachers, homework and term papers and all those other things we think of when we talk about school. This is an alternative school, and other countries have their own training facilities very much like ours. This isn't a Hollywood spy thriller. This is the real thing. Some of it is glamorous, some of it is not. At the Academy, you really only had the basics. Now you get the advanced course. You learn the arts and sciences of espionage. Surveillance techniques, photography, communication, documentation, coding, decoding, analysis, linkage, lateral thinking, extrapolation. All of these and much more: Islamic culture; nationalism; oriental philosophy; communism; capitalism. And above all, you'll learn to remember the simple philosophy of World War II, 'Loose lips sink ships.'"

The cabin lights came on at the same time as the "Fasten Seat Belt" sign. She sat back, closed her eyes, and listened to the sounds of the engines. She was pushed back into her seat as the plane roared down the runway. She started counting when the pilot accelerated . . . 33, 34, 35, 36, rotation, airborne, a pause, then wheels up and climbing.

Rod pointed out the small refrigerator with some sandwiches and drinks, a jug of Starbucks coffee, and the latrine. When the fasten seat belts light went off, she excused herself and went to the lavatory. She splashed water on her face, touched up her makeup, then paused to look at herself in the mirror. It was the same old Christie, but she felt unexplainably different.

Voices In The Fog

I've made a huge change in my life and it'll never be the same, she thought. She took a deep breath and returned to the cabin. She pulled a Styrofoam cup from an overhead container and poured a cup of coffee, taking time to savor the steam and aroma before putting it to her lips and sipping the strong, delectable taste. She rolled the warm cup gently between her hands, noticing that the sheet of paper with her new self fell on the floor. She reached down and picked it up. She looked at the name they gave her; Ann Marie Beaudet. What a beautiful name. She caught herself biting her lip, a bad habit since childhood whenever she was miffed or puzzled. I wonder how they decide names? What kind of logic do they use, or is it just a computerized, random chance?

McCarren loosened his tie and opened a folder across his knees. His arms were folded over his chest and he seemed to be engrossed in whatever he studied. For the first time, she really looked at him without feeling self-conscious. He wasn't cute, she decided. He was handsome. Eyelashes, the same shade of blond as the lock of hair that fell across his forehead were long enough and thick enough to make any woman envious. Who was he, really? Where did he come from? How long had he been Rod McCarren? Who was he before? She acknowledged that she probably would never learn the answers to those questions. She eased herself into the seat next to him, and their shoulders brushed. It felt good. He glanced up and smiled.

"Why don't you go ahead and start memorizing that?" He nodded at the paper in her hand. "Then we'll talk about it."

She flicked on the light above her seat and began to read. Whoever wrote her new life story didn't stray too far from the old one. The content was basically a reflection of her life, but the geography was dramatically different. Ann Marie Beaudet graduated from Pearlman High School in Salt Lake City, then on to Brigham Young in Provo for a degree in Elementary Education. Not too far from the truth, except they left out her training in teaching special needs students. There was no mention of the baby. She smiled to herself, visualizing the picture Alfred Williams let her hold for too short a time. Justin Christopher.

She let her mind float free from rational thought. Who selected her new name? And why? And why Utah? The second question was easier than the first. Utah would be simple. The Mormons ran their own form of conservative government and had a genealogical library unsurpassed anywhere, which might explain her new name. Was Ann Marie Beaudet already tucked away somewhere in the Mormon archives? She thought back to her studies of Howard Hughes and his henchmen, and what some referred to as the Mormon Mafia. When they wanted something done, it was done. Clean! Swift! No questions!

"Hmm," she wondered aloud. "No questions."

The flushing of the toilet startled her. She glanced at the seat beside her. Empty. Rod went to the bathroom and she hadn't even noticed. The door opened and Rod came out. "Did you say something?"

She took the last sip of cold coffee and put the cup in the trash bag affixed to the side of her seat. "Oh, nothing. Just thinking out loud." It seemed logical though. If Uncle Sam could turn to anyone to help set up phony records and guard them with their life, it would be the Mormons. How much more were they in on? Anybody's guess, she thought. But if you can't trust a Mormon, then who is left?

Voices In The Fog

Rod lowered himself back in his seat and twisted sideways to face her. Their faces were inches apart. She liked the scent of his aftershave.

"Are you ready for your first quiz?" He gave her that dazzling smile, but she knew he was serious. "Tell me about Miss Beaudet."

The rays of the sun falling obliquely across the cabin reminded her that she hadn't eaten anything that day except a couple of éclairs and a carrot stick. "Can't we eat first? I'm starved."

He got up and went to the small cabinet that served as a galley. "Me too, now that I think about it. Let's see. We have salads." From under the refrigerator, he took two plastic enclosed salads in Styrofoam bowls which he placed on trays he pulled from under the counter. "Then we have sandwiches. Would you prefer chicken salad or - -" He examined the four sandwiches. "Or chicken salad?"

"Oh," She laughed. "If I have a choice, I think I'd like chicken salad."

He grinned at her over his shoulder. "Excellent choice, madam. More coffee? Or would you prefer a cold drink?"

"Coffee, please."

She took several bites of her food before speaking. Then she took a swallow of the fresh coffee. "Before we start the quiz, can you answer some questions for me?" she asked.

"Such as?" he retorted.

"Such as, where are we going? How far is it from Washington?"

His hand shot up in front of her face. "Whoa, right there. You'll see what you need to see, and hear what you need to hear at the right time." He shook his head. "Sorry, but I can't discuss it now. Everything we do is on a need to know basis."

"Can you at least tell me how much longer we're going to be flying? For crying out loud, it's not like I can give away any state secrets. I deserve the courtesy of knowing how much further we're going."

"Okay, fair enough. We change aircraft in about four hours, give or take a bit, then about another twenty minutes to our destination. How's that?"

She glanced at her watch. It was eight o'clock. She realized she hadn't checked the time when they took off and had no idea how long they had been in the air. Two hours? Three? She calculated quickly. Graduation was over at eleven o'clock. The reception by noon; how long with Williams? An hour? That made it three o'clock. Another hour to lift off. That made it four o'clock. So they had been in the air about two hours. Once again, she whipped out her mental calculations. Three hundred-fifty miles per hour for a guess. Fourteen hundred miles en route somewhere, but where? And two more hours to go. So they would land fifteen hundred to eighteen hundred miles from Washington. Unless they were flying in circles. But she was able to see the lowering sun for the first part of the trip, so she was sure they were headed west. But where?

She shook her head in frustration, looked him in the eyes, brushed her hair back and smiled. "Okay. Do I need to know where I'm going after I finish this school?" she emphasized the verb.

" 'fraid not. Next question?"

She wanted to ask him about himself, with all the questions that ran through her mind since she first saw him. Who was he, really? Instead, she asked him something else. "What can you tell me about Mr. Williams?"

He shrugged. "Not much. He's been in this business a long time and he has a lot of clout."

"Is he your boss?"

"You might say so." He shrugged.

She hesitated, then asked, "Was he FBI before - -?"

Rod looked at her quizzically. "Before?"

She frowned at him. "You know. Before he started doing this?"

"Couldn't say." Rod answered around a bite of his sandwich. "We don't talk about 'before' much, although he knows everything there is to know about me, of course." He grinned wryly. "As you are well aware. But I think he got his training in Viet Nam."

"What about you?" she ventured.

"Not much to tell," he answered. "Now, let's talk about you, Ann Marie Beaudet."

She felt a clutch around her heart and she didn't know if it was fear or anticipation. She drew a deep breath and let it out slowly.

"Okay. Shoot," he directed.

So Ann Marie Beaudet told Rod McCarren all about herself.

Before he was satisfied with her story, she heard the groan of the wheels being lowered. She felt the plane roll slightly to the right, then the nose dipped as the engines slowed and the NASA jet began its descent to refuel. She had no idea where they were. Maybe they were over Canada or maybe the Deep South. Maybe they were in a slow turn ever since darkness fell and were right back where they started. She was lost, and that's all she knew. Except who she was, and now she knew that. She said it a hundred times in the last few hours. Ann Marie Beaudet.

Voices In The Fog

The whine of the engines slowed, then just a soft bump and they were on the ground. The plane braked hard, turned, and came to a halt.

"We'll be about fifteen minutes and up again," Rod said.

She unhooked her seat belt, stretched, and got up. Still hungry, she took a few minutes to browse through the refrigerator. Another sandwich, a couple of fresh apples, a six-pack of Perrier, some Cokes and Dr. Pepper, and a Dilly Bar in the freezer. "Not bad," she thought when she sat back with a bottle of water and the Dilly Bar. "They know me. They know what I eat. My God, what else do they know? They even knew about him and I didn't even know if it was a boy or a girl. They just snatched my baby away and were gone. I never got to see him. Never got to touch him." She fought back stinging tears and bit into the ice cream.

She allowed her mind to free float; to daydream. "Whoever they are, they know their business, but the day will come when I'll be able to do everything they can do, but I'll do it better and faster." Amused at herself, she nevertheless welcomed that sense of confidence. "If they're this good and they picked me to join them, then I have to be pretty damn good, too. That's a fact. I'm good and not ashamed of it. I'm not cocky, but I can pull my weight."

She checked her watch when the plane lifted off. Nine forty-five. Eastern time, but what time zone were they in now? Couldn't be Mountain, but might be Central. She took a deep breath, feeling the frustration building up in her chest. Never before was she stuck in a time warp. It was unnatural, and nobody should be crammed into a nearly total sensory deprivation like this. The minutes ticked by: five, ten, fifteen, twenty. Too much time to be in a vacuum.

Voices In The Fog

The tension built in her chest. "This is too weird," she thought. She looked at Rod, absorbed in paper work again, and anger rushed through her. "Son-of-a-bitch," she mumbled under her breath.

Exasperated, she flipped the finger at the bulkhead in front of her, and suddenly was embarrassed at her frustration. She was mad at them, but even worse, she was furious with herself. "What a dim-witted thing to do," she thought. "They probably have the whole thing on tape. That's it. This whole damn thing is a charade just to check me out, and I acted like a spoiled baby." She sat quietly in her seat, composing herself, regretting her attitude. She acted foolishly and knew it, but she supposed they were used to it by now if everybody needed to go through this hocus-pocus routine.

She allowed the rest of the flight to drift by, reviewing her Beaudet bio again and again, until the engines slowed and they began their descent into never-never land.

*****

Rod opened the hatch and held out his hand to her as she stepped onto the top step. His grip was warm and reassuring. She grasped the cold steel of the handrail and felt its chill run the length of her body. She shivered and felt the icy cloak of suspense wrap itself around her.

The night was pitch black, broken only by the runaway lights and a few buildings a couple hundred yards away. A helicopter hangar stood near the other buildings, but none were the size you might expect to find at a commercial airport. Obviously, they landed at a small private airstrip, but one with a runway long enough to land a jet. The air was cool but not cold enough to account for the chill of goose bumps she felt crawling slowly over her body. Everything was so strange, so secret. Everybody was friendly, but at the same time, it was as if she was alone on a desert island. That's it, she thought as she quickly looked around again. There were no trees. They were in the desert. New Mexico? Texas? Maybe Arizona or even Nevada. As she thought about it, she immediately knew that she never before considered how many desert states there are. She had no idea where she was.

Her thoughts were interrupted when McCarren spoke, "Come on, Miss Beaudet, they're ready to crank up our machine." Her eyes followed the sounds from the hangar and saw a two-person crew inspecting the helicopter. She fell in behind and followed McCarren toward the bird. "*Déjà vu.*" she thought. Only hours earlier she followed him on the first steps of her new life, and here she was following him to yet another phase of this adventure.

"Take a look at this baby," McCarren said when they walked into the hangar. "A Bell 206 B Jet Ranger. One good-looking machine if I ever saw one. It's fast, too. We'll be there in no time." He stepped alongside the aircraft, pausing to help her climb in.

"Wow," she remarked as she took a seat. "We could have a party on this thing." McCarren took a seat beside her while a ground crewman hooked up a tractor and pulled the helicopter free from the confines of the hangar. Minutes later the rotors began a slow churn, then went into a smooth hum as the craft tilted forward and lifted off into the inky black sky. Once again she found herself in an aircraft without windows. She still had no firm idea where they were or where they were going. She looked at her flying mate and their eyes locked in the dimness of the solitary light in the rear bulkhead.

Voices In The Fog

"I know you're curious, but we'll be there in about twenty minutes or so. Then you'll start to get in on everything."

"Where are we?" she asked. "Can't you at least tell me that much, or is that a national secret too?"

"No, it's not a national secret," he said in a businesslike tone. "It's just not for me to say. When someone thinks you need to know, then they can tell you." He shifted in the seat and looked at her. "Here's a free lesson for you," he said firmly. "Need to know, and right to know. Keep those two terms in mind forever." His gray eyes pierced her like polished steel daggers. "Need to know, and right to know," he repeated. "If that's all you learn today, then at least you've learned an important basic lesson."

*****

She caught herself grabbing the armrest and feeling a sinking sensation in her stomach when the chopper descended quickly toward their landing spot. They came in steep, she knew that much. Out here in the desert if you come in steep, it must mean that you went into some mountains or canyons. Two can play this game, she thought. Even though she couldn't see, she could feel the machine near the ground, hover for a second or two, then turn slightly to the left, and land with the touch of an expert pilot. Wherever she was going, she just arrived.

She and McCarren sat in silence while the rotors slowed, giving the helicopter a gentle, steady bounce as the engine came to a halt. McCarren was the first to unbuckle his seatbelt, reaching out and sliding the cabin door open.

She sat for a moment after he jumped out, giving her time once again to compose herself for whatever lay ahead.

"Ready?" McCarren asked, sticking his head back into the cabin.

"You bet I am," she responded. She made an effort to put a positive ring in her voice. "Damn right I am." She unbuckled, made her way to the door and climbed out onto a smooth, well-trimmed grassy area. She looked about and saw that they were on what appeared to be the lighted fairway of a golf course, maybe fifty or sixty yards out from an elegant old house or an old hotel. Its lights pierced the dark of night.

McCarren stood silently while she found her bearings. They were isolated! Golf course or whatever, they were far from anything else. No other lights or buildings were to be seen. She breathed deeply and spun around, taking in all that she could see. They were alone. Away from anyone else. Just Ann Marie, Rod McCarren, the helicopter crew, and who else?

The quiet of the night was broken by the sound of a door being shut at the hotel. Ann Marie turned to see an elderly woman tottering carefully down the steps from the porch onto the grass. "Hi folks," she shouted. She crossed the fairway to meet them. She came around the helicopter, waving to the crew as they were shutting down the engine. "Rod, you devil," she said. The old lady threw her arms around him. "Welcome back, you rascal."

McCarren hugged her, then turned to Ann Marie, and gestured, "Millie, this is our new guest."

"Hi." Ann Marie studied the woman as she extended her hand. She was tall, white haired, and fit. She was a woman who took care of herself. "I'm Ann Marie Beaudet. Nice to meet you."

Voices In The Fog

"Let me show you to your room, sweetie," Millie said and started back toward the house. "Rod, you've got your old room back, so you can find your way." Millie took Ann Marie by the hand and spoke as if she was Ann Marie's very own grandmother. "Come on honey, I know you've had a long day. I've got a little sandwich fixed and will bring it to you. Now, you just get in your room and get a good bath. The boys will get your bags to your room, but you can unpack tomorrow." Millie led her into the building with its check-in counter, down the hall with the hardwood floors echoing every step, past several rooms each with an identifying name on the door – Dry Gulch, Coyote, Apache, and on to her room, Desert Lily.

"Can you tell me about this place?" she asked when Millie opened her door.

"Not much to tell," the old lady replied. "As you can see, it used to be a grand old resort, but anything else you'll have to learn later on." Millie turned on the light. Ann Marie was glad to see a soft, feminine room. There was a double bed with an elegant headboard and footboard, all in dark, oiled mahogany. A nightstand with an antique lamp stood on a doily stood beside it, and an old Turkish rug covered the hardwood floor. "Nothing," she said aloud, "like the Academy. This place is unreal. It's so beautiful."

"Your private toilet is through that door," Millie said, pointing to a door. Ann Marie opened it and stepped back in time fifty years. An old tub and washbasin, but all spotlessly clean. Sparkling white towels hung on a brass rack on the white tiled wall. The flush box and pull chain hung above the commode. She stepped forward and pulled the chain, then stood there like a child. The toilet flushed as though it were the newest model on the showroom floor.

Voices In The Fog

"It's beautiful," she said as she turned back to Millie. "The whole place is so aristocratic. I love it."

"Thank you child," Millie said. She reached out, took her guest's hand in her own and patted it. "This is a wonderful place, and anything I can do to make your stay comfortable, you let me know." She turned and started to leave, then looked back to Ann Marie. "I'll be back with your sandwich and a drink in a second," she said and closed the door.

*****

Ann Marie took the last bite of her sandwich, turned on the hot water and filled the tub. She dumped a small handful of bubble bath under the tap and sat on the edge of the commode, undressed, and watched the bubbles billow up like so many cumulus clouds reaching into the heavens on a mid-day's afternoon, rolling over each other until they were nearly flowing over the edge onto the floor.

From the direction of the golf course, she heard the slow, rhythmic whop-whop-whop of the helicopter. The rotor blades began to churn, slipping their dagger-like edges through the still air, gaining momentum, pulling the chopper upright from its skids, laboring against the pull of gravity. The whoping sound gradually changed to a smooth flowing whop-whop as the craft raised itself away from Christie Cole and Ann Marie Beaudet, and into the desert darkness, leaving her to the warm solitude of her bath.

She pulled a towel from the rack and wrapped it around her head, being careful to tuck her hair beneath it as she gingerly stuck her toe through the bubbles and into the steaming, hot water. She allowed her body to slip slowly into the water, covering herself up to her shoulders, then leaned her head back against the lip of the tub. She took a deep breath and let it out slowly as the soothing water eased the tension from her muscles.

"What a day," she thought. "Never, never could I have imagined a day like this. From student to agent. From agent to? To what?" She had no idea what she was or where she was: no idea of her title, if she had one. She didn't even know for sure what time it was. But, wherever she was, she knew she was in for the adventure of a lifetime, a world beyond her wildest imagination. It was a domain that would terrify people if they had any idea it existed. She thought of it as a place of intrigue and mystery, a maze of governments within governments, a blur, a mixture of the real and the unreal, and a mosaic of truth and deception. Goose bumps crept down her spine, into her hips, down her legs and into her feet. It was frightening, but it also was exhilarating. Ann Marie Beaudet, she mused mentally. That's who I am now.

CHAPTER FOUR

Ann Marie shoved her head under the pillow to muffle the chime of the alarm clock. She rolled onto her stomach and eased her hand from beneath the sheets, then ran her fingers up the side of the nightstand and across the top until they found the clock. She carefully tucked it into the palm of her hand, flicked off the alarm, and pulled it under the sheet where she could lie for a few more minutes. Then she would dress and go to breakfast. Guessing she was in the Mountain Time zone, she set her clock back two hours and went to bed at midnight. It really didn't make any difference what time it was, she decided. Millie told her Sunday breakfast was served all morning, so whenever she got to the dining room would be fine. According to Millie, today would be her free day. She would have something to eat, unpack, maybe meet a few people, then spend the remainder of the day exploring her new environment.

It was seven-thirty by the time she strolled down the hall, following the sounds of a few clattering dishes and the rich scent of bacon floating through the house. She found half a dozen tables in the dining room, each with a view looking out over the golf course and the rugged mountains in the background. It was picture-perfect, a postcard from the 1930's. Everything was in its original condition. There were tables, chairs, and the sundeck beyond the dining room windows. Everything. It was a step back in time. It was, she thought, a quantum leap backward to an age when the world moved at a much slower pace, a pace more in tune with a body's natural ability to deal with whatever challenge it encountered. It was as though she was offered an escape from the passing of the millennium. It gave her a brief look back before being absorbed into the whirl of the twenty-first century. She decided this was the calm before the storm, a touch of nostalgia, a gentle reminder of a kinder and gentler day. But whatever it was, she would take advantage of the amenities. She might never again see the likes of this jewel of the desert, so she decided to wear it with all of its historic elegance.

"Good morning, Miss Beaudet," Millie said, coming through the kitchen door with a plate full of biscuits and eggs that she placed in front of a sleepy-eyed woman about Ann Marie's age. "Morning Millie," Ann Marie replied, studying the other woman, the only other person in the room. A little younger than she, but probably not as tall from the way she sat at the table. She had certain similarities: fairly broad shoulders, and athletic looking. Her hair was blonde, cut in a smooth cap that covered her ears. She looked as though she went to an all-night party and just arrived home. Ann Marie walked over to the table where the glassy-eyed woman sat poking at the egg yolks. "May I?" Ann Marie asked.

The woman looked up and smiled. "Please do. I'm sorry if I look like hell. I'm April McDermott." She offered her hand and they shook briefly.

"Ann Marie Beaudet. I'm glad to meet you," she said as she pulled out a chair opposite April. "Have you been here long?" Ann Marie asked.

"Five weeks today, but I'm suffering with this micro-surveillance stuff. Stayed up all night, but I think I finally got it right. I can ace most of this stuff, but electronics is all new to me. Hells bells," she laughed, "all I ever had to do was turn on the coffee pot or plug in the toaster. Anyway," she stopped to gulp her coffee, "I heard your chopper come in last night, but I was up to my tail in wires and lenses and couldn't stop to say hello. Sorry," she said, tossing a quick glance toward her new colleague.

Ann Marie ordered her breakfast, sipping juice and coffee while she watched April slouch over her plate, mopping up the runny yolks with a biscuit. "Can you tell me anything about where we are, or what we're doing?"

April looked up from her plate, smiled and wiped her chin. "I'm sorry. I know you must think I'm rude, but I've been working my butt off, and hardly getting any sleep at all. This schedule is tough. They don't cut you much slack. On the other hand, you'll be learning from the best. The very best," she exclaimed. "It's just that I let myself coast too much the first couple of weeks when I should have been studying, and you know how that goes. You get behind, then have to bust a gut to catch up. This micro thing caught me off-guard. So I've been going about a quad-zillion miles an hour to stay up."

April laughed at herself and scooted back from the table. "Tell you what," she said. "Have your breakfast. I'll meet you in the lobby in thirty minutes and show you around."

*****

April sat on the bottom step of the front porch, sipping coffee from a Styrofoam cup when Ann Marie stepped outside. She took a deep breath, held it for a second, then let it out slowly. "My God," she exclaimed, "fresh air. No cars or motorcycles. What kind of place is this? I didn't know there was an unpolluted corner on earth anymore."

"Yeah. Welcome to Millie's House. That's what everybody calls it. Probably has, or at least had, a name at one time. But, who knows? Anyhow," she said. She let out a little moan and got up, rubbing the small of her back. "Damn, I feel like an old lady. C'mon. I'll show you around." She set off for the golf course, her tank top and khaki shorts revealing a nice tan and well-honed muscles. They walked the nine-hole golf course, with its manicured and well watered greens, and sand traps to snare a few errant balls. The out-of-bounds looked like it would challenge a snake-charmer's luck to dig around in the cactus and rocks among the rattlesnakes for a lost ball. In the midst of this desert landscape was a spring-fed pond on the fourth hole - exactly one hundred and eighty-five yards from the tee box. It was well placed and just enough to catch the average hacker's drive. Someone spent a lot of money to bring their hobby with them to this oasis in these scorched, barren mountains.

It was perfect, Ann Marie thought, for the rich people who perhaps came here in the 1930s, maybe even back in the 20s. It was certainly a quiet retreat far from Wall Street or Washington, or wherever they came from, but surely, a safe haven from the rush and clatter of the big city pressure.

April stopped on the ninth tee box, taking time from this, the loftiest place on the course, to look out over the house and the mountains in the background. "Beautiful, isn't it?" she asked. She stretched her arms over her head, breathing in the dry desert air. "I can only guess the house was built around the turn of the century, probably Victorian. Look at the gingerbread trim"

The beauty was almost beyond description. Porches ran the length of the first and second floors; the entire house was trimmed with what was the most elegant gingerbread trim of the time. Its lacy fingers gripped the fascia board like so many embroidered stitches. Terra cotta flower pots on the porches were filled with the several hues of geraniums. Colorful wandering Jews were draped from hanging pots beneath the cool shade of the porches. Daisies and sunflowers were laid out in beds along the sidewalks and beside the house. Giant saguaro cacti stood like sentinels on the hillside, their twisted arms giving evidence of their ability to survive the ravages of time. By whatever name this place was previously known, there could have been neither finer retreat nor more perfect spot where one's soul could be soothed from the burdens of the time. It was nothing short of a masterpiece tucked away in the purity of the clean desert air.

"Is there a third story" Ann Marie asked, noticing the sun reflecting off a small window high up under the eaves. "What's up there?"

"Who knows?" April continued stretching, working on her legs now. "Attic, I guess. But nobody goes up there. At least the trainees don't."

Ann Marie looked at her quizzically.

"None of us peons are allowed above the second floor. Access is secured behind dead bolts."

"Hmm," Ann Marie mused. She shaded her eyes, trying to get a better look at the small window. "Wonder why?"

"Storage. At least that's what I hear," April replied.

They stood silently and enjoyed the peace and quiet of the Sunday morning. A soft warm breeze caressed them with gentle kisses. The white, two story house stood out in stark dissimilarity against the backdrop of a rocky bluff that reached several hundred feet into the air. Its crags and crevices defied the laws of nature as saguaro and flat-leafed prickly pear found root and reached out for the gift of light and an occasional raindrop. To the front of the house and stretching out several hundred yards in either direction was the crisp, green golf course, and the sweet smell of freshly cut Bermuda wafting in the early morning air.

There was so much in contrast with its surroundings, the desert and the mountains, the golf course, the house and the work that took place there. It was concealed behind the deceptive antique beauty; yet everything fit together like the pieces of a puzzle.

She decided that was part of the game. This was a puzzle. This place had a secret. Isn't that what she was told? Everybody has a secret? This was her challenge – find the secret of Millie's House and she would know who she worked for and how all of this came together. Find the secret and find the trail to the voice in the fog.

April broke the silence. "And now for the best part of this place," she said, grabbing Ann Marie's hand and leading her away from the golf course. They walked quickly around the side of the house and onto a rocky trail leading up a narrow canyon. Its granite walls reached up toward the small, puffy clouds that floated against the unpolluted blue sky. They only went a few dozen yards before they came to a small pool of water no larger than a child's wading pool carved through the ages into the rock, yet as smooth as a tea cup

"Try this," April said, pulling off her sandals and stepping into the ankle-deep water. "A natural hot spring up there," she whispered, pointing further up the canyon. "This is the coolest pool, and as we go up toward the spring, each one gets a little bigger and hotter. Actually, the top pool at the spring is too hot to use, but the other ones are great."

Ann Marie followed April's lead, taking her own sandals in her hand and stepping into the water. They walked along silently, moving deeper into the canyon, wading and kicking up the warm, clear water as they enjoyed the peace and tranquility of the isolation in which they found themselves. They climbed up the smooth rocks and over the lip to a larger pool, this one the size of a backyard pool. "Stays about ninety degrees," April said. She scooted over the rocks and into the water. She looked back at her new friend, hesitating at the edge.

"Gotta get wet, kiddo. Ain't any other way to get to the top of the canyon." April laughed at Ann Marie who stood at the water's edge, then dipped her toe into the water.

"What the hell," she blurted. She jumped in, making a splash that soaked her from head to toe.

They moved on through two more pools before the reached the top pool where they sat in the shade of a mesquite tree to let the air dry their clothes. Even in the warm dry air, steam rose from the water and drifted like a thin veil up the canyon side, gradually disappearing as the sun's heat radiated off the rocks, squeezing the moisture out of everything like a giant oven. The tree jagged out from a crack in the rocks, throwing ample shade over a smooth boulder that centuries ago fell from the cliffs and came to rest at the water's edge.

"So fill me in," Ann Marie said. She slipped out of her shorts, and began to wring them out. April paused for a second, then got up and stepped around the mesquite tree, being careful not to slip on the smooth rock and fall in the hot water.

"Hope you don't mind," April said. She stripped naked and spread her clothes on the warm rocks, then lowered herself gently onto her stomach, letting the desert sun shine upon her nakedness.

Voices In The Fog

"This will be the only time for another week that I've got to relax. Once we get back to the house, I have a ton of studying to do. This is my day, then I'll give them their time. But for now, I've got to let it all hang out, so to speak," she giggled. April folded her arms and nuzzled her head into them. She spoke in a muffled tone and told the organization's newest employee what lay ahead for her: Eastern European Nationalism; Judeo-Christian conflict in the Middle East; Islamic fundamentalism; the history of conflict between India, Pakistan and Bangladesh; the Sino domination theory; Mexican politics and revolutionary groups; Central and South American dictators and the narcotics trade; American organized crime; and, perhaps most intriguing of all, a course entitled, Inside American Democracy: The Price of Elections.

"What it actually means," she said, looking up at Ann Marie and twisting her face in an expression of her discontent, "is that he who has the biggest pot of money and isn't afraid of how he uses it, or who he buys, wins! It doesn't get much more basic than that. It's American politics at its best. But, I guess most people have more or less figured it out on their own, so they vote or don't vote and the world still spins."

"But only if we can see through the fog," Ann Marie responded quickly.

April laughed. "You've been talking to Williams. I recognize the lecture."

"But he's right," Ann Marie protested. "Imagine what it would be like if one side held the power. All of it. My God, it's scary to think about. Imagine what they could do. Total domination! Isn't there something in the Bible about that? Isn't it in Revelations? Something about seven years of domination, and then what? I think our world is in a delicate situation. Not that there haven't always been forces trying to do it one way or the other, but it's worse now because of the technology available to us – to everyone in the world, just about. Whether it's the bomb or computers, or germ warfare or genocide. The thing that concerns me is not that there are depraved people, because they have always been there. But with the speed that things can happen now, once they get started, it may be too late to stop them. That's alarming."

April gradually lifted her weight onto her elbows and rolled over. The remaining droplets of water on her body reflected the sun's rays like little diamonds dancing on an invisible string. "What alarms me right now is that I'm dying in the course on surveillance and countermeasures, and I'm about lost. I'll make it, but it's a dog, and they have really worked my tail off. Tiny cameras and high tech listening devices. It's all that James Bond crap, you know."

"Actually, I'm afraid I don't, but I have a feeling I will before too much longer," Ann Marie said. She stood and pulled he shorts up over her waist. "Shall we?" she asked. She gestured back down the canyon.

"Yep! I'm ready as I'll ever be," April replied. She peeled her dry clothes from the rocks and began putting them on.

The lone figure lay quietly on the canyon rim, focused the crosshairs, adjusted the lenses, and filled the camera with images of the pair as they lazed away what they thought was the pristine solitude on the desert mountains.

*****

Ann Marie spent the rest of the day getting settled in, lining the dresser drawers in her room with butcher paper

Voices In The Fog

Millie gave her, ironing a few pieces before hanging them in the closet, and in general having a pleasant, casual afternoon. As the evening sun threw its last bright rays over the scabrous mountain peaks, April and Ann Marie met in the dining room. They found a table near the window and seated themselves as Millie poured each of them a glass of ice water. Half a dozen men, also trainees, she surmised, sat at the other tables, each of them already deep into their Sunday dinner. They ignored April and Ann Marie.

"Tell me, Millie. Meatloaf?" April asked. She slipped her arm around their hostess and gave her a tender, gentle hug.

"It's Sunday, isn't it?" Millie replied with a smile before turning to go back to the kitchen.

Ann Marie laughed. "If I didn't know better, I'd think my own grandmother was cooking dinner. Every Sunday, we always ate the same dinner. Meatloaf and mashed potatoes with gravy. I swear I never got tired of it. Besides," she mused, "if her hair wasn't snow white, she would remind me a lot of Granny. How old do you think she is?"

April unfolded her napkin, placed it precisely across her knees, and lined up her silverware like soldiers at inspection. "Pretty old, I guess. In her seventies, at least. Maybe older than that. She's been here almost forever. At least, that's what I hear."

Ann Marie looked around the room. Four men about her age came in, followed by an elderly couple. The two parties seated themselves as though they performed this routine a million times. "Fill me in some more. Who are these folks?" She gestured with a nod of her head at the men, each sipping their glasses of ice water, carefully holding their pinkie fingers extended away from the glass.

"I don't think I've ever seen such nerdy looking guys. Look at them and their scraggly hair. Good grief, their clothes look like they are straight off the rack at Goodwill. Didn't their mothers teach them how to dress?"

April, focused on spreading a light coat of margarine on her bread, but didn't look up. "Analysts. Whatever that means. Just bits and pieces I've picked up, but I think this place is loaded with computers, and those guys go in there and ejaculate or something." She laughed as she was swallowing a bite of bread, nearly choking. She sputtered for a minute and took several sips of water. "This outfit is loaded with geniuses, and I think those are the guys who do some of the research on new recruits. People like you and me."

"You don't mean one of them named me, do you?"

"Take another look at them and decide for yourself. I think there may even be a little method to their madness. See the jerk with the maroon T-shirt and green shorts? The good looking guy?" she wisecracked. "Well, I was walking down the hall in the office area and got a quick peek when he came out his door. Guess what? The little runt had a Texas A and M pennant on his wall. Get it? He's an Aggie. I'm April McDermott, and you're Ann Marie. Doesn't that make you sick?"

"Now that you mention it, yeah. But that's silly, isn't it?" She thought for a moment, then said, "Maybe not. I once knew a guy who graduated from A&M." She knew better than to tell the other woman she was an A&M grad. "He was scary. His first car after law school was A & M maroon, that deep iridescent maroon that was popular a few years ago. His living room furniture was covered in maroon leather. When he got married, he and his attendants wore maroon ties and cummerbunds. I thought that was the weirdest thing I ever heard."

April laughed. "Texas A & M must make people do strange things."

This was an appropriate time for her to keep her mouth shut, Ann Marie thought. She picked up her glass of ice water and slowly spun it, watching the clear ice cubes twirl in an easy rhythm, around and around. Always in motion, but going nowhere. Always going back to the same place where they started, then following the same route again. Around and around, following the invisible axis of the laws of physics.

"For everything there is a reason: for everything there is a season," she said softly. She looked away from her glass, taking in the final orange and gold and deep purple of the sunset, letting them hold her in their grasp as they faded in the twilight. She glanced quickly at April and smiled. "And for every secret, there is a reason."

She nodded toward the older couple. "And what about gram and gramps over there?"

"They're the house and grounds keepers. Good Mormons. I figured that out all by myself. They take their car and leave on Friday afternoon and come back on Sunday evening. Don't cuss. Don't smoke. Don't seem to get upset about anything. Nice people." She broke off another piece of bread. "A couple of weeks ago, I found Herbert, that's Gramp, reading the Book of Mormon on the front porch. Then I overheard his wife, Lottie, talking to him about the kids in Salt Lake, so I figure it's pretty safe to say they're Mormons. Wouldn't you say so?"

Ann Marie did not respond, but let her gaze float across the room to the couple. Mormons? What was this? The second or third time in less than twenty-four hours the idea of Mormons surfaced in her new employment? Maybe it meant only that they were in one of the western states where the Mormon population was high.

Ann Marie and April were finishing their crumb crust apple pie when Rod McCarren strolled into the dining room, stopped for a moment to give Millie a hug, then walked directly to their table.

"Ladies. May I?" he asked politely. He pulled out a chair and seated himself without waiting for a response.

"Please do," Ann Marie said. "And to what do we owe this honor?"

"Well, you are just about the luckiest woman on the face of the earth." His quick and easy smile swept across his face. Their eyes locked onto each other, neither willing to surrender, then continued, "I'm your mentor, you lucky devil."

"I'm not sure what that means, but I think you're about to tell me, so why don't you go ahead? Oh, by the way, let me introduce April McDermott. April, this is Rod. Rod, April."

"How do you do, April? Been here long?"

"Few weeks. What about you?"

"A few years. I come back to Millie's from time to time. I love it here," he said. He paused for a moment, nodded his head in approval, and looked with satisfaction around the dining room. "Come back every chance I get. So when they gave me a shot at being a mentor to my good friend, I couldn't pass it up. Which brings me to the reason for this chat." He leaned forward and looked directly at Ann Marie. "Every student has a mentor, somebody to check in with them and see how they are doing. You know, kind of a big brother thing. How are you doing? What can I do for you? We don't want you to feel alone out here in the middle of nowhere. I'll spend the first couple of days with you. Going to classes with you, that kind of stuff, then I'm out of here and back to my regular assignment. But I won't forget you. I'll check back off and on to see how you're doing. That brings us to the moment," he said. He slipped an envelope from his pocket and handed it to her. "This is your schedule for the first week." He shoved back from the table and bowed a good evening to them. "Perhaps I'll see you for breakfast. Right now I've got some work to do. Anyhow," he said, "I'll catch you at eight o'clock tomorrow in the old smoking room. By the way April, I think that's on your schedule, too. See you guys then."

*****

Ann Marie and April finished their breakfast in time to grab their notebooks from their bedrooms and hurried to into the dark paneled, high ceilinged room that at one time was the private chamber where gentlemen talked politics and investments while they smoked their cigars.

Rod was already there, re-arranging the furniture. "Ladies, your timing is perfect," he quipped, but his smoky eyes weren't smiling.

"I guess it's down to serious business now," Ann Marie thought.

"This morning's topic is on surveillance and counter-surveillance measures, so why don't you take a seat and make yourself comfortable while we go through this. It won't take long."

Ann Marie quickly scanned the room. It was nothing less than ancient refinement. Dark paneled walls, two sofas, two matching overstuffed chairs, a coffee table with a vase of fresh flowers. At the head of the room was a baroque desk such as might be found in the private study of some famous tycoon, maybe a Rockefeller or Kennedy. The walls were decorated with Monets and Picassos. She wondered if they were originals. A small mahogany table in the corner supported a delicate ivory carving, something whose value she could not even guess, but was probably worth more than she made in a lifetime. An exquisite mahogany armoire with delicate scrollwork stood like a silent sentinel against the far wall.

"McCarren opened the doors to the armoire which turned out to be an entertainment center with a television set as its focal point. Using a remote control which he took from another shelf in the armoire, he turned on the television, inserted a DVD and almost immediately the screen was filled with the words: BEING PREPARED.

"Now what we have here, ladies, is a short course on the very credo of our jobs. That is, always be ready to snare someone when and where they least expect it. Conversely, always be on guard lest someone else should be trying to snare us."

He turned toward April, his smile fading to a harsh stare. "And were you not on a surveillance alert this weekend, Miss McDermott?"

Startled, Ann Marie glanced at April, who looked as surprised as herself. April swallowed hard. "Yes sir."

"Would you be so kind as to explain to our new student exactly what that means?" Rod's stern voice requested.

Nodding her head, April spoke as though she was a child caught stealing cookies. "An alert is what we are given if someone in the organization has reason to believe that somebody outside the organization is spying on us; that is, somebody is seriously trying to figure us out. Our position may be in jeopardy, so we are to take all means to assure that we cover ourselves. Be vigilant. Be alert. Lay counter traps to see if they walk into them. Bottom line: be vigilant."

"During your course of study here, do you receive alerts so you can practice how you should respond?" Rod asked

Ann Marie watched intently, reading the body language of both the man and the woman. Rod was stalking like a cat. It was clear he was going to have April for breakfast. But what was not clear was how and when he was going to do it. "If this is something that April screwed up, why am I here?" she wondered.

"Well?" Rod fired again at April. "Did you receive an alert Friday? A forty-eight hour alert?"

"Yes sir, I did," April replied meekly.

"Will you please explain to our new colleague what that means, so she can learn from this lesson?"

"An in-course alert means that for the next forty-eight hours we are subject to absolute scrutiny. Total! Sight and sound. The only off-limits area is in the bathroom. Other than that, we are fair game, so we need to try to figure out if anyone is watching. If so, who is watching, where are they. That kind of stuff."

"Now do you want to explain this?" Rod fiddled with the remote clumsily, intentionally playing out the drama so his students would have plenty of time to let their minds anticipate what he was about to do.

With each click of the control, a view, in full color, was beamed back to them from the screen: The two women wandering about the golf course, climbing up through the hot springs to the mountainside. There was Ann Marie taking off her shorts and tossing them onto the rocks; she glared angrily at Rod, her face feeling hot and flushed. Then Ann Marie on the screen dissolved into April lying naked, her buttocks shining in the warm sun. The last one was the most humiliating of all: April stretched out on her back, fully exposed to the digital camera with its telephoto lens, exposed to Rod McCarren. A close up of every inch of her body; her eyes, her lips, her breasts, the drops of water clinging to her pubic hair. There were no secrets from Rod McCarren, or from her new friend. She was totally exposed and utterly embarrassed.

April's head dropped and she bit her lip. She didn't speak. Ann Marie had a few choice words she wanted to hurl at him, but she clamped her jaws shut and seethed.

"I'm sorry I had to do this to you, April. But you knew about the alert and you should have been prepared. What if you had been in the field and as unaware of surveillance as you were yesterday? What if I'd been an enemy with a gun instead of a friend with a camera? You both have to learn, and sometimes the lessons are hard and embarrassing. But better to be embarrassed than killed."

The silence stretched out. "Friend with a camera, my ass," Beaudet thought. She would never call him a friend.

He popped the DVD out of the player and tossed it to April. "Here. Take it. It's yours." He grinned, but suddenly Ann Marie was immune to his smile. "Yours to destroy. Or, you have to admit, they're pretty good pictures. You may want to keep the DVD." His frown faded and he touched her shoulder. "There are no copies. I promise."

Tears were flowing down April's cheeks. Without a word, she grabbed the DVD and hurried from the room. Ann Marie gave Rod one last withering glance and followed April.

Voices In The Fog

*****

Four men completed their training during Ann Marie's second week at Millie's House. She barely met them, but nevertheless, she showed up for a farewell party in the dining room where good cheer and fellowship flowed. Millie served cold beer, chips, roast beef sandwiches, and some veggie dip as teachers and students celebrated the completion of the school and the beginning of the four new careers. None of them ever discussed their previous lives with Ann Marie, and she did not broach the topic with them nor with April. What was behind them were unwritten histories, an era void of any personality, replaced by what she believed were their secret lives. Lives created by the U. S. government and documented by the Mormon Church. Lives about which any inquiry would set off alarms all the way to Washington. Lives which would become state secrets, known only to a handful of the best clandestine operatives in the world.

The party gradually petered out, and Ann Marie and April went out for a walk in the gathering dusk. The green hues of the golf course darkened to black.

"What about you?" asked Ann Marie. "You're next. When are you leaving?"

"Probably a week. Maybe two. I'm working on some specialized things right now, and as soon as I finish it up, I'm out of here. Kind of gives me cold chills to think how the world really works and that I'm going to be part of it. But, I'll do okay. I'd love to stay in touch with you, but I know it doesn't work that way. Don't know if we'll ever see each other again, but I want you to know how special you have been to me. Especially with the way we got started on the Sunday walk. I was really down, but you were a good friend when I needed one the most. I think that is the only

71

thing that scares me after I'm out there - - wherever *there* is. We all need somebody to hang on to from time-to-time. All I can say is, if you have a chance, look me up."

"That's a two-way street. It scares me, too. I'm not sure how I'll function as a lone wolf. They've got to have some way that we stay in touch with somebody somewhere."

"Probably. Time will tell," April commented. She looked at the purple shadows creeping down from the mountain peaks and across the golf course, "but all I can say now is that it's getting dark, and if we don't want to be out here with the rattlesnakes, we need to scoot back to the house."

*****

Ann Marie was getting in bed on Saturday night when she heard the chopping sound of the helicopter and immediately knew that the newest student arrived. Like her, he or she would be dazzled and bewildered about their new life. "What the hell." she thought. "I'm not about to get dressed to go out and greet them. I'll find 'em tomorrow. At least I'm not the rookie anymore."

*****

Ann Marie and April found their newest colleague at breakfast the next morning. He was the most beautiful Black man Ann Marie ever saw. Close-cropped black hair framed a broad forehead and strong jaw. His brooding dark eyes drew her into their depths when he welcomed the women to his table. He smiled and his whole face lit up. His dark eyes danced and strong white teeth brought a glow to his ebony skin.

"Did anybody ever tell you that you are the spitting image of Tiger Woods?" April asked.

"Sometimes. Helps me pick up women," he teased. "Except I don't play golf. I'm Adolphus Morin."

Ann Marie and April glanced at each other and didn't even try to smother their laughter. Adolphus Morin glanced from one to the other, frowning. "What's so funny? Oh - - " he relaxed. "It's the ridiculous name, isn't it?"

"We think some Texas Aggie named us." April chuckled.

The now second newest spy extended her hand. "I'm Ann Marie Beaudet and this is April McDermott. Looks like we got tagged by an Aggie."

"So that's it," Morin said. "I've been wondering."

"We're not positive," April said, "but it seemed logical." She related the incident of seeing the man's office decorated with Texas A & M banners.

"I have a feeling we're going to see a lot of things even stranger than that around here," Morin said.

After breakfast, they took him on the obligatory Sunday walk, going through the house, down the golf course, and ending up soaked to the bone at the upper pool. But, this time no one shed any clothes.

During the following week, Ann Marie and Adolphus had class together, studying European nationalism along with an introductory course of discreet audio and visual surveillance.

Fred Lynn, their instructor in electronic surveillance, was a frumpy, tired and disorganized looking man. Whenever she saw him around the house, he always wore the same wrinkled white shirt, smeared with tiny samples of every meal he ate since he last washed it. But his knowledge and enthusiasm more than made up for his appearance. He loved his work, and it showed whenever he started talking. His face lit up, his voice was inspired and full of fire, and he could hardly contain himself until he showed them in excruciating detail how everything worked.

"I can't believe this stuff," was Morin's first comment when he got his hands on the thousands of dollars worth of equipment that was issued to each of them. The Regency Sound System looked like a standard portable compact disc player, no different from those which millions of other people wore on their belts while they listened to their favorite music. But oh, what a difference. The Regency earphones were micro-powered directional listening devices, strong enough to hear a heart beat from twenty feet, and most assuredly, strong enough to pick up a whispered conversation from one hundred or more feet.

"No doubt, my good friends," Fred told them, "this will be one of the most valuable tools you will have. Even a whisper in the adjoining room of a hotel cannot escape being heard on your Regency."

He went on to show them the various attachments that went with the Regency, since it would not always be feasible to wear a CD player and head set. The power unit could be tucked away in a coat pocket or purse, and a hearing aid slipped into their ear would serve the same purpose as the headset. "Whatever you choose, I guarantee. You will hear things you never thought possible."

To go with the hearing device was the perfect match for surveillance equipment: the MoTrac Viewer. "No secrets," the instructor said. "You will see people at their rawest. Essentially, naked as the day they were born. The MoTrac was developed as a night vision tool, but we discovered its potential quite by accident. It won't see through too many layers of clothes. For example, it won't go through a heavy overcoat, but given a person's normal daily wear, you put these on like a pair of glasses, and good grief, you'll see them in all of their glory, albeit in various shades of green." He gave an embarrassed giggle as he slipped a pair of glasses from a case and started to put them on.

"What do you think you're doing?" Ann Marie yelled, hastily crossing her arms in front of her body. "Put that thing away!"

"Just kidding," he laughed. He slid them back into the case. "I'm an engineer, not a peeping tom. I don't get off looking at naked people, but there will be times when this is exactly what you will want. You might be looking to see if a person is wearing a wire, or maybe even carrying a gun. Who knows how you will use it? But I caution you against its improper use. It wouldn't be fair to size up, so to speak, a new date to see what's real and what's not."

If Fred hoped to get a laugh, he was disappointed. She glared at him, and Adolphus, watching her, gave her a conspiratorial smile.

The last device they received was the Regency Mark IV Interceptor, the granddaddy of their covert listening devices. "The Mark IV," he said as he held up the wine colored leather briefcase holding the various components, each securely stowed in a tight-fitting foam rubber container, "will take you to the heart of a person's private conversation. Most of all," he said with a broad smile that showed his nicotine stained teeth, "what you will like about it is that you can be anywhere from four-hundred to six-hundred yards away, and hear the most intimate conversation. Simply affix the directional microphones to a stable base, maybe something like a telephone pole, point it at the window of a house or office within one-hundred feet, sit back and turn on your tape recorder up to six hundred yards away from the microphone, and bingo! You will hear every vowel. . .every syllable. You will hear a gentleman profess his love in the most tender words, or you may hear a hushed conversation between some of societies most hardened scoundrels as they decide some poor person's, or even a nation's, fate. Amazingly, extraneous noises, such as street noises surrounding your target, are filtered out. You hear only from the spot you're focused on."

The professor, as he liked to be called, held their attention with complete silence. He stood before them, holding out the little microphone for them to look at, allowing his words to play-out their full meaning: there are no secrets.

"You will overhear spoken words that would send chills down the spine of Edgar Allan Poe. You will hear the raven, knock, knock, knocking at the door. You will hear men and women at their very worst, yet you will not be their confessor. No! You are their adversary, and you will use your newly found information to right a wrong: to balance the axis so that our children and grandchildren can enjoy the fruits of our labor."

CHAPTER FIVE

Ann Marie lay in bed, listening to the soft raindrops dancing and swaying in the midnight darkness, slapping gently against the windowpane. Nature's symphony was playing an encore to a sleeping audience.

Only one week to go and she would be on her own. Tomorrow she would learn of her first assignment. Rod made his usual Saturday night drop-in by helicopter and gave her the news over Sunday morning coffee. Ever since the morning when he showed the DVD of her and April at the springs, she kept her distance from him, still uncomfortable about what she considered his spying on them. In spite of his protests otherwise, she still thought he could have gotten his point across in a less embarrassing way. So their contact was limited to brief visits each weekend when he critiqued her work. Still spying on her, she thought, admitting to herself that it really was his job to keep tabs on her progress.

She would have one last week of intense review, plus a heavy indoctrination on the subject of her case. Friday would close this chapter of her life, and Saturday would begin a new chapter, one she somewhat dreaded to see. What would she be doing? Where would she go? She kicked back the sheet and wiggled her toes in the night air — too tense to sleep; too excited about what lay ahead; anxious to meet the challenge head-on, yet sorry to see that somewhere out there was somebody or something working tirelessly to destroy everything she stood for. Here she was, innocent little Christie Cole, literally about to take on the world.

She thought about that FBI agent who was like her guardian angel all her life. He saved her life, then disappeared. Even though she barely remembered him, he was her inspiration. Where was he now? What would he think of her decision to join the group Alfred Williams led? For an instant, she felt lonely, as if she lost him. The moment passed and she smiled in the darkness. She was exactly where she was meant to be.

She rolled over, reached for her clock and tilted it in the dim light that shone through the rain-spattered window. Three o'clock and she hadn't even dozed since she went to bed at eleven. She was too keyed up because tonight she was going to execute a plan she formed over several weeks. Every time she had the opportunity to wander around the grounds, she paid particular attention to the attic windows she noticed on the first day. The four windows were never opened. They always were shuttered and showed no signs of ordinary use. There was an attic, possibly, but at least four hundred square feet of useable space. Something must be there, and tonight she would find out.

Late one evening, when she and Adolphus Morin returned from a walk at dusk, she looked up at the windows and was sure she saw a faint glow, perhaps a light, through the shutters. So maybe the room was in use after all. Or maybe, she scolded herself, it was where Millie kept the spare bed linens and toilet tissue.

She didn't really believe that, though. Intuitively, she knew that behind those windows lay the secrets of this grand house. Maybe secret, high level meetings were held there. Maybe Millie's real office, where all the secret files were stored, was tucked away in that office. Maybe her romantic notion of intrigue was getting the better of her. Ann Marie smiled in the darkness. Nevertheless, tonight she was going to find out what was behind that attic door. She was cursed with the need to know everything, she thought. Not in the sense that Rod McCarren defined "need to know," meaning what he thought she needed to know, but she had a strong curiosity about everything and everyone, and she, Ann Marie Beaudet, really needed to know what was going on around her and why. Immediately upon her arrival at Millie's House, she started to work on pinpointing where the house was located. Freshman astronomy carried her this far. From maps in the library, to some rough measurements with her compass as she watched the night sky, she made some best-guess calculations. Putting that together with the rocks and saguaro cactus, a meager amount of rain up until tonight, and for good measure, throw in some thoughtful conjecture about airliners passing overhead and she reached a conclusion. Phoenix. More or less fifty miles to the southeast. It had to be. She might be off a few miles, but she was confident that she was in some rugged, maybe unnamed mountains in central Arizona. A place that once was a resort for the rich and famous, but now a clandestine training ground. But how and when did it all come together? If she was ever going to know, now was the time.

She took a deep breath and let it out slowly while she counted to ten. When she hit the magic number she rolled over, tossed her feet over the side of the bed and on to the floor. If the answer was under this roof, she was going to find it.

From her briefcase, she took the lock-pick kit her employers generously provided, then grabbed a pen light from her bureau drawer. She held it tightly in her hand and stepped to the door of her room, opened it slowly, and listened for any sound. A light from the lobby at the end of the hall provided a gentle glow, just enough that she could walk without bumping into anything. Her bare feet stepped lightly on the hardwood floors. She held her breath with each step, waiting for the slightest creak, but there was none. Nothing but the sound of the rain and the gentle sweeping sound of her robe flowed against the still air. Everyone was asleep. She passed quickly beneath the light at the front desk and stepped into the darkness of the hall to the administrative offices. Even here, she thought, would not bring her to what she wanted to know. There wouldn't be anything of significance on the organization's background in everyday working offices. But upstairs, in the attic. If it was anywhere, that's where it would be.

Ann Marie passed by the last office door before flicking on her penlight, its narrow beam slicing through the dark until, at the end of the hall, it fell on a door, its sterile white paint shattered only by the stark word PRIVATE painted across its face in bold black letters. Her heart pounded. Sweat droplets ran down her back. She stood there in her robe, looking like anything but a master spy about to break into the inner sanctum of her employer's closet. What ghosts of the past might it hold?

She glanced nervously over her shoulder toward the reception desk, convincing herself that she was alone. She was as alone as she had ever been in her life. It was deathly quiet. Not even the sound of the rain could be heard here. It was as if she was wrapped in a cocoon of damp, silent, still air and hidden away from the rest of mankind.

She stuck the tip of the penlight between her teeth, tilting her head so she threw the beam into the palm of her hands as she opened the compact sized lock-pick kit. She slipped the tubular pick from a sheath and snapped the kit shut. She slid the pick into the skeleton lock and went to her knees as she shut the light off, listening in the daunting quiet. Slowly, she turned the pick, first to the right, then back slowly to the left. Less than a half-turn later, she heard the lock snap open. Her heart hammered. This was her first real covert entry. Her heart raced like the pistons of a car as she reached for the doorknob with her empty hand, still holding the flashlight between her teeth. She glanced again over her shoulder as she slowly twisted the doorknob. Then, praying the door wouldn't squeak, she eased it open. In the thin beam of the penlight, she made out a steep staircase.

Tucking her light into the palm of her hand, she allowed her eyes to become accustomed to the darkness of the stairway beyond. She tilted her head slightly, listening for any sounds that might indicate that anyone was moving about, but the house was as still as a tomb. She strained her eyes in the darkness, looking around the door and the staircase for the dim red light of a silent beam which, if broken, would arouse the household of an intruder. There was nothing. The door and stairs were sterile. She let out a slow, deep breath. She was inside!

She flicked on the penlight and pulled the door shut behind her, taking a moment to reach back and twist the old lock shut, and then stepped onto the first step. Walking slowly, each placement of her bare feet an intentional, calculated maneuver, Ann Marie moved closer to the landing at the top – closer to the secrets of Millie's house. She counted the steps to herself - - nine, ten, eleven, twelve, each of them silent. At last, she was at the top. She swung the beam of her light in quick, short arcs, taking in brief glimpses of an ordinary, dusty, cobwebbed attic. Cardboard file boxes; aged, military green, four drawer file cabinets. Everything was neat and orderly, in its place, looking like it had been there for years, undisturbed. A few silky cobwebs draped over items like delicate stitching between the boxes. Mouse droppings were at the foot of the first file cabinet that she came to. All signs indicated the place had not been used in a long time.

She walked slowly up and down the rows, noting that none of the boxes or drawers carried any markings that might identify its contents. If she was looking for easy answers, she wouldn't find any labels to guide her search. She couldn't go through everything if she had a year, so any quick answers would be as much a matter of luck as anything else. Guessing that files might be in some form of chronological order, from the back to the front, she carefully tiptoed through the dusty aisles, her robe sweeping the dust from the boxes and file cabinets when she eased past them. The stale air was stifling. The dusty, moldy odors clung to her nostrils; sweat poured down her brow and the back of her neck.

She neared the back of the attic. A mouse chattered softly and brushed against her bare foot before it scampered into the darkness between the boxes. She choked back a scream and felt a cold chill run the course down her spine. "Damn it," she muttered. Mice, spiders and snakes were her absolute torment. There wasn't a two-legged creature alive that could drive her off, but a creepy, crawly thing might be the death of her. However, there was no turning back. She came this far, and would finish the job.

Ann Marie scooted aside the top box in a stack of four, and quickly followed with the next two, coming at last to the bottom box. This, she hoped, had to be the first box, where the oldest files were kept, and the first written memory of Millie's house. She eased her fingernail under the crispy, dry strip of tape that was used to seal it shut so many years ago and opened the top. A dirty, gray puff of air shot up from the box, following the path of the box top.

Voices In The Fog

She caught herself in mid-sneeze and swallowed hard, choking as she held back the sneeze.

The tiny beam from her light danced over the yellowed papers that were neatly stacked and tied together with string. She slowly picked up each stack, looking carefully at the top sheet of paper before setting it aside until she completely emptied the box. They all appeared to be handwritten minutes of meetings held decades ago. Each individual pack appeared to be the minutes of separate meetings in March, April, and May of 1933. Records of people and issues that were part of the world long before she was born. She struck a bonanza! Slowly, gingerly, she untied the knot around the pack of minutes from the very bottom of the first box. She laid aside the top paper that was inscribed with only one word, SECRET.

Beneath that one sheet, Ann Marie found the clandestine history of Millie's house. Minutes written and signed by Maureen O'Connor, Private Secretary to the Vice-President of the United States of America, John Nance Garner. The minutes recorded a meeting when "Cactus Jack" Garner spoke on behalf of President Franklin Delano Roosevelt and his concern with how unscrupulous powers were taking advantage of the world's disastrous economy.

Ann Marie shifted the boxes around, arranging a place where she could sit in reasonable comfort while she read each page of the one and only packet that she would have time to review. Beside the Vice-President, others at the meeting were Herman Goldstein of the Wall Street firm of Goldstein, Drachman, Attorneys-at Law; Richard Dreyden, Special Assistant to the President; General James Tornbow, United States Army; Frederick Dunn, representing the

Voices In The Fog

Governor of the State of Utah; and Mr. William Young, Librarian, Salt Lake City.

Her heart raced even faster than her eyes as she read the minutes reflecting the President's concern that foreign and domestic powers unfriendly to the United States were racing to fill the pockets of brokers, bankers and politicians with enough money to choke an elephant. With the money, those unnamed powers were gaining influence into the very fiber of American government from Wall Street to the labor unions; from the price of oil and wheat to the election of aldermen and city councils. Their influence was "tilting the balance of power," as Tornbow described it. Or, as Garner said, "It is as if they are bound and determined to swathe the world with a cloak of fog to conceal their scandalous conduct."

That was a similar description she had heard so many months ago in what seemed like a different lifetime. "Voices in the fog." It hadn't changed in the ensuing years.

Too quickly, she came to the next-to-last sheet of crispy paper: the outline for the future. To assemble a small, secretive body that would operate at the will of the President, and whose task it was to identify those persons or organizations who worked to disrupt the democratic government of the United States.

She looked carefully at the final few sentences. A cold chill slithered like a snake over her skin as she reread the charge that Garner expressed on behalf of the President.

"The operatives of the United States shall never be identified publicly. They must move in the shadows of legitimate government, and shall bring to bear whatever force is necessary for the good of our nation, even at the cost of their lives."

Voices In The Fog

Tears formed in her eyes as she again read those dynamic words, spoken so many years ago. And yet, even with the passage of time, nothing changed. The forces of good and evil, some overt, others covert, were still engaged in the unending struggle for power and domination. Would it ever end?

She finally set the page aside and shone the light on the last page, a letter from the President of the United States.

"Greetings to those gathered together on this somber occasion,

"I send my personal representative, the Vice-President, to speak on my behalf. These first one hundred days of my office as President of the United States have been most trying. Nevertheless, I hold great hope for the people of this nation to rally together to help us overcome our adversaries. Whether it be armies of domination, unscrupulous carpetbaggers or common criminals, the very foundation of this great country is in peril. Therefore, I charge each of you to hold forever in silence the outcome of your discussions and conclusions, and to work in eternal secrecy to bring our foes to their knees while at the same time raising the glory of our great country to the heights that we know it can again ascend. I say this to you individually, and as a body. We must work with haste, but never at the cost of our honor and integrity.

May God in heaven bear witness to your honorable work.

Signed,
Franklin D. Roosevelt,
President of the United States."

*****

Voices In The Fog

Rod sat on the edge of the bed, swatting the alarm clock that wouldn't stop its incessant chirping. His eyes finally focused, and he saw that it was eleven minutes after three, the middle of the night! "Damn it," he blurted as he spun around on the bed, flicking on the nightlight and reaching for the alarm panel on the table across his bedroom. It wasn't the clock. It was a security breach.

Three tiny red lights flashed as the audio alarm continued its nerve-wracking little bleep. The file room. Somebody was in it. He paused for a second, taking in a deep breath to clear the sleep and give himself time to logically analyze what was happening. There were compression pads beneath the first, third and ninth steps leading to the file room, and each of the flashing lights indicated someone stepped on them. Nobody, absolutely nobody was allowed in the file room alone, and never in the middle of the night. Somebody would pay dearly for their transgression.

He pulled open the dresser drawer and grabbed his .40 caliber semi-automatic, taking a quick glance to make sure the clip was in it. He started toward the door, dressed only in his boxer shorts before he paused, then went back to the dresser and flipped quickly through his equipment and found his MoTrac viewers, the perfect tool for nighttime surveillance.

With his Glock in one hand and his viewers in the other, he padded quickly down the hall to the reception area, taking time to find the light switch and turn it off. He smiled to himself as he put on the viewers and saw everything come into focus in various shades of green; tables, desks, carpets, doorways. It was as though he was a cat. He moved quickly down the hall, taking care not to bump into anything. He moved in silence. It would be only a matter of seconds until he found out who entered the attic. He already had a good idea of who it was, but nobody would get away with anything on his watch. Somebody was going to pay hell for this.

He stopped when he approached the closed door to the staircase. Quietly, he took the doorknob in his hand and twisted . . . nothing! It was locked. Whoever it was took time to lock it from the inside. "Shit," he whispered. Rod spun around and started back down the hall toward the reception area, then stopped in his tracks.

"Bullshit," he muttered, and tuned back toward the staircase. "Bullshit, you asshole. You're in for the surprise of your life." He walked slowly back to the closed door, pressed himself up against the wall, and waited.

*****

Ann Marie folded the papers back together, carefully re-wrapping the strings around the bundles before putting them back in the box. She stood, dusted the grime and dirt from her robe, and carefully put the boxes back into a stack like she found them. She knew the secret of Millie's house. She would slip back down the stairs and get back into bed, her soft, warm, comfortable bed. But she knew she would not sleep. Her discovery darted around in her brain like lightning flashes. She was involved in something far larger than she ever imagined. She was actually on a quest initiated by the President of the United States.

Her feet padded softly on the floor as she retraced her steps around the files and boxes to the landing at the top of the stairwell. She paused, flashing the tiny light back through the darkness of the attic, taking one last glance at the history of a lifetime.

She gripped the handrail lightly, flicked her light off and started carefully down the darkened stairs. Counting the steps, she reached out into the inky blackness and touched the latch. Turning gently, she listened for the click of the lock, then gently pushed the door open. Instantly, she knew that something was wrong. She should have seen an indirect glow from the reception desk, but there was nothing. The light was off. The hallway was in complete darkness.

Rod watched as the doorknob, eerily green as seen through the MoTrac viewers, turned and the door began to open. His heart quickened. He lifted his gun and thrust it into the face of the woman as she stepped through the doorway.

Ann Marie's scream caught in her throat as she felt the cold gun being jammed into her cheek. "Help! Help! Don't shoot."

Rod stopped the gentle pull on the trigger in the instant he recognized her, "Shut your fucking mouth, Miss Beaudet," he commanded in a loud whisper. "Just shut up."

"Oh God, is that you Rod?" she muttered as she reached in the darkness and pushed the gun away.

"Shut up and don't move a muscle," he commanded. He stepped back and looked at her. "You know this is off-limits. Why were you up there?"

Ann Marie fumbled with her light as she tried to turn it on, but Rod raked the gun barrel across the back of her hand, sending the light crashing to the floor. She wanted to cry, but swallowed it, trying not to show her fear or the sting in her hand. "Okay, damn it. You caught me. Now what are you going to do with me? Arrest me? Kill me?"

Voices In The Fog

She heard a quiet laugh and imagined Rod smirking because he caught her with her hand in the cookie jar. "So what now?" she asked. She squared her shoulders and stood defiantly in the doorway. She couldn't see anything in the darkness, but heard his breathing no more than three or four feet in front of her.

The rain stopped. The sound of silence filled the hallway. "Rod? Rod? What are you doing?" Her mind raced through all sorts of conjecture about her mentor.

"Looking at you," he replied softly. God, she was beautiful. They stood there without moving; she listened to his breathing; he looked at her nakedness, bathed in the green glow of the night viewer. He forced his mind back to the matter at hand, but it was hard.

"I could have killed you. You know that, don't you?"

"Yes," she whispered. "Yes, I know you could have, but you didn't. So what happens now?"

Rod took off the glasses and flicked the switch, turning on the hall light. They stood silently for a moment, looking at each other, then she glanced at the glasses he held in one hand, and the gun in the other.

"You! You were spying on me with those? You bastard! How dare you!"

He ignored her outburst. "Did you find what you wanted?"

She took several deep breaths and suppressed her outrage. "I think so," she said finally. "Have you ever been up there and looked through those things?"

He disregarded her question and pulled the door shut behind her. "Out there in the real world you would be dead right about now. Do you understand that?"

"Yeah, I do. So I ask again, what happens next?"

"I can't say right now. It isn't my call. I guess you'll find out in the morning when you get your assignment. If you get one."

Ann Marie felt sick to her stomach. "You mean I might wash out? For this, I might be thrown out of the whatever we're in?"

"For this!" Rod exploded. "Miss Beaudet, you deliberately disobeyed instructions. You broke the rules. You broke in a place you didn't belong. What did you expect?" He stopped. His breathing was labored. "You should know by now that no one 'washes out.' We couldn't send you back out in the world, knowing as much as you do about us. What would you do? You couldn't be Miss Beaudet anymore, because she belongs to us. You couldn't be Christie Cole, because she doesn't exist. So where does that leave you?"

She tried to swallow the lump that threatened to choke her. "What will I do?" she whispered.

"I don't know." He grinned sourly. "We do have our equivalent of Siberia. Now go to bed. Maybe I'll see you in the morning then maybe not."

CHAPTER SIX

Beaudet sat on the edge of the bed, shoulders slumped, matted clumps of long dark hair clinging to her neck and cheeks. She tossed and turned all night. She couldn't explain her compulsion to discover all she could about her new employer. It was just there. She had to know! And it might have cost her everything. Rod indicated she might get sent to some out-of-the-way post. The group probably had people to do the grunt work somewhere. Maybe she would spend the rest of her life as a file clerk in Boise.

She finally dozed for a while, then woke up late. She missed breakfast, but if she hurried, she could grab a glass of juice and go to her briefing session. This is what she worked for during the last nine weeks, but now she was more scared than excited. In another hour or two, she would find out where she would be going, and if she still had a promising career as an ultra-secret spook. She shook the grogginess from her head and went to the bathroom, hoping a hot bath would clear the cobwebs from her tired brain.

*****

Ann Marie stood at the juice bar, tucked her notebook beneath her arm, and filled her glass with fresh, cool orange juice, just the way she liked it, full of pulp. She was ready to go. She left the dining room, walked quickly past the reception desk and down the hallway, the same hallway where Rod surprised her only hours earlier. Now, it was so different: peaceful and welcoming. A touch of the days when the Vice-President of the United States walked its length. So long ago when the world was different, yet startlingly similar. Shiny, waxed hardwood floors, a mahogany end table covered with a doily sat beside an occasional chair, beckoning a passerby to pause and enjoy a few minutes of quiet relaxation. It was a step back in time, before everything was so pleasant and deceptive, as well as swathed in the fog of deception.

She stopped at the conference room door for a moment to calm her racing heart, and to cling to the remaining moments of her previous life. She felt like a condemned killer about to enter the death chamber at Huntsville, known as The Walls Unit. Those huge, foreboding, red brick walls deep in the piney woods of southeast Texas. A gurney was waiting beyond the door. They would strap her down; give her a chance to say a few last words. Or maybe not. Painlessly, they would inject her with a sedative. That would be the beginning of the end, and all she had for a last meal was a glass of orange juice.

She remembered a time when she was in college and went to Huntsville as part of a sociology project, not about the person about to be put to death, but about the crowd that gathered outside those old, towering brick walls. Some were there to cheer. Others came in silent protest. It was, she decided, a macabre scene. Something was there for everyone. There were hotdog vendors, reporters, television lights, candles flickering in the sticky, humid air, policemen and security guards, and priests and nuns saying the rosary. The most curious of all was a woman standing silently beneath an old oak tree, holding an infant to her breast as she stared with blank eyes – gazing at nothing in particular.

Not since then had she felt so alone, yet in the midst of so many people. She took a deep breath and opened the door. *Deja vu*! Alfred Willams sat at the far end of the conference table, chewing the stem of his unlit pipe.

"Good morning, Miss Beaudet." He got up and walked around the table to shake her hand.

Her heart pounded. Rod said he wouldn't be the one to decide what would happen to her. Was her future in Alfred Williams's hands? "Good morning," she replied. "We meet again. Somehow, though, I'm not surprised to see you."

Williams returned to his chair, gesturing to her to sit across the table from him. "I thought you might be expecting me. Won't you have a seat?" He pulled a sheath of papers from his open briefcase and slid them over to her. "Not very dramatic," he commented. "No big lead-in or anything, but here is your case."

Ann Marie glanced furtively at the papers, then back to Williams. Surely, there would be some preliminary butt-reaming before he shipped her off to Outer Mongolia.

"You can read them later. Right now I will summarize your assignment for you. We seem to be having a problem with our Supreme Court. Not that the government has always been happy with some of their decisions, but we think this is different. It seems as if Justice Gonzales has done more than a one-eighty over the last two sessions. Something's happened. We don't have any idea what changed him, but something obviously has. He went from being the most conservative of the Justices to being liberal. More than liberal. Hell, even left-wingers don't know where he is coming from. It's like he's lost his mind. I've brought some of his old cases for you to read, and you'll see what I mean." He indicated a large cardboard box at the end of the table.

Ann Marie swallowed hard. Why didn't he just get the reprimand over with? The suspense was killing her.

Voices In The Fog

Seemingly unaware of her discomfort, Williams continued his briefing. "The first five years he was on the bench, he was one mean, son-of-a-bitch. Tough as hell. Even the President was surprised, albeit pleasantly, at how conservative he was. Then, bang! Like a shot in the dark. For the last two sessions he has been coming on like he was on the ACLU payroll or something. Even when he is on the low side, real low, like an eight-to-one vote, he carries on like a deranged man." Williams pulled his tobacco pouch from his pocket and scooped a bowl full. "He's no nut. Not by any means. He's as smart as they come. A damn genius. He knows the law and the constitution from A to Z, but his decisions are so out of whack with his history that we think something is wrong."

"Couldn't that be the explanation?" she asked. "Everyone knows how intelligent he is. Couldn't it be that he just studies his cases harder than anyone else, and can very logically come to these conclusions? I mean, can't a person change without the government suspecting some type of conspiracy?"

Williams considered her thoughtfully. "Some change over a span of years might not seem unusual, but this is different. It's too sudden and too radical. Like the difference between black and white. No, somebody has gotten to him. That's where you come in. We want to know who got to him and why. And most of all, how." Williams lit his pipe, sucking deeply, savoring the chicory taste before letting the smoke drift slowly upward. "Maybe you're right, but by damn, you're going to have to prove it. Either way. You're going to have to prove what has happened, or conversely, prove to us that a zebra can change its stripes."

94

Voices In The Fog

Relief flooded through her body. Maybe she was getting a reprieve from only God knows where. Temporarily, anyway. She nodded. "I'm sorry, go ahead."

"Ricardo Huerta Gonzales is sixty-two years old. He is the son of a copper miner, born and raised in Bisbee, Arizona, went to Stanford on a scholarship, then on to Harvard Law. He got a job in Houston with a big firm doing civil cases, but then was hired as a special prosecutor on one of the federal scams that scooped up a couple of congressmen who got wrapped up in some oil deals and a little off-shore banking. One thing led to another, and pretty soon he ended up as a federal prosecutor in the Northern District of Texas. About five years later, he was appointed by the President as a Federal Judge. He was a good one, too. Democrats and Republicans alike voted him in. He was solid. That was for damned sure. So, seven years ago the President nominated him to the Supreme Court. He flew through the hearings like a gentle ocean breeze and landed on the highest court in the land, and almost everybody was happy. You know how that goes. A few members of the loyal opposition tried to take a shot at him, but he handled it with aplomb. Everything was great.

"Until recently, that is, and nobody can explain it. Of course, nobody can simply walk up to a Supreme Court Justice and ask him what the heck is going on in his mind. But this guy has gone fruity. Not crazy, you understand, but fruity. He has been making a mockery of the system, and that's something we can't tolerate. We have to live with screwy decisions from time to time, but this is different. We're convinced somebody has gotten to him."

"Can't he be impeached or removed somehow?"

"Find a crime, and we can get rid of him. But there is a bigger picture than this one member of the court. I propose to you this scenario. If someone can reach out and touch a Supreme Court Justice, what else can they do? Who else can they touch? We live in a delicate balance and cannot handle too much undue influence. Do you understand?"

Williams sucked on his pipe and continued. "This guy is a bachelor, but there's no evidence of homosexuality. That was the first thing we checked out. He's more or less a loner. The man likes to read, enjoys a bit of fly-fishing, goes up to Wyoming once or twice a year, goes to the opera, and eats out a lot in restaurants. He lives alone, but has a maid in weekly. The bureau has checked her out, and everything is kosher. No problems. No gambling. No drugs. No weird sex. Nothing. That's the problem. On the surface, he's as clean as a whistle, but by damn," Williams said as he slammed his fist on the table, "there is something there. A secret, Miss Beaudet. A secret. Go find it."

Still no word of reprimand. What was going on? Hadn't Rod reported her late night foray into the inner sanctum of Millie's House? Why hadn't Williams confronted her? Stifling the questions, she made her exit as quickly as possible, vowing to Alfred Williams there was nothing to worry about. She would solve the riddle of the Supreme Court Justice.

She lay across her bed into the wee hours of the morning, reading and re-reading Gonzales's life history; court case after court case; opinion after opinion; every word that was written by or about one of the most powerful people in the United States. His was a rags-to-riches story – the American dream – from the squalor of the slag heaps of Bisbee to the Supreme Court of the United States. It's the stuff books are written about.

"Yeah," she mumbled to herself. "There'll be a book or two written about him by the time this case is done."

Voices In The Fog

The days and nights became a blur. The aspiring young espionage agent read almost non-stop except for an occasional snack, but otherwise becoming acquainted with the Justice better than she knew herself. She reviewed copies of news clippings, baby pictures, old family albums, college transcripts, FBI background papers when he was nominated for the judgeship, and later for the Supreme Court. To say he was squeaky clean was an understatement. He was untarnished in every form of the word. He was a hard working judge and a believer in the rule of law. Nobody could be excused – king or pauper.

She thought she could have seen him two hundred years earlier. He would have been a combination of all the things the framers of the constitution sought in a leader. Honesty. Fairness. Integrity. Purity. Equality. Everyman's dream for the way things ought to be. That was Justice Gonzales seven years ago, but not the same man now. Not even close to it.

A radical's radical is how a Washington Post editorial described him after his most recent decision, a minority one at that. Even the two other dissenting Justices did not join his opinion in *United States v. Londell*. The case was simple enough. A fourth amendment question of the legality of a stop and frisk by the police when the officer "feels" through the defendant's outer garments what the officer believes "feels" like contraband.

Gonzales raged for page after page about the framers' intent of protecting the citizenry from the ravages of the "king's agents, descending upon them like a pack of wolves, tearing at the backbone of freedom . . . their right to privacy."

It went on, case after case. Well written. Astute. Articulate. Logical to the point that it went all the way around, three hundred and sixty degrees, to the point of being illogical. It seemed almost as if it were a different person from the conservative, independent thinker who joined the court only seven years ago.

What went wrong? How could a person make such a dramatic swing out of the blue? Surely he didn't forget his roots. Where was everything he stood for only two or three years ago? He always was intelligent and independent, but this was uncanny. Elephants don't fly. Suddenly she caught herself repeating Williams's comment, "And zebras can't change their stripes."

Saturday morning found Secret Agent Beaudet, as she dubbed herself, once again seated across the conference room table from Williams as they shared bagels and cream cheese, a mound of documents scattered in disarray between them.

"Well, what do you say so far?"

"I think he's some kind of a nut," she replied.

"Yeah, well you're in good company. But why? What happened to bring a man like him around to such a strange point of view? Did you see anything there we missed?"

"*Nada.* Zero. Zilch. Zip. Just out of the blue. At the start of the session two years ago, he came out swinging. Not that he hadn't been assertive previously, but this was different. It was totally different, with nothing to give a hint as to why. Something really inexplicable has happened, and you're right. If they can get to a Supreme Court Justice, then who is next? Scary, isn't it?"

"I believe you've hit the nail on the head, Miss Beaudet." Williams began bundling the papers into a briefcase, obviously deep in thought. When he finished, he shoved the case across the table toward her. "There you go. It's yours. Ready?"

"Ready as I'll ever be," she responded, pulling the briefcase into her lap. "Let's do it."

"You're on! Okay, here we go with the new you, Miss Beaudet. Your *adversary*," he emphasized the word, "Justice Gonzales lives in a beautiful, two-story row house on Union Street in Alexandria by Founder's Park. It's across the river from Washington D. C. It's a wonderful place, really. He has a porch on the second story and can sit out there on Sunday afternoon and watch the yachts on the Potomac. In the springtime, he can look across the tidal basin and see the cherry blossoms. We would have to call it one of the better places in Alexandria. He likes to go for walks along the river, visit the little tourist shops, coffee places, browse, that kind of stuff. He eats out quite a bit in some of the fish houses along the riverfront. All in all, he seems to lead a pretty nice life and enjoys himself. He likes to read the paper on the park bench on the weekend. Not a bad life at all, and that's what makes all of this crap about him seem so strange.

"On a good day, he can get to the office in twenty minutes or so. A driver, one approved by the FBI, the Marshal's Office, and the Secret Service, picks him up and takes him home. We have checked the driver every which way but loose. Clean as a whistle. Name is Winchester Tubfield, from a long line of slaves, merchants, and a few politicians. Folks who did pretty damned good for themselves. Winchester retired from the Post Office about ten years back, and has been a driver for the Court ever since. He's clean, and we don't figure him to have any involvement in this, one way or the other.

Voices In The Fog

"We've arranged for you to have a nice little place on the corner, just catty-corner from Gonzales' place. The first floor is your new art gallery. A place we've named Heritage Art Works. You'll have a reasonable collection of American art. A few names I'm sure you recognize; Hurd, Wyeth, O'Keeffe and a few others. Your apartment is upstairs. We already have the gallery set up, but a sign on the door says that you're open by appointment only." Williams laughed. "You're a high-priced lady, Miss Beaudet. Anyway," he continued, "that's your cover. You're a very selective collector of American heritage art. You studied a little of that in school, didn't you?"

"Yeah, sure did. Never could afford it, though."

"Well, you're in it now. That is about where I leave you. Here," he said. Williams reached into his jacket pocket and pulled out a set of keys and slid them across the table to her. "There are the keys to your kingdom. Now go get him."

"And what if I run into trouble? Need some advice or some kind of support? Anything like that?"

"Good questions. Remember, you may feel alone, but we're never too far away. There's a little flagpole next to your front door. Normally, you will fly the stars and stripes. Got a problem? Run up the Virginia flag. In a bad bind? Real bad bind? Put out a trash sack by the front door. We'll find you and take care of you. I promise. Don't worry about it."

*****

The sun long ago set over the rugged peaks. Ann Marie sat on the edge of her bed in the growing darkness, waiting for the sound of the helicopter. Even this late in the game, she would not be allowed to go in the daylight where she might see enough to identify exactly where she was. As they said so many times, "Right to know, and need to know."

Before the new day's sun rose over the Potomac, she would be home. Home in Old Town Alexandria. Across the street from Ricardo Huerta Gonzales, Justice of the United States Supreme Court.

CHAPTER SEVEN

Four-thirty a.m., November 1st, Ann Marie heaved the last of the heavy boxes onto the landing at the top of the narrow stairs. "Welcome home, Ann Marie Beaudet," she murmured to herself. Out of breath, she leaned against the narrow railing that ran around the perimeter of the small landing outside the door of her new apartment over the art gallery. *Her* art gallery, now. Heritage Art Works. She allowed herself a wry smile. She knew as much about art as two courses in art history had taught her.

It was a long night, one in which she reversed her trip to Millie's house. First, the helicopter ride from the golf course to the airstrip; then the NASA jet to National Airport, where she was met by the smiling Irishman in the Evergreen delivery truck. Everything the same. Only backwards. The only difference was that on this trip she was alone. Not only was Rod McCarren not there, he didn't even come with Alfred Williams to see her off. She hadn't seen him since the night he caught her returning from her stealthy visit to the attic file room in Millie's house. That worried her a lot. She didn't believe for a minute that he would let her rule infraction slide. He must be planning some sort of retribution. But what?

Ann Marie dragged the last box into the small, furnished living room and shoved it into one corner with the rest of her possessions. The boxes were loaded into the van driven by the Irishman when he picked her up at the airport. He helped her unload them downstairs in the gallery, but left her to get them upstairs on her own. She gazed at them and shook her head. "Not much to show for thirty-three years of living," she thought.

Voices In The Fog

These were the boxes she saw in William's storeroom office the day she left the FBI Academy and started her new career. The gall of Williams. He had someone go to her home in Texas and pack them, even before she accepted his proposition. He must have been very sure of her. Of course, there was the picture he showed her. He must have known the sight of her son would soften her up.

Williams told her they packed nothing that would connect her with Christie Cole. So, she knew that when she unpacked, she wouldn't find her diploma from Texas A & M. None of her basketball trophies were there. Not even her grandmother's scrapbooks that chronicled the Cole family through several generations. Most likely, she wouldn't find Amos, the soft and cuddly brown bear that was her favorite possession since Granny gave him to her years ago. She didn't take Amos with her to the Academy. He was her companion in her college years, but she knew space would be limited and her roommate might not think a stuffed animal appropriate for an Agent Trainee. She brushed away a fleeting melancholia, tossed her Nikes on top of one of the boxes, and flicked off the lamp. Seconds later, she was in a deep sleep on the sofa.

Somewhere close by, bells rang. Deep melodic chimes that seemed to be inside her. Reluctantly, she opened her eyes, but didn't move for a moment, somewhat disoriented. The room was flooded with light and she closed her eyes against the glare. Where was she? Then she remembered she was in her new home. She opened her eyes again and glanced at the clock on the mantel. Eleven o'clock. Now she recognized the sound of the Sunday morning call to worship in Alexandria, Virginia's churches. She had slept nearly six hours, exhausted and out of gas. She was mentally and physically worn out.

Voices In The Fog

She decided to unload her boxes, and spend the day much as she had on the first Sunday at Millie's, exploring her surroundings. She heard much about the charm and beauty of Old Alexandria, but she didn't have time to explore while she was at the Academy. Now, she lived in the heart of the old city.   She would explore the neighborhood. Have lunch at one of the cozy cafes along the river. Maybe find a bookstore and have a cup of coffee.

She stretched, enjoying the pull of muscles stiff from the long trip and her late night, to say nothing of heaving a dozen heavy boxes up those stairs. No work today, though. She wouldn't even think about Ricardo Huerta Gonzales or the Supreme Court. Nothing. This would be a day to pamper herself. The Academy demanded her time, morning, noon, and night; weekends and all. Then Millie's place nearly overwhelmed her with classes, hands-on practice with gizmos of every kind, tons of literature to read at night, every moment absorbed in work. But not today. This would be her day of leisure. She might even spoil herself with a lobster dinner tonight, and to hell with the cost. She could afford it. Why not have a little fun and spend some of her new wealth.

After a long hot shower, she dressed in jeans that were not too wrinkled from the suitcase, and a long-sleeved, teal T-shirt, in case the afternoon got cool later. She decided not to dry her hair, and the damp ringlets left faint spots on the T-shirt, but once she was outside, they would dry soon enough.

She decided to put off unpacking until later, but she rummaged through one of the suitcases, looking for the photographs of her parents and her grandmother with the grandfather she never knew, which stood on her dresser at home. In the small dorm room at the Academy, there was only a small shelf to hold them. She found the pictures and gazed at them for a few minutes, realizing that in her hands she held all that was left of her former life.

Unexpectedly, tears spilled from her eyes and slid down her cheeks. She brushed them away with the sleeve of her T-shirt and gently placed the photographs on the dresser.

Ann Marie carefully set the burglar alarm with the code Williams provided her, locked her new front door, and strolled onto Union Street. Williams told her she had a car that was kept in the garage attached at the back of the gallery. Today, though, she wanted to walk.

Union Street was crowded with people who looked suspiciously like tourists to her. She was a little surprised at first. Early November wasn't the typical tourist season. Then, in the nation's capital and its environs, she supposed every season was tourist season. Since Alexandria was just across the Potomac from Washington, D. C., and claimed Mt. Vernon, George Washington's home, the city probably swarmed with tourists year-round.

The crowd, mostly amiable and friendly, fascinated her. Tourists with backpacks slung over their shoulders wandered in and out of shops, ran between the cars that crept along the narrow street. Shopping bags dangled from the crooks of arms. Toddlers held onto their mothers' hands as they were tugged along.

It was good to be back among ordinary, regular people. No spies, no government in crisis, no project reports due in the morning. Nothing!

She meandered through the shops in the Torpedo Factory, and after a while, decided she needed an ice cream cone. She sat on the edge of a sidewalk flowerpot, savored the soft creamy chocolate, and people-watched – one of her favorite pastimes. The afternoon sun was warm. People were smiling and having fun, and all was right with the world.

Ann Marie finally found herself exactly where she wanted to be, at a bookstore at the far end of Union Street. She discovered the coffee shop on the second floor offered a view of the river. She grabbed a magazine from the rack, ordered a café Mocha, and found a table by the window where she could watch the boats as they cruised the Potomac. She was a little surprised when she realized how good she felt, how happy she was with her life, with the choices she had made, and what she was doing. How many people could say the same thing about their lives?

On her way back down Union Street, she noticed a small window display of stuffed animals. She stood in front of the window a few minutes, examining each toy with satisfaction. Impulsively, she went inside and was delighted when the lone clerk, doing busy work behind the counter, let her browse unmolested. After a few minutes, she found what she was looking for. About a foot tall. Plush and brown and oh, so soft. Eyes that seemed to meet hers. She took the bear in both hands and held him at eye level. "Hello, Amos Two," she murmured in delight.

As she prescribed for herself, she was home by six o'clock and immersed in a hot bath with bubbles overflowing the tub. If she was going to spoil herself, she was going to do it in style and have fun, too.

She decided that, for her first real meal in Alexandria, she would enjoy lobster at one of the elegant old restaurants along King Street. Lobster, a Caesar salad, and a glass of white wine. For dessert? Something light and sweet, followed with a cup of deep, dark coffee.

Voices In The Fog

*****

Hours later, she crawled into bed. "Not bad for a first day," she muttered to Amos Two. She tucked him snugly under the sheets next to her. It was, indeed, a good day. "Tomorrow," she thought, "will take care of itself."

She lay back on her pillow. Her mind floated back over the days at Millie's, and the people she met, the old-time elegance of the house and grounds, and the intense weeks of her training. When she was almost asleep, she recalled one of Williams' last bits of advice: be patient, careful and methodical. Don't try to rush things. If you need us, we'll be there. Otherwise, do your work and you'll find the secret, whatever it is. It's just a matter of time.

*****

By chance more than plan, Ann Marie sat at the breakfast nook early Monday morning, eating a bowl of Cheerios and sipping a glass of orange juice. Not fresh and pulpy, the way it was served at Millie's House, but for the A&P, it would do. From the window over the table, she could watch the hustle and bustle of Union Street below. It gave her an unobstructed view of Justice Gonzales's home, catty-corner across the way. As she was scrutinizing his neat, two story brick house, a black Lincoln Town Car pulled to the curb in front of it. Ann Marie glanced at the clock on the wall next to the small refrigerator. Eight-thirty exactly. No more than a minute passed before the front door opened and a man in a black topcoat came out, turned to lock the door behind him, then headed toward the waiting car. She gave thanks for her 20/20 vision. She recognized him immediately from pictures Williams showed her; black hair slicked back from a broad brow, tall, broad shoulders. Mr. Justice Gonzales. He moved quickly, purposefully, but before he reached the car, the driver got out and came around to the passenger side to hold the door for him. "This must be Winchester Tubfield," she thought. Typically, Williams was precise in his description of the Justice's driver in his briefing to her.

She grabbed a scratch pad from the kitchen counter and made some notes: Monday, November 2. Black Town Car. Gonzales in dark suit. Topcoat. Briefcase in left hand. Gone in less than two minutes after the car arrived. Later, she would enter her notes into the permanent case book she would use throughout the investigation. Her new life was underway.

Ann Marie watched the car nose into traffic, going north on Union, then a left on Oronoco Street, where it disappeared from sight. She finished her breakfast, cleared the table, and went to the bedroom to dress. Snug jeans, a cranberry colored lightweight pullover, and Nikes. Her uniform for the day–and many days–she thought, unless there was an appointment downstairs in the gallery to show a painting to an unsuspecting client who thought she was dealing with a reputable art dealer. She quickly pulled her dark hair back and secured it loosely with a scrunchy at the nape of her neck. She added a touch of color on her lips and she was ready.

Today, her surveillance of the Justice would be loose since she had a few more preparations to make before getting down to serious business. First, she wanted to get the lay of the land and develop a comfort zone with her surroundings.

She mingled with the tourists and shopkeepers for a while, in and out of stores and alleys. She had no specific destination in mind, except that she had one type of store in mind, a florist. When she found what she wanted, the clerk inside raised her eyebrows when Ann Marie told her she wanted two medium sized clay pots filled with pansies – potted, not cut. Perfect, she thought, when she saw the finished arrangement. The purple and yellow flowers made a riot of color against the terra cotta; she had a touch of beauty to brighten up her balcony. However, she had an even more important use for the pots. They provided the perfect cover for her Regency Mark IV Interceptor. With her purse slung over her shoulder, carrying a pot of pansies in each arm, she started home.

She stood back and admired her handiwork. The pansies looked bright and cheerful, perched on the wide railing. She was glad she bought them. Propped on a brick wedged snugly between the two pots, her Mark IV Interceptor was directly on a line with what she was sure from the diagram of the Justice's house provided by Williams was the window to Gonzales's second floor bedroom. From this moment forward, the Justice would no longer have a private life. With this little gadget, she would listen to his every sound. She would know what television shows he watched and every word he muttered in his sleep. She would hear his portion of every telephone conversation he had, no matter where he was in the house.

Ann Marie suggested to Mr. Williams that they – whoever *they* were, whoever *she* was – that they bug his phone, but that idea was nixed immediately.

"Too much risk," he'd said. "We don't know who he is working with, or for, and we don't know who's handling him. Someone may be blackmailing him for all we know. If he's being used by someone, then whoever it is may sweep his line from time to time and our bug would be discovered. That would be disastrous. We just can't take that chance."

So Ann Marie monitored the house day and night. When at home, she could keep the speaker on, a low undercurrent to everything she did. In addition, the sounds coming from Gonzales's house will be recorded, so she would miss nothing when she was out of the apartment. Her first priority when she returned was to listen to the digitally recorded sounds, mostly the whispers of an empty house. "Except on Fridays, when the housekeeper came," she reminded herself.

Satisfied that the Interceptor was working, Ann Marie gazed at the house across the street. It was time she got a closer look. She hurried downstairs and out to the sidewalk. When there was a break in traffic, she crossed the street and paced slowly past the house. An empty carport, looking as if it had not been used in years, huddled beside the house. No door led from the carport into the house. There was no room for a car, even if the Justice owned one, which he didn't. He didn't even drive. The small structure was filled with flower pots containing a motley assortment; one sickly looking hibiscus, a night blooming jasmine that didn't look as if it bloomed in a while, and some red bougainvilleas. There was an old park bench and beside it, a barrel turned upside down which made a rough table. From the looks of things, Gonzales was a bachelor through and through. No artsy touches except the pots and flowers placed without much attention to aesthetics. No thought of things such as space, size, color; chaos versus order. Although, some would say, chaos is nothing more than a different type of order.

"Secret Agent Beaudet," she mused to herself as she walked past the house to the end of the block and turned right. Halfway down the block she came to a paved alley that ran behind her target house. A dumpster stood opposite the gate. "Maybe a Justice rated a little extra convenience," she considered. A low white picket fence enclosed the tiny back yard, where a few remaining dandelions poked their scrawny necks up through a reasonably good stand of well-trimmed grass. Not a big yard, by any measure, but in these neighborhoods where space was at a premium, any grass was considered a luxury.

Late that afternoon, after making sure the Mark IV Interceptor was working, she got a Perrier from the refrigerator and sat down in the breakfast nook to wait for Gonzales to come home. Precisely at 6:30, the Town Car wheeled up to the curb and eased to a stop directly in front of the door. Gonzales got out of the back seat, leaned over to say something to the driver through the passenger side window, then walked toward the house. He juggled his briefcase from hand to hand as he fumbled for his keys. He stepped inside and reached for something with his right hand. Although Ann Marie couldn't see his hand, she realized he was disarming his alarm system. Within seconds, the door closed behind him. "Probably home for the evening," she thought.

Via the Mark IV Interceptor on the balcony, the government agent listened to the sounds coming from across the street. Boring, she thought, five hours later when his bedroom light went out. She waited and listened a bit longer. He listened to National Public Radio, then watched the late news on television. All the while, Ann Marie heard the rustling of pages as if he read. Or, maybe he brought work home from the office. Now, he was snoring – loud enough to wake the dead. "Maybe that was why he'd never married," she thought, amused.

Voices In The Fog

Through Friday, Mr. Justice Gonzales did not vary his routine, except that one night he watched a John Wayne western instead of listening to public radio. The Lincoln arrived exactly at eight-thirty every morning to pick Gonzales up, and it deposited him on his doorstep promptly at six-thirty each evening. "His bachelor life could only be described as boring, maybe even more boring than hers," she thought wryly. She heard that stakeouts were painfully dull and long, and even though she wasn't confined to a car or a lamp post or even one particular spot, she was confined to a lonely existence. Her only company was the sounds made by a man who didn't even know she existed.

On Tuesday morning, she initiated her planned surveillance of Gonzales' daily drive to work. She knew, or assumed she knew, where he spent his days – in his office at the Supreme Court Building. Nevertheless, she wondered if he might occasionally make an interesting stop along the way. The two-year old navy blue Chevy her employers provided her was perfect for undercover work. Nothing too obtrusive. An easy hide in everyday traffic. Just an ordinary car driven by an ordinary woman.

She followed Winchester Tubfield and the judge as they drove demurely along a route that was not necessarily the shortest, but certainly the most scenic, and for the judge, probably the one that reminded him of his sworn duty to protect and uphold the Constitution of the United States.

They crossed the Memorial Bridge, curved around the Lincoln Memorial, drove up Constitution Avenue where they traveled through the very image of all that America stands for. To the right, the Washington Monument; to the

112

left, the White House. The last few minutes took them past the Capital Building before the Lincoln pulled up to the Supreme Court Building and the private entrance reserved for the Justices of the United States Supreme Court.

Surely, she thought, he looks at these beautiful manifestations of American history as a reminder of the awesome power he wields; power he can deliver with the stroke of a pen.

For the rest of the week, Ann Marie followed the Judge, as she began calling Gonzales, back and forth to his office, always taking the same route, and the trip always took precisely the same amount of time – forty minutes. Maybe he wasn't contacting anyone during his commute, she decided – at least he hadn't this week. Unless he was using a cell phone. She hadn't been following closely enough to tell if he was using a phone or not. Her notes from Williams showed no evidence of one, but that didn't prove anything. There were all kinds of throwaway phones, phones that could be registered to someone else.

Beaudet was glad when Saturday morning came. Maybe the judge would do something interesting over the weekend. The November temperatures dropped during the week, so she dressed warmly in case he decided to go out – a heavy sweater over jeans, and her Nikes. A beige windbreaker lay on the table in the breakfast nook, along with her purse, her keys and the MoTrac viewer. She watched his front door while she sipped her orange juice. Whatever adventure he was about to embark on, she realized it was on foot when he came out of his house, locked the door and set off down the street. His head was bare, but he wore a hip length tan all- weather coat over dark trousers.

Voices In The Fog

She grabbed her things off the table and hurried out of the apartment. When she reached the street, he was more than half a block away. She thought of herself as reasonably athletic, but when she tried to stay up with the judge, she was a first class piker. Gonzales was not an athletic looking person, but when it came to walking, he could cover the town from one end to the other and never slow down. Ann Marie was sure they were going to see every corner of Alexandria that morning. He wasn't particularly fast, but his pace was grueling – go, go, go. No wonder he didn't have a car. He didn't need one. He could cut through city traffic on foot faster than most people could in a car. She just hoped that he was so engrossed in his walk he wouldn't notice that one other pedestrian was never far away. Finally, he came to a more crowded area and slowed. She drew within seven or eight yards of him. He didn't stop to talk with anyone or make any effort to deliver a message or do anything suspicious, but she needed to know if he was concealing something beneath his coat – a recording or receiving device, a cell phone, anything.

She slid the MoTrac glasses over the bridge of her nose and fitted them safely on her ears. They weren't exactly a pair of Gucci frames, but they would do for what she wanted to see. More than she wanted to see, she realized immediately. "Oh, my God," she whispered. "He's naked. A skinny, hairy butt and a scar along his lower spine. Damn! This is sickening. I think I'm going to puke."

Before she could get the glasses off, a nauseatingly obese woman, probably in her forties, stepped between her and the judge, nearly causing Ann Marie to stumble over her own feet. She yanked the glasses off, but not before she

114

saw heavy rolls of flesh tumbling against each other as the woman jostled a shopping bag from one arm to another. Her immense, sweaty nakedness glistened in the noonday sun.

God, she thought. I don't care what the s.o.b. does. I'm not looking at his naked body again. Or anyone else's. She laughed quietly, amused at the results of her clandestine operation – a hairy butt and the winner of the Mrs. Doughboy contest. She turned on her heel and went home.

*****

When the judge started out on foot again Sunday morning, Ann Marie was ready to go. However this time, without her MoTrac viewer. The temperature dropped ten degrees overnight, so she put on a wool pantsuit of a rich, hunter green. The jacket, which came to her knees, covered a soft sweater of pale green. No Nikes today, but a pair of rich tan ankle boots worn over thick socks. She braided her hair into one long braid and put on a green knit hat with a soft, sassy brim. "No way did she look like the woman who had power-walked the judge over hill and dale yesterday," she hoped.

It was 8:00 a.m. when Gonzales left his house and headed north on Union, then west on King and north again on Washington. From the brief glimpse of his shadow as he walked, she saw he wore a dark suit under his topcoat. "Uh-oh," she breathed. "What is he up to, now?" Maybe he was going to meet someone important. Progress at last.

The judge's destination was a fifteen-minute walk from home, and Ann Marie didn't realize they arrived until he abruptly turned and started up the steps of the old Christ Church. She hesitated, not knowing whether she should follow him inside or wait and hope she didn't miss him in the crowd that would surely erupt through those massive doors when the service ended.

The government spy couldn't remember her last time in a church. She believed in God and practiced what she thought was a good, moral life. When she was growing up, Granny and she were in a pew of First Methodist Church of Sunnyside, Texas, every Sunday morning and evening, and on Wednesday nights. Since Granny's death, however, Ann Marie hadn't been in a church. She had a fleeting thought of her parents and grandparents in heaven, and she hoped fervently that they were happy with her. Today, she would go to church again.

After church, the Judge wandered along Washington Street a few minutes until he stopped abruptly in front of a small café, then went inside. She debated briefly about whether to go inside. So far, the Judge seemed unaware he had a tail, so she didn't want to expose herself. Finally, she followed him into the café and was shown to a table tucked away near the kitchen. Fortunately, the room was small enough that she had a fair view of her quarry, seated alone at a table for two by the window. She ordered a bagel and cream cheese from a waitress in a black polyester uniform with a white collar and jaunty white cuffs on the short sleeves. Gonzales took his time perusing the menu, then gave his order to a redheaded waitress in the uniform of the day. He waited patiently for his food. When it came, he ate deliberately, apparently enjoying his meal. Idly, he watched the people passing the window, but Ann Marie saw he wasn't interested in anyone in particular. No one approached his table except the thin, redheaded waitress.

She reached for her purse when she saw him fold his napkin and place it on the table, extract a ten-dollar bill and lay it on the table. The Judge spoke to the redhead, handed her the money and waved away the change. He seemed in no particular hurry on his way out, but he didn't pause at any table or speak to anyone or pay particular attention to any other patrons. Ann Marie let him get a short head start and followed him.

The Judge's walk today was more leisurely than it was on Saturday. He stopped frequently to gaze into shop windows, but didn't go inside. Eventually, they wound up at the same bookstore she found the previous Sunday. He wandered the aisles for the better part of an hour, occasionally leafing through a book, then putting it back on the shelf. Beaudet was a little surprised when he spent an inordinately long time examining suspense and legal thrillers. She never took him for a reader of light fiction. He chose several books off the shelf – books by John Lescroart, John Grisham and Ridley Pearson – and settled into a comfortable arm chair provided for browsers. She kept out of sight in the stacks and watched him scan a few pages in each book. Finally, he replaced the Pearson in its proper place on the shelf and took the Grisham and the Lescroart to the check out counter.

From the bookstore, his walk turned more purposeful, and it soon became apparent to her that the Judge was headed home. When his front door closed behind him, she hurried up the stairs to her own apartment, longing for a hot shower, a pair of comfortable sweats and a mug of jasmine tea. Or maybe something a little stronger. She had the makings for margaritas. Maybe she would indulge herself - - just a little.

Curled up on the sofa with her half-finished margarita and her week's notes on the surveillance, Secret Agent Beaudet wished she knew more to report to her handler when he made the first of his scheduled Sunday night calls. So far, she uncovered exactly nothing suspicious about Ricardo Huerta Gonzales. Outside his office, he seemed to live the quiet, innocent, actually boring, life of a loner – one who didn't feel the need to interact with other people. She heard that becoming a Supreme Court Justice sometimes curtailed one's social life because of the need to stay uninvolved and to appear unbiased, and to give the appearance of total objectivity. To Ann Marie, that was a high price to pay for the exalted position. Maybe he got his kicks vicariously, through books, she thought. Maybe, in his mind, he was a bold, fearless, trial attorney like the ones he read about. A fighter for justice and the American way of life.

True, his recent Court decisions might make him seem like a nut to some people, but what she saw this week only seemed to underscore everything she read about him. He was dedicated to his work and his love for America. She was beginning to doubt that subversives of any kind had reached him. On the surface, he lived a sterling life: simple, honest, hardworking. So, maybe as he got older and more experienced as a Supreme Court Justice, he saw things in a different light. "People can change," she mused. "Can't they?"

Ann Marie reviewed her options. She chafed at her inability to learn anything helpful about Gonzales. She continued making the daily commute to and from work with the Judge, but his timing was so precise she doubted the prolonged benefit of that. Nevertheless, she continued with the Mark IV Interceptor surveillance. So far, that was the most boring aspect of her job. He got few phone calls and made even fewer. She found herself rather enjoying the music on public radio, but was tired of westerns. She would be a happy woman if she never heard John Wayne's voice again.

She couldn't get a look at his mail because the postman slipped it through a slot in the Judge's front door. That brought her to his trash. She had no hope he would dispose of an important letter, but maybe an envelope, a receipt, or maybe even a phone bill. She determined that garbage was picked up on Tuesdays and Fridays, so on Monday night, she would see what she could find to begin her duties as a dumpster diver. "You're dreaming," she told herself. But this was something that had to be done.

In her final briefing, Alfred Williams told her that every Sunday night at ten o'clock she would get a phone call on her secure line for a report on her week's activities. He didn't tell her who her contact would be, or where the call would come from, but she didn't care. She just wanted to talk to someone. As time for the promised call approached, she found herself watching the kitchen clock, mentally urging the hands to move faster. This time last Sunday she was so excited to have a real, honest-to-goodness undercover assignment that she didn't give a thought to how isolated she would be. Her week was busy, but her lengthiest conversation was with Amos Two, and she was tired of talking to someone who never talked back. She kind of liked banter and teasing and the exchange of ideas. "Admit it," she thought. "You're ready for some human companionship, even if it is long distance from God knows where."

She took her shower and smoothed fragrant lotion over her body. Now, she sat in her nighttime t-shirt, men's size large, with the A&M insignia on the back; an oversized T with A&M on either side, originally in bold letters, somewhat faded now from repeated washing.

At ten o'clock, the phone rang and she grabbed it. "Hello?" Questioning. It had to be her contact; her phone hadn't made a peep all week, not even a wrong number.

"Ann Marie?"

She almost squealed with delight when she heard Rod's voice. She hoped he didn't notice. Not that it was because it was his voice, she told herself. It was just that she *needed* someone to talk to. Then she remembered their last encounter as they stood in the hallway at Millie's House, and he was holding his MoTrac viewer in his hand. Damn him.

"You seem happy for a woman who's been on stakeout for a week."

Rod sounded amused, and she almost saw a smile play around his lips. She erased that picture in a hurry and got down to business.

"Just trying to hide the fact that I have absolutely nothing to report," she said. "Your Justice seems to be clean as far as I can tell. He leads the most boring life. Almost as boring as mine," she said wryly, then hoped he wouldn't think she was complaining.

"You're not getting tired of the job already?" he asked sharply.

Oh, Lord, he did think she was whining. "No. No, I'm not. I just wish I were making more progress."

"Maybe you are," he soothed. "Just tell me. There may be more here than you realize."

Stung, Ann Marie wanted to snarl at him. "So you think I am just a neophyte, too ignorant and inexperienced to interpret what I see," she thought to herself. Instead, she took another deep breath and began to recite the events of the week. Day by day. Minute by minute. She didn't leave out a single detail.

Voices In The Fog

"So what do you think?" he asked when she finished.

"Ha! Now he wants my opinion." She paused and gathered her thoughts. "I don't know. It could be he just changed his mind about a lot of things over the years. Maybe he saw that things were not working the way they are and he wanted to fix them. People can change, can't they?"

"Maybe." Rod said, sounding doubtful. "I see what you're up against, but it's too soon to let him off the hook."

"How long am I supposed to keep tabs on him? Until I find something? That could take forever." She hurried her words to get them all in, more to keep him on the line that to get an answer.

"You'll stay as long as it takes," Rod said.

She sighed. "I still think it would be worth the risk for me to get into his house and look it over."

"No! Absolutely not. Didn't Williams tell you not to do that?"

"Yes, but - -"

"And he told you why you can't just go waltzing in there?"

"I don't intend to waltz. At Millie's Place, I learned how to get in and out of places like that with no one the wiser."

"Except you didn't do so well at Millie's," she reminded herself. She hurried on, hoping he wouldn't mention that embarrassing episode. "And yes, he told me there might be cameras or hidden microphones, or even someone else watching the Judge; someone like me."

"Right. So stay out."

"Why did you teach me all that if I'm not going to use it?" she demanded.

"You'll use it someday. Just not on this case. And you'll learn that you will *not* use every skill you've developed, not on this stakeout, anyhow. You use the tools that fit a particular situation, and it'll vary from case to case. You got that?"

She let her breath out slowly. "Got it," she said finally. "I guess that means that tomorrow night I steal the Judge's trash."

"You're a quick learner, Miss Beaudet." Rod laughed "I'll be looking forward to hearing all about your forays into the dung heaps of the high and mighty in the nation's Capitol."

"Oh, Lord, I'll never live long enough to dig through that much garbage," she said.

For the next hour, Ann Marie felt restless, energized. She replayed Rod's instructions over and over in her mind, not because she thought she would forget, but because she simply wanted to hold onto the sound of his voice. Then, almost cheerfully, she brushed her teeth and slipped into bed beside Amos Two. "Maybe I'll find something important in the Judge's trash," she told the furry brown bear. He didn't answer, but lay all night with his glittering marble eyes open, almost as if he watched over her.

CHAPTER EIGHT

Monday night, November ninth. Mark it in your notebook, Super Secret Agent. You're taking a step worth noting. She smiled as she listened on the Mark IV until the she heard the unmistakable sounds of the Judge getting ready for bed. Then the light went off and in five more minutes, the snores battered the Mark IV like waves against the rocks.

Another cold front moved through that day, so Ann Marie wrapped herself in a long wool coat, then grabbed her own overflowing trash bags from beneath the kitchen counter, tucked them carefully in her empty backpack and strode purposefully out the door. No time to set the alarm. Hurry. Get this over and be back in less than a minute.

The brisk air stung her face. She wrapped her collar as high as it would go over her face and crossed the street, quickly covered the half block toward Lee Street and cut into the alley. Only four paces brought her to the dumpster. Like a thief in the night, she paused, taking time to look over her shoulder down the dark alley. The dark and the wild thumping of her heart were reminiscent of her foray into Millie's attic. She was completely alone. She lifted the lid quietly, hesitated again to scan the alley, then lifted out two small plastic bags holding the Judge's garbage, she hoped. She laid them at her feet, slipped the pack from her back, dumped her trash bags in the dumpster to replace the Judge's just in case anyone should wonder why he hadn't thrown out his trash.

She stuffed his garbage bags into her pack, and without taking time to put the pack on, slung it under her arm and walked hastily back onto the street.

Voices In The Fog

Now came the fun part. Fun if you get your kicks from sorting through somebody else's trash and garbage, instead of getting a good night's sleep. She spread two layers of newspapers on the floor and carefully unzipped her pack. The odor wafted up to greet her nose – cold, soggy, putrid. She could almost see the color of the stink, a greenish yellow. She gagged and swallowed, hopped up, lit a scented candle, took a box of Baggies from the cupboard, and slipped one on each hand. She surveyed her backpack in dismay. Never again would she wear it except for these dismal excursions to the Judge's alley in the middle of the night.

She took a deep breath, sat down Indian-style on the floor, and reached in the pack. Carefully, slowly, she emptied the sacks, one item at a time. Obvious garbage like coffee grounds, egg shells, bits and pieces of cantaloupe and the rotten remains of what at one time was juicy tidbits of a meal, were unceremoniously dumped on the newspaper. Other things, newspapers, junk mail, and hand-written grocery lists were separated and laid out. Some needed to dry. All needed to be scrutinized to determine their merit, if any at all.

It was nearly dawn when she lay back on her kitchen floor. She was exhausted, too tired to go to bed. She stunk. Her apartment stunk. She felt as filthy as ever. Contaminated. Squalid. And all for nothing. Not one damned thing! Gonzales drank a lot of coffee and even more hot chocolate; was nearly addicted to vanilla; wrote out his grocery order for the store to fill when the housekeeper came on Fridays; and had to be one of the most boring people on the face of the earth.

Definitely not under pressure from somebody to be the damnation of the United States. Not this guy. He made a nerd look like the life of the party. Maybe the Judge caused some people to be uncomfortable with his decisions, but sure as hell, nobody was pressuring him to do anything. Of that, she was sure.

*****

The days ticked slowly by. They were routine, ordinary, and so uneventful Ann Marie wished something, anything, would happen to break the monotony. Gonzales continued to leave his house at 8:30 every morning and returned each evening promptly at 6:30. His routine never varied, and he never made stops along the way. Ann Marie was tempted to stop her surveillance, but she convinced herself that as sure as she missed a day, that would be the day he would make contact – if he had one, which she was beginning to doubt. It was a beautiful drive from Old Alexandria to the Supreme Court Building, one she never tired of. She was tired of the traffic and of the lack of results her surveillance produced.

Weekends were only slightly less boring, and no more productive than workdays. Even though the days were colder, the Judge began every Saturday with a leisurely stroll along Rock Creek Park, and then fed the ducks in the yacht basin. After that, he ate a light brunch at his favorite café, followed by browsing several bookstores. She stayed as close to him as she dared, especially in the café and the bookstores, both of which provided excellent opportunities for him to make contact with his conspirators, but no one spoke to him nor did he speak to anyone, except restaurant and bookstore personnel.

Every weekend she tried to alter her appearance as much as possible to lessen the likelihood of his recognizing her. She wore different outfits; sometimes jeans under a pea coat and knitted cap, and her Nikes. Other times she wore slacks, a sweater, an all weather coat that reversed from beige to black, and a woolen scarf. She even went so far as to buy a cheap wig in an indeterminate shade of brown. Her disguises appeared to be working, because Gonzales never seemed to notice her, even in the close confines of bookstores. His apparent lack of suspicion about being followed fed her growing conviction that he was what he appeared to be – a middle aged Supreme Court Justice, nondescript and unassuming.

Gonzales frequently capped his Saturday excursions with an early movie; it didn't seem to matter what the movie was about or who was in it. After the movie, she followed him home where he had a solitary supper, either reading or watching television.

Sundays started with the early service at Christ Church, followed by brunch, and usually a couple of hours at the Alexandria Public Library where he didn't seem to have a particular interest in any one subject or section, but wandered through the stacks and the various rooms randomly. Sometimes, he stopped in one or two bookstores on the way home.

His Sunday night routine at home followed the pattern set for every other night of the week. A solitary meal and, usually, a movie. Ann Marie wondered how many John Wayne movies were in existence. The list seemed endless. From her notes, she knew that he watched movies at least four nights a week. Once or twice, he abandoned John Wayne for Jimmy Stewart, a welcomed relief for her.

Every day she wondered how long she would be assigned to this fruitless venture. Surely, she observed Gonzales long enough to convince Rod and Alfred

Williams that the Judge hadn't been corrupted. By Thanksgiving, she was ready to give it up as useless.

She was pleasantly surprised when Rod called her on Thanksgiving night. She had made her weekly report to him Sunday night and he said nothing about changing the time for his weekly call. She'd already taken her shower, put on her A&M T-shirt and wrapped herself in her warm red terry cloth robe. Carrying Amos Two, she poured herself a glass of merlot, settled in one corner of the green and white striped sofa, and was rereading her notes on Gonzales.

The sound of Rod's voice sent a small jolt of electricity through her chest, which she promptly squelched. "What's going on?" she asked, hoping he was going to tell her they had a break in the case, or that he was pulling her off the surveillance.

"Nothing on this end," he said. "I just wanted to talk to you. Thought you might like a little company on Thanksgiving, even if by phone."

For an instant her heart sank, then that electric shock started it again. "Oh," she squeaked.

"What do you mean, 'Oh'? Or do you already have company?" His voice sharpened.

"No. Of course not. Who would I have? Undercover agents don't have friends, remember?"

He ignored her sarcasm. "What did you and Gonzales do today?"

She tried to make her voice light. "We had a lovely lunch at Fontaine's. Believe it or not, they had traditional Thanksgiving dinners, complete with pumpkin pie and whipped cream. Although the Judge turned up his nose at turkey and went for the prime rib. Then he walked from one end of this city to the other. I consider myself athletic, but today he didn't slow down for anything. Of course, his favorite bookstore was closed, as well as was the library. He didn't even look for the ducks."

"Must have been invigorating." Rod tried to keep the amusement out of his voice.

"Oh, sure. I really enjoyed the bracing forty-four degrees and the mist drizzling into the collar of my coat."

Rod laughed. "Don't tell me you're getting bored with your fascinating life as a spy."

Ann Marie sighed heavily. "Just don't tell me I'm going to be doing this for the rest of my natural life."

"Oh, no," Rod answered cheerfully. 'Your next assignment could be spying on a movie star. Or a sultan. Or, maybe, even a foreign head of state. Who knows?"

"In other words, I should remember to pack my Regency IV when I leave this place - - if I ever do leave it."

"And don't forget your Mo Tracs," Rod teased.

"Oh, God, no. Never again." she moaned.

"Never say never. That's one sure way of bringing about the thing you never want to do."

"Speaking of the Mo Tracs," she queried, "what did you find out about the scar I saw on the Judge's back, It's the one and only time I ever used them, and the only time I ever intend to use them."

"We couldn't find any records showing Gonzales had ever been injured or had surgery anywhere. The only thing we can conclude at this point is that he was injured somehow and didn't receive treatment."

"That scar looked as if it was stitched, what little I saw of it, what with all the hair and how quickly I jerked those glasses off. I think I may have closed my eyes for a few seconds, too. Yuck."

"We'll keep looking, but I don't think we're going to find anything."

"So. How much longer?" she asked.

"As long as it takes," she thought. She'd heard that answer every time she asked the question, which was every time she talked to Rod.

This time, he surprised her. "Don't know. We're talking about what to do next," he added.

"Great. I'm glad we're looking ahead." She swallowed a sip of wine.

"Then its back to the grind tomorrow?" he queried. As if he had to ask.

"Pretty much. The Judge won't be going into the office because it's a holiday. I hope he doesn't decide to take another walk. That reminds me. I have an appointment in the gallery tomorrow. A woman saw our sign in the window and called, wanting to know if we had any Andrew Wyeth or Georgia O'Keeffe."

"Good. Maybe you'll make a sale."

"But I have to be in the gallery, so if the Judge goes out, he'll be alone."

"Don't worry about it. He's had plenty of opportunities to make contact on his walks, and since he hasn't, I don't think tomorrow will be any different. Nothing else unusual is happening. Other than the gallery appointment, I mean?"

"Not a thing."

"All right. I'll talk to you Sunday."

"So soon? Do you think I'll have something new to report by Sunday night?"

"Nah. But I'll call anyway," he retorted.

Ann Marie didn't even try to quash the warm feeling that spread through her at those words. It's just that you're so isolated, she told herself sternly. You need to hear a familiar voice. Nevertheless, she burrowed into the corner of the couch, one arm wrapped around Amos Two, holding her wine glass in her free hand, and sighed in contentment. Suddenly, she felt better than she had in days.

The Friday after Thanksgiving, she sold two works by Andrew Wyeth to her first client at the gallery since she moved in. The woman chose Wyeth's "Fortune Teller," framed in beautiful rosewood, and a smaller work, "Around the Corner," framed in wood with a burnished gold finish. Ann Marie felt a glow of satisfaction as she watched the woman walk out of the gallery, obviously pleased with her purchase.

Over the next few weeks, she had several calls from clients wanting to see her art, two of them as referrals from her first client. She sold four more prints – another Wyeth, a Maxfield Parrish, and two Georgia O'Keefe's. Being in the gallery was a pleasant break from the drudgery of watching and listening to the boring life of Ricardo Huerta Gonzales, and the noxious task of examining his garbage, piece by piece, twice a week.

By December 23rd, she was thoroughly disillusioned about the exciting life of a G-man. Okay, a G-woman. She thought of the documents she found in Millie's attic, of the awe that overcame her when she read the fateful words written on the stationery belonging to the President of the United States. Words that created the organization that put her in this place. "Surely, this is not what you had in mind," she told that long-dead President.

*****

Gonzales did not go to the office on the morning of December 23rd. Ann Marie knew from her research that the other Justices took Christmas holidays, some lasting a couple of weeks, but the Judge went into the office every day until today, when he stayed indoors all day. At about six o'clock, when she heard the familiar sounds of food preparation, she decided it was safe to go grocery shopping. She decided she might even pick up something festive to brighten what loomed before her as a dreary Christmas day. An hour later, she was back, carrying her frozen Christmas dinner complete with turkey and dressing, fruit for a salad and half a dozen frozen dinner rolls. She opened some canned veggies and another bottle of merlot, lit the large red candles mounted on a glittery golden sleigh, and enjoyed her first Christmas as a U. S. Government secret agent.

She played the digital recording the Mark IV made while she was out as she put away the groceries. At first, she heard only the sounds of cupboard doors opening and closing, the rattle of silver and the clink of glassware. There was a faint whistle from a boiling teakettle, then silence for a few minutes. The Judge's dinner preparation was interrupted by the jarring ring of the telephone. Ann Marie looked at the digital readout on the Interceptor's recording. The call came at 6:45. She barely missed it.

She listened, frustrated because she could hear only the Judge's side of the conversation, which amounted to a few yes and no responses.

"All right," he said, finally. "I appreciate you letting me know about the *barbacoa*. No one prepares it the way you do. Yours is always the best. You prepare it the way it is supposed to be prepared. Not some American fast food version."

"What was that?" she wondered. What did he mean about American fast food?

131

Voices In The Fog

As soon as he completed the call, he made another one. "Yes. I want a cab to pick me up as soon as possible." He gave his address, then told the dispatcher he would be going to Georgetown.

Ann Marie listened intently, but the only sounds she heard were those of the Judge putting away his unfinished dinner. Shortly afterward, she heard the sound of the front door closing, then nothing but the silence of an empty house.

She strode back and forth in her tiny kitchen, frustrated. Could this call be what she was waiting for all these weeks and she missed it? Then again, maybe it was exactly what it seemed to be. A restaurant featuring the Judge's favorite dish. She had only a vague idea of what *barbacoa* was; some kind of Mexican barbecue, she thought. She'd heard it was popular in Southwest Texas. Maybe it was a code word.

She sat down at her computer and logged onto the Internet. After typing in *barbacoa,* she waited a few seconds and a web page appeared. The first of about a hundred, she saw. Scrolling down, she clicked on one that indicated it included recipes for *barbacoa*. The original *barbacoa*, she read, used *cabeza*–cow's head, stripped of eyes, ears and tongue, slow roasted with yellow onions and spicy seasoning. Done the original way, in a brick-lined pit, the dish took two days to prepare and was extremely labor intensive. From his remarks on the phone, she inferred that it wasn't served every day. No wonder. Ann Marie grimaced. So the Judge liked barbecued cow's head. She never met anyone with that particular taste before, but evidently it was a popular dish in some circles. Reading further, she discovered that modern day *barbacoa* is sometimes made with chuck roast instead of the cow's head. It was an improvement, as far as she was concerned, but maybe that was what the Judge called American fast food.

For two hours she alternately prowled the small apartment and posted herself at the window that overlooked the Judge's front door, willing him to come home. She tried to convince herself he simply went out to enjoy one of his favorite foods. Just a simple dinner, one he didn't get to have often because the restaurant didn't want to invest the time and labor required to serve it regularly. Repeatedly, she listened to the digital tape of the Judge's phone conversation, but there was nothing to suggest the call wasn't exactly what it purported to be.

At nine-thirty, she sat in the breakfast nook, sipping hot chocolate, having decided to forego anymore wine. She gazed out the window toward the Judge's house when a cab careened down the street and came to a bone-jarring halt at Gonzales's brick walk. He was gone two and a half hours – about the right amount of time required for a cab ride to Georgetown, a leisurely dinner and the return trip. As she listened to the familiar sounds of the Judge resuming his nightly ritual, she tried to persuade herself she was getting frustrated for no reason. People went out to dinner all over the city, all the time. However, Justice Gonzales didn't, or hadn't, in almost two months. Ann Marie couldn't shake off the feeling she missed something important, but there was nothing she could do about it at this point.

She was more vigilant than ever for the next few days, leaving her apartment only for necessities and trying to make the trips short. Gonzales stayed at home throughout the holidays, except for Christmas Eve, when he went to the special midnight service at Christ Church. Ann Marie, knowing about the service from the church bulletins, was ready to go when he stepped through his front door. She was bundled up with practically everything warm she owned, so she wouldn't freeze during the short walk to the church.

*****

On Christmas Day, a small delivery van drove up to the Judge's house, something she hadn't seen before. She watched keenly as the driver hurried up the walk with several packages in a wire carrier. The Judge invited the driver in, and a few minutes later, the man came back outside with an empty carrier. Puzzled, Ann Marie watched the driver get back into the van and drive away. Then sounds from the kitchen clued her in. Apparently, the Judge ordered a Christmas dinner delivered, either from a restaurant or a caterer. Ann Marie hadn't been able to read the lettering on the van, so she didn't know where the food came from.

She prepared her packaged Christmas dinner, but even the combination of food, wine and candles couldn't ease her loneliness. Her second Christmas without Granny. She wished she could talk to her grandmother. She wished Rod would call, even though it wasn't Sunday. The instant that thought flitted through her head, she knew that was what she really wanted. She needed to talk to someone, and that someone was Rod McCarren. She shook her head, trying to dislodge that idea. Theirs was a professional relationship. Nothing more. She might as well accept that. She drained her glass and poured a little more wine into it, then focused on the transmissions being beamed to her from Gonzales's house. They were boring to the ultimate degree.

Voices In The Fog

New Year's Eve was on Thursday. Ann Marie listened on the Mark IV while the Judge watched the Times Square festivities on television; the ball falling at midnight; Dick Clark spouting meaningless prattle when the old year rolled out and the new one rolled in on a frigid, fifteen-degree midnight in New York City.

Finally, when the only sound from the Interceptor was the Judge's snoring, she sighed. It was time to tackle his trash again. She'd heard him go out his back door just before he went to bed, so she was sure he placed his garbage in the dumpster, even though there would be no pick up the next day, January 1. The outstanding fact she'd discovered about Gonzales so far was that he was a creature of habit, doing the same thing the same way, day after day. Wearily, she put on her pea coat and watch cap and got her smelly back pack off the balcony where she placed it so it wouldn't make the apartment reek. She put her own small bag of garbage inside it and left by the back door.

By now, she had this routine down to a science. Cross the street, hurry the half block to Lee Street, and dash into the alley. Quietly but efficiently, she replaced the Judge's trash with her own, put his bags into her backpack and hurried back to the street. At the intersection, she stopped for a group of New Year's Eve revelers who were in no hurry to cross the street in front of her. One, an oversized bull with huge arms, grabbed her arm. "C'mon, baby. Let's party." He wrapped his big hand around her shoulders. "Gimme a kiss!"

"Fuck off, asshole," she barked. Without thinking, she slapped him across the cheek with the back of her hand.

"Fuck you, bitch," he yelled as he released her. "And fuck the horse you rode in on."

135

Voices In The Fog

The instant she was free, Ann Marie squared herself in case he came at her. She dropped the pack on the sidewalk. If he took one step toward her, she was going to give him the thrill of his New Year. A solid kick to his balls, spin and catch him again on the side of his head with another kick as he went down. She hadn't spent all that money over the years learning Karate for nothing.

"Ah, damn it, Freddy. Let's go. Leave her alone," the lone woman in the group pleaded, grabbing the oversized jerk. "Let's have another drink."

"You don't know what you missed, bitch," Freddy said. He turned and joined his friends as they staggered away, weaving on and off the sidewalk.

Ann Marie scooped up her pack and bounded across the street. Locking the door behind her, she ran up the stairs and tossed the pack on the floor by the sink. She checked the clock. Good. Very good. Even including her encounter with the horny drunk, she was gone only about two minutes.

What a fun way to spend New Year's Eve, she groused to herself as she began the odious task that was familiar by now. The end result was familiar as well. Nothing. The man's garbage was as innocuous as he, himself, seemed.

Ann Marie got up and paced restlessly around the house. She didn't know what else to do, and that feeling of helplessness irritated her. She watched him for two months now, and absolutely nothing out of the ordinary happened. Unless she counted the one night he went out to a restaurant for dinner, and that probably didn't amount to anything. He might simply have developed a new perspective toward the law and the Constitution as he got older, but he was clean. That was the bottom line.

Voices In The Fog

A week later, Ann Marie found nothing to make her change her mind about Gonzales. When Rod called that Sunday after New Years, he sounded less sure, as well. She told him about the Judge's jaunt to sample the *barbacoa* on December 23, and Rod agreed with her that it was suspicious only because it hadn't happened before. Nevertheless, they agreed that she would continue to stay close to Gonzales by way of the Interceptor, as well as one-on-one surveillance, as before.

About six o'clock on Thursday, she heard Gonzales take a telephone call that was interestingly reminiscent of the one in December. In fact, as she listened, she could well believe it was an exact replica.

"Yes . . . no. Good. I'm hungry for your *barbacoa*," he said. He terminated the call and immediately made a quick call for a cab.

This time, she would find out exactly where the Judge got his *barbacoa*, if indeed, that was what he was going for, she decided. She grabbed her all-weather coat and her keys, and dashed downstairs to the garage. Her car idled at the curb when the cab arrived for the Judge. A one-car surveillance is not the easiest thing to do, especially in metro traffic, but she got in close to the cab when it pulled away. Surveillance driving was one thing, but staying up with a D.C. cab driver was something else. Soon she was convinced she was going to get killed in the process. The cab changed lanes, whipped around traffic, screeched around double-parked cars, and raced to catch the next light. The cabbie drove like this was the last fare in the world. They zipped across the Memorial Bridge and made a quick move into the left lane, then onto Virginia Avenue. She nearly lost them when she was blocked momentarily in traffic, but was able to squirt through a small break and kept them in sight through Foggy Bottom and onto M Street.

She finally breathed a sigh of relief when they got caught up in the evening traffic crossing Rock Creek before going into Georgetown. Traffic was at a crawl. Pedestrians hopped on and off the curbs, taking their lives in their hands as they raced back and forth across the street. The cab pulled to the curb near Thirty-Fourth Street, almost at the foot of the Key Bridge.

Ann Marie drove slowly by them. Gonzales climbed out of the back seat, tossing money at the driver as he went. Luck was with her. Less than a block away, she found a parking place that gave her a decent view in her rear view mirror of the Judge as he darted among the cars crossing the street to a building with a sign in bright blue neon: *Mi Tios Restaurante.* Gonzales swung the door open and went inside.

Ann Marie sat in her car, trying to decide what to do. She could go in and see if he actually was ordering dinner. But what if he turned around and came right back out while she was away from her car? Then she would be stuck and would lose him. Of course, his cab left, so he wouldn't have transportation anytime soon. Unless he had friends in the restaurant who might drive him somewhere. She thought about it for a minute, remembering that the last time he went for *barbacoa,* he was gone for more than two hours. There was nothing to prove he was actually at the *Mi Tios* that long, but he came home in a cab, just as he left. She made her decision. She would wait in the car and see how things went. She didn't want to sit out here in the cold for hours, but she couldn't see any other solution. The wait seemed interminable. She kept shifting around in the front seat, never taking her eyes off the restaurant door. At first, she kept the motor running so she could keep warm. Finally, it was too hot, so she turned off the engine. If Gonzales called a cab, she would see it drive up in time to get the car started again. Then, she got cold and had to run the heater again. Not only was she uncomfortable, she was also bored because she was convinced she was on a wild goose chase. Or a wild *barbacoa* chase. She laughed. She knew that every job had its drawbacks; one aspect that one really didn't want to do. For her, that was surveillance. There was nothing worse.

Finally, after almost an hour and a half, the Judge came out. Apparently he was standing by the door, and when a cab pulled up, he hurried out and got in. Ann Marie pulled away from the curb. To follow them, she would have had to make a U-turn, but, feeling confident she knew where the cab was going, she drove around the block. The cab was gone, so she retraced her drive over Rock Creek, the Potomac, and back into Virginia.

By the time she parked her car and went upstairs, the Judge's lights were on. She flipped the Mark IV from "record" to "play" and listened. He was in the shower. Twenty minutes later, he was in bed, but he wasn't asleep. He was making sounds she hadn't heard before, but she wasn't sure what they were. It wasn't his usual snoring. Of that she was sure. She tilted her head – what she called her "good ear," and sat very still, listening. Suddenly, the sounds tore through her like a thunderbolt.

Supreme Court Justice Ricardo Huerta Gonzales was crying.

*****

Voices In The Fog

When Ann Marie gave Rod McCarren her weekly report on Sunday night, he thought about it for a minute. She held her breath. She hoped this might be her last week on this dreary assignment, and his prolonged silence didn't sound promising. He was thinking about the restaurant too long to suit her.

"Okay," he said at last. "We need to check this out some more."

"Oh, no!" She groaned.

"Listen, Miss Beaudet. Doesn't it seem strange that for six weeks, he doesn't go out, then within a two week period he goes for *barbacoa* twice?"

"Maybe they make it more often during the holidays." she said hopefully.

"Or, maybe something is about to happen. Maybe the Judge and his pals are about to make a move of some kind. These restaurant visits could be planning sessions for whatever the Judge is going to do next. Do you have any idea what appeals he might be working on?"

"There are several," she answered, "but no way of knowing which one might be significant at this particular time. We're just going to have to wait and watch a little longer. See if *Mi Tios* makes *barbacoa* anytime soon. I'll tell you one thing," she said, "This time I'm going in. I'm going to watch his every move and see who he talks to, and I'm going to have some tacos."

$$*****$$

Three more weeks of tedium passed before she got her opportunity. The Judge's phone rang at about 6:30 that Friday night and she knew immediately what it was about. The Judge grunted a few times: "Yes. No. Uh-hum." Then he disconnected and called a cab. Ann Marie didn't wait to hear any more. She grabbed her keys off the kitchen counter, the portable sound system out of the closet, and raced down the steps to her garage.

She backed into the street just in time to see a cab slowing in front of the Judge's house. She was tempted not to wait; she knew where they were going, but caution prevailed. *Barbacoa* might be simply a code word, and the meeting might not be at *Mi Tios Restaurante,* as it had been the last time. She squelched her impatience and fell in behind the cab and the two vehicles raced through the traffic into D.C., through Foggy Bottom and over Rock Creek until they were in the heart of Georgetown. She watched Gonzales enter *Mi Tios Restaurante,* found a pay parking lot a block the other side of the restaurant, and minutes later was hesitating in the foyer, trying to see where the Judge was seated without being seen herself.

Other than Gonzales, who was already seated in a booth in a far corner of the small dining room, there was only one other customer. An old man, a Georgetown intellectual type, who sat at a table near the door, engrossed in a book. Apparently *barbacoa* was not very popular. She wasn't at all surprised, considering how it was made. How could it be worthwhile for the restaurant to make it? Unless . . . Agent Beaudet's internal radar pinged. Unless, the *barbacoa* was not what actually brought Gonzales to *Mi Tios.*

There were several empty booths and tables, including a small table next to where Gonzales was seated, facing the door. He appeared to be studying a menu. Ann Marie asked the hostess if she could have the table near the window, which was close to Gonzales. Trying to be inconspicuous, she followed the slender, dark haired hostess and sat where

141

she could see the Judge's back. She stuck the sound system on her belt and plugged the earpiece into her ear, looking to anyone who cared like a woman listening to her favorite music. She had to twist herself around a few inches to the right to get a good alignment, but immediately caught the sounds of his breathing, surprised at how labored it sounded. She ordered a margarita, then began perusing her own menu.

When the woman returned with her margarita, she also delivered an iced tea to Gonzales and then excused herself. Ann Marie watched her go through the kitchen doors, into an ear-piercing clatter of dishes and pans. Seconds later, a tall, mustached man of about forty, she thought, came out of the kitchen and sat down across from the Judge. Ann Marie sat very still, straining to hear.

"Right on time," he said in a low voice.

"Am I not always?" the Judge responded. Ann Marie thought his voice sounded raspy, choked. "How's the *barbacoa*?"

"It'll be out in a minute. But here, I've got something for you." Ann Marie peered over her menu and past the Judge's shoulder. She watched the mustached man pull a single sheet of paper from his shirt pocket, unfold it, and slip it across the table to the Judge. "A letter from your wife."

Ann Marie choked on her margarita, sputtering and spraying liquid on the table. His wife? If her research was good, Gonzales was not married.

"Oh, miss. Are you okay?" asked the waitress as she ran around a table, passing a fresh napkin to her.

"Yes. Yes. I'm fine. Just choked on a piece of ice," she said. "Now, how about some tacos and a plate of refried beans?"

"Sure thing, miss. Be out in a minute."

Ann Marie watched the waitress go to the kitchen. She was chagrined to see the man from the Judge's table follow her out of the room. What did she miss? For several long moments, the Judge sat quietly, reading and re-reading the single sheet of paper, ignoring the waitress who placed a plate of food in front of him. The agent scolded herself for sitting too close to the Judge, but she wanted to make sure she heard the conversation. Now, she wished she took a table across the room so she could see his face. Her mind reeled. Something was definitely wrong, but she didn't have any idea what was going on. Something, or someone, was definitely screwed up. The Judge had a wife nobody knew about.

*****

Agent Beaudet fiddled with her dinner, sipped another margarita, but never took her eyes off the Judge. Plainly, he wasn't hungry. She saw him raise his fork only once. Finally, the man returned from the kitchen and once again sat down. As he did earlier, he slipped a sheet of paper from his pocket and handed it to Gonzales. "Read it quickly, then you have to go," he commanded.

Ann Marie saw Gonzales look at the paper, fold it up, and give it to the man.

"Okay," he said. "I can do that. I'll re-write that decision and use stronger language to underscore those issues".

The man slid out of the booth. "Nice to have you join us for dinner, sir. Hurry back."

Ann Marie heard the Judge tell the waitress to call a cab for him, then went to the door and put on his hat and coat. Should she follow him, or was he simply going home? She fretted over the decision. Logically, whatever the man wanted was related to Gonzales's work at the court, so he probably was headed home. There was no hurry. She waited a little longer. Her mind slipped into low gear, grinding back over everything she had read about Gonzales. Nowhere was there a mention of a wife. Something was wrong. Very wrong!

She paid her bill, then walked slowly along the street, staring blankly into the shop windows. The cold night air refreshed her, but brought tears to her eyes as she squinted into the wind. Try as she might, her mind could not make sense of the events of the last hour. Maybe things were worse than Williams thought they were. Could it be that Gonzales was not Gonzales at all?

CHAPTER NINE

Ann Marie slammed the door shut behind her, walked up her darkened stairway to the kitchen and slumped into the breakfast nook, her mind still in a spin.

"No way," she muttered. "No damned way, whatsoever." She gazed out the window, across the street. The Judge's lights were out. The sound system was picking up some little noises. Paper? Something being rustled? She couldn't make it out, but whatever he was doing, he was doing it in the dark.

"Screw you!" she mumbled. She got up and walked the few steps to the refrigerator and flung the door open so hard she knocked off some of the magnets that held notes she wrote to herself. "Screw this whole damned world," she thought. She looked at the magnets on the floor, and in disgust, kicked them beneath the refrigerator. She pushed things aside on the top rack and found a bottle of Fosters Ale buried in the back behind the milk and some unidentifiable green thing in a plastic dish. She sat in the dark of her living room and looked out at the nearly deserted street. She sipped from the frosty bottle and listened to the sound of the sleet that started to fall. She shook her head angrily. She was almost to the point of believing in him. That was her problem. He betrayed her. She wanted him to be what he wasn't. A wicked smile crossed her lips. "Yeah," she said aloud. "You betrayed me and the whole damn country."

She stood at the window. The cold glass reflected the bitterness of her voice back to her. "I don't know who you are or what you're doing, but I'll find out. I'm going to stick with you like glue. I'm going to be your worst nightmare."

Voices In The Fog

She slept little for the next two nights as she studied, analyzed, and reviewed everything that was written about the Judge. How in the world could these kinds of background checks not turn up a wife? What about children? How could such a mistake have been made? It couldn't. Absolutely impossible.

Even the thought of it made her cringe. Who else knew about it? The FBI? Maybe the CIA? You can't hide a family during a background check. They would have to show up. But the question becomes, why didn't his? Why did they do it? Who are "they?"

"Oh shit," she muttered. "This is about too much for me." Maybe it was time to call in reinforcements. She thought for a minute of running up the Virginia flag, maybe even putting a trash bag by the door. But no. Not now. Work through it. Find the secret. That was the answer.

"That's right. I'll find your secret, you bastard. You hypocrite." She made a pot of coffee and spread her files on the table. "I'll do it," she said aloud.

The first light of dawn slowly erased the darkness of night. Ann Marie packed away her files. Three leads. That was what she must work with. First, the family. How did they get missed? Second, the surgical scar on his back. There was no mention of surgery in his files. That would have come in during his mandatory screening. Why didn't it?

Third? *Mi Tios Restaurante.* That was the place to start.

*****

A Monday morning telephone call to the D. C. Office of Tax and Revenue gave her a name. Not a whole lot, but

146

it was a starting point. The property that was now *Mi Tios* was bought three years ago in the name of Jose Espinoza Martinez. No lien was filed, so he paid cash for the building, significant in itself, because few people have that kind of money. Especially for a little restaurant that could only seat about twenty people at most. So there was a little more information to tuck away in the back of her mind. Where did Martinez get his money? Was it his, or was someone else behind him?

"Lots of questions," she thought.

Her next call was to the Health Department. Public records are just that, and she was entitled to get the information she asked for. The clerk on the other end stalled and stammered, but finally realized that she liked her job better than what Ann Marie threatened to do about it.

"Jose E. Martinez," the girl said. "Do you want his Texas driver's license number? That's what he showed for ID when he filed for a permit for the restaurant."

"Yeah, sure. Go ahead with it."

The clerk read off the numbers, then repeated them to make sure she got them right. "Can I do anything else for you?" she asked.

"No thanks," Ann Marie replied. She hung up the phone and smiled.

Immediately, she dialed a third number, one given to her by Alfred Williams. A soft, feminine voice answered. "Resources, Incorporated."

"I'm looking for something in Jasmine," the agent said. There was a click, then a dead pause.

Finally, a man spoke one word in a light baritone: "Jasmine."

"I'm A-M-B-274," Beaudet responded.

"Go ahead. You're clear," the man answered.

She looked at her scratch pad, read out the numbers on the Texas driver's license, and waited for what seemed like an eternity.

"Okay, gotcha here," the man said, finally. "You've got a guy named Jose Espinoza Martinez, date of birth December 28, 1965. Let's see – five feet, eight inches tall, weighs around one-seventy. The address on his license is 2028 Rio Grande Drive in Laredo, Texas. Sound like your guy?"

"Yeah, I think so. Except he's not in Laredo. He's in Georgetown. Or was Friday night. Hey, can you do a little more for me? Like run him through records. You know. Do the whole thing. Local, state and national?"

"Sure, glad to. Stand-by. It'll take a couple minutes," the man agreed.

Ann Marie looked at the clock on the wall, counting the minutes as they ticked away. Three. Four. Five.

"Sorry it's taking so long. Computer's slow today."

"You could have done it by hand," she thought.

"Okay, here we go. Look, I ran Texas, Virginia, where you're calling from, and through national in D.C. Nothing there. Zilch. Sorry. He's never been busted or even got a ticket."

"Hang on a minute," Ann Marie pleaded. "Give me another minute." She needed time to think, to sort things out. There had to be something somewhere.

"Look," she said. "I know we're missing something, like what if he got in trouble outside the States? Can you check DEA or FBI suspect files while I wait? If he's only listed as a suspect in something, then he wouldn't pop up in a regular records check, right?"

"Right. Hold on a second, and let me see what I can do for you. Do you have time?"

She laughed. Just what she needed was a guy with a sense of humor. "Time? Yeah, that's all I've got. I'll wait." She held the phone in the crook of her neck and shoulder as she made a cheese, lettuce and tomato sandwich and poured a glass of milk, waiting as "Jasmine," whoever he was, did some more work for her.

She finished her sandwich and rinsed the glass when his voice came back on the line. "I think you're on to something. Got your pencil and paper ready?"

A quick jolt shot through her chest. "Shoot. I'm ready."

"Okay, there wasn't anything in any of the regular places, but I tried a link with the National Central Bureau."

"Interpol," she said, breaking into his comments.

"Yeah. So get this. They linked me up with their headquarters in Lyon, France. That's what took me so long. Anyhow, I got three notices back. They give them by color codes. First, I got a gray one. That means they have information Martinez may be involved in international organized crime. Then up popped an orange one. It's different. Orange really is about organizations, companies, corporations, that kind of thing. Martinez's name is there as possibly being associated with the Ling Nuy organized crime outfit in China. Supposedly, they run all sorts of covert operations around the world.

Ann Marie, writing as fast as she could, noticed her hand trembling. Excitement? Nervousness?

"Then last, but not least, a FOPAC."

"FOPAC? What's that?"

"Actually, that's the program we can run to give us information about international money laundering. So, I guess what it is telling you is that this Martinez guy is multi-talented. International organized crime and money laundering, and who knows what else."

There was a long, eerie pause as the line went quiet. She couldn't think what other questions she should ask.

The man broke the silence. "That's all I have for you. I'm looking at your file on my computer, and I see you have a fax. As soon as we hang up, I'll send you a copy of his driver's license. Okay?"

"Yeah, thanks," she said absently, her mind frantically trying to absorb this new information.

In a few moments, the fax began to whir, slowly spitting out Jose Espinoza Martinez's driver's license. Ann Marie watched as he was gradually pumped out of the fax, head first. Dark hair; eyes staring into the camera; pursed lips. Nobody ever looked decent on a driver's license picture. Then, there he was. The man who spoke to Ricardo Huerta Gonzales at *Mi Tios* on Friday night. Jose Martinez, restaurant owner. Possibly, the owner of the bench of the Supreme Court! They, whoever "they" are, actually penetrated the highest court in the land. Ann Marie sat on the floor and looked at his picture. "How could it be?" she asked. "How, in the name of God did this happen?"

By now, it was past noon. She spent the entire morning on the telephone, and it was a fruitful four hours. Now the question was: what to do with the information she gathered? She re-read her notes from her conversation with Jasmine. It was clear that Gonzales was involved in something shady simply because of his connection to Martinez, and probably to the Ling Nuy organization. But why? She looked again at her notes about Ling Nuy. A Chinese conglomerate, ergo, a Chinese government organization? The idea excited her, but she still couldn't make the connection to Gonzales. For the next hour, she paced the floor, discarding ideas almost as soon as they originated. Finally, she came up with a plan she hoped might work. She was going to take them head-on. She knew how she was going to do it. A little luck was all she needed.

She grabbed her notes, stacked them neatly on the table, laid out a tablet and a ballpoint pen and the phone book, and she was in business. A few long distance calls, a slip-up by the other side, and she would be in: she would know who was who, and where they were.

"The power of positive thinking," she muttered, punching the numbers into the phone.

The Laredo, Texas, Tax Appraisal Office listed the Golden Eagle Corporation as the property owner at 2028 Rio Grande Drive, in Laredo, Texas, Jose Martinez's residence address. Another call to the Texas Secretary of State, the bureaucracy that maintains Texas' corporate records, showed the officers of the Golden Eagle Corporation as Jesse Rodriquez, Rodolpho Martinez, and Willie Lim. "Gotcha!" she exulted. A firm China connection here.

She made another call to "Jasmine." A gold mine was the compliment she wrote on her scratchpad. An absolute gold mine. He told her Interpol came back with a FOPAC and Orange notice of Golden Eagle Corporation of Laredo, Texas. Then he ran the three names through DEA and came back with another hit. Willie Lim was a suspected class one violator of China white heroin being brought into the United States.

"Let me call you back after I get some more stuff on this Lim guy for you," Jasmine said. "This is fun. I don't know what you're up to, but you sure are getting into something big."

Ann Marie stretched, rubbed her eyes and took a deep breath. She was on the phone for hours without a break. She ached from her neck to the soles of her feet, but she wasn't complaining. Only forty-eight hours earlier, she was ready to call it quits. On Friday, she thought the Judge was squeaky clean, but now she was convinced he was involved with some major international criminals.

She walked onto her balcony and watched the sunset over Alexandria. A brisk breeze penetrated her light blouse and her skin broke out in chill bumps. She shivered and wrapped her arms around herself. She looked fixedly across the intersection with a feeling of satisfaction. She moved from being the passive observer to being the aggressor, and it felt good!

The sound of the telephone sent her scurrying back inside. "Hello," she said.

"Beaudet, this is Rod."

She was startled. She wouldn't have been surprised if Jasmine had called, but why Rod?

"Hi Rod. What can I - - ?"

He interrupted her. "Just be quiet and listen to me. Did you make some inquires directly to Texas?"

"Sure. Why?"

"You tipped your hand, that's why. These people have folks on their payroll all over the world. So do we."

She listened as he took slow, deep breaths. She knew him well enough to know that he was getting his thoughts together.

"They don't know where you are, but they're on to you. Apparently you've triggered an alarm somewhere. They're running background right now trying to figure out

152

who you are. More importantly, they want to know *where* you are."

The phone went quiet again, neither of them sure of what to say. It seemed like an eternity. Finally, Rod broke the silence. "We've got to meet. Ten o'clock at the Lincoln Memorial. Be there."

"Sure, but what's going to happen?"

"Get off the phone and get your ass out of there. We'll talk later."

*****

The breeze turned into a heavy wind coming off the river. The parking lot next to the massive figure of Abraham Lincoln was empty. Ann Marie made a swing around the lot and parked in the middle. Nobody would be able to slip up on her. The wind took her breath when she stepped out of the car, so much that she turned her back for a few seconds while she adjusted to the biting cold. Not one to take careless chances, she carried a .40 caliber Glock when she was uneasy about her surroundings, and this was one of those times.

She carried it not so much out of fear on her job, but as a fact of life in America. A woman must be able to take care of herself. She tucked the gun under her sweater and walked toward the monument. The solemn figure of Lincoln, sitting tall in his chair gave her goose bumps. She stopped at the bottom of the stairs. Nobody was there. She was alone. She started up the stairs, but stopped short of the top.

Could someone, someone other than Rod, be in the back? Behind Lincoln's chair? You could put a small army back there. "Not going up there," she whispered as a means

153

of self-assurance. She looked around and squinted into the wind. If she stayed on the stairs, she was at least thirty yards from anything. Nobody could slip up on her. If they tried, she would shoot them. It was as simple as that. She twisted her arm around in the light from the monument and checked her watch. Ten o'clock. Right on the dot.

"You gonna get out of that wind?" someone asked.

She spun around. Rod stepped out from behind Lincoln's chair. "It's freezing down there. Come up here out of the wind," he shouted. He gestured for her to join him.

"Damn you, Rod. You scared the crap out of me," she said as she climbed the last step.

He grinned, wrapped his arm around her shoulder and pulled her into a more sheltered spot. "Tell me what you have before we both freeze." He didn't offer to release her, and she stood close to him, sharing his body warmth while she explained what had happened. *Mi Tios;* the Health Department; the calls to Texas. Everything.

He looked down at her somberly. "You're on the right track, that's for sure. And for damn sure, you've stirred up a hornet's nest."

"But what went wrong? How did they find out what I was doing?" She stuttered through her chattering teeth.

"It's like a big puzzle. They pay people to watch our people, and we pay people to watch their people watch our people. Simple enough?" He smiled grimly. "Anyway," he continued, "they know someone has made some inquires about Golden Eagle and they're trying to find out who was asking questions. They haven't had much luck so far, if that's any comfort." He looked at her.

She read his features and body language. He was concerned.

"What does that mean? Am I in danger?" she asked.

Voices In The Fog

He kept his arm around her shoulder and led her down the stairs and across the parking lot. "I don't know," he answered honestly. "Nobody does, so all we can tell you is to follow the Marine Corps manual."

"What's that?"

"Keep your butt down, and watch your flanks."

Ann Marie unlocked her car with the remote device, then slid inside, glad to escape at least some of the cold air.

"Look," Rod said. "Be careful." He took her hands in his and eased her toward him, resting his cheek against her hair. "Be careful," he whispered again, inhaling her clean fragrance. She pulled her head back until she saw his eyes. Then she leaned forward and pressed her cold lips against his. Neither of them moved for the longest time. Ann Marie Beaudet forgot the frigid temperature, forgot her anxiety and her fear, conscious only of a deep, inexplicable connection she never experienced before.

When she pulled away, reluctantly, his eyes locked with hers, drawing her within him. He held her in his arms, and their lips met again, and again that sweet sense of connecting, of belonging, swept through her.

*****

She locked her car and walked slowly up the stairs, pausing to listen for the slightest hint of something out of place. There was nothing. Only the sound of her footsteps broke the silence. The phone was ringing when she went inside. She stumbled over a chair, her heart pounding. Rod again? More bad news?

"Hello?" she answered, making it a question.

"Jasmine here. Got your pencil ready?"

155

"You're working late," she said, flipping to a clean page on her notepad.

"We just scratched the surface this morning. One thing led to another and I couldn't find a place to stop. Listen to this."

Her excitement grew as she listened. The DEA files showed that Willie Lim owned a ranch in Mexico, just south of the Texas border. Only a few miles south of Laredo. The theory was that tons of heroin passed through there before heading north into the United States and into Canada. Even more disturbing was the information that there was a strong suspicion that Lim was backed by the Chinese government, whose long-range plan was to bring about the destabilization of the American government.

"Shit," she said.

Jasmine was quiet for a long moment, then he spoke grimly. "I think you need to be careful. We've never met, but I think you might be getting in too deep if you're working this case alone. Do you understand?"

"Yeah, sure do, and thanks." Suddenly, more frightened than she had ever been in her life, she took the Glock from her coat pocket and put it on the table in the nook. Her fingers trembled as she gently placed it beside the salt and pepper shakers.

CHAPTER TEN

Ann Marie sat at the table for hours after the phone call from Jasmine, scratching and doodling, trying to put the pieces together. Jose Espinoza Martinez worked for Golden Eagle. He probably was no more than a figurehead on the papers of incorporation. Golden Eagle was a front for the Ling Nuy organization. And Ling Nuy was a front for the Chinese Communists. So what about the Judge? Where did he come in? What about that unknown wife of his?

She rubbed her temples and squinted, a habit she picked up in college when she crammed for an examination. Now, she focused on everything she knew about doing background searches. It was unbelievable they missed this much. She knew the Bureau wasn't necessarily genius in everything they did, but they couldn't screw up this badly. She drew a row of question marks across the top of her paper. There was a multitude of questions to be answered. Maybe more than she could handle. She thumbed back through her notebook and came again to the comments she wrote about the Judge the day she saw him with her MoTracs. What about the scar? How did it get missed in his background checks? She smiled, of course. No one found it because it wasn't there. That's why it was missed. And the wife? Same thing. She wasn't there, either. And if they didn't exist when Ricardo Huerta Gonzales was back-grounded before his appointment to the Supreme Court, how could they exist now? She shook her head in disbelief, afraid of her own thoughts. They weren't there because the man across the street from her wasn't the Judge. He was an imposter. Justice Gonzales was gone. Dead? Maybe. Probably. Where did "they" hide the Judge? Or, an icy chill raced through her, where did they get rid of his body? Which brought up the most important question: who was the man across the street? How did he get there?

*****

Ann Marie continued to sit in her nook, listening to the Judge snore. She looked around her darkened apartment. A shiver crept up her spine. There was one last thing she could do, she decided. It was now or never. The street was dead quiet. She could do it now and have it over in a minute or two, then she would have something to work with. Something tangible. She laughed grimly to herself. A real clue. That's what she needed.

There might not be much time left. Somebody knew about her. They knew she was asking questions about the Golden Eagle. When they discovered who she was, they would come after her. She would have to make her move now before she lost her nerve.

She slit the large manila envelope with her fingernail file and pulled out the sticky-gummed legal sized paper. It would be a one-time shot. Get to his door, wrap the sticky side to the door knob, peel it off, and get out of there with fingerprints of whoever was using the Judge's front door.

She stood at her own front door and scanned the deserted street. Sodium lights painted a soft, yellow glow over the storefronts. Not a solitary soul was to be seen. She breathed deeply and stepped outside. The cold air hit her like a hammer. She ducked her head as she walked across the street.

"Don't run," she whispered over and over again. "Don't do anything to attract attention." "That's stupid," she thought. "Out in freezing weather in the middle of night, and thinking I can do it without somebody seeing me and not thinking I'm out of my mind." She reached the porch, and in one smooth swing of her hand grabbed his doorknob with the coated sheet of fingerprint detection paper. Folding it smoothly over the cold, brass knob, she held it for a moment, then peeled it back. She whipped around, stepped off his porch, and counted the steps to her front door. Forty-six steps and she was inside. She was sure she had someone's prints.

She laid the paper flat on her table and watched as the chemicals in the gum slowly developed the conglomeration of prints and smudges she lifted.

"Damn it," she uttered. She wasn't an expert, but knew enough to know there were too many smudges but not much in the way of clear, readable prints. Nevertheless, it would have to do. It wasn't exactly a crime lab she was working in, and there might not be another chance.

The call to Resources, Incorporated went through in a matter of seconds, but each one still seemed like a lifetime. Jasmine transferred her call to the fax, and she plugged her phone into the modem. Whoever's prints were on that paper, Jasmine would have them on file. Now, it was a matter of time. She hung up after the fax went through and began the wait. How long would it take? Maybe a minute. Or an hour. Or maybe there wouldn't be anything at all.

Ann Marie took the phone with her into the bathroom, turned on the hot water, and dumped a handful of bubble bath into the tub. The suds rolled and tumbled, higher and higher, reached up to the rounded lip, and stopped before they folded over and out on the floor. The mirror steamed over. She stood there and looked while her reflection gradually disappeared in the fog. It felt good. Warm, like a blanket covering her and hiding her from everybody and everything. It made her feel secure. It was just what she needed.

She slipped out of her clothes, tossed her panties into the hamper, and stepped slowly into the hot water and bubbles. It seemed forever since she let herself relax totally. She let her mind float free, then dozed off while the bubbles massaged every inch of her skin.

The phone rang, startling her awake. She scrambled out of the tub, wrapped a towel around her and grabbed the phone on the third ring.

"Got your stuff," Jasmine informed her. "Tell me when you're ready to write it down."

"Hold on a sec." She dried her hands on the towel, wrapped it more securely around her and padded, dripping, to the breakfast nook where her notepad lay. "Go ahead," she replied. "I'm ready."

She wrote in her personalized style of shorthand. There were a few smudges, but the majority of the prints she collected from the Judge's front door belonged to Juan Reynosa Duarte, a Mexican citizen and lawyer for some of the narcotic traffickers in Mexico. He was arrested once in Nogales, Arizona on some kind of a trumped up traffic offense, but it was enough to give DEA a set of his fingerprints. He obtained a court order to have everything purged, so there weren't supposed to be any fingerprint cards left. It seemed that least one set got missed – accidentally, of course.

"Duarte dropped out of sight about five years ago and hasn't been seen since," Jasmine concluded. "DEA intelligence records list him as 'probably dead.'"

"Family?" She inquired.

"Yeah," Jasmine said. "I'm sorting through a bunch of junk on the computer – hang on a second. Here it is.

Voices In The Fog

Married. Wife named Marisa. No kids. DEA got in his house in Nuevo Laredo, Mexico, after he dropped out of sight. The house looked like they went out for a walk, but would be back a little later. Everything there like it was supposed to be, just no people. Poof! Gone. DEA figured he must have gotten himself crossways in a deal and got wiped out. Of course, when that happens, they kill the whole family. It all made sense then."

He paused for a moment and cleared his throat. "Now, of course, you throw their guesswork out the window. Well, good luck. Need anything else?"

"No, you've been a big help. Thanks." Ann Marie hung the phone on the cradle and looked out the window. The windows in the house across the street were still dark, even though it was nearly dawn. Juan Reynosa Duarte apparently was sleeping well, unaware that his secret life was discovered.

The government agent, so alone in the world, yet in the midst of the nation's capital, was too keyed up to sleep. She would have to work through it. She sat on the couch with the tablet on her lap while she retraced who was where with whom. Where did they come from? Where did they go?

"Hmm," she mumbled. "Where do I go now?"

"Yeah, where do I go?" she thought. "If Duarte is here now, where is his wife? The ranch in Mexico? Maybe. Makes sense. It's near Laredo. Martinez is from Laredo. Duarte goes to see Martinez and gets a letter from his wife. Sure. Makes a lot of sense," she thought.

But what about the Judge? Probably dead. Or, he could be at the ranch, too. Don't know. Lots of things I don't know. Somehow, she would have to come up with a better answer. How was the switch made? How long ago? And the biggest question of all: *why?*

Voices In The Fog

Suddenly aware that it was broad daylight, Ann Marie looked at her watch. Almost 8:30 in the morning. She looked out the window and sure enough, the Towncar was parked in front of Gonzales's house. He came outside and got in. The imposter, she thought bitterly. How long was he in-place? And how the hell did they pull it off? The Towncar pulled away from the curb. She watched it go down the block. A yellow Volvo slipped through traffic and fell in behind it. Both cars made the left turn at the intersection and were gone.

She took her pad into the living room and sank into the cushions of the couch, her mind still whirling. For certain, the public would be outraged if they found out someone had kidnapped and killed a Supreme Court Justice. Worse yet, they replaced him with an impostor. That's not the kind of thing you want to see in the morning paper. Talk about a lack of faith in government. Hell, they might revolt. Nobody would believe anything anymore. Not after Clinton and Monica, the Gulf Wars, or all of the FBI screw-ups on about a dozen high-profile cases. Not many people had a whole lot of trust in Washington. If they heard about this, the whole thing —everything might come unwound. Then she thought of the Chinese. According to Jasmine's information, that was exactly what the Chinese government wanted. To destabilize the American government.

"Son of a bitch," she moaned. Maybe she played right into their hands. Maybe they wanted Duarte to be found out. He was no more than a pawn. Let him be exposed. Let people know how their government is out of control. Totally screwed up. Honest, God-fearing citizens would be up in arms. Crap, they could even start a revolution. Every right wing idiot with a gun would come out of the cracks.

Voices In The Fog

No. Somehow, she needed to get the whole answer. She closed her eyes, and a blanket of sleep swept over her.

The sound of traffic on the street woke her. The angle of the shadows on the living room floor told her she slept away almost the entire day. After a quick trip to the bathroom where she splashed water on her face and dried briskly to restore circulation, she scrambled some eggs and fixed a pot of coffee. There is nothing like breakfast at five-thirty in the evening.

She sat with the paper spread across the table as she sipped the last drops of coffee from the mug. Right on time, the Judge came home. Six-thirty. A pang of anguish sweep over her. Where was the Judge? The real Judge. What happened to him?

As quickly as usual, the car pulled away from the curb, the Judge unlocked his door and went inside. A yellow Volvo passed by at a crawl, moving too slowly to escape her attention. She remembered seeing it that morning.

This could not be a coincidence. Someone was keeping tabs on Gonzales, and she knew enough about surveillance to know that no American agent – not the Bureau, not CIA, nobody on our side, would tail a subject in a yellow Volvo. Too noticeable. She made a note in her book. "The Judge grew a tail. A yellow tail."

Ann Marie went to the closet and took out the Virginia flag. It was late in the day, but never too late to call for help. Things were happening, and she needed to move fast. They, whoever "they" are, might be getting too close.

The last rays of sunlight reflected off the Potomac. From her rear window, she saw the huge monolith of the Washington Monument standing tall. Erect. The very symbol of American history.

Voices In The Fog

The downstairs doorbell buzzed shrilly in the silence of the apartment. She hurried to the living room window overlooking the gallery entrance. In the shadows under the gallery's small portico, she saw two men, and for an instant was frozen with fear. Then the taller man stopped back and looked up at her window, his features dimly illuminated by the night light. Rod. Her breath caught in her throat. Alfred Williams stood next to him. Finally! It was more than two hours since she sent her SOS and she was fast coming to the conclusion that no one saw her signal.

She paused to take the keys from the top drawer of the cherry wood chest by the door, then caught a glimpse of herself in the mirror over the chest. Her blue eyes glittered and her cheeks were flushed. Several strands of hair escaped the pony tail and dangled against her cheeks and neck. Moving swiftly, she jerked the scrunchy off the pony tail and shook out her natural curls with a sharp shake of her head. She grinned, tore through the door, and raced down the interior stairway to the front door. When she flung it open, Alfred Williams stepped in first and clasped her hand in his strong grip.

"We came as quickly as we could," he said.

"Thank God!" She managed a weak smile. "I decided I'd been abandoned."

"Not a chance," Rod said, right behind Williams. In spite of his light tone, his forehead was furrowed with concern. Williams let go of her hand and moved quickly up the stairs and into her small living room.

She looked up into Rod's smoky eyes. "Hi, there."

He smiled at her. "How are you holding up?"

She shrugged. "Okay." She reached out and placed the back of her hand against his, and for a moment neither moved. If Williams noticed the brief exchange, he ignored it, apparently absorbed in examining the room.

"Nice." He turned toward her, smiling reassuringly. "Almost like home."

Williams nodded. "Let's see what we have."

Ann Marie indicated that he should sit in the emerald green Queen Ann chair that sat at a right angle to the green and white striped sofa. She sat at one end of the sofa and Rod sat at the other end. In neat stacks on the glossy cherry wood coffee table were all the reports and information she accumulated over the past three months. The weekly summaries she prepared for Rod; accounts of each day's surveillance, including her regular visits to the Judge's dumpster; and summaries of the information Jasmine sent her, including all the material he faxed her.

Williams read through the material quickly, pausing several times to ask for clarification on specific points. Finally, he put down the sheaf of papers and leaned back in his chair, his cold pipe clenched between his teeth. "This is totally different from any case I've ever worked," he said. "It seems clear to me that the Chinese are involved in this mess. In fact, considering how widespread the Ling Nuy drug operation is, I'd say they're running the show."

"But we aren't looking at blackmail here, are we?" she asked, knowing the answer.

"Hell, no," Rod interjected. "They're not blackmailing anybody. They went out and got themselves a new Judge."

Williams nodded, an expression bordering on disbelief in his deep set eyes. "You're both right. They've actually replaced a Justice of the Supreme Court with someone they can control." He shook his head. "Unheard of, in my experience. Never in my life have I encountered anything like this."

Voices In The Fog

"They must have made the switch quite a while ago, at least two years ago," Rod pointed out. "That's when we first noticed the abrupt changes in the Justice's decisions."

Williams lit his pipe and took a deep pull on it. "You know the implications here, don't you?"

Beaudet knew where he was going with this line, but sat silently, waiting for him to go on.

"Who else have they got? Senators? Governors? Financiers?"

A chill raced through her. Impossible! But was it? Really? "What are we going to do?" she asked in a tight voice.

"I don't know, yet." Williams drew a deep breath and seemed to draw inside himself at the same time. The three sat through a heavy silence that seemed interminable to her. Finally, Rod spoke.

"There is one thing." He looked at Williams. "You know that situation I covered a few months ago at Alamogordo?"

Williams nodded, a grim smile beginning to form at the corners of his mouth. "Concerning the compound in China?"

Rod nodded. "Maybe we should meet with those people again, possibly in Roswell. We can find out if they've learned anything more about the compound, and we might find a way to use some of the," he hesitated a moment, "some of the resources at Roswell." He cast an oblique look at the young female agent as if reluctant to say more in her presence.

Noticing Rod's hesitation, Williams nodded at Ann Marie. "I think we can speak freely here," he said. "Hell, she has landed us in the middle of the biggest case we've ever worked"

He turned to her. "Have you ever heard of Roswell?"

"Who hasn't? I'm from Texas, remember? Practically next door to all those moon men who dropped into New Mexico sometime in the 1940s. Can't say I buy any of it, though."

"Miss Beaudet, what you've heard about Roswell is true. Some of it anyway. But the whole truth never got out." He shook his head. "There was a lot of conjecture and bullshit, but the truth, the real facts, are still locked tight. It's safe. And the few people who really know the truth are dying out. Soon, there won't be any of us left." He smiled sadly, much like a father telling his only child that Santa Claus doesn't really exist. "Rod is right, young lady. We should go to Roswell. All three of us."

He got up from his chair and wandered to the window, turning off the light as he passed the switch. Deep in thought, he stood quietly, sucking gently on his pipe, gazing across the street at the home of a Justice of the Supreme Court. Finally, he turned to face his colleagues, and began outlining a plan that was coming together as he spoke. "Rod, get a crew over here first thing in the morning, I want this place sanitized. Not a speck of dust is to remain. Not a fingerprint. Nobody, and I mean nobody, must ever be able to find anything, either up here in the apartment or downstairs in the gallery that might lead back to Miss Beaudet."

He motioned toward the window. "I want a top surveillance crew to cover whoever is living in that house. Cover him like a wet blanket. Watch his every move, but don't let anything happen to him. Also, get some identification on that perp in the yellow Volvo, which, incidentally, is down there right now. Take a look."

Voices In The Fog

Ann Marie and Rod joined him at the window. The Volvo was parked down the street from the Judge's house, and far from the nearest street light. Even so, she made out the dim profile of the driver, smoking a cigarette, its red tip glowing in the darkness.

"Do they know I'm here?'

"I don't know, my dear, but we can't take a chance. Not this late in the game. Nevertheless, I'm going to guess they don't. The way I figure it is they know somebody is wise to Golden Eagle, and they're covering all their bases. I simply don't think they have enough right now to put two and two together." He looked at her and smiled. "But, of course, that's only my guess."

"I'll check it out," Rod said, putting his topcoat back on. He checked his watch. Two-thirty a.m. "Send the cavalry to the rescue if I'm not back in ten minutes," he quipped.

He slipped out the back door, went around the block, and, staying in the shadows, came close enough to the back of the Volvo to read the license number in the dim glow of the street light at the corner. Five minutes from the time he left, he was back. Williams remained at the window, sucking on his pipe. Ann Marie sat on the couch while Rod placed a call to Jasmine. She watched that quirky little smile light up his face as he listened intently.

"What I figured," he replied to Jasmine. He hung up the phone, plopped down next to her, and put his feet on her coffee table.

"Stolen plates?" she asked.

"Yep, three weeks ago in Woodbridge. Just covering their ass and figure they're safe for the time being."

CHAPTER ELEVEN

It was mid-day before the NASA jet sped down the runway, rotated, and climbed to thirty thousand feet. Ann Marie and Rod sat in the Coleet seats at the rear while Williams scooted into a seat at the console. They no sooner leveled off than Williams got busy on the radio. "We've got discreet frequencies," he said, looking over his shoulder at her. "We need to get as much done as we can before we hit the deck, and I mean it. We're going to hit the deck running."

His voice was lost in the whirl of the jet engines, but Ann Marie knew he was deep in conversation with somebody at the other end. He was making notes, going back and forth between his cellular phone and the radio. He was frenetic and engrossed, and she wondered if he finally met his match.

She twisted in her seat to speak to Rod, but he wasn't there. He was curled over in the seat, sleeping like a baby. "Probably not a bad thing to do," she thought. Who knows when we'll get another chance? She loosened her seat belt, slipped down in the seat, and squirmed about until she found a comfortable place for her head. The drone of the engines hypnotized her. She felt her body begin to drift away, so light and free. Sleep crept up on her and took her away into a deep, inviting journey, and dreamless sleep.

She jerked awake when the landing gear dropped and locked down. Rod was already awake, sipping a cup of coffee. He leaned toward her and brushed some matted hairs from her cheek. He smelled good, a pleasant musky scent.

She rubbed her eyes and stretched. "Did I snore?"

"Nope. But you're beautiful when you sleep."

"Hold down the noise over there," Williams barked. "Can't you let a guy get a little shut-eye?" His head was buried in the crook of his arms, folded down on the console. He lifted his head and looked at them. "Just kidding. We're about there. Ready?"

"I hope so," Ann Marie replied. She smiled and stretched again. There was no doubt Williams was the boss, but he exhibited a smoothness and kindness she did not see in many men. She liked him more every time she saw him.

The wheels touched down smoothly, with only the slightest bump. It was absolutely perfect.

"Where, exactly, are we?" she asked.

"Outside of Roswell. It's an old military base. Got shut down a few years ago with all the base closures, but now they use it for a government training center. We won't be staying here, though. We'll have some transportation take us to our place – a ranch about an hour away. That's where we'll put our plan into action."

"What is our plan?" Rod asked.

"You'll see. Just hang on," Williams replied.

An inconspicuous sedan awaited them, and the three stowed their bags in the roomy trunk. Williams got behind the wheel and Rod indicated that she should take the front passenger side, while he got in back and stretched out his long legs. Obviously, Williams was familiar with the city, zipping quickly out of the airport and turning onto the highway.

She didn't know what to expect. She read and heard of Roswell, but did not have any preconceived ideas what it might be like, so she wasn't disappointed. A Dairy Queen, a Sonic Drive-in, Rexall Drugs on what she assumed was the main intersection of the little downtown.

Voices In The Fog

Williams drove along the main street, passing the county courthouse and rows of small businesses, half of which hung models of little green men in their display window. ROSWELL ALIEN MUSEUM, flashed in the window of what appeared to be an old church.

"What the heck?" she said, craning her neck to watch it long after they had passed by.

Rod gave her one of his high voltage smiles. "Everybody has to make a buck. So the Martians were good for Roswell."

They drove quickly through town, northbound on the highway. It had always been a game she played with herself: memorize street names, highway numbers, that kind of thing. They were on Highway 285. Next town, Vaughn. Ninety-five miles.

Rod seemed to read her mind. "Long way to anything out here," he said.

Twenty minutes later they crossed a bridge over a dry riverbed, passed a mini-van pulling onto the highway, then turned left onto the same gravel road the van left. "Fasten your seat belts," Williams quipped. "It gets a little bouncy from here on."

Ann Marie saw a towering, snow-capped peak far ahead in the distance. "What's that?" she asked, nodding toward the mountain.

"El Capitan Mountain, but we won't go quite that far," Williams replied. He looked at her out of the corner of his eye. "We'll be way the heck out in the boondocks, though. Nobody to spy on us."

"Right," Rod quipped. "Nobody at all."

A cowboy, or at least a man who looked like he should be a cowboy, was waiting for them at the gate. He opened it and they passed through. Ann Marie looked back and saw him climb into his truck and follow them up the road. She guessed they rode at least ten miles on the dirt road after leaving the highway, and still no buildings were in sight. To say they were in the boondocks was an understatement.

Another ten minutes of bumping and bouncing brought them to the house, a nondescript, single story ranch house with a couple of barns, a stable, and that was it. At least as much as she could see in the gathering darkness. A cold wind swept down off the mountains, but it was the stars, millions of them, that sent a chill racing through her body. It was beautiful. The sky changed to a deep, ink black, except for the stars. Never in her life had she seen so many of them. Each one sparkled separately. It was breathtaking.

She grabbed Rod by the arm as they walked to the house. "Was it a night like this when the Martians landed?"

"Don't make fun," he said, half joking; half serious. "You never know."

The cowboy met them on the porch of the ranch house, and Williams introduced him, but Ann Marie, focused on the beauty of the night sky, missed his name. Inside, the cowboy, whom she immediately nicknamed Cowboy Joe in her mind, showed them to their rooms. His slow drawl bespoke his apparent lack of concern or hurry. "Here ya go, folks. Not too fancy, but it'll keep ya out of the weather."

It was nothing, Ann Marie noticed, like Millie's place. A simple ten-by-ten bedroom with a shower stall in the corner; a metal bedstead; a two-drawer night stand; and a three drawer chest of drawers crammed between the bed and the wall.

"Toilet is down the hall," the cowboy said as he pointed to the end of the dark hallway. "We'll have a bite for y'all in the dining room. Whenever you get there. Just some cold cuts and iced tea. Guess I can make you something hot to drink if you need it."

"No. That will be fine," Williams interjected before the others could open their mouths. "Did the others get here yet?"

"No sir, not yet. But I expect them pretty soon. Think they ran into some bad weather coming over the mountains from Los Alamos. Shouldn't be long, I reckon." He pointed to their rooms. "Go ahead and dump your stuff, and I'll see you in the dining room."

"Who are you talking about?" Ann Marie inquired after the cowboy sauntered off.

"Colleagues from Los Alamos. Quite astute," he emphasized. "They are nothing short of genius in what we'll be taking on. Just wait and see. These two men will help us immensely. But, that's for later; right now let's relax while we can. Once we get started, it may be non-stop and very tiring. Get your stuff put away, and we'll gather in the front room." He offered a warm and genuine fatherly smile. "You'll need your rest for what's coming."

*****

They sat around the fireplace in the living room and finished the last tidbits of their sandwiches. The cold wind whipped down from the mountain and banged the shutters. The old house groaned and creaked. Ann Marie shivered as she drank the last of the tea, then got up and sat on a log by the roaring fire.

"Freezing my tail," she said somewhat apologetically. She propped her feet up to the blaze, "Ahh, now this is the life." She looked at the cowboy, sitting silently in the shadows across the room, leaning back on the legs of his chair, his worn boots propped up on the edge of a table. "Would you happen to have a little Kentucky sipping whiskey around here?" she asked.

He almost fell off his chair, laughing. "My God, lady, you're my kind of woman." He leaned forward, pulled the table drawer open, and lifted out a flask. "Jack Black do?"

"You're my kind of cowboy." She got up and took the well-used, leather-bound flask from him. She started to twist the cap, then stopped to look at the inscription. It was a cattle brand. The letters, HJ; worn but readable

The cowboy spoke before she had the chance to inquire. "Glasses are in the kitchen if you need one."

Ann Marie curled in close to the fire, the flask cupped in her hands. "Nope. A good sip and a warm fire are all a lady needs." She twisted the top, raised it to her lips and tipped it slightly, allowing the strong, stiff drink to warm her to the bottom of her feet.

Rod caught the cowboy watching wide-eyed as she took the drink. He laughed aloud. "If you knew her like we do, nothing she does would surprise you." They all chuckled and passed the flask around.

They said little as they listened to the cold north wind sweep in from the mountain. The house creaked and groaned. Ann Marie took charge of tossing an occasional log on the fire and stoking it with the poker. Rod excused himself to go to his room and shower. He came back wearing his Levis, a Georgetown T-shirt, and a pair of white gym socks. He sat across from his new counterpart. "Got a drink for a guy?"

"Here you go," she replied.

Rod took a long belt and swallowed it slowly. "Jeez, that's good," he said after he caught his breath. He leaned back and looked at Williams. "How are we going to get started?"

Williams nodded his head from side-to-side. "Not now. Tomorrow,"

He steered the conversation, what there was of it, free from their case. They covered the Middle East situation, who the opposition might be in the upcoming presidential election, and the cowboy's real concern about the quality of quarter-horses that might be running at Ruidoso next summer.

Ann Marie watched quietly. She understood this was the place but not the time for work.

Williams finally stood up. "I'm calling it a night," he announced. "See you in the morning."

"Good night." Ann Marie said as she watched him disappear through the hall door.

Rod leaned forward, his hands on his knees. "Probably good advice for us, too. What do you think?"

"You go ahead. I'm too wired to sleep. I think I'll sit by the fire a little longer."

"Okay." He reached toward her and took her hand in his for a moment, creating a streak of electricity that shot up her arm. "Good night."

"Good night," she answered, her voice barely above a whisper. When he left, the newest spy in the government network looked at the old mantel clock when it hit the stroke of midnight. "Think they'll get here tonight?" she asked.

"Yes ma'am. Reckon they will. Running late, but they'll get here." Cowboy Joe rocked back and forth in his chair, then eased himself up to his feet. He stood tall, buttoned the top button of his shirt, and took his coat from the hook. He was looking up at a soft, green light flashing over the doorframe. "They ought to about be getting to the gate in fifteen or twenty minutes, so I have to go. Good night ma'am. Enjoyed visiting with you." A blast of arctic air raced through the open door when he left.

Ann Marie screwed the top onto the flask and put it back in the drawer, then walked lazily to her room. She showered, put on warm pajamas and, as she crawled under the blankets, heard the sound of a car and the cowboy's old truck when they banged up to the front of the house.

All the players are here, she decided. Tomorrow will be our big day. She was suddenly struck with what some might call "a foxhole conversion." Might it be too big; not just for her, but for Williams, Jasmine, or even the bureau itself? She closed her eyes and prayed.

CHAPTER TWELVE

After breakfast, Williams, Ann Marie and Rod gathered once again in the living room. A light dusting of snow covered the ground outside, reflecting an occasional ray of sun that pierced through the clouds. A strong wind blew down from the mountain, whipping the flakes like an invisible broom sweeping the landscape. Ann Marie looked at a thermometer that hung on the windowsill. It read twenty-four degrees. It was so cold - - too cold, even for February. She hoped this wasn't some harbinger of things to come.

Two men came down the hall. Actually, trudging would be more like it, each with a briefcase in his hands. She thought they looked as if they had been up all night. They looked wretched. The older of the two appeared to be in his late sixties, a gravelly, yet distinguished face. He wore a rumpled gray suit and was in need of a shave. He must not have changed or rested since his arrival last night. His bloodshot eyes looked as if they were going to fold themselves closed any second. The younger man was probably about forty. Otherwise, he looked much like his counterpart — exhausted. She casually studied him as he walked into the living room. He wore an eye patch over his left eye. He didn't have on a jacket, but wore a vest. Something about him struck her. She knew him from somewhere before; a person couldn't forget that ruddy, hero-type image. Then it struck her. He was younger, but the spitting image of John Wayne, a real true grit kind of man.

"Miss Beaudet, let me introduce you to our colleagues." Williams gestured to the older man, "This is Dr. Hammond. He specializes in aerial surveillance." Turning to the other, he said, "This is Harold Gosbeck. He does organizational analysis, among other things. Right, Harold?"

"Yes sir," Harold replied. He shook hands with her and continued, "The doctor and I have been going over your files, and frankly, your findings and the tentative conclusions are exceptionally alarming." He looked around the room and took a seat close to the fire. "We don't have any time to waste. We think we're facing a critical situation."

He looked first at Ann Marie, then Williams, and continued. "Without trying to sound like an alarmist, and while making every effort to remain objective, we must raise the possibility that the United States conceivably could go to war over this. It was not an overt and dramatic blow like Pearl Harbor or September 11th, but nevertheless, it was a sneak attack at the heart of our system. Someone, apparently the Chinese, is trying to overthrow our government from within. Furthermore, the worst part is this. We don't know how many others have been corrupted in a similar fashion."

"Indeed," the doctor broke in. "I believe we must move with the utmost speed. Our device has been tested under the direst conditions, and has performed almost flawlessly." He smiled confidently. "I believe we are in position to launch our aerial surveillance system without further delay. Indeed, I propose the suggestion that any delay should be considered as a setback to the overall accomplishment of our mission. The only question I pose to you, Mr. Williams, is this: Are you, or those you are in contact with, prepared to do what is required to counteract this aggression?"

Ann Marie's heart pounded. The palms of her hands became cold and clammy. Aggression? War? How did it get this far? This wasn't war. We can't go to war over this, however bad it might be. She started to speak, but at a glance from Williams she decided otherwise. She was the novice. It was sage, old advice. You have two ears with which you listen, and one mouth to speak. Shut up, and learn.

"You're convinced you can do it?" Williams asked the doctor. "This is not a thing for routine satellite surveillance?"

"Not for what we need. The satellites will give us very good visual pictures of our target, but not the audio or explicit detail we need." He paused and took a deep breath. His bloodshot eyes glanced around the room. "With our device, we will slip in and literally become their intimate company, albeit unannounced." He smiled at Ann Marie, obviously enjoying his role. "Their secrets will soon be ours."

Williams nodded his head in approval. "Ready?"

"Absolutely. Shall we?" Hammond gestured toward the door.

The cowboy, who stood in the back of the room, moved quickly to the door and opened it. "Follow me," he directed as he pulled his sweat-stained Stetson down over his head. Ann Marie grabbed her jacket and followed behind, watching the men as they tromped through the deepening snow toward the barn. "What else did you find out?" Williams asked Gosbeck.

"They're for real, that's a certainty." He shook his head, and continued. "Let's get one thing at a time, though. We'll get the device launched, then talk about what else is steaming on the stove."

Cowboy Joe opened the barn door and held it against the wind while the others passed into the darkness of the unlit barn. "Straight back," he commanded while he pulled the door shut and barred it with an iron rod. "Back to the last stall on the left."

Hammond led the way, a sprightly bounce in his step for a person who, less than twenty minutes ago, looked like he could fall asleep. Dim rays of gray, subdued sunlight slipped through cracks in the boards. The wind whistled, picking up bits of straw, flinging the dank stink of manure in a swirl through the cracks and crevices of the stalls. Ann Marie knew her career as a "spy" would lead her to challenging frontiers, but this one became surreal. It was grotesque to think that they made a quantum leap from the warmth and charm of Old Alexandria to a frank discussion of war, all in a matter of only twenty-four hours.

Hammond pulled the stall gate open, gave a stout tug on a wooden lever on the wall and stood back. She gasped as the entire straw covered floor began to lift up, bringing a gray, metallic box with it. It was an elevator. She stood transfixed as the door rolled opened. Hammond led the way, turning to the others, "Come on, let's go. We're wasting time."

She followed Williams, Gosbeck, and Rod into the elevator, then turned to Cowboy Joe. "Coming?" she asked.

"No ma'am. I'll be here when you get back." She saw him reach for the lever, and the door closed.

"Hit three, please," Hammond directed.

Ann Marie looked at the panel – seven floors. There was an entire complex beneath the barn. Her mind raced back to her first conversation with Williams the day he told her she would encounter a world most people never thought existed. How right he was; she was in the middle of it.

The elevator stopped with a gentle lurch and the doors quietly opened. Hammond led the way down the sterile hallway; the echo of their footsteps reverberated off the cold tile. He unlocked a door and led the way into a large, bright laboratory. Electronic equipment was packed into every conceivable inch – dials, gauges, digital readouts, and computer terminals. From somewhere, the gentle, steady hum of electricity was heard. It looked to her like a combination of a radio repair shop and an operating room, complete with a gurney in the middle. Bright flood lights hung above it, throwing a blinding glare down on an egg-shaped disc that looked something like two oval serving platters. Ann Marie estimated them to be about twelve by eighteen inches that were welded together by their inverted edges. She blurted out before she could catch herself, "My God! A flying saucer."

Hammond laughed. "Oh, no, my dear. Not a flying saucer. You've been reading too much rubbish."

"So this is it?" Williams asked.

"The Scout," Hammond replied. He grinned from ear to ear. "An airborne magnetic powered surveillance device. The only one in the world."

"Sorry, but I have to plead ignorance. Can you explain it to me?" Ann Marie asked.

"By all means. I thought you'd never ask," he joked. "I do not have children. But this," he said, patting the icy-looking disc, "this is my child. I have given my whole life to it, and it works. I guarantee. We've tested it here, over at White Sands, the Antarctic, you name it, we've tested it." He patted it gently, stroking it as though it were his prize kitten. "You want to see this Chinaman's ranch in Mexico?" He grinned at the incongruity. "You want to know how many are there and how to get in and out? This will tell you, without a doubt. We'll see them and hear them. Everything. No secrets can be hidden."

Voices In The Fog

Ann Marie pulled up a stool and sat alongside the gurney, inspecting the disc under the glare of the lights. "I'm not an engineer, Doctor. Can you explain it in lay terms?"

"It's very simple, really. Did you ever play with magnets when you were a child?"

"Sure. Lots of times. We'd play games with them. You know, see how close we could scoot one to the other before it flipped around. We actually could feel the magnetic power in our fingers when they got close together."

"A good description. What we have here is not all that different from a commercial magnet. However, it is compressed slightly more than eight hundred times the density of your run-of-the-mill commercial magnet. Inside are receptors that allow us to control the magnetic opposition, as well as the effect of magnetic north." He smiled in satisfaction and continued, "This will completely revolutionize travel. We don't need to rely on fossil fuels. We no longer shall need internal combustion engines. First, we will see it in limited action such as we're about to do today. Later, it will replace the need for an air force as we know it. Then, you will park one in every garage." He laughed a deep, self-satisfied laugh. "Not in our life times, I would think, but not all that distant in the future."

"Look here," he said, pointing beneath the lip of the object. "This shield opens on command, allowing us to use a telescopic lens to focus on the target, as well as aim a powerful listening device at it. We can see with a fair degree of clarity from thirty thousand feet in altitude. When we move closer, we can see with total clarity. Even through walls. Our Scout is equipped with a Forward Looking Infrared Radar that can easily penetrate a typical residential wall. Of course, we are not able to have clear pictures through a wall, but we can detect the forms of people and objects exceptionally well; the same is true with sound. We can move the Scout as close as is needed and tune in to the lightest whisper."

"I assure you, Mr. Williams, and you, too, Miss Beaudet. We can pilot the Scout from here to your dinner table with one hundred percent accuracy. You want to see who is at that ranch? How about an eight by ten color glossy portrait?. I assure you, the Scout will deliver."

Doctor Hammond folded his arms triumphantly over his chest. "We can deliver every whisper. Every sound. Nothing can escape. Absolutely nothing!" He glanced at Gosbeck.

"You've heard from Holloman?" Hammond asked.

"Yes sir. They said they'd have an aircraft up at oh-four hundred. I never heard back, so I'm sure they're airborne."

"What's that?" Williams asked.

"Holloman Air Force Base in Alamogordo. They sent up a plane to do a recon flight over the ranch for us. We should be getting some computer images back any time. That will give us the lay of the land, as well as precise longitude and latitude. We will download their data into the computer, and then we will launch."

"How fast will Scout go?" Ann Marie asked.

"On paper, faster than we can deal with. Unfortunately, we have not yet mastered the metallurgy for the magnets, so we have to go quite a bit slower. Still, we can cruise comfortably at seven hundred knots per hour. Not bad, wouldn't you agree?"

Gosbeck turned to a computer terminal and pulled up a seat. Ann Marie looked over his shoulder and peered at the blank screen. "Holloman?"

"Right. We should get their stuff right about now. Assuming everybody's computers are up and running." He typed in a password, followed it with a screen full of commands and sat back. "Should take a few seconds." No sooner had the words left his mouth than the monitor came alive with photos. Dozens of them rolled across the screen so fast she could not count them.

"We'll download them, then take our time and scroll through them. We can pick out a couple that we want to keep and print them out. I'll store the others on a disc in case we need them later."

Williams and Rod stood alongside her, watching as Gosbeck went back through the photos – all appearing in shades of green and black, a result of infrared shots in the dark. Nevertheless, it was clear what was there. It was a main house, a garage and an outbuilding. "Maybe something like a guesthouse," she thought. Then, what looked like a barn.

"Is there a better shot of the barn?" she asked.

Gosbeck continued to scroll, stopping at a shot from a different angle. "That?"

"Yeah," Williams responded. "It's a hangar, not a barn. Do you agree?" he asked, turning to Ann Marie and Rod.

"Look," Rod pointed out. "That's a runway running parallel to the road. It leads right up to the hangar."

They scanned the pictures until at last they were satisfied they had a good feel for the ranch. "So what it looks like is that, besides the main house, we need to see who or what is in the guesthouse," Rod said.

"Then check to make sure the other building is a garage; try for a better look at the it; and keep a close eye on that building, about a mile east of the ranch house," Hammond injected.

Voices In The Fog

A pickup truck was parked alongside it, more or less blocking the road. "What do you think it is? A gatehouse?"

"A reasonable guess," Williams said. "Makes sense that they have at least one – maybe two guards out on the road to stop anyone from coming up to the house."

"Are you ready, Doctor?" Gosbeck asked.

"Lock and load, as they say on the firing line," Hammond answered. "Madam, gentlemen? Shall we launch?"

They eased the gurney through the door and onto the elevator. As promised, Cowboy Joe was waiting for them in the barn. "Got my horses fed. Y'all ready?"

Hammond nodded his head. The Scout was ready. He was ready. There was nothing more to do except roll it outside and set it underway.

"So unceremonious," Ann Marie murmured to Rod. "A jillion dollar project, and we're going to take it out in the snow and send it off. There ought to be a band. Maybe some speeches or something. Damn it, one minute we're talking about going to war. Now we all have horse shit on our heels, and we're going to stand out in the snow like kids flying a kite. It just doesn't seem right."

Rod wrapped his arm around her shoulder, blocking some of the falling snow as they followed the others outside. "Truth is stranger than fiction, isn't it? You're right, though. It does seem an injustice to such a noble cause for there to be no fanfare whatsoever. Be that as it may, there's no romance in war, and that's a hard, cold fact."

"No romance? Never?" she asked in a husky voice.

His one-sided grin slipped across his face. "Almost never."

Abruptly, the wind dropped and the snowfall became just a light sprinkling of flakes. "A good omen," she

185

thought. She stopped to take in the natural beauty of the ranch. A horse stood in the corral, his scruffy winter coat caked with snow. Behind them was the towering peak of El Capitan Mountain. Below, in the valley as far as she could see, was rough, rolling cattle country. The buffalo grass, stubby and tarnished gold, stuck through the thin blanket of snow, high enough to scratch the cowboy's stirrups when he rode his horse across the prairie. The air was crisp, but not cold. The thought of a country Christmas card passed through her mind. Peace. Goodwill to men. Her solitude was broken by Hammond's voice.

"Lift off!"

She stood still, mesmerized. Hammond punched commands into a tiny computer no bigger than a Gameboy. The Scout began to wobble, then raised itself an inch or two and stopped. It was like a magic show where the magician levitates a volunteer from the audience. It hovered momentarily, then lifted itself silently – slowly. Almost like a feather caught in the breeze, gradually rising up beyond the barn roof. Suddenly, with a burst of speed, not like a bullet, but like a dove taking flight before the hunter's gun, the Scout tilted into the wisp of wind and moved away.

Doctor Hammond, Harold Gosbeck, Alfred Williams, Rod McCarren, Ann Marie Beaudet, and Cowboy Joe stood silently with their private thoughts as the silver disc moved farther and farther away. It slipped effortlessly beneath the path of a red-tailed hawk that swooped in unseen currents of air, eyes toward the ground, waiting for a mouse to move and surrender its life in the unending struggle of the food chain.

Ann Marie realized that a metaphor played out before her eyes. The hawk and the Scout. The mouse and the ranch. Not life imitating art, nor art imitating life. Neither of those at all. This was science imitating the laws of nature. It was the predator and the hunted. One dies that the other may live. But, who, she wondered, must die?

"I'll take it from here, Doc." It was Cowboy Joe who broke them from their trance.

"Thank you," Hammond replied. "The rest of you, let's get inside and talk. We've got a lot of ground to cover, so to speak."

Ann Marie sat on the edge of the hearth and pulled off her jacket while the others busied themselves getting something warm to drink and finding a hook to hang up their coats. Doctor Hammond sat on the couch and propped his feet on a stool next to the fire. "You have a question, Miss Beaudet? I can tell by your expression."

"The cowboy. Who is he? I just assumed that he was an employee to keep up the place."

"Oh, yes. He is that, too. But, we gave him a real job. One more in his line of discipline. Cowboy, you called him?" Hammond chuckled. "Actually, you honor him. He loves his horses. But, you see, our cowboy friend is Doctor Edmond Rucinski. One of the most brilliant physicists on the face of the earth. His is one of the many unseen faces that give us a quantum leap over every other nation in unmanned flight. We don't dabble in little green men or anything like that, but we are capable of going to the outer reaches of the solar system and back. We are not God. We certainly have our imperfections, but we work with all of our hearts and souls to perfect man's ability to understand the whole of the universe. We do this not for the sake of war. To the contrary, we understand the evil of the world and believe that our effort, however humble it may be, might take us one step closer to universal peace."

Voices In The Fog

Hammond turned his attention to Gosbeck. With only the slightest nod of his head, the young organizational analyst took the lead from the elder statesman. "I have some things of more than a passing interest to all of us. What we've learned is a serious concern for our national interest. In fact, it should be of interest for the whole world." He unfolded a map and laid it out on the floor for everyone to see. "Here is Beijing." He pointed with the tip of a pencil. "Now, directly north and slightly to the east is the city of Linshi, a rather nondescript community in the mountains. Certainly not a place tour guides would recommend for you if you were to take a vacation. It is really out of the way. It's cold, isolated and almost inaccessible. The local people survive almost entirely on what they can grow. A few crops and animals, and that's about it.

"Nevertheless," Gosbeck continued, "the isolation serves the government very well. The CIA and the NSA were not aware of this for quite a while, but not until we inquired, in some detail, about Ling Nuy did they share their intelligence data with us. Fortunately, we were able to confirm some of this overnight with a satellite flyover and have retrieved some incredibly good pictures. Look here," he said.

Gosbeck passed around three pictures, each taken from an altitude high above the stratosphere – photographs of a long, multi-story building on the face of a mountain, hanging precariously on the edge. "This building is isolated, even from the community. It is an intelligence academy. Furthermore, they've included a significant program that we do not have in the free world, but definitely one of interest." He pointed to a wing of the building, and continued. "This is their hospital. That in itself is not so unusual, but the type of work they do there is extremely important." He referred to his notebook on his lap. "They have a surgical system that allows them to duplicate a person."

Ann Marie gasped involuntarily. Gosbeck glanced up at her.

"My reaction, too. But I don't mean duplicate, such as cloning, but surgically duplicate a person. In this case, it appears they have duplicated a member of our Supreme Court. A CIA source, one that is highly trusted, has provided proof of what goes on there. The simplest way to explain it is they find a person who meets the basic physical, cultural, and educational parameters of their target. They remove that person from his normal habitat, take him to Linshi, and reconstruct him physically. Supposedly, that is the easy part. From there, the person undergoes an extended period of time in the academy itself. He, or she, has to learn everything that allows them to be substituted for the original, including mannerisms, and all of the unique characteristics that every one of us has. Hobbies, foods, entertainment; everything. Our CIA source is not aware of any non-Oriental passing through Linshi, but given the great secrecy of the place, that is something our intelligence people recognize as being reasonable. The bottom line is this; we have great faith in their source. The person I spoke with, and I know her personally, said she would bet her life on what the source said."

"What I have here," he said, pulling a sheath of pictures from his briefcase, "are some photos of Justice Gonzales and of Mr. Duarte at the time of his arrest in Nogales."

A gasp went up as he placed the photos in front of his audience. The two men could pass as brothers. "As you see, a remarkable similarity. And this is prior to Duarte's undergoing the process at Linshi. Extraordinary, isn't it? There's no detailed intelligence information, other than DEA reports, that indicate when this specific case was implemented by the Chinese. I believe we can assume it might have been five years ago when Duarte allegedly was killed. Obviously, he wasn't. We may surmise that he went to China, spent about three years in Linshi, then was substituted for Gonzales. Of course, we have no idea how they kidnapped the Judge and inserted their replacement. Quite a trick, but they pulled it off very well. As for the real Justice, it's anybody's guess. He could be dead or alive. We are assuming he is at this ranch in Mexico, I take it?"

"We hope," Williams assented.

Hammond spoke. "It is imperative that we obtain good information from the ranch. There is no time to waste. If the Judge is alive, and I pray he is, then there are two likely places for him to be held – Linshi or the ranch. The worst-case scenario is if he is at Linshi. I see little likelihood of our being able to rescue him from there. The ranch is a different story. We can get him out of there. Don't you agree, Alfred?"

Williams tossed a log on the fire, stabbed effortlessly with the poker, then turned to Doctor Hammond. "I concur, Doctor. Linshi is out of the question. The ranch may be difficult, but it is within our reach."

Since it would be an hour or more before the Scout came back, Ann Marie went to her room and lay across the bed. She needed to be alone so she could assimilate all she learned that morning. Eventually, she allowed her body to drift away, far away into a deep sleep. A place where her mind washed itself clean and fresh from the overload she witnessed in such a short time.

Voices In The Fog

*****

"We've got the Scout back."

She shook her head, cleared the cobwebs from her brain, and rolled over. Rod shook her feet. "Time to get up. It's back."

Hammond, seated at the computer in the underground bunker, smiled when she came and stood at his shoulder. "For a first run, it looks like we did well. Very well, in fact.

"We had live-action pictures coming back to us. So what I have done is edit them down to some still shots that we might be interested in looking at a little closer. Then, depending on what we see, we can plan our next sortie."

Slowly, he scanned the pictures through the computer and allowed the group time to get an overview of what they wanted to look at more clearly. They were a couple dozen to scan – all taken from the predetermined altitude of one thousand feet above ground level. Low enough, Hammond determined, that they would be close enough to see things well, yet high enough that the Scout would not be noticed by anybody on the ground.

By consensus, they settled on the bird's eye views of the ranch they wanted to download and observe in more detail. They started with the gatehouse. It was a stucco, eight by ten, flat roofed house at the edge of the road leading to the house. One pickup truck, a battered Chevy was parked in front, the rear end protruding into the road and essentially stopping anyone from getting by without going into the ditch on one side or hitting the building on the other side. Other than a door facing the front and a window on either side, the place was about as plain as might be expected. Inside, out of the weather, they

assumed, would be a simple place with a single purpose —
to stop unwanted traffic to the house. No one moved.
Whoever was there was probably sound asleep, or at least
lazing away the day.

The hangar was about fifty yards to the right side of
the house. The doors were closed, but it appeared to be
about the right size to shelter a small- to mid-size plane,
maybe about a six-place Cessna. It was definitely too small
to hold a cargo plane that might come in loaded with dope.

The guesthouse sat to the left rear of the main house.
There was probably no more than thirty feet from its front
door to a rear door into the main house. Williams made a
few rough calculations, determining its size to be about
forty feet by forty feet, or roughly, sixteen hundred square
feet under roof.

The main house faced the east. It was larger – probably
twice the size of the guesthouse. It was surrounded by a
low stucco wall around the yard. The front, sides, and back
also took in the guesthouse. Both houses appeared to be
stucco, topped with tile roofs.

"Very typical," Gosbeck commented. "Mexican tile,
stucco, patio wall – about what we would expect in the
southwest and down in Mexico."

The garage also appeared to be a modest, yet utilitarian
building. It had three closed overhead doors.

"That's it for now," Williams commented. We'll go
back around dusk and try to pick up some movement and
see who is around. We'll keep the Scout at about the same
altitude, then drop it as low as we want after dark. That's
when we'll get our first close-up. Real close-up."

*****

Voices In The Fog

Gosbeck sat at the control pane. The others gathered tightly around him. The monitor picked up a distant shot of the ranch on the horizon. Scout was coming in from the west, the falling sunlight at its tail. The ranch was dead ahead on the flat prairie. As smooth as glass, the Scout slowed to little more than a hover only a quarter of a mile from the house, holding steady at one thousand feet. The camera picked up a man in the back yard, sitting in a chair, casually watching smoke rising up from a barbecue pit.

"Serene, isn't it?" Gosbeck commented.

"Yeah, but look there," Rod said. A second person stepped into view. A woman came from the house and approached the man, remained a few seconds, then went back inside.

"We're too far away to get a good look at them in this light. We'll have to wait until it gets darker, then we will slip in for a closer peek," Hammond said.

Gosbeck scooted the Scout in a long, circular swing around the house, then out to the gatehouse. All was quiet. Nobody moved; other than the man at the barbecue. Gosbeck swung the camera around in time to catch the man take whatever he cooked from the grill and carry it inside on a platter.

They elevated the Scout higher and allowed the sun to slip below the western horizon before easing it down, much lower than previously viewed. Williams watched the screen intently, guiding the surveillance device lower and lower and, at the same time, closer to the house. Williams read off the altimeter as the craft descended, finally barking out a command, "Stop! Low enough."

Ann Marie looked at the altimeter. The Scout was hovering at fifty feet, peering directly at the back of the house. Gosbeck guided it around to the right. Lights were on in almost all of the rooms. Then it was there! A view directly through a window to the dining room table where two men and a woman sat. The man and the woman were easily recognizable as the people who were seen in the back yard.

The third person, a smaller man, had his back to the window.

"Maybe?" Ann Marie uttered, almost as a prayer.

"Shh. We'll wait and see." Rucinski whispered as he reached for a switch. "Let's listen." He adjusted the squelch and turned up the speaker. The sound of silverware scraping on the plates filled the room. The three people at dinner spoke in Spanish, which Gosbeck quickly translated for the others. There were a few soft comments between the bigger man and the woman, but nothing of significance – the steaks; need to get gas for the car tomorrow; the weather; nothing more than the dinner table chatter. The smaller man ate in silence, adding nothing to the conversation.

The larger of the two men pushed back from the table and patted his belly. "*Estaba bien, Marisa. Muy bien.*"

"Marisa?" Rucinski asked.

"Yeah, I guess that's her," Hammond replied. "Duarte's wife must be keeping house for Ling Nuy while her husband fills in for the real Judge."

Ann Marie and the others huddled around the computer screen until, at last, the small man pushed back from the table. He excused himself, and said he was going to have a cigar before he went to bed. Gosbeck tilted the camera lens and followed him when he went out the back door and sat in the chair by the barbecue pit.

Ann Marie held her breath when he unwrapped a cigar, bit the tip and held it in his mouth. She saw Duarte follow this ritual precisely. Not in restaurants, of course, but outside, in the park, on the street. This man did not hurry. Indeed, he was relaxing after dinner, about to enjoy a good cigar in the refreshing, crisp, desert evening air. He flicked a match that burst into flame, and just as quickly was fanned out by the wind. He hunched over against the breeze, and lit a second match. He held it to the cigar tip and puffed lightly as the flame exposed his face in the darkness. In the glow of the match hung a disembodied face, the exact replica of Duarte.

"It's him!" Williams shouted. "It's the Judge. We've found him."

"Yeah, we've found him, all right," Rucinski said. "But, that was the easy part of the operation. Step two will be a bigger challenge."

"He looks awfully relaxed, don't you think?" Ann Marie asked, more rhetorically than anything.

Dr. Hammond smiled and shook his head. "I'll offer a conjecture to this situation. He has been their prisoner so damned long that he is pretty much what we call in our prison system, a trustee. Face it, he is about five miles from the highway, and if he should make it that far, then he is a good sixty miles from Nuevo Laredo. Even if he went south, it would be another sixty miles or so to Sabinas Hildago. There is nowhere to turn. Will he run? If so, where to? Who will he run to? Every cop down there is on *la morbida*. You know what I mean – the bite, the take.

Hammond shook his head in disgust. "My friends, that poor man is a lost and trapped soul. To add to his misery, he believes nobody has the slightest idea he is missing. Imagine that, if you will. Out in the middle of the desert, and nobody even knows you're there. God, what a horrible, lonesome feeling it must be to him."

195

They sat silently around the screen, watching while the Judge finished his cigar and ground it out beneath his foot. Gosbeck guided the lens as Gonzales walked back to the house, stopped in the kitchen for a drink, then went to his bedroom.

The Judge stood in front of the window of his sparsely furnished bedroom. Nonchalantly, he undressed to his underwear and went to the sink in the corner to brush his teeth.

"I'm sorry, but I can't stand here like a voyeur and watch this poor man. Let him have his dignity. Please," Ann Marie pleaded. "Let him undress and go to bed. There's nothing more for us to see there," she said, pointing to the window.

"Yes, I agree," Rucinski replied.

Gosbeck controlled the Scout as it silently backed away from the house. "Let's look at things from another angle." He switched on the Forward Looking Infrared Radar, and allowed it to scan the house much as a radiologist performs an X-ray or an MRI patient. The forms of a man and woman could be seen, still sitting at the dining room table. As the scan moved forward, the shape of a third person, a very big person, was seen sitting in the living room. Gosbeck moved the Scout completely around the house and felt relieved that no one else was there. He spun it around to the guesthouse, and again felt the tension ebb from his shoulders when they found it empty. "To the guard shack," he commented, guiding the Scout along the road until the gatehouse came into view. Gosbeck slowed the scout and allowed the radar to scan the circumference of the house. As expected, two men sat inside and the pickup truck was still parked in the front.

Voices In The Fog

"So far, we've got four men, a woman, and the Judge. To the hangar?" he asked Williams.

Williams nodded his approval. "Let's give it a go."

Gosbeck was having fun, playing with the Scout as he ran it around the Mexican landscape, peering into windows, running the radar through the buildings, all from the anonymous safety of his belowground vault beneath the El Capitan Mountain.

The Scout moved stealthily in the dark night along the road, silently veering to the left as it approached the house. He brought it to an abrupt halt directly in front of the hangar. "Are we taking bets? What do you want to put on it? Is there or is there not a plane inside?" he asked.

"Just quit farting around! You're like a little boy playing a game," Ann Marie said. She was getting impatient. The Judge's predicament was too distressing; too sad.

Gosbeck turned slowly and looked over his shoulder into her eyes. His right eye, the one without the patch, pierced her professional armor. She caught herself taking a half-step back.

"I do my job well. Very well, in fact. And if I have to 'fart around' as you say, to find a bit of humor in this fucked up world, then more power to me. When the shit hits the fan, I'll be out front. I always have and always will - - until the owl calls my name, I'll bust my balls doing what I do. So, *excuuuse* me," he emphasized, "if I try to get a little humor while you're in the corner, biting your lip, in pain, hurting, because you can't stand to see that miserable Judge watching his own life pass him by."

Gosbeck flicked on the radar, turned and looked at her again. "You should have taken my bet. You would've won.

Look," he said, gesturing toward the screen. "No plane. Nothing. *Nada*."

He swung the camera around and scanned the garage. There was a Suburban and two sedans and nothing more.

Hammond took a deep breath and rubbed his blood-shot eyes Then he said, "I'm tired. Bring it home and let's get some sleep. Every one of us needs it. Tomorrow's another day. I think our investigation is pretty well wrapped up. It's time to put some boots on the ground."

CHAPTER THIRTEEN

Ann Marie sat on the sofa with Rod. Their stocking feet were propped on the footstool. A sliver of moonlight parted the drapes and wove a thread of light across the hardwood floor. Golden red flames in the fireplace danced and licked themselves around the mesquite logs, throwing a natural, hypnotic trance into their sleepy eyes. The house was dark and deathly quiet. The others long ago went to bed, leaving them to sit side-by-side in comfortable silence. Their shoulders touched, sorting out where they were, but even more importantly, where they were headed. "They found the Judge, but now what?" she thought. Ride in like the cavalry? Hardly. There were two counter-balancing variables to think about, not the least of which was the Chinese. How would they react when their hostage disappeared? They had to have a "Plan B" in case they were exposed before they achieved whatever goal they had in mind. What would they do?

"And," she mused, "how do you explain to the American people that an imposter was sitting on the Supreme Court? To make an even worse case scenario, how many others are there? Congressmen? Governors? Maybe the Federal Reserve Chairman?"

"Hell, we've really gotten into a pickle on this, haven't we?" Rod asked. "It hasn't quite worked out like we thought it would when we first got started. Truthfully, every time we start a case, we each develop our own particular vision of how it might turn out. We come up with a handful of scenarios, and then in our own minds, try to anticipate how we can deal with them. I never envisioned something like this, and I'm sure neither Williams nor the others did either.

199

Voices In The Fog

I hate to say this, but there might not be too many alternatives. What're we going to do? Rescue him and call a press conference? Then we could re-introduce the Judge to the people? Oh yeah! Sure. They'll understand and have a lot of sympathy."

Rod offered a soft chortle and continued. "If you believe that, then I've got some good swampland in Arizona I'll sell you. I tell you," he said with a twinge of sarcasm, "it might be so unsettling and disastrous to the whole of our systems that we can't return him to the bench. Never!"

"Exactly what do you mean by that?" she fired back. Her voice rang with stinging venom.

"What if? Just what if we left Duarte on the bench and compromised him?" he responded. Rod leaned over and looked directly into her eyes. He watched the reflection of the flames dance on her face. They were so beautiful, innocent and honest. Her expression was trusting, but very naïve about the evil in which she found herself.

"Precisely what are you saying?" she asked.

"Make sure that Gonzales never leaves the ranch. Not him or anybody else. All but Marisa. She becomes our leverage. She's the one we hold over Duarte to make sure he swings around and does things our way."

Ann Marie pushed Rod back away from her. "Have you lost your mind? That man is a Justice of the Supreme Court, and you'd leave him to rot down there?" she queried. She felt the anger move up her neck. Her face flushed. "You bastard. You filthy bastard." she blurted out. She jumped up from the sofa, spun around and looked down at him. "Which side are you on? Aren't we supposed to be the good guys? Wasn't it our job to make things right? That seems pretty damn simple to me, and. . . ."

Voices In The Fog

Rod put his finger to her lips and stopped her in mid-sentence. "Slow down. Just slow down for a minute and think about this. I'm not saying we send a bomber down there and kill him, but I am saying this; we have to come up with a list of alternatives. With each alternative, we have to itemize the potential outcomes – good and bad. Nothing more than basic economics. What is our return on investment? What do we get for whatever we do? Who does it impact? How will they respond? How will we respond to how they respond? How far does it go? Damn, if it was as simple as eliminating him and having it over, I'd vote to do it right now. Then we would arrange some simple little accident and take care of Duarte, too. How does that sound? Bim-bam, thank you ma'am. It would be over just that fast, and we get on with the President naming a new Justice. Nobody would be any the wiser." He smiled more to himself than to her. "Well, almost nobody."

"Return on our investment? Rod, shut up and listen to yourself for a minute. Return on our investment? Like so many cattle and so many cents for a pound of liver? Or maybe a good certificate of deposit? Maybe it would draw eight percent. How's that for a return on our investment?" Ann Marie replied.

She stared down at him, her clenched fists pressed against her hips. With vengence in her voice, she blasted McCarren. "This isn't a debit or credit. This isn't something you can put in your accounting book. This is a human being. He is a member of our Supreme Court. He's one of the most important people in the land, and you just want to write him off? Is the world really this evil? This mean? I can't believe we're having this conversation."

She shook her head in frustration: her hair whipped against her cheeks. "What in the hell has come over us?

What would happen if we stopped for a minute and thought like Superman. You know. Truth, justice, and the American way? We rescue the Judge. We arrest Duarte. We tell the whole world about the Chinese: we're open and honest. Is that too much for people to handle? What if their government told them the truth instead of some adulterated smoke and mirrors by a government spinmeister? Can't people handle the truth, pure and simple?" she looked at Rod and asked.

Rod shook his head. "No, they can't." He reached out, took her hands in his and guided her back down onto the sofa. "Welcome to the real world: no holds barred. To the victor goes the spoils, and second place means you're the first one to lose. No, people can't handle the truth when it hits them like an atom bomb. We'd have riots. They wouldn't know who to trust, so they would be better off if they didn't trust anybody. Everyone for himself. Chaos. That's what we would have. Total chaos. They would suspect everybody; their banker, their city alderman, the cop in the doughnut shop. There wouldn't be any limit to it. They'd go crazy. It would be like some ghostly science fiction. A real class B movie. You know, creatures from outer space who invade us and take over people's bodies." He paused to give her time to think about what he said. "But, there's more. What about the Chinese? Isn't that really their goal? To upset the applecart? Well, we sure as hell would play into their hand, wouldn't we?"

Special Agent Beaudet, as lonely and confused as she ever was, sank back and rested her head against the back of the sofa. She pulled a pillow on top of her and wrapped her arms around it, squeezing it tightly, feeling protected and safe in its warmth. "What kind of a mess are we in?" she asked through the pillow.

Voices In The Fog

"Bad. About as bad as anything I've seen," Rod replied. He jabbed around in the fire with the poker, giving a breath of fresh life to the dying flames.

Like Ann Marie, he slipped down low in the sofa and let the tension flow free from his muscles. Neither of them spoke about anything. They watched the waning fire flicker its last gasp, then settle into soft, glowing coals. Rod's breathing slowed. His eyes grew heavy. The last thing he remembered was the sensation of her hair brushing against his cheek, and they fell asleep.

Somewhere in the night, a coyote howled. Rod opened his eyes, disoriented for a moment. The quiet of the night returned. A single coal shone beneath the ashes in the fireplace. Ann Marie slipped down and nestled onto his lap. He brushed her hair from her face, leaned down, and kissed her cheek.

"I'm not asleep," she whispered. She opened her eyes and her smile illuminated the dim room. She put her arms around his neck and pulled him close. Their lips met and the electricity was created to fuse them forever.

*****

The agents and scientists spent the next day around the dining room table, each laying out a thought. Each of them offering their options. Brainstorming. No abstraction was too good or too bad, too bizarre or too conservative. Cover the spectrum. Williams was the facilitator, carefully jotting notes on his yellow notepad, taking time to challenge the others. Prompting them into a higher level of thought. Encouraging them to look beyond the obvious. Think of the big picture. The REALLY big picture. This was more than an uncomplicated procedure of rescuing Gonzales and restoring him to his rightful place. That was far too simple. There were too many ramifications. What did the Chinese have up their sleeve? Who knew? Maybe this was their one and only trick: their last shot. A shot in the dark, so to speak. Inspector Clouseau at his best. What if that was their strategy all along? To be found out? Create distrust in the American government: induce havoc in the institutions; banks, the news media, churches? Wouldn't that accomplish their objective? Bring down the government from within?

What about everyday people? The soccer moms and NASCAR dads, teachers, plumbers? The bureaucrats that keep our systems running? Do we try to keep it a secret from them? What if it gets out? Or, should we tell them up front and publicly proclaim our ability to hold fast to our ways and to ferret out the evil that others try to inflict on us? Then what?

What if the press or those same everyday people get provoked enough to demand military action against the Chinese? There always are a few hawks that spend their entire life looking for a reason to kick somebody's ass. Do we go to war over this thing? Not a very bright perspective.

They went non-stop all day, breaking briefly for a lunch of Cowboy Joe Rucinski's famous chili. Finally, with the late afternoon sun glaring through the windows, Williams tossed his pencil on the table. He leaned forward on his elbows and dug his fingers into his eyebrows and temples to release the pressure of his headache. Ann Marie watched him rub away the pressure from his brow, then looked across the table toward her.

"Quite a secret you found. Wouldn't you say?" He gave a short, brittle bark, intended to be a laugh, and gazed slowly around the table, absorbing the body language of his friends and partners. Nothing like a crisis to draw people together. Individually, and as a group, they were exhausted. Ann Marie stretched out. The back of her head rested on the edge of the chair; Rod held his forehead in one hand and played solitaire tic-tac-toe on his notepad; Rucinski stared blankly out the window; Gosbeck picked at invisible lint on his Pendleton shirt. Hammond looked at each of them and gave a tired, grim smile.

"Frankly, I'm so damned tired that I think I'm going to fix myself a nice martini and take a nap."

"What say, my friends, let's call it a day before we're totally brain dead?" Williams asked, shoving back from the table. "I'm going to get my jacket and take a walk before it gets dark. I'll breathe some of your clear mountain air," he said with a nod toward Rucinski.

"I have to feed my horses," Rucinski replied as he, too, got up and headed for the door.

"It's a shower and a cold beer for me," Gosbeck commented in a mild whisper. He eased himself slowly from the chair and moved down the hall like the walking dead.

Ann Marie looked at Rod. "What about you? Do you want to take a little hike? Get some fresh air? Maybe go up on that knoll behind the barn and watch the sunset?"

He nodded. "Let's get out of here. I want to forget this whole mess, even if it's only for a few minutes." He took their coats from the hangers by the door and held hers so she could slide her arms into it. Her fingertips touched Rod's hands as she slipped her arms into the sleeves. She held them tightly, then pulled them around her and clasped them to her chest. She felt his body quiver. Neither spoke. They stood in the quiet room and held on to each other, searching for warmth and comfort from the world they faced. She inhaled a slow, deep breath and took in the scent of his cologne. She held her breath and turned around slowly with his arms still wrapped around her until they came face-to-face, looking at each other, before she raised herself on her toes and put her lips to his.

*****

After dinner, Hammond and Williams returned to the barn, down to the third level, down the cold hall to the last door on the left, where once again they found their only weapon, the Scout. It was a "him," not a "her," according to Hammond.

"Ships are females. Planes, too; but not scouts. Just read your western history. Lewis and Clark and the rest of them. Scouts and explorers were men. Real men! Tough hombres. Mean sons-of-bitches," he boasted. "Loners, for the most part. They got in, did the job, and zipped back to the fort. That was their job. Now we call it intelligence gathering, but it's the same thing. Slip in real quiet like, see what the rascals are up to, then get out of there and get back."

"Well, what do you say? Shall we talk about him, or should we send him down to Mexico and see what is going on tonight?" Williams asked when he turned the gurney toward the door.

"Let's get it done," Hammond replied. "South of the border, down Mexico way," he sang. "Just a little incursion to see what the bad guys are doing." He chuckled as they went up the elevator. "What the hell do you think the Mexicans would say if they knew what we were up to?"

"That's their problem, not ours. I won't tell them if you won't."

Voices In The Fog

Williams stood back as Hammond punched the commands into his hand-held computer. The Scout lifted itself slowly from the gurney, paused and wobbled, then slipped quietly into the night, on a southeasterly course, over the lights of Roswell in the distance.

The two men went back into the barn, prepared to spend the next few hours at the computer as the Scout flew in eerie silence over the mountaintops, across the desert, and on to the border, a boundary it wouldn't recognize. It sailed on the evening breeze until at last it came to the ranch. Then, silently, but with exact precision, it glided in and explored the innermost privacy of those who lived there. The Scout looked, listened, and recorded, and when the work was done, he slipped away. Back to the fort on the third floor beneath the barn. Then the cavalry would ride in, bugles blowing and guns a-blazing, and the good guys would win again. That's the way it's supposed to be.

*****

Ann Marie was the first one up in the morning. By mutual agreement, they delegated the first person up as the coffee maker and the distributor of the half-dozen boxes of cold cereal on the counter top. Wheaties, Raisin Bran, Cheerios, Fruit Loops, Shredded Wheat, and a local concoction called *Chacumba*, a grainy wheat and rice dish the Navajos made. Something for everybody. For those who wanted a hot breakfast, there was an old stand-by, Pop-Tarts. Not that any of them considered this to be a particularly healthy breakfast, but if nobody wanted to cook this early in the morning, which they didn't, then it was cold cereal and Pop-Tarts, or nothing.

Voices In The Fog

It was close to six-thirty, and nobody else would be up and around for another hour. She carefully measured out twelve tablespoons of coffee into the basket, then held the pot under the faucet and filled it to the top line.

A narrow slit of morning sun poked over the horizon, throwing the first rays of light over the rolling hills and prairies of eastern New Mexico. The gray morning gradually took on all the colors of nature. Buffalo grass, mesquite trees and patches of snow that fell during the night reflected the light like so many mirrors. Tiny icicles hung by their fingertips to the strands of barbed wire; a pair of white-winged doves cuddled together on a branch. It was a fresh new day and a new beginning.

That is when it hit her. As clear as the sun. It was there all the time. It just took a fresh eye to see it – the peace and quiet of the morning, and it was there. She had the answer. Nothing simple, but nobody said life was easy. It would be a challenge, but was attainable, and that's all that counted. It would work. She knew it.

The smell of fresh coffee filled the kitchen. She poured a bowl of Cheerios and covered them with half a dozen slices of fresh peaches, wondering where Cowboy Joe got them in the middle of the winter. It was a good day. She enjoyed the solitude of having her breakfast alone. No conversation, no clatter of dishes, nothing but the sounds of silence. It was an opportunity to examine her startling idea from every angle before she mentioned it to Williams and the others.

It had been a long time since she felt so relaxed and confident. The grind and gruel of the academy; the secrets and mystery of Millie's grand old house in the desert; the days and nights spent watching the Judge who wasn't the Judge. It all seemed so long ago. Now, for the first time in many months she felt as if she controlled where she was, and even more importantly, where she was going. She met the best of them and won. It was only a matter of time.

It was after eight o'clock by the time everyone finished breakfast and was ready to take on the new day. The table was cleared; the dishes were washed and put away. Williams gathered his little flock around the table, each taking the same place where they were seated the day before. He made notes while Hammond recounted Scout's observation the night before.

Marisa finished the dinner dishes, then went to the guesthouse. She read a book for about an hour, took a bath and went to bed. The two pairs of guards swapped places. The men from the quarters on the road were in the main house; the other two went to guard the road. The Judge went to his bedroom about ten o'clock where he sat at a desk until almost midnight, writing who knows what? The two men in the main house played dominoes until almost two o'clock in the morning. The two at the guard-house turned out the lights and were in bed around eleven.

"A pretty ordinary evening," Gosbeck commented.

"What about Gonzales?" Rod asked "What would he be writing? A diary, maybe?"

"What about this?" Hammond interjected. "What if they shipped the real cases from the court to him? What if they have him write opinions? You know, get his actual words on paper, twist them around, but still keep his basic writing style. From his manuscript, they develop it into their own writing and come out with some of these bizarre opinions we have been reading for the last couple of years."

Rucinski was the first to respond. "A month ago, I'd have said you lost your mind. Pretty damned farfetched, but now I think you may have something. It makes sense. But it raises another question. Why would he be willing to do it?"

"Because he wants to stay alive. That's why." Ann Marie shot back. "Pure survival instincts. As long as he's alive, he has hope. Remember, he doesn't have any idea that anyone has the foggiest notion that he's missing. If some way or other, we could get our hands on his actual writings, we might be able to decipher some sort of code he has worked out. Maybe he's been trying to tell us all along, but we never saw whatever it was he wrote."

"You may have something there," Williams commented. "He's an exceptionally intelligent person. That would be right in line with his personality. He was never a quitter. He came up from the barrio. Pulled himself up by his own bootstraps. Had lots of ambition and drive. You may have hit it head on."

He shrugged. "But we don't have any idea what he has been writing. Maybe his last will and testament. Who knows? In fact, right now, it really doesn't make any difference how he got there. The fact is, he's there, and it's our job to get him back; to make things straight. To get things back on keel, so let's don't lose our focus."

"I am focused," she said. "Never more so than I am right now, and I can see it clear as a bell. How to get him out! How to make things straight."

Williams looked at her. An inquisitive grin crossed his face. "You've found something we've missed, haven't you? We couldn't see the forest for the trees? Something like that?"

"Something like that. It hit me this morning. It seems so simple, but I know it's not." She looked at each of them, carefully making eye contact. "M-A-D. Remember that? The cold war? Mutually Assured Destruction? We didn't push the button, and neither did they. All of us had enough missiles and bombers to blow the world to smithereens, so just the threat of it kept us out of nuclear war. Well, why can't we do something like that now with the Chinese?"

"Blow them up?" Rod asked skeptically.

"Hardly," she replied. "Look, they have our Judge, and we have their stand-in, right? Well, what about this? We get their Premier. Maybe even their top general. How about their ambassador to the United Nations?"

Rucinski nodded his head. "Ma'am, I'm not sure where you're headed with this, but it sounds like you've lost your mind completely, or you've come up with one hell of an idea." He gave a nod of approval. A smile crossed his grizzled face. "I suspect you probably have such a wild idea that it would knock their socks off and scare the crap out of them. Let's hear it."

She leaned forward, confident as she took control of the discussion. "I was watching the sunrise this morning. Gradually, ever so slowly, things started to take shape, to take on color. Take on life. Things looked different in the light, and they weren't at all what they appeared in the night. That's when it hit me. Things aren't always what they appear to be. So I said to myself, 'Why don't we do to them what they have done to us?' Except, of course, we don't have two or three years to mess with. Maybe two or three months, but that's all. So then I started thinking about Hollywood. You know, the movies. Science fiction. All that. What if we called their hand? What if we created a few of their top people, just like they did ours? Of course, they'd know that we had not yet replaced their people with our stand-ins, but that's okay."

She continued. "Look, they have a closed society, but we could still cause as much havoc for them as they

could for us. What if Spielberg or – what's his name?
Lucas. George Lucas. He's the guy who does all that
fantastic computer animation in "Star Wars." They could
create some look-alikes for us, and we could shoot them on
film or video. We go digital. Voices, their whole bodies.
Everything about them. We create them from the top of
their head to the soles of their feet. Mannerisms, dialects,
expressions, absolutely everything. We create a film of the
Chinese Premier discussing with his top advisers the
invasion of Russia?" she proposed. "What about them
launching a missile attack on Moscow. We show our video
to the Chinese, and tell them we have videos of a dozen
more of their top leaders planning all sorts of crap. Maybe
a germ warfare attack on England or France. How about
they're joining up with Iraq or Iran to take over Kuwait and
Saudi Arabia? We're only limited by our imagination. Tell
them we can arrange to have these people shown looking
like they're coming right out of Beijing. We can bring the
whole damn world down on them."

She laughed to herself. "Or better yet. Show them the
films, and tell them we're going to give them to the
Russians. That ought to get the Ruskies' attention. We
could get a full-scale missile attack on Beijing within the
hour.

"Or how about this? Maybe we create a film of the
Chinese army planning some ethnic cleansing of their
Moslem people. That would create a stir, wouldn't it?
Might create a whole new civil war for them.

"But, of course, we don't really want to have a war. We
want to meet them at the table and discuss the destruction
we can do to each other. Mutually-Assured-Destruction.
The only thing we don't know is how many more stand-ins
they have. But if we can convince them that we have

212

developed our clones of their people, and that we are prepared to use them, that we're ready to encourage the Russians to attack Beijing, then maybe, just maybe, they will fall for it." Special Agent Beaudet gave a modest grin. "Who knows? Maybe it will work."

"That's bold," Hammond said. "Maybe just bizarre enough to create sufficient doubt about whether or not we would go through with it. Could they take the chance that we wouldn't? Interesting thought, isn't it?"

"I'll take it a step further," Gosbeck responded. "I've worked a lot of black operations in the last four or five years, and think we can go one better. That's how I lost this," he said as he tapped the patch that covered his left eye. "Afghanistan. But that's a story for another time. Anyhow, I think we could have a pretty good chance of finding out exactly how many clones they have. Of Americans, anyway." He shrugged his shoulders and started making notes to himself. "We can go all the way back to Vietnam. Hell, we had Navy Seals swim up the sewers of Hanoi for years. We knew more about what was going on in Hanoi than most of their own generals knew. More recently, in the Gulf – Iraq, Iran, all over the Middle East. We have people all over that area feeding information back to us. Granted, it's not always perfect, and a lot of times we have to take some odd pieces and extrapolate out of them what we think is the whole picture. But it works in the long run. We keep good intelligence on damned near every despot and nut in the world. Some of these operations have been going on for years, and nobody has ever gotten any the wiser about them. Even the Chinese." He shook his head. "I was caught off-guard by this Linshi thing, but obviously, some other agency wasn't. Anyhow, let's don't get in too big of a rush. Let me have time to talk to some of my contacts and see what they can do for us, okay?"

Williams stopped writing his inevitable notes and gazed out the window, deep in thought. Finally, he turned and looked at Gosbeck. "How much time?"

"Don't know. A week or two at least. Remember, we don't just hop on the e-mail and ask the hotel clerk at Linshi who he's got registered. These things take time. I can only give you an educated guess right now. For starters, I have to make a couple of contacts back east. Then they will have to bounce it off a couple of people up the chain of command. If everything is a go, and they don't see it jeopardizing some bigger operation, then they have to get word to whomever it is they have at Linshi. You have to keep one thing in mind. That place is really isolated. It wouldn't surprise me if they didn't have to do some off-the-wall tactic to get word to their person. Then that person needs some time to get an answer for us. After that, that same person has got to feed the information back down the pipeline. Eventually, it will get sent to our people in D. C. They'll have to take some time evaluating it, trying to separate the wheat from the chaff. Once they are done with it, they give it to my contact, and she gets it to me. Then, we should have a pretty good idea if Linshi has produced any more American substitutes."

He laughed at himself and shook his head. "I know that sounds like a bunch of bureaucratic mumbo-jumbo, but that's a fast overview of how it'll go. If it goes at all. This thing can get upset anywhere along the line. Somebody gets sick. Maybe somebody chickens out and is afraid to stick his nose into this mess. Maybe somebody just drops dead. Anything could happen, and I have to tell you, I've seen lots of these things start out smooth and look like a slam dunk, but go to hell in an instant. That's just the business we're in. Win some; lose some. He who has the most toys at the end wins the game. That's the rule."

Ann Marie stared at Gosbeck. She saw him in a light that was alien to her. A cold-hearted bastard, she thought. As if he were talking about playing a game, not saving people's lives.

"Do I have the time?" Gosbeck asked Williams.

"You do!" Williams said.

CHAPTER FOURTEEN

It was Saturday and Ann Marie's turn to take a pickup truck and go to Roswell for groceries and whatever particular wants or needs someone had. They had an equitable sharing of jobs, and this was far better than mucking out the stable and barn as she did last weekend. Besides, she just might take the time to find a movie where she could simply relax and enjoy a bit of private time.

She moved quietly through the kitchen and pantry, barefoot, dressed in Levis and her tired and aged white Eddie Bauer button-down blouse. Even though it was freshly washed and ironed, it saw better days.

Her hair was pulled back in a ponytail and danced to and fro as she swept from cabinet to cabinet, refrigerator to freezer, spice drawer to vegetable bin, and back to the pantry. She used her private version of shorthand and made quick written notes of their needs; bread, butter, margarine, milk, buttermilk for Rucinski, lime flavored corn chips for Rod, hamburger meat, steaks, chicken, pork chops, fresh and canned vegetables, paper towels, toilet paper, soap, toothpaste, and a final note, "me," for her special little things.

She pulled out a kitchen chair and sat down. Her reflection in the microwave window caught her eye. She could pass for any other thirty-something mom going up and down the aisles at Safeway doing her Saturday shopping, but oh, they would never know how her life was so different from theirs. She leaned back and scrunched her lips. She forgot something. What else was it that someone mentioned to her to be sure and pick up? She looked down at her painted toenails. What was it? It hit her – batteries. C cells for their flashlights and AAA for Rod's CD player and some of the other portable things they used.

Voices In The Fog

A whispered voice from behind her suddenly broke her thoughts. "Hey, hey, hey. You were really zoning."

She looked over her shoulder and was taken aback by his million-dollar smile. He reached out and began to massage her shoulders.

"You're beautiful when you're in your own little world. I could stand and watch you all day. What're you doing?"

"Grocery shopping," she replied as she held the note pad up for him to see.

The massaging slowed as he leaned down to read her scrawl. "Don't forget the batteries."

"I won't. I just remembered them when you came in." She leaned forward away from the magic of his fingers, placed the pad on the table and noted C and AAA at the bottom of the list. "Sleeping a little late this morning, weren't you?" she asked.

"I was down there until after midnight – my turn to watch the perimeter detectors and the HVAC controls. Make sure nobody spied and pooped around the ranch, and that everyone else gets a good night's sleep."

"I've never had to put in an all-nighter in the control room. Isn't it pretty boring?"

"Oh, yeah, but it has to be done. When there's not anyone like us here, they keep a three-man team up here at the ranch. It was some of those guys we saw the first day we got here and they were pulling out onto the highway from the ranch road. Remember? They were driving a mini-van?"

"Oh, yeah," she replied. "Williams mentioned them and gave them a wave."

"Right," Rod continued. "It gives them a place to run around and practice, plus keeps enough staff here to watch the monitors and controls. Rucinski installed the detectors around the ranch a few months ago. If anyone gets within their search field, it'll show up on the monitor. Not much action, actually. Every once in a while some hunter will trespass and trip a signal, or some kids hiking. Once we had a group from the university doing some UFO research. But, we can't have anyone snooping around looking for landing sites or even getting on our property by accident. If we get a hit on a sensor, we go out and find'em and send them packing."

"What about that team? Are they here all the time when Cowboy's by himself?"

"Just about. They're a big help with all the work this place takes. They're pretty decent guys, but all I can say is that they're different from you and me. Special operations type of folks. Quick in; quick out; and, deadly as hell. They're stationed at the Roswell base but are fast responders just about anywhere if someone needs them. When Rucinski is alone up here, he arranges for a team of them to come up. The guys like it; it gives him some company; and, they help with the maintenance this place needs."

Rod stepped around the table and pulled out a chair. She looked at him for a moment as she inhaled his persona: disheveled hair, unshaven, a frumpy Chicago Cubs t-shirt, and Tevas on his feet. His appearance was that of an overgrown college boy, but a man of a million experiences in an ugly world. He was the next generation of Williams and Company.

Ann Marie propped her feet in his lap. "More massage?" she begged.

His hands were strong but gentle as he rubbed the soles of her feet, then her toes, one at a time.

Voices In The Fog

She leaned further back in the chair and interlocked her fingers behind her head for support. "Where is this going?" Her voice was soft and feminine, yet had a tone of thoughtful introspection.

"You know the game by now. Our side does what we can. Sometimes it goes like a bat out of hell. Others," he paused. "Other times, it drags on for what seems like eternity."

She pursed her lips and shook her head. "This," she said as she gestured ever so slightly with her finger as she pointed toward him, then back to herself.

He stopped rubbing and pulled her feet deeply into his lap. "Where are the guys?"

"They went to the lab about an hour ago. It's just us - - you and me. They won't be back for a while." She smiled coyly. "Are you afraid here with me?"

Rod smiled, leaned down, and kissed her toes. With his lips still to her feet, he cast his eyes up toward her and smiled. "Nope. Not at all. Not afraid of you or any of the bad guys in the whole world. Just bring'em on," he joked.

She pulled her feet back with a start. "Seriously, Rod. Can't you be serious for a minute? What about us?" she demanded.

His smile disappeared. "I know you're special. I've never felt like this about anyone – ever!" He nodded his head. "Yeah, it scares me. I can't sleep at night 'cause I've got you on my mind when I should be thinking about my job, but damn it, you're always there. Do I love you? Hell, how should I know? I've never been in love, so I don't know how I'm supposed to feel." His voice reflected his exasperation. "What about you?"

She reached out and took his hands in hers. "I like you, I know that much. Love?" She laughed softly. "I like you and may even love you, but I'm in kind of a twirl." She gestured around the house. "This is all so bizarre, so unreal. It scares the crap out of me. I don't want to be alone, but I'm afraid if I say I love you that I'm just looking for someone to hold me and take care of me. That's not the real me. I'm my own person. I don't want to make a mistake and get hurt or hurt someone else."

She got up and went to the stove. "Coffee?" she asked.

Rod slouched like a limp rag in his chair. His eyes slowly drifted the length of her body . . . her hair and face. Her cute nose and soft lips; her long legs and shapely body; her pretty feet. But, there was so much more than that. She was smart as hell and filled with a passion for life. He loved her and everything about her.

"Yes, I'd love a cup of coffee and yes, I love you."

"What was that last part?" she asked as she tipped the coffee pot and let the strong, aromatic steam rise up into her face.

"I love you." Rod took a deep breath, stood, and took her into his arms.

*****

They walked arm-in-arm to the cowboy's crusty old faded yellow Ford pickup truck. Rod held the door while she slipped behind the wheel. "You sure you can handle this four-on-the-floor stick shift?" he asked as he closed the door.

"Sure, mister," she responded with a forced southern drawl. "Been driving these old critters since I was knee high to a grasshopper."

Voices In The Fog

They laughed in unison as she depressed the clutch and hit the starter button on the dashboard. The engine cranked, paused momentarily, then started with a roar. "See you in a few hours Mister McCarren. Say, what are you doing to earn your livelihood today?"

Rod frowned. "Cleaning the gutters."

"Have a nice time," she quipped. She gunned the engine and pulled onto the dirt road leading away from the safety of El Capitan Mountain and away from the safety of Rod's strong arms.

*****

She looked at her watch. Over an hour since she had left the ranch and she hadn't accomplished much. A Dairy Queen, and that was about it.

Movie choices in Roswell didn't quite match up to Houston or D. C. Three theaters and six different films between them. None worth the seven dollars it took to get in, so she decided to forego them before she headed to the Southgate Mall. It wasn't much more than a strip shopping center, but it was someplace where she could get a couple things for herself, then on to Safeway before heading home. She smiled. Home. She actually thought of that Doctor Strangelove world as home. She had come a long way.

She left Rita's Ladies Apparel with a package of some new undergarments and a bottle of perfume, then jogged across the driveway of the parking lot toward the truck. Out of the corner of her eye she noticed a Red Jeep Cherokee. She saw it when she parked and it was pulling into a slot just a few parking places from hers. It didn't seem like much. She noticed a little Hispanic man driving and maybe one or two other people in it. So? It was

Saturday, and people were out shopping just like her. But, it was still there and the people were still sitting in it. That struck her as unusual. She checked her watch. She was in the store about fifteen minutes, maybe twenty. That seemed like a long time to be parked and no one get out.

She opened the door of her truck, tossed the bag across the seat and climbed in. With her right hand she reached up and adjusted the mirror. They just sat there.

Paranoid, she thought. I'm paranoid. Poor guys are probably waiting for someone to finish shopping so they can get back to doing something worthwhile.

She hit the starter, shifted into second – low was too low for the flat ground – and pulled out onto the street. Five minutes later she pushed an empty shopping cart into the bread aisle at Safeway. She looked over her shoulder. No one was there. She laughed to herself. "Even paranoid people have a right to look over their shoulder," she thought.

Nearly an hour passed by the time she checked out, paid with cash, and walked with a pimply-faced teenager as he pushed the fully loaded cart to her truck. "Just put them in the back," she said as the youngster unloaded her sacks. He stacked them neatly up against the back of the cab, and with a faint, "Have a nice day," turned and pushed his cart back toward the store.

Once again, she cranked up the tried and true old Ford and guided it back to the street and onto the highway toward El Capitan. She zipped past the last traffic light and accelerated slightly. At the same time, she reached up to adjust the mirror since she had failed to re-adjust it when she left Rita's.

She saw it immediately. The Red Cherokee was about ten car lengths behind her. She couldn't make out the features of the people, but could count the heads – three of them, just like at the mall. They weren't shopping. They were following her.

Ann Marie pulled her purse from across the seat where she had tossed it and popped it open. She knew it was there, but had to check anyway – and it was. She had her gun. Her hand slipped into her purse and lifted the gun from its holster, and with the ease of a professional, she flicked off the safety and laid the instrument of death on the seat next to her leg.

She cruised at the speed limit for ten minutes. The Cherokee maintained its distance, then she saw the blue and white highway sign, "Rest Stop Two Miles." That's where she would test herself and them. She would pull in, but not kill the engine. If the Cherokee pulled in, she would pull out, make a U-turn, and drive back into town and directly to the police station.

If it went by, she would let it go, still make her U-turn, and go back to town. She didn't want to panic and go to the airport and ask for help. After all, there could also be the possibility that it could be nothing more than mere coincidence, although that was unlikely.

She slowed as she approached the exit to the rest stop. She saw in her mirror as the Cherokee also slowed. She guided the old truck to the side near the restroom. Her hand rested on the butt of her gun. Suddenly the Cherokee accelerated and zipped around her, cut to the right, and boxed her in. The rear seat passenger jumped out.

Ann Marie's mind went into fast forward – a Hispanic man; clean shaven; something in his left hand; I can't see it; he's coming directly toward me. The front seat passenger is another Hispanic man; can't see him; he's moving to the passenger side of my truck. The driver is staying put.

Her right hand lifted the automatic and she fired toward her passenger side window. The glass exploded. Suddenly, gunfire erupted from everywhere. It was too fast too comprehend. The man who came toward her door disappeared. She spun around to look out the rear window. People were there. They were everywhere.

A casually dressed man with an automatic rifle moved slowly but deliberately past her door and went toward the Cherokee. He gave his gun a quick burst of fire.

"Miss Beaudet, you're okay. We've got you covered." Ann Marie swung around toward where her side window was previously. It was another man holding an automatic rifle. Sweat dripped from his forehead. He ducked his head through the shattered glass.

"We've had you covered all the time. Sorry it got so close." He opened the door and climbed in. "Head to the ranch. They'll take care of everything here." He paused and extended his right hand. "Just call me Danny. I know who you are." He gestured to the others. "We keep track of you El Capitan folks when you're away from the ranch, but I have to say, you're a pretty hot number." He shook his head. "It isn't usually like this."

"What about them?" she asked as she gestured to the two men on the ground on either side of the truck. She couldn't see the man in the Jeep, but assumed he was dead.

"You drive, or let me, but we have to get the hell out of here."

She slammed the clutch down, crunched the gears, found reverse, went around an SUV that was parked near her left rear quarter panel, and pulled back on to the highway.

Voices In The Fog

Danny brushed the broken glass from the seat with his bare hand, scooted around so he could see out the rear window, then placed his gun on the floor. He turned back around and made himself reasonably comfortable in the midst of the chaos of the last few minutes. "Don't speed. Just take it easy and get us there in one piece," he commanded as he leaned over and looked at the speedometer – eighty miles an hour. "We're in a hurry, but don't get us stopped by the cops."

Ann Marie slowed and took the opportunity to look at her savior. Anglo, about her age with long dark hair combed back and a three-inch long, scraggly beard. He wore tan denims, a long sleeve teal shirt, a tan baseball cap, and hiking boots. "Who are you?" she asked.

"Danny. I'm a guy who takes care of people. That's all you need to know." His voice was soft, but an acerbic tone was detectable.

"Are you from the base?'

"Sure. You can guess that much. Sorry, Miss. But idle conversation isn't my thing."

"I suppose killing people is?" she fired back.

He didn't answer immediately, but turned slowly and peered out the rear window again. "Okay, we're fine now. The others caught up to us and will stay with us up to the ranch."

She looked in the mirror. The SUV was barreling down on them. "Is that them?"

"It's the hand of God. That's what it is," he quipped.

*****

Williams presented himself as a person of complete command and control. Dressed in faded jeans, a t-shirt and

225

hiking boots, he stood near the fireplace and rested his elbow on the mantel. He presented himself as a five-star general. He was in charge and no one had any doubts about it.

Gosbeck and Rucinski were "down there," as they referred to it. Ann Marie sat on the couch. Hammond sat at the opposite end. His face was ashen; his clothes rumpled as they usually were; Rod stood stoically behind the couch like her guardian angel. His eyes darted back and forth from Williams to Ann Marie.

Williams spoke. "This was an exceptionally close encounter, and one that we cannot afford to duplicate. Nevertheless, I extend our sincere respect and appreciation to these fine gentlemen." He lowered his head in a salute to them as they sat at the table, each nursing a cold drink. "Let me introduce you to them." He nodded again in respect. "This is Danny. Fresh back to our New Mexico confines from one of his quiet adventures elsewhere in the world." He smiled knowingly. "Of course, Miss Beaudet, you've already met him, but let me introduce you to the others." He nodded, this time to the casually dressed man who came to her side of the truck before he fired into the Cherokee. "This is Michael, and he is one of our regulars here at the ranch."

Ann Marie looked at him. He could pass for an insurance agent or realtor; short-cropped hair, clean-shaven, wearing a Ping golf shirt, denims, and loafers – anybody's neighbor out for his Saturday shopping.

"Last but not least," Williams said as he acknowledged the middle-aged Hispanic man who had tilted back in his chair. "This is Rodrigo – the team leader. Right *amigo*?" he asked.

"*Seguro que si,*" he replied. A hint of a smile spread across his grizzled face.

To Ann Marie, he was the only one whose looks alone could frighten her – not small, but not tall either; muscular, but not a steroid freak; dark, oiled hair combed straight back; an acne scarred face; a Fu Manchu mustache; but most noticeable of all, a jagged scar streaked up from beneath his shirt collar to his right ear. He had been slashed to the point of nearly being beheaded. His short sleeve sport shirt revealed massive, hairy arms. He was a living powerhouse who looked like he could snap her in two – and probably did it a few other times in his life.

"Tell us about it," Williams inquired.

Rodrigo responded. "Another one of our units picked her up when she got to the highway, and we took over the surveillance when she left the Dairy Queen." He smiled again. "They weren't very good. We spotted them when they parked by her at the mall." He shook his head. "They were pretty amateur. None of us knew them, but they stuck out too much. Shit, they should've put up a sign that they were out to get her. So we let them go, but stuck pretty close – surprised myself a little they didn't spot us, but they were too intent on her. So, when they whipped in we just followed them and kicked their ass." Rodrigo looked down at the floor and gave a soft chuckle. "They were a bunch of dumb asses and paid the price."

"So what about the crime scene?" Williams asked.

"We're always ready. We keep enough undercover supplies with us to cover just about anything. I stuffed a couple ounces of cocaine under their front seat and a thousand bucks in the driver's pocket. The cops will think it was a dope deal gone bad." He chuckled again. "Yeah, it was a bunch of dopes, and sure as hell, it went bad on them."

"Any witnesses?"

Rodrigo tilted his head and cast a disappointing glance at Williams. "You know better than that. Come on, don't insult us." He emitted a soft chortle.

"Not an insult, but a damn important point."

"Yes sir, I know." Rodrigo wiped the Cheshire cat grin from his face. "But you already know my answer. I hit the stopwatch when we pulled off the highway – fifty-nine seconds exactly before we got back in our vehicle and were pulling out on the highway. Bim-bam, thank you ma'am. In and out. Job done."

Williams smiled. "Yes, I knew the answer, but we've got to cover all the bases."

"Right," Danny interjected as he took a last sip from his drink. "I checked the odometer when she hit the road, and it was four miles before we passed a south-bound car."

"Exactly," Rodrigo joined in. "It was two and a quarter miles before we passed it. So, that means they took at least two or three more minutes before they reached the rest area. If they didn't stop, it didn't look particularly unusual. We pulled the two guys to the far side of the Cherokee and anyone passing by probably couldn't see them unless they pulled in – no witnesses, I guarantee."

Williams looked down at Ann Marie. She leaned back in the couch and stretched her legs out in front of her and crossed her ankles. Her arms were folded across her chest.

"How are you doing?" he asked.

She shrugged her shoulders, titled her head, and threw a sour grin at him. "Hell, just another day at the office. A bunch of guys tried to kill me, that's all." She acknowledged the men at the table. "And along came God in a SUV and killed the bastards." She looked back at Williams and forced a smile. "How am I supposed to feel?"

"Probably about like you do," he replied.

Rod interrupted. "How about a break? I could use some air."

Williams nodded approval. "Good point – take fifteen and let's get back together."

*****

It was more like thirty minutes before everyone was back in the living room. Danny moved the SUV into the barn, and Rodrigo took their guns to the kitchen and started stripping them down on the counter for cleaning. The scent of bore cleaner and gun oil permeated the room.

Rod pulled an occasional chair from the rear of the room and scooted it up to the couch next to Ann Marie as she resumed her place on the couch. Williams returned to the front of the room.

"Let's go over a few things and call it a day." He looked at Rodrigo. "Your SUV needs a rest. We don't need it back on the highway for a few days, just in case someone saw it. We'll keep it here and get you a ride back to the base in the other pickup we've got. We'll also keep the guns here just in case you get stopped on the way back." He propped his elbow on the mantel, sucked on his pipe, and continued. "This was too close for comfort, but we'll learn from it and move on. We'll get the data on the dead guys in a few days. Our contacts will have all of it from the crime reports after they're all typed up. Nevertheless, I don't have any great expectations about who they were or what they were up to."

Voices In The Fog

He looked at Ann Marie. Her fingers were digging into the arm of the couch. Otherwise, she was completely stoic. "New Mexico is one of the most sparsely occupied states in the Union, but it has the third highest ratio of espionage agents to their population. Just behind New York City and Washington."

Ann Marie shook her head slightly. "Why?'

"Look around you for starters. Then there is Los Alamos, and White Sands, then Holloman, and us. Of course, there's the history – true and false – about 1947." He smiled a fatherly smile. "Spies watching spies. That's what we have in the Land of Enchantment."

"But what about me? How did they find me?"

"Conjecture, of course, but this thought has run through my mind. After your phone calls in Alexandria, they knew someone was on to them. Then there was the Volvo, and we never did learn who that was. Anyhow, I decided you were compromised, so we closed down, took a plane, and came here."

"Okay, but you've lost me," she replied.

"The flight information is public information. Every spy worth his salt knows the base in Roswell is a cover, so all they had to do was compare that "N" number of the plane that left Washington and see where it landed. It was pretty damn simple. They concluded you were on it, and probably had your photo from their own surveillance photos even though they didn't know who you were at the time. Anyhow," he continued as he shifted and sat on the edge of the fireplace in front of her, "they spread your picture out to some of their guys around here, and bingo. Today, they found you. They were just in the right spot at the right time."

Voices In The Fog

"Correction," Rodrigo interrupted. "They were in the wrong place and the wrong time."

Williams glanced at him and smiled. "I stand corrected."

"So what's the next step?" Rod asked.

"We get these guys back to Roswell tomorrow and its business as usual for us." He tossed a glance at Beaudet. "Still with us?" he asked softly.

She smiled, leaned forward, and took his hand in hers. "A good night's sleep and I think I'll be okay."

Williams rose from where he sat and looked to Rod. "Let's call today done. Why don't you two get some fresh air and relax? To our faithful friends from Roswell," he said as he stepped across the room and shook their hands. "There's plenty of food and drink. Help yourself."

Rod and Ann Marie went only a few steps from the porch when she faltered. She stopped and looked at her own feet, choked back a cry, wet her lips and took a deep breath. She took a strong stance with her fists on her hips, glanced at Rod and began to cry. "My God, I could be dead right now," she stammered. "They were going to kill me." She began to shiver. Sweat dotted her forehead.

He took her hand and led her away from the house. They walked in silence for a few minutes; then he stopped and swung her around and kissed her and kissed her again while she wept. Tears streamed down her face. She gasped for breath, then simply sat down in the dirt and looked up at him. "On Rod, I need you."

He leaned down and took her hands, pulled her upright and wrapped his arms around her. His cheek brushed her hair as he whispered. "You're okay, baby. It's over. We - - I'll take care of you. I promise. I love you, and that's my promise forever."

Voices In The Fog

*****

The morning sun slipped through the window and caressed her sleeping eyes. She kept them closed and allowed her face to bathe in the warmth of the day. He was right. It was over. She was okay. With a flick of her arm, she tossed back her blanket and sheet and felt the fresh air against her naked body. It was a wonderful night.

Wearing her jeans, an old but comfortable sweatshirt hanging loosely around her hips, and her white sweat socks, Ann Marie walked lazily to the dining room. The house was void of human activity. She saw a note tucked beneath the base of the coffeepot.

> *"You are a brave lady.*
> *We are proud to have served you,*
> *Sincerely,*
> *Rodrigo and the guys"*

She smiled, took a cup from its hook beneath the cabinet, and poured it full of tasty, hot coffee. It was going to be a good day. She strolled across the room and looked out at the high rolling grass country that stretched to the horizon. It was beautiful.

The warmth of grace and peace filled her body and soul.

CHAPTER FIFTEEN

"Goose, it's been three weeks today," Ann Marie said.

Gosbeck shook his head. "I know it, but I told you up front, you can't hurry these things. They happen or they don't, and that's all there is to it. You have to remember, I don't have any idea who the agency has in Linhsi, or how to communicate with them. As far as I know, it's a slow boat to China. We hang on for the ride, or we get off. It's that simple. We don't have any control over how fast this goes, if it goes at all."

They stood on the porch and looked out over the rolling foothills. Shadows slipped silently over the land and snuffed out the colors of the setting sun. Somewhere in the distance, a coyote's lonesome wail echoed across the vast countryside. Ann Marie looked forlornly at Gosbeck. "Will it work?"

"It can. It might. We just have to hang on and see where it goes. If push comes to shove, and we go with Rod's idea we sweep in, clean everyone out – *Mi Tios*, Golden Eagle, the ranch, and see what happens. Of course, there are the folks back east. They may come up with a whole new game plan. We'll just have to wait and see."

She knew the "folks back east" were Gosbeck's superiors. She pulled her sweater tightly around her shoulders, warding off the late afternoon chill. "It seems like we're stuck on high center, not moving forward or backward. Not going anywhere. We keep sending Scout down there, nosing around, but nothing changes. They eat, they sleep, the guards go into town every few days for supplies, and the Judge sits at his desk from time-to-time and writes who knows what."

Voices In The Fog

Gosbeck offered a half-hearted chuckle. "You're frustrated. We all are, but that's the business we're in. Hurry up and wait. Why don't you find a couple of good books on oriental warfare, especially the philosophy of guerrilla warfare? You'll see why Asians have been so successful, and it's no small part because of their willingness to be patient. Good things take time."

She knew he was right, but she was never a patient person. The truth of the matter was now she couldn't get her mind off Rod. She loved him like she never loved anyone before. Nevertheless, she was an impatient person, not a great quality for someone in the espionage business.

She forced herself to focus on the moment. "I went to town a couple times when I first got here," she reminded Gosbeck. "I visited the International UFO Museum. What an education that was. From the front, with the Marquee and the lights, I thought it was a movie theater showing the latest sci-fi film."

Gosbeck grinned at her. "Was it really that bad?"

"Better than I thought it would be when I first walked in," she admitted. "When I was welcomed by that giant fake alien in the lobby, I almost turned around and left."

"Fake alien?" Gosbeck asked, amused. "You mean, as opposed to a *real* alien?"

She punched his shoulder. "You know what I mean. The dummy alien. Speaking of such, when I saw the display of a figure held aloft by his antennae, and it was labeled "Dummy," I thought maybe it was me. Maybe I was the dummy for even being there. "

"But it got better?" Gosbeck asked.

"I read every scrap of information there, and there was a lot, so that shows you how bored I was out here. It was interesting. Fascinating, in fact. I particularly liked the section on the alleged cover-up."

"As a part of the U. S. government now, I would think you wouldn't support any cover up," he said.

She glared up at him. "Do you mean to tell me that we don't hide things from the people when it suits us? What in hell do you think we're doing here?"

Gosbeck was saved from replying by the slamming of the screen door behind them. The unexpected noise startled her. She spun around and came face to face with Rod, who looked past her to Gosbeck.

"Rucinski called on the intercom. You need to get down there right away; you've got some e-mail coming in. Maybe it's good news."

"Would be nice," Gosbeck commented. He paused to take time to watch the sunset over El Capitan Mountain. A few final golden rays poked through the narrow canyons near the peak; the late spring snow reflected the dying rays of the setting sun. He walked slowly toward the barn, stopped, and looked over his shoulder at Ann Marie. "How come you've never asked about the other levels under the barn?"

Before she thought of an answer, he turned and was gone. She watched the barn door close behind him. "Why?" she thought. "Why haven't I asked?" What was on the other floors? Why seven floors? She was taken only to the third. What else was down there? Why didn't they tell her?

"I'm cooking dinner," Rod said. "See you later."

She sat in the rocking chair and watched the approaching darkness sweep over the land. Her mind drifted back to one of her first conversations with Williams and McCarren, and later with Hammond and Rucinski. There was something about Roswell. No little green men, but Roswell was true. What else was there? She shivered, not from the night air, but from the very thought of the tales of Roswell. What was the truth? What was down there beside the third floor?

She could ask. It might be as simple as that. Or, she could explore. Just like she did at Millie's house in the desert. What would happen if she got caught? What would she jeopardize? What was down there, and how badly did they want to guard its secrets?

Why did Goose ask? Was he tempting her, or was he letting her know it was there for the asking? "Damn it," she muttered. "Too many secrets. Not theirs, but ours."

*****

Hammond wrapped a sheet of foil over a plate of enchiladas and beans and carried it to the barn for Gosbeck and Rucinski while Ann Marie and Rod cleaned up the kitchen. The group's life fell into an unplanned routine with chores being shared equitably – house cleaning; cooking; except for Ann Marie, going into Roswell for groceries and other odds and ends that were needed from time to time; staying up at night to watch the control systems and monitors.

Rucinski cared for the Scout and sent it on its nightly mission, then watched until the ranch fell silent after everyone went to bed. Occasionally, he sent it on its way in the early morning in time to have it in position when the guards and the Judge got up and went about their day's routine. Even with the camera lens' ability to see from significant distances, Rucinski was careful about letting the Scout get too close to the ranch during the day for fear someone might see it. After all, a twelve by eighteen inch metal disc hovering around the ranch might look suspicious to even the most dull-headed guard. To say it would cause a problem if somebody saw it would be an understatement.

"What's on the other floors?" Her question caught Rod off guard. He threw a quick glance at her, then continued putting the clean dishes on the shelf.

"Well? Are you going to tell me, or do I have to find out on my own?" she asked.

"The way you did at Millie's?" Rod shot her a sharp glance.

"Maybe," she countered, putting her fist on her cocked hip. "I found out what I wanted to know."

Rod put down the platter he was holding and gazed at her. "You found out what Williams wanted you to know," he said slowly.

"What do you mean?" she queried.

"It was part of the test," Rod said. "You were supposed to go hunting. It showed initiative and ingenuity and a certain degree of curiosity, all the things you need in this job."

Anger rose in her. Her face flushed; her throat was dry; she stared angrily at him. "I suppose your surveillance with the MoTracs was also part of the test."

Rod had the courtesy to look embarrassed. "I took them off when I saw it was you," he reminded her.

"Yeah. Yeah. But how long did you look before I caught you?"

He grinned that heart-stopping grin. "Not nearly as long as I wanted to."

She thought a moment. "What would have happened if I hadn't gone snooping at Millie's?"

Rod went back to cleaning the kitchen counter. "I don't know. Williams probably would have given you a different assignment, though."

Silence hung in the air while she digested his comments. "Thank goodness you caught me snooping, then. He might have sent me to stake out somebody in Minot, North Dakota and I'd really have frozen my butt off." She grinned. "Now, back to my original question. What else is going on here? What do we have on all those underground levels?"

Rod gnawed his lip. "I guess I can tell you. I just thought Rucinski or Hammond would handle it."

He tossed the tea towel over the drain board before he looked her in the eye. "Let's take a walk, okay?"

"Sure. Let me get my coat. Going anywhere in particular?"

"Nope. I just want to walk. C'mon," he said. The early April moon loomed over the eastern horizon, its soft brilliance shone down over the rolling prairie. "We won't need a flashlight. I'll try to put a little light on what goes on here. It's time you knew, I guess. You've paid your dues and then some."

"You make it sound scary."

"It is scary. If it doesn't traumatize you, you're missing the point of this place and all it stands for. Where do you want me to start?"

"In the beginning? Isn't that what you told us out at Millie's place? What about a name? What do we call this? The ranch?"

"Actually, Rucinski named it. Not officially, but since he runs the place, yeah, they let him name it. He calls it the High Jinks."

"What?"

"You heard me. High Jinks! Remember Buffalo Bill?"

"Sure," she replied. "William Cody."

Voices In The Fog

"Well, as you've noticed, Rucinksi is a real groupie of the cowboy and Indians thing. Of course, Buffalo Bill is right up there at the top of his list of western folklore heroes. High Jinks was the name of Buffalo Bill's ranch somewhere down in Arizona around the early nineteen hundreds. So, Rucinski called this place High Jinks."

"Sure, now I've got it. The flask, right? The HJ brand?"

Rod flashed his smile. "Yep, you got it. Can't get anything past you," he joked.

"Okay, so much for our western history, but what about some facts, starting with how we've all ended up here."

"Fair enough. In the beginning, there was this lady; a really sharp schoolteacher. But because of her first meeting with an FBI agent when she was really young, she always wanted to join the Bureau. She didn't - - "

"Wait a minute! How do you know about that?"

He looked at her and his smoky eyes grew dark. "You need to ask Williams about that. Anyway, to get back to my hypothetical woman, she didn't have any family; she was brilliant; she was eager and patriotic; she was reasonably assertive, if not downright aggressive; she was honest and loyal; she had the highest level of integrity; she was moral; and, she was of childbearing age. Succinctly, she was perfect for this career change. She was chosen, and of course, she accepted."

"*Excuse* me!" she bellowed. "Child bearing age. You can't gloss over that so easily. You owe me one hell of an explanation!" Her face flushed.

Rod tossed a quick glance at her and continued down the dirt road. The flat leaves of the prickly pear cactus reflected the moonlight like so many reflectors along the

239

roadside. "You said you wanted to know, didn't you? From the beginning? Didn't you say that?"

Ann Marie was furious. She bit her lip and caught up to Rod. "You know damned good and well what I mean, but go ahead with this sordid little tale of yours."

"You've heard Williams talk about how our world is so delicately balanced on its axis; how there is a veil of fog obscuring reality. One side or another is always trying to tip the scales in their favor. Sometimes they get close. Sometimes we do, too. The bottom line is, we pretty well keep each other in check, and the world keeps right on ticking. Nevertheless, common sense plus a lot of different projections by quite a few sources say that maybe someday soon, some character is going to screw it up. Maybe bigger than anything ever seen in the history of mankind. When that happens, there'll be pandemonium."

"Do you mean nuclear war?"

"That's one theory. Germ warfare is another. Electronic annihilation is another. Of course, there could be general revolution throughout the world. People get so disgruntled with their governments that what we see now as regional conflicts like Israel, Iraq, the Kurds, Bosnia, Ethiopia, Serbia, the old Soviet Union," he ticked them off on his fingers. "All those places take off like wildfires raging out of control. This thing about the Judge is a good example. Is he the only one? Are there others? Are the Chinese going to help us turn ourselves inside out? Even Hammond has the jitters since it came out a while back that the Chinese are getting classified information out of Los Alamos. Plus some sort of allegations about a former President who may have been tied in with the Chinese. Hard to believe, but what the hell do we know? Is he one of theirs? Probably not, but he's human and can make some bad policy decisions."

Ann Marie shivered and tucked her hands in her pockets. The evening air swept down from the mountainside. The scrawny leaves of the mesquite trees rustled. The cold air slipped down the back of her neck. She felt overwhelmed by emotions too numerous and tangled to sort out: anger, fear — even love.

"And there's more," Rod continued. "Some extremely thorough research by military historians, political scientists, and economists, just to name a few, plus volumes of work done by Christians, Jews, Moslems, and even a couple of agnostics – very thorough research by highly respected scholars has indicated a tendency to believe mankind is on the verge of a phase of catastrophic international events, but not the end of the world. Even the Brits have a working project on this."

He kicked a stone and watched it bounce into the cactus at the road's edge. "It's not a pretty picture. I don't have the foggiest idea who is working on the British project, but I can tell you what I read in the executive summary. The year 2050! That's what they say. A fifty-fifty chance of a world-wide catastrophic event or chain of events." He looked at his beautiful colleague. His eyes were cold and emotionless. "Each of us did our research independently and came up with very similar findings."

He shook his head, put his arm around her shoulder and drew closer. "Brrr. Colder out here than I thought." She leaned into him cautiously, afraid she was offering something he hadn't invited. He drew her closer to his chest and she felt the thumping of his heart, like a timpani.

"Not the end of the world, but the end as we know it today," he continued. "National boundaries, cultures, economics, and governments are at risk. The phrase they use is 'the end times,' like in the days of Noah's Ark. That wasn't really the end of the world," he emphasized. "It was a cleansing and renewal. A re-start of what nature, or God, depending on a person's belief, started in the first place."

She shook her head. "So this," she gestured, "is Bible-based theory?"

"No, no. It's well founded on research of current and historical political, monetary, and military trends. The research projects covered those issues, but went back in time periods – one hundred, then two hundred years. Then the biblical issues were researched, and it all came together.'

"The research suggests that in the next fifty years, more or less, it's going to occur again. Maybe some idiot will start planting bombs or anthrax, or dumping some other insidious evil on mankind. Somebody will respond. Another side will respond to that, and it will go on until there are only losers. No winners. Maybe even no one left at all. If there are survivors, then, mankind will try to get it in gear again and see if we can do it right the next time."

A chill, not from the cold air, shuddered through her and she huddled closer to him. "So how about this place?" she asked. "How does it fit in? What about you and me? How do we fit into this picture?" She swallowed hard to control her voice and emotions, but she was angry and upset: mad at Rod for the way he dumped all this on her so unexpectedly; upset at the thought that things could change so drastically – so abruptly, and she was in the middle of it. But, she thought, "Better to be in the middle of it than left out altogether. Better to calm down and take it one step at a time."

Voices In The Fog

"Simple enough," Rod said. "I'm not sure how many places like this our side has, but probably about a dozen top-secret sites. I've only been here and one other. I think we started building them around the end of World War Two, Korea — right in that time frame. The main haven is up in the Wasatch Range in Utah. They're scattered around the country. Each of them will hold ten to twenty people underground for up to seven years in relative comfort, if you can call living below ground in comfort. Just like you and me, those people were assigned to a place where there's a fairly good chance of their being able to ride things out while the world is going to hell in a hand basket, so to speak. Each safe haven is independent of the others. Theoretically, each place can re-start the human race."

He looked at her and shrugged his shoulders. "I think that's a stretch of the imagination, but the theoretical possibility is there."

"Oh, my God. You're not serious, are you?" she asked with a hard lump in her chest.

"Serious as a person can be. Each haven is staffed with a variety of people. Teachers," he said with a quick smile at her. "Physicians, blacks, whites, Asians, men and women, philosophers, engineers, chemists. Pretty much a mixture of what it would take to get us going again."

She drew away and looked into his eyes. "This is the sickest thing I've ever heard. You're out of your mind if you think I believe this insanity. This is absurd; utterly impossible."

Rod interrupted her before she continued. "I didn't think you'd like it, but it's the truth. Each site has two goals. The first is to support our government's efforts to detect and deter the enemy's efforts to overthrow us. The other is to provide a safe foundation for the reestablishment of our way of life if we fail with our primary goal. Pretty scary, isn't it?"

Ann Marie tucked her hands deeper into her pockets and walked in silence a step ahead of him. The full moon climbed high in the sky and swept the rolling plains with a gentle brush stroke into a sea of tranquility. It was so contrary to the world in which she found herself immersed. They walked back to the gate before she allowed herself to speak.

"This is terrifying. This isn't the way things are supposed to end. What happened to us that we should end up living like - - ? What was the name of that movie? Planet of the Apes? Do we go underground and come out to find the animals in charge of the world?"

"Probably not. If it happens, it'll be ugly, but survivable. That's why we have the seven stories underground. We'll survive. We'll do okay, and our way of life will endure to live another day," Rod said.

"You want me to be like a brood mare? Keep pumping out kids to re-populate the world?" she demanded angrily.

"I wouldn't describe it in such a crass portrayal of your role, but yes. You and others will be responsible for having children. We don't know, but have to consider the worst-case scenario that only our sites will survive. That means that maybe ten or twenty women in a dozen or so locations will have to have babies for the future."

"Oh God, Rod. This is horrible beyond description. It's absolutely appalling."

"I told you it was outrageous, and it is. All we can do is look at the bright side. We work like crazy to detect and deter the bad guys, and if that fails – well; we hunker down and wait it out." He put his arm around her shoulder when they started back to the ranch house. "And there is one more possibility."

"I don't know if I'm up to it, but go ahead."

"Asteroids. Meteors. Things like that. Probably not much of a likelihood, but if we saw them coming, this is where we would head. It's happened before. It could again, so we are more or less prepared for it."

"Could I ask a question, especially since it's a personal thing with me?"

"Sure," Rod responded.

"If I'm supposed to be one of the herds and have the babies, is the stud just assigned at random to the various women?"

Rod threw her the cold look he gave to her earlier. "That's a pretty disgusting way of putting it. No. Not at all." He looked again at her and shook his head. "You don't make this easy for me, do you?"

"How about you not making it easy on me?" she asked.

"Remember, you asked. This wasn't my idea. You couldn't wait to find out for yourself, or ask Rucinski or Hammond, could you? No, you had to come to me, and now you don't like the answer, so you want to kill the messenger."

They walked in silence again, each alone with their thoughts. The lights of the house glittered in the distance before she spoke. "I'm sorry. Go ahead. How does it happen?"

"I don't have all the answers. Rucinski would be in charge. If something happened to him, then it would fall to Hammond. Anyway, they have it documented how it must come together. Who would be with whom. That kind of thing. But, they understand how you and I have developed a relationship. That's about all I know about the social anthropological environment we would be in down there, on the seventh floor."

"Okay, I'm sorry for what I said and how I said it." She took his hand in hers and squeezed. "I was wrong. I shouldn't have put you in that position and I knew it, but I thought it would be easier to get it from you than from the others. Anyway, I'm sorry." She raised his hand to her lips and kissed it. "Friends?"

"Friends," he replied. He opened his arms and she stepped into them hungrily, her mouth turned, seeking his. Somewhere, in the heart of their kiss, they allowed their fingers to explore each other. Her mind raced. She was afraid of the unknown and was afraid of facing the world without the first man in her life she truly loved. She unzipped his jacket, unbuttoned his shirt, slipped her fingers beneath it and massaged gentle swirls on his chest. She felt him tense, then felt his cold hands slip under her shirt, unhook her bra, and touch her breasts. Her nipples were hard from the cold, but also from the heat of her passion. Rod raised her shirt and put his lips to her breasts. She felt the softness of his tongue when he caressed her, then the clumsiness of his fingers as he groped her belt buckle. In spite of all he told her, here in his arms, her world was at peace.

Reluctantly, she backed away. "No, not now," she whispered. "Not here. I know how we feel about each other, but we don't know each other. Not really. We need to take our time."

He smiled his thousand-watt smile bright in the desert moonlight. "Um hum, you're right." He stepped back, never taking his eyes off her as he buttoned his shirt, then his coat. "I know you, but you don't know me. That's not fair."

Voices In The Fog

"So tell me who you are."

He started to respond, but she put her finger to his lips. "Not the company line," she said. "The true story. The real story."

"Fair enough," he replied. He jammed his hands in his pockets, looked down and kicked a stone like a little boy kicking a ball. "The real me? Okay! Daniel Raymond Patterson; son of Rodney and Tobie Patterson of Oak Park, Illinois. Dad was a full-fledged alcoholic and skipped out on us when I was a baby; Mom worked two or three jobs as long as I can remember. I was a freshman at Southern Illinois when she died. Breast cancer, a long, hard death." He paused, looked up at the moon, and gulped in the fresh air. "I dropped out and went to work at Sears selling men's wear; socks, shorts, that kind of big ticket item." He tried to make it sound funny.

"Great job," he joked. "I did it for a while, then went back to night school and graduated by the skin of my teeth. Damn, it was hard working odd jobs and going to school. Anyhow, I got through and got a job in Chicago working food stamp fraud. I made a couple of organized crime cases; made a few good collars; just did my job, and slapped a couple of home runs. At some point I got some attention from the big guns, but of course, I didn't know it. One day, out of the blue, this guy is waiting for me when I got back to my apartment, and the rest is history."

He paused and gulped in another breath of cold, fresh air. "Time goes by so damned fast. Seems like it was yesterday, but it's been ten years." He looked at her and wrapped his arms around her waist. "I never met anyone like you, Christie, I mean Ann Marie." He laughed. "I'm not supposed to slip up like that."

"You never married?"

"Nope. The job was part of it, but I never met anyone I ever really wanted to spend time with. Until I met you, and then it all changed." He kissed her lightly. "I fell in love with you." He took her hand and started back up the road toward the house.

"Now let me tell you about the seven floors, if you haven't figured it out already."

"I've probably gotten the big picture, but go ahead."

"The first floor is the armory. Not that we plan on using it, but just in case. Small arms, handguns, ammunition, environmental hazard suits. Quite a bit of safeguard material in case we have to go out for short time periods before it is safe. The second floor is the library. About everything you would ever want to know. Pretty much a complete Library of Congress, plus complete libraries of chemistry, mathematics, religion, etcetera, etcetera," he quipped. "Everything on CD Roms, floppy discs, digital equipment, and Ipod stuff. Plus a whole network of computers to tie it together."

"The third floor, of course, is the scientific laboratory. This haven specializes in audio/visual surveillance. We have nearly one hundred listening devices spread throughout the western states, mostly high in the mountains. Anyhow, the object is to be able to listen while the world self-destructs. Going down to the fourth floor, we come to the nuclear power station that will keep us going. The fifth floor is water in-take and recycling, plus a seed and plant nursery: just in case we need to re-seed mother earth when we come up for air. The sixth floor is our warehouse. Food, clothes, household items, movies, real books. Actually, that floor is the largest of them all. One side is the warehouse; the other is a clinic. It's well equipped, to say the least. You probably couldn't get a heart transplant there, but they could fix a broken leg."

"Or deliver a baby," she interjected.

"Yeah, for sure, they could do that. Anyhow, last, but not least, is the seventh floor. Home. Actually, they're pretty decent apartments along with some common areas for meals and leisure. Also, from the seventh floor are two escape tunnels. Both of them run about a mile – one uphill toward El Capitan, the other down toward the highway. Just in case the barn comes crashing down on our elevator."

They stopped at the front stoop and she stared at him, aghast. "You asked," Rod said. He took her hand to his lips and kissed her.

*****

Williams taped a note on the door directing them to come to the third floor as soon as they returned.

"Maybe we're finally getting somewhere," Rod said. "Let's get down there." Moments later, they found themselves huddled around a table. Gosbeck organized his notes, but the smile on his face told them that he had his answer from Linhsi. Ann Marie noticed, though, that Hammond was troubled. He pulled up a stool and sat off to the side, taking a backseat to Gosbeck's excitement. Clearly, he did not share in the enthusiasm, but he would hold it to himself, at least for the time being.

Gosbeck spoke. "I'll start by giving you a brief historical backdrop to Linhsi, then proceed to where we think we are today. Geographically, Linhsi is located on the frontier, nestled in an extremely desolate region between Manchuria and Nei Monggu, or what we commonly call Inner Mongolia. The spoken language in that region of the world is Mongolian, the Hoshot dialect, but I'll come back to that later.

"The buildings we saw in some of the satellite photos were originally constructed in the 1860's by Christian missionaries, but eventually were taken under the administration of the British and became an army hospital. Over a period of years, a number of additions were made to the original facilities, and of course, the British were finally driven from the area. After they left, the Chinese developed the hospital into a research center. They devoted a considerable amount of work to biochemistry, immunology, and cytology. As a segment of what they referred to as the healing arts, they developed a major program in the psychology of healing. All of which means, of course, they had a significant investment in the number of sociologists, psychologists, and other eastern philosophers that were entwined with their holistic health program. Their goal was to become a premier cancer research institute, and to some degree, they achieved what they set out to accomplish. Unfortunately, the isolation of the hospital led them to abandon their goal. They were too far away from transportation systems and other research facilities to coordinate their research, or to exchange research papers with other scholars. But, they had too much in the way of capital assets, to say nothing of the number of researchers and scholars to close the facility, so they re-directed their efforts to what we see today."

Gosbeck shuffled his notes and continued. "I spoke briefly of their language. That is what originally caught the CIA's attention. The spoken language in that region of Inner Mongolia is the Hoshot dialect, but telephone transmissions accidentally picked up by a satellite scanning one of their military maneuvers was not in Hoshot at all.

Voices In The Fog

The language being transmitted in a routine phone call from the hospital was Putonghua, or what we usually refer to as regular Chinese. So some young language intelligence analyst began going back to that frequency from time to time to monitor it because it seemed to be out of the ordinary. The more he monitored it, the more he became convinced he stumbled on to something. From that point, they put it on a regular monitor and have been doing so for several years. The information they shared with me is that they intercepted seventeen messages over a period of four years about a Latin man. The CIA never determined what was important about the Latin man until Miss Beaudet ran into this mess." He grinned up at her. "That has been the only communications about a non-Asian, so it is an educated guess that he is the only one. Hopefully, they don't have any other moles that have been inserted into an Anglo government.

"I don't know exactly how long our side has listened to their conversations, but I estimate that the place has been under surveillance for at least five years. I haven't been told that our side has a person working inside the institution, and I doubt that we do, but our information strongly suggested that Linhsi had more or less become a Manchurian Candidate site, if you remember the movie, a Richard Condon novel. Remember old blue eyes? Frank Sinatra and Janet Leigh? It was released in 1962 during the cold war, which added to its impact on people."

"I remember it as Denzel Washington and Meryl Streep," Ann Marie interjected.

Williams smiled at her. "Nice to have some young people around who don't remember the sixties." He turned to Gosbeck and nodded. "Continue, please."

Voices In The Fog

"The original Manchurian Candidate was a touch of realism, albeit set with the dramatic background of the Korean War and what the press called the Yellow Horde. The tidal surge of Chinese Communist soldiers ready to sweep across Asia. The movie's theme was about an American soldier, captured in the war, who was taken to Manchuria for several days and nights of intense experimental drug and hypnotic conditioning. Supposedly, the treatments would turn him into a human time bomb. Then, he would be released and sent home where, at a later date and given the right trigger, he would explode."

Rod was the first to respond. "Goose, if I'm putting all of this together correctly, what you're saying is that they've escalated from a 1960's movie to a real-time and real-life science horror story. The truth is stranger than fiction."

Hammond spoke softly. His voice was barely audible. "I must interject another point to add a new dimension to this picture that causes me great trepidation. It has been confirmed that a colleague at Los Alamos has performed a grave act of treason. I will keep it simple for you. He stole and gave to the Chinese government the very heart of our nuclear capability. A system known as the Lagrangian Codes. I shall not try to explain what all of this means, other than to say he brought the Chinese from being decades behind the United States to being up to, or possibly ahead of us. The impact of his treachery is almost beyond measurement."

Dr. Hammond paused and removed his glasses. His eyes were watery and red. "The picture is calamitous. To go with what we have learned recently, I must share with you some other disturbing information. Ling Nuy has slipped quietly into the Panama Canal while our government slept. They have signed a contract with the

Voices In The Fog

Panamanian government to 'manage', as they refer to it, the port at Balboa which controls the Pacific side. Furthermore, they have another contract to manage the port of Cristobal which controls the Atlantic side. They also obtained the option to procure Rodman Naval Station, and Howard Air Force Base at the canal. As if that were not bad enough, remember that during the base closures we shut down almost all of our naval facilities on the west coast. Tragically, Ling Nuy is bidding to lease our former naval shipyards in Long Beach.

"To link this to what we currently learned about their program at Linhsi brings us to consider the most disastrous consequences. They may be ready to strike us internally as well as externally. They have penetrated the heart of our government, and have nuclear capability to strike us at will. It's a colossal setback to us, and a puissant coup for them. The question that remains is, what response do our elected leaders want?"

Williams poked his unlit pipe between his teeth and bit down. "I'll be in conversation with the appropriate people tonight. I have some thoughts, as I'm sure each of you do. Of course, everyone who is involved in this matter has some ideas of their own. We shall see."

"War or peace?" Ann Marie asked.

"I surmise we shall soon activate High Jinks," he replied. "Never have I witnessed such a high level of covert aggression. Truly, I fear that our nation is in jeopardy. We have moved far beyond making an effort to determine why our Justice was making so many unusual decisions."

Ann Marie looked into his eyes. She read his body language; the tone of his voice, and his expression. Beneath his professional veneer, she saw a loving and compassionate gentleman; a man of honor and integrity.

Voices In The Fog

When he spoke to her, his delivery was gentle. "It is most fortunate you made your discoveries when you did. Little did we anticipate the depth of this case when you started your investigation. But now?" He paused and looked down at his feet, then back at her. "Now? My dear, we may be on the brink of war."

CHAPTER SIXTEEN

Williams and Rucinski sat quietly in front of the fireplace. The few remaining flames danced valiantly, trying in vain to gather themselves into a burning rage. With a gasp and a flicker, they surrendered to inevitability: first shrinking into glistening coals, the terminal signs of life before they breathed their last and deep gloom fell over the room. Only a lamp at the farthest end of the hallway gave the slightest hint of light to the living room. The quiet darkness matched their somber mood.

In the quietness came the sound of slippered feet padding down the hall. Rucinski looked over his shoulder as Ann Marie came in.

"I couldn't sleep either," she said. She pulled up a chair and curled her feet beneath herself. Her faded red terrycloth robe was draped loosely around her shoulders. Her hair hung limply to her shoulders. She appeared as they had not seen her before, mentally and physically exhausted.

"I'll be leaving in the morning," Williams said. "Any last bits of wisdom for me?"

"Be gone long?" she asked.

"I don't know. Maybe a couple of days. Maybe longer."

She sighed heavily. "This is bad. But not worth involving us in a war. Not yet, at least. I still think we can pull off some sort of masquerade. Even if we have to turn the Russians against the Chinese and let them nuke each other into oblivion. I hate to see it come to that, but if it's them or us, then to hell with them. We have to protect ourselves."

"Coming from you, that's hard talk," Williams said.

She nodded. "I never thought about having to make that kind of choice, but here it is." Silence fell over the room again. Finally, she continued. "We have to go get the real Judge. We can pull it off. I don't know how, but we have to put him back on the bench."

She paused and nodded her head. "I know we can do it. We can rescue Gonzales from the ranch and get him back where he belongs." She shrugged, mostly lost in the dimness of the room. "Then you guys can figure out what the hell to do with all the people at the ranch and at the restaurant. We can't just let them go on as they are."

Williams heaved a huge sigh. "You're right. For more than one reason. We need to eradicate, or at least damage the Ling Nuy cartel. Second, we need to silence those involved in the kidnapping. It must be done at the same time we raid the ranch so no warning can be given. They will all disappear in a single night. No one must be left to answer questions."

She shook her head and sucked in a deep breath. "I see that. All in one fell swoop. Convince the Russians that the Chinese are planning a surprise attack. Let them get at each other's throat, and if they go to war, so be it. At the same time, we get down there and get the Judge back and take care of Duarte."

"Just what do you mean 'take care of Duarte?'" Williams asked.

"I don't know. That's not my business. It's yours."

"Are you saying we should kill him?" Williams demanded. "Or, would you rather put it in some more diplomatic terms? Eliminate? Yes, how about that? We eliminate him. Or maybe neutralize him? Do you like that?" The tone of his voice was flavored with a hint of sarcasm.

"Look, damn it," she blurted. "I don't care what the hell happens to him. Let's just do it and not look back."

Voices In The Fog

"Miss Beaudet," Rucinski interjected. "We're all aware that we may be on the brink of a nuclear holocaust, or - - " he paused "We may be just bright enough, just clever enough, just gutsy enough to pull this off. Probably not without loss of life, but this is undeclared war. But remember, every minute, it is war. With war, there are casualties. I think we all understand that much. Given that, now we have to calculate ways to minimize our losses. Theirs too, if we can. No one wins if the world gets blown to pieces. So we must accept some degree of human tragedy, but try to maintain some semblance to the world order as we know it."

He looked to Williams. "Go ahead. Tell us what you'll be recommending.

"In a nutshell? Pretty much as she has laid it out for us," Williams said. We provoke a major confrontation between the Chinese and the Russians. Hopefully, they won't go for an all out war, but anyhow, they'll have more than their plate will hold. While they're occupied with that, we pull a switch." He glanced at Ann Marie. "We get Gonzales back where he belongs, and everybody else dies. It must happen fast and cold. There can be no mercy and no negotiations. Nothing!"

He stood and put his back to the remaining warmth of the fireplace, his hands behind him. Even in the semidarkness, she saw a transformation taking place in him; a new surge of energy and thought. His eyes were focused, but not on anything in the room. His mind was in the distance. He raced to keep his train of thought, yet not bound by conventional wisdom. Ann Marie noted he gazed at her for a long time. Slowly, he nodded approval to his private thoughts before he spoke.

"You, too. You're going with me. Basically, it's your idea, and this is your assignment. There'll be questions; brainstorming, emotions, attacks, and counterattacks." He gestured toward her. "It's your game and you just as well see it through. There's no sense in your sitting on the sidelines." He turned to the fireplace, hunkered down, and rubbed his hands together over the dying warmth from the ashes. He spoke without facing them.

"I've got a reservation tomorrow on American Airlines leaving from Midland, Texas. We need to travel separately. Rucinski can take you in one of his trucks to Albuquerque and you can take a flight from there. I don't care which airlines. Pay cash for your ticket. Go to Dulles Airport and take one of the shuttle buses from there to Crystal City. Stay at the Potomac Bay Hotel. I'll talk to you when we're ready." He turned and looked at her. "Welcome to the big leagues!"

"What about my return ticket? When?" she asked.

"Give yourself a week," he replied.

"What about you?" she asked as she sat upright, her feet planted firmly on the floor. A quick thought raced through her mind: we're planning the fate of the world and I'm only wearing a pair of panties under my robe.

"I'll go through National Airport and meet the people I need to see. It might take me an hour or two; maybe a day or two, but don't stray far from your room. When we're ready, you be ready."

*****

Ann Marie yanked her bags off the carousel and made her way though the crowd toward the exit turnstile. An emaciated little man, his skin as white as though he had never seen the great outdoors, leaned against the rail. He glanced nonchalantly at ticket receipts and luggage stubs;

258

his wrinkled blue uniform hung like an old shirt on a clothes hanger. He observed about a million people too many. He checked her ticket against the numbers on her bags, gave her a weak nod, and passed her through to the exit.

"You make me feel so safe," she mumbled to herself. She stepped to the side of the walkway to take the shoulder strap out of the hanging bag, affixed it and tossed it over her shoulder. She then pulled the handle out of her roll-along bag, adjusted the weight, and stepped toward the exit to find the shuttle bus, another step in her journey of intrigue, she thought wryly.

It was nine o'clock at night by the time she dumped her luggage on the bed. With what was becoming a practiced art, she unpacked and placed her clothes in the drawers and closet. Ten minutes later, she stood in front of the bathroom mirror and looked at herself. It was twelve hours since she and Cowboy Joe left the ranch for the drive to Albuquerque, but surprisingly, she looked fresh and sharp. Her navy blue jacket held its crease and hung smartly over her white blouse with its crisp, button-down collar. She had a small smudge on her matching slacks, but with a quick whisk of the washcloth, she felt presentable, at least for the hotel coffee shop for a late snack. She freshened her lipstick – a new color for her, Berry Freeze. Something she bought the last time she was in Roswell. She brushed her hair back and thought it was about time for a haircut. She couldn't remember the last time she had one. She placed her toiletries on the counter, turned and looked over her shoulder at her image in the mirror, then gave herself a big smile. She felt good, even if a little nervous. But she was ready for whatever lay ahead.

Voices In The Fog

A quick spray of Amarige on her neck and she was out the door. She was halfway through when the phone rang. She was startled for a moment, not expecting anything this soon. She darted back, closed the door behind her, and caught the phone on the third ring. It was Rod.

"Hi. How was the trip?"

"Rod. I wasn't expecting you. The trip? Long, but I made it. I was just going out the door to get a bite of dinner. Wish you were here. It's a gorgeous place - -" She paused and looked at the king-size bed. Beyond, through the window, she saw the city lights. "It's beautiful, but I'm tired. Just going to get a light dinner, maybe a glass of wine, then get intimate with my pillow."

"I'm proud of you, Annie girl," he quipped. "You've done well. You're a hell of a good trooper." He paused. "You packed your gun didn't you? Not that you'll need it, but it's always good to have it around. You know, like a good insurance policy," he teased.

"Nice of you to care what happens to me," she replied.

"I'll always care." He paused, and with a nod of approval, continued. "I'll always take care of you." He paused again. The silence droned for seconds.

"Is everything okay?" she asked.

"I love you." His voice was little more than a delicate whisper. "Be careful."

Her heart beat so hard she hardly heard his words. "I love you, too, and yes, I'll be careful." She opened her purse to reassure herself that she took the gun out of the suitcase. "Checked the paper work with TSA, and my little friend and I made it fine."

"Good luck, honey," he said softly.

Voices In The Fog

He never called her 'honey' before. Was something wrong? Did he know something she didn't? A cold chill ran down her back. "Rod, is everything okay?"

"Yeah, sure," he said. "It's just that you're really playing major league stuff now. You'll do fine. I just don't like being this far away from you, so maybe I worry a little bit after all you've been through. That's okay isn't it? To worry about you?"

"I want you to worry about me," she thought.

"No need to worry," she assured him. "I'm going down for dinner and will be back in an hour." She sat on the edge of the bed and twisted the phone cord around her finger, then lay back across the bedspread, wishing he were with her. "Rod, is there anything I need to know?"

"No. Not really. It's just that I want to be with you; to smell your hair; to touch you and hold your hand." There was a long pause. "Damn it, Ann Marie. I love you and I don't like being all the way across the country from you."

Warmth flooded her body and she smiled. "I love you, too. Call me in the morning and we'll have coffee together. Just the two of us." She chuckled and kicked her shoes off. "We'll have coffee in bed, just like the rich people. Of course, we'll be a couple thousand miles apart, but real love transcends distance. We'll be together. Just you and me."

"That's what I love about you, sweet thing. You're so damned cute." His voice was little more than a whisper. "Goodnight, Love."

"Goodnight, big guy," she responded

She sat upright and placed the phone back on the cradle, slipped into her shoes and got up. She stepped toward the door, and on a whim of instinct or training, she didn't know which, stopped, opened her purse again and

261

closed her fingers around her.40 Caliber Glock, model 27. A ladies' gun; 3.46 inch barrel, cozy and light-weight at nineteen ounces to fit a woman's grip, and deadly accurate. Safety on. Loaded with nine rounds. She took a deep breath. She was as ready as she would ever be and filled with self-confidence, relaxed but fully charged with energy. She opened the door.

The man caught her by surprise. His massive hand gripped her throat, lifted her up, and slammed her against the wall. In the flash of a moment, he shut the door, pulled a handkerchief from his pocket and shoved it down her throat before she could scream. Her attacker was huge! Gross, acne scarred face. Bulbous nose. Heavy overcoat. Felt hat.

"I've got some questions," he growled. "And you'd better have the right answers."

Ann Marie shook her head violently. She had to do something fast, before she was totally dominated. She remembered the words of her defensive tactics officer at the Academy: Recover within two seconds, or you're likely to be down and out. She jabbed her fingers like bolts of lightning at his eyes, but he reacted even swifter and blocked her attack. She felt his iron-like grip on her wrists. Instinctively, she thrust her knee toward the ceiling as she had been taught–don't swing to the target; swing through it. With all the power she could muster, she buried her knee in his groin and drove it halfway to his heart.

A woeful groan emanated from his throat. He tried to maintain his grip on her, but was powerless. She pulled free from his grasp and twisted away from him. He made a feeble attempt to grab her, but was met with a karate kick across the bridge of his nose. The heel of her shoe caught the corner of his eye and blood spurted over his face and shirt. His head drooped to his chest. He crumpled and fell in agony on the floor. He landed on his back. She wrapped her arm around his neck in a carotid chokehold and counted steady, measured numbers; one, two, three, four, five, then released him. Unconscious. Five more seconds of that and he would be dead.

Her mind raced with bullet speed through the last few weeks of her life. First, Roswell. Now Alexandria. Nevertheless, better him than me.

How quickly a life can be extinguished, she thought. Thank God, he was only unconscious.

She got up from his limp body and caught a glimpse of herself in the mirror, no longer crisp and clean. Her jacket hung off one shoulder and her blouse had come un-tucked from her slacks; splatters of his blood were sprayed on its white edge. Her lipstick was smeared from cheek to cheek; her hair a tangle of spaghetti. It all happened in no more than fifteen seconds.

She moved hurriedly while her attacker was unconscious. She threw the bedspread and pillows on the floor, and with a sweep of her arms, pulled the sheets away from the mattress. Like the good Girl Scout she had been, she tied his hands and feet with a double knot; then with a bath towel, she tied the bindings together. He was hog-tied and helpless.

She got up just as he began to moan and squirm, and just as quickly as he did, she took the handkerchief he put in her mouth and stuffed it down his throat as far as she could. She stood and looked down at him, like a cowgirl standing over a helplessly tied calf at the rodeo.

She leaned over and checked the knots. He wasn't going anywhere, and he knew it even though his mind was clearing from the kick and choke hold. She stepped back and looked at her trembling hands. Her mouth was dry. She was scared as never before in her life. What do I do now? Who do I call for help? Then she remembered. Jasmine.

She reflected again on her training – how to block a person from hearing. She kicked off her shoes and raced to the bathroom where she found two bars of soap. Her fingers tore into the wrapping paper that she threw on the floor as she turned on the water and filled a glass. Moments later, she stood over her prisoner, and with her fingernail file, peeled slivers of soap into his hairy ear. She tapped the soap slivers down with the hotel's complimentary ballpoint pen, then slowly dripped water onto the soap and tamped it down further until soap filled his entire ear. Then she turned his head, and gave the same treatment to his other ear. She was glad to see this one wasn't as hairy as the first one. Within minutes, she was finished. She looked triumphantly at him and managed a smile, then leaned close where he could read her lips. "You bastard," she said slowly and distinctly. Then, for good measure, she wrapped the bath towel twice around his head, so he couldn't see.

Ann Marie paused to take measure of herself. "Did good," she said aloud, reassuring herself, glad to hear a voice, even if it was her own. Now she could call Jasmine without worrying about the son-of-a-bitch hearing her. She went to the phone and dialed the number. Once again, a soft feminine voice answered.

"Resources, Incorporated."

"I'm looking for something in Jasmine," Ann Marie replied. There was a brief silence, then another woman answered.

"Jasmine. Can I help you?"

"Help is what I need, and a lot of it," Ann Marie said. "I'm A-M-B 274, and I've got a problem."

Voices In The Fog

"Give me a minute." Silence. "Okay, go ahead. I've got your file on my screen. What can we do for you?"

"I'm at the Potomac Bay Hotel in Crystal City, Room 407, and I've had an intruder." She paused and took a deep breath. Suddenly, she began to shake as she looked down at the attacker at her feet. He wasn't moving, and with his face muffled by the towel, she couldn't hear him breathing. Her own breathing stopped and she couldn't speak. Then, with a sharp inhale she said,

"I think I've killed him. Please - -"

"Hold on. Stop for a second. I'm getting help on the way. Are you okay?"

Ann Marie lowered herself onto the edge of the bed. Tears seeped from her eyes. She was torn between removing the towel from around the man's face to see if he was alive, and the fear of loosening his bonds and discovering he was dead. Her hands weakened as shock raced through her mind and body. Her entire body trembled. The telephone tumbled to the floor. Somewhere in the distance she heard a voice calling her from far away. Her head spun, and she lay back on the bed. She gasped for breath and struggled to control herself.

"Miss Beaudet," the voice called. "pick up the phone."

Realizing she dropped the phone in mid-sentence, she rolled over and looked for it. It was on the floor, nestled between the man's back and the edge of the bed. Cautiously, she reached down. Her hand brushed against his coat as she slipped her fingers around the telephone.

"Yes, yes," she muttered. "I'm here. I'm okay, but I need some help."

"Listen carefully. A woman should be there in fifteen minutes. Maybe a little more. She'll come to your room. Her name is Regina. She'll know what to do. Okay?"

"Okay," Ann Marie replied in a dry, whispery voice.

"You've got to help me," Jasmine commanded. "Check his wallet. Look in all his pockets for anything, but be careful. Don't take any chances. If something happens, just get out of there."

Ann Marie sat upright, looked at the helpless blob at her feet, and stood. She stepped across the room, still holding the phone, but regaining her composure.

"Okay, I'm with you. Just give me a minute. I'm moving the phone away from him just in case, but I'm all right." She laughed grimly. "Yeah, just fine. Hang on a minute."

She removed the gun from her purse and, holding it in her left hand, she lifted his coat up over his waist and slipped her hand into his hip pocket. It was wet. He had urinated; an involuntary action at death. She slipped her hand around the soggy wallet, pulled it out, and went to the bathroom where she lifted the extension phone from the cradle.

"Got it, but give me a few seconds." She placed the wallet and phone on the counter, turned on the hot water and soaped and rinsed her hands, then held them for good measure under the hot water until it was about to curl the skin from her body.

She looked in the mirror as she dried and thought of news photos of combat Marines; how haggard and dirty they looked, even in victory. *That's me.*

"Look," she said as she put the phone in the crook of her neck. "This billfold is soaked with his piss. Will Regina have some latex gloves or something so we don't have to handle this animal's waste products?"

"I think she'll have everything, so just hang in there."

Voices In The Fog

There was a long pause while she looked around the corner at the lifeless body, then stepped back into the bathroom to look at her own weary body. "Will you be making the calls to the right people?"

"We've got all that underway. Stay with me. Help should be there pretty soon. In fact, Regina is parking in your driveway right now. She was close by and she'll know what has to be done, so just listen to her. Everything will be fine."

Sure. Easy for you to say. I've probably killed some guy in a hotel, and his body is lying at the side of my bed, but everything will be fine. "How do I know its Regina, and not some other bad guy like this creep?"

"Good point. I've got her on my screen. She's fifty years old; five feet, four inches; one hundred thirty-five pounds. You can ask her for a password, and she'll tell you 'Riverside.' Anything else, well, let's not go down that road. She'll be there any moment."

Ann Marie looked at the cold, gray gun in her hand and flicked the safety off. If it's not Regina, whoever is there is going to meet Jesus Christ in less than a second.

She heard the soft rap on the door and her heart pounded. Still, she felt a surge of confidence fill every fiber of her being. She turned off the bathroom light, then stepped around the body on the floor and turned off the lights in the room. She paused to allow her eyes to adjust to the darkness, then went to the window and pulled the drape shut, painting the room in total darkness. That would be her advantage.

She stepped softly to the side of the door, pressed her back to the wall, and peered out the peephole. It was an Anglo woman; middle age. Nevertheless, still fulfilling her promise to herself to be careful, whispered, "Password."

She flattened herself closer to the wall, realizing that whoever she was, if it wasn't Regina, could fire through the door.

"Miss, I've been down at the Riverside and came up to see you. Jasmine sent me."   Ann Marie, realizing she was holding her breath, exhaled slowly and turned the doorknob.

Regina stepped quickly inside and shut the door behind her. "Good for you," she said. "Glad to see you're being careful. Now, let's see what we have," she commanded as she started turning on the lights.

Ann Marie watched as the composed veteran walked through the room, examining, taking in the totality of the scenario. She wore comfortable, grandmotherly black shoes, a well-worn beige overcoat with a faux fur collar, a wool scarf tossed casually around her neck, and had a black purse hanging from her shoulder. Her salt and pepper hair was cut short and combed back; not very stylish, but practical in her line of work.

She took a long-handled dental mirror from her purse, got down on her knees, and leaned over the corpse. She pulled his head free from the towels and glanced over her shoulder at Beaudet. "Good job."

Ann Marie nodded acceptance of the compliment, then raced to the bathroom to vomit, retching every last morsel and drink she had taken in the last twenty-four hours. She rested on her knees over the commode, slobbering down the front of her already soiled jacket and blouse. Tears flowed heavily down her cheeks.

She was responsible for killing another human being. It was nothing like what they show in the movies or on television, nor what it was like on the highway in Roswell. There was no turning back. However much she prayed, she could not undo the last hour. It was over, and so was her innocence.

With her hands steadying her on the counter, she pulled herself up and leaned over the sink. She trembled as she turned on the water, then doused her face with cold water, over and over again, trying to wash away the stain of her sin. "But, it's not a sin," she said to herself. "It's not a sin."

She looked squarely at herself in the mirror, breathed deeply and took a careful self-measure. She did the right thing; now she must move on. With a quick whip of the towel, she wiped the front of her clothes and went back into the room.

"Good timing. Come here and give me a hand with this lug." Regina pointed toward his legs and feet. "Help me flip him onto his back where I can take a good look at him."

Ann Marie leaned down, and with all the intestinal fortitude she could manage, untied his feet and twisted him onto his back while Regina maneuvered his shoulders – at least two hundred-fifty pounds of dead weight.

Regina tilted his head around to a position where she could place the mirror first to his nostrils and then close to his mouth. She held it there for a few seconds, then slipped it back into her pursue. "You're right. He's not breathing. Come on, let's take a look in his wallet."

"I've got it in the bathroom," Ann Marie replied. She realized the faintness of her voice. Shattered by her experience, and at the same time impressed with the cold professionalism of her rescuer, she led the way into the bathroom. The wallet lay like a dead soldier on the counter, shoved in the corner behind the little bottles of shampoo and conditioner. With practiced efficiency, Regina put her purse on the closed toilet lid, retrieved a pack of latex gloves, and peeled them off. Two for Ann Marie and two for herself. She lifted the wallet carefully and held it over the sink where it dripped the last remaining drops of yellow-tinted body fluid into the drain. Then, with a slight twist of her fingers, she wrung out the final drops and turned on the faucet.

"Okay, Miss, you take mental note but don't write anything down. Just pay close attention so we both keep a pretty good mental inventory of anything special we find," Regina said.

Ann Marie nodded her understanding, even though she wasn't sure what that was all about. But, I'm about to find out, she thought.

Regina opened the bill section and pulled out several wet bills and spread them on the counter. Two twenties, two tens, one five, and seven ones. "Seventy-two dollars," she said. "Got it?"

"Got it. Seventy-two dollars," Ann Marie replied.

Regina flipped open the credit card and identification card flaps. No pictures. No driver's license. No credit cards. Only a coupon for Starbucks coffee. Otherwise, the wallet was worthless. Regina slipped her fingers around the creases looking for hidden pockets, but there were none.

"Pretty clean guy, but we'll figure him out. Going to need a little time, that's all."

Ann Marie checked her watch. Ten-thirty. "We've got maybe ten hours before housecleaning comes by. Can we make it?"

Regina looked at her with a grandmotherly smile and nodded her head. "We'll make it. Don't you worry."

The buzz of a cell phone caused Ann Marie to jump.

Voices In The Fog

"Mine," Regina said as she pulled her phone from her purse.

Ann Marie listened as Regina did little more than nod her head and gave a few grunts of acknowledgement before she flipped the phone off.

"Okay, get your things packed. We have some people on the way here. They'll escort you to a safe place for the night, and tomorrow is business as usual."

Ann Marie shivered. "What about him?"

"Not your concern. You did your job; we do ours. Remember that first lesson we all received, 'Right to Know and Need to Know.' Well, young lady, you've done a bang up job here, but where things go from this point on falls in that category." She smiled and gestured nonchalantly, "You've got no right and no need, so clean yourself up and get your things together and be ready. They'll be here any minute."

*****

Ann Marie sat quietly in the darkened back seat of the car. She brushed her hair back and let it dry with its long flowing curls dampening her jacket. Sans makeup, she wore only a white t-shirt and a set of Texas A&M maroon and white sweats, plus her jogging shoes.

The two men who came to the room and helped with her luggage sat stoically in the front seat. The smaller of the two, an Oriental thirty-something like herself, guided the car out of the parking garage and into the flow of traffic. She caught him looking into the mirror at her and he responded with a smile and glance over his shoulder.

"Okay, ma'am?" he asked.

"Yes, I'm fine." She leaned forward, laying her arm across the back of the front seat so she could see his face when they spoke. "Where are we going?"

271

"Marriott Key Bridge," he replied. He looked back at her with a reassuring nod. His freshly starched white shirt and dark business suit belied his task for the evening. He was neat and professional and a true gentleman.

She turned to the passenger, a stout man in his late forties, burly, yet nicely dressed in a dark sports jacket, slacks, and a light blue turtleneck sweater. He had the same build as Rodrigo, but was much more suave. She spoke directly to him. "What about him?" she asked as she gestured back toward the hotel.

"Those things happen, Miss. We don't necessarily like it, but that's the cost of doing business. You did what you had to do to save yourself. Nothing more." He turned in his seat and looked directly into her eyes. His voice was strong, but not threatening or challenging. "You did what any other lady in your situation would do if they could. Just thank God you had the skill and nerve to do what you did. Unfortunately, so many people either don't have the ability, or they're just too scared to do it."

He nodded his approval. "I know it wasn't easy, and it's not going to get any easier. You won't forget tonight, but you'll adjust to it." He reached up and rested his hand on her arm, surprisingly gentle and comforting for a man who looked as if he could break her in two if he wanted to. "You did good!"

Thirty minutes later her bags were spread across the bed of another hotel. Her two companions bade her good evening as they pulled the door shut behind them and left her alone once again.

She shuddered. It all raced back at her – his huge hands and face; that ugly nose; the handkerchief; the suddenness. Death. Jasmine. Regina. The two men whose names she didn't know. And now, it was like it never happened. Unpack, but forget the late night dinner. She was alone. It was deadly quiet in her hotel room. She sat at the foot of the bed, slipped off her shoes and stretched her toes, then turned on the television and flicked the buttons as randomly as any man until she found a music station.

She stripped out of her clothes and threw them in a wad on the floor. Minutes later, she was submerged in the tub and kept the water running until the bubble bath nearly overflowed the rim. Her muscles slowly relaxed as she folded a towel and rested her head on it and allowed the bubbles to sooth her from the tips of her toes to her chin. Finally, between the soft music and the warm bath, she dozed off until her hands fell from the rim of the tub and slashed in the water.

She roused, flailing, pushing the heavy weight, her knee poised for a hard kick. With a start, she pulled herself slowly upright and dried off, then went to bed and cried herself to sleep.

CHAPTER SEVENTEEN

Sleep eventually came to her, but it was elusive, remaining for a few minutes, then escaping, leaving her to toss in the unfamiliar bed. Then it claimed her again, only to flee as suddenly. The cycle repeated itself until the darkest hours of the morning when she finally subsided into a deep unconsciousness.

The piercing ring of the phone roused her. She tried to reach for it, but her arms and hands were numb from being tucked under while she slept on her stomach.

The ringing was incessant. She rolled over, tossed the blanket aside, and swung her feet to the floor, wringing her hands to bring the flow of blood back to her dead fingers. She brushed her hair back, and with her hands gradually starting to feel alive once again, lifted the phone to her ear.

"Hello." Her voice was dry and cracked.

"Good morning." She recognized William's voice.

"Yes, well I guess that depends on your perspective," she grumbled.

"I'm sorry about what happened last night, but that's why I wanted to touch base with you. How are you?"

"How do you think?" she said bitterly.

"I know it's hard. I won't tell you that you'll get used to it. You won't. But you'll learn to live with it."

She sat silently, barely holding onto the phone.

"If there's any consolation, hopefully you'll never have to do that again."

Never have to kill a man, he meant, although he didn't put it so crassly.

"We need to move forward on the business that brought us to town," he continued.

Voices In The Fog

She heard him rustling papers and sipping his morning coffee while he prepared her for the worst. They know all about me. They're trying to kill me and get me out of the way.

She lifted her cold feet back on the bed, tossed the sheet over them to warm them up and lay back on the pillow, braced for whatever was to follow.

"He was Anthony James Scordato." There was a pause.

Ann Marie took a deep breath. Here it comes.

"Regina printed him and we checked them against all the databases." More silence. She waited. She knew what was coming. They, whoever they were, found her out and planned to kill her.

"He's worked for a couple of different organizations, what we call a private contractor operative. We use them, so does the CIA and just about everybody else. He worked for the Department of Defense in Afghanistan for a few months, and before that he was in Slovenia."

She heard Williams flipping pages in his notebook.

He coughed, then continued. "He was working for a large contractor. An outfit called Government Corps. They do all types of jobs for governmental agencies. Of course, they have to meet our specifications. But, they do almost everything; trucking, air transport, construction, armed security, and a few espionage jobs from time-to-time. Basically, they'll contract out to do almost anything. They hire a lot of guys out of the service – Special Forces, that kind. Anyhow, he worked for them up until a couple of years ago when they fired him. What they called a loose cannon. They figured he was working both sides of the fence, so they cut him off and sent him back to the States."

"So how does he come into our case?"

"Well, we're not positive he does, but it certainly is likely. He played both sides against the middle."

"What do you mean?"

"GovCorps – that's what they go by – thought he was a solid employee, but they found out he'd made a couple of trips to Okinawa. Trips that weren't authorized by GovCorps. So, they put two and two together and started doing a little spy work themselves. They couldn't prove anything, but they spotted him with a couple of known Chinese agents. That's when they sent him packing. He was just too much of a detriment for them."

"You mean he was working for us and for the Chinese government?"

"That's the working theory right now." Williams cleared his throat and continued. Ann Marie listened to the sound of his breath. It seemed to last forever.

"GovCorps had his car in storage for him when he was overseas, and he got it out when he came home."

"Don't tell me," she replied.

"Yeah, a 2001 Volvo. Yellow."

"So it was him watching the Judge. Or me."

"Probably," Williams said. "After we got that information, we set up some search parameters and found the car in the Metro parking lot a few blocks from your hotel."

"They know who I am, don't they?"

There was another long pause. "I think so," he replied. His voice was soft, almost apologetic.

"How did they find out?" she demanded.

"It's only speculation, but we think they could have checked out the phony Judge's neighbors. Typically, in an operation like that, you take photos of neighbors, meter readers, people like that. Mostly just ordinary people, but you have them on file just in case. Then, as we suspected after the Roswell incident, when you disappeared overnight, they latched on to you as a target. When you booked a flight on a commercial airline out of Albuquerque, they fingered you."

"How did they do that? Of all the flights and the thousands of people arriving here every day, how did they find out I was coming?" Her voice grew shrill but she didn't care.

"I'm assuming the Chinese government has the same access to computer information that we do. They probably had your name flagged in their database"

"So their computer geeks are superior to our computer geeks?" she said wryly.

Williams allowed himself a grim chuckle. "As least as competent as ours," he agreed. "So when they got a hit on your name yesterday - -"

"They – he was waiting for me."

"I'm afraid so," Williams murmured.

Ann Marie drew a deep breath to keep her voice from shaking. "I'm not safe, am I?"

"I wouldn't go so far as to say that. I think we've passed the immediate problem. They didn't plan on what happened to that asshole last night. I know this isn't easy for you, but now we need to refocus our efforts."

His voice was grim. "We can be fairly certain they know we're on to them, but we don't think they have any way of knowing where you are now. I think you're okay. How about you?"

She closed her eyes and swayed to-and-fro on the edge of the bed. "As okay as I can be now that I'm a killer."

"I know," his voice softened. "But it was self defense. Don't forget that. You only did what you had to do."

Voices In The Fog

She heard him sucking on his pipe. He was taking his time, calculating his answers. The phone grew silent. She waited, then breathed deeply and leaned back on her pillow. "So what happens now?"

"Don't pack. Get some breakfast and I'll meet you in the lobby around eight."

The thought of food sent a wave of nausea through her. "I think I'll skip the breakfast. She placed the phone back on the cradle and felt only marginally relieved. Maybe he was right. Maybe she was going to be okay. But that didn't change the fact she killed a man.

*****

"Where's this meeting?" she asked Williams as the neatly dressed, uniformed chauffeur opened the rear door of the black Cadillac. She slid across the soft leather seat as Williams followed her into the car. He didn't answer until the driver was behind the wheel and closed the privacy glass between the two seats.

"We have a meeting room in the Old Executive Office Building across from the White House." He loosened his tie and ran his finger inside the collar of his heavily starched white shirt.

Nevertheless, he looked every bit a top-level executive in his black pin striped suit; a man for whom lesser men would step aside and allow him to pass. He folded his hands across his chest and spoke. "There'll be three other people besides us. I won't introduce you to them, but they know everything about you, and they know about last night."

She felt a chill. It was frightening, yet rewarding to be here at this particular moment, doing this precise thing.

Voices In The Fog

"It'll be a very unusual setting, but don't be cowed by it. It's not meant to intimidate you, but it's the way we conduct business. The others will be more or less in a darkened part of the room. In fact, you'll probably be sitting in the only light there is. There'll be one woman and two men."

He leaned forward and turned to look directly at her. "This isn't any child's game. This is for keeps," he emphasized. "Our nation's future could be decided today, and I say that without trying to be melodramatic. You have to know what to expect, and don't be too dazzled by where you are and what you're doing."

The novice agent sat quietly, looking into his eyes. Like her mentor, she was dressed in a dark business suit plus a white blouse, low heels, delicate gold earrings, and a touch of Amarige for courage. Her hair was twisted into a neat swirl at the back of her head. With unspoken words, they acknowledged their trust in each other. She turned away and took in the beauty as they passed the White House. Then she looked back at Williams and beyond him, toward the Old Executive Office Building, one of the most elegant buildings in the Capitol. It was one of the last examples of French Second Empire architecture, cast iron details, and mansard roof pavilions marking the corners and framing the doors. She remembered her college history class. It was here more than sixty years ago that Secretary of State Cordell Hull met with the Japanese emissaries after Pearl Harbor. Now, it houses the offices of the National Security Council. Of even greater importance, it houses the office of the Vice President of the United States of America.

Voices In The Fog

Today, in some quiet, secretive fashion she would meet to discuss a worldwide crisis looming on the horizon -- one that might have the magnitude of Pearl Harbor.

On the inside, the building seemed to her to be what a seat of government should be; somber, yet attractive, elegant, yet not cold. Gasoliers, replicas of early 1900's gas chandeliers, hung from the lofty heights above with coved, stenciled ceilings and mahogany floors of the old library; nothing less than historic elegance, reminiscent of the sophistication of Millie's place, but much more overpowering than the rural grace of that desert hideaway.

Williams led the way up the broad, curving expanse of the south stairwell to the second floor. He nodded toward a mahogany bench. "Have a seat for a minute and I'll be right back."

Ann Marie watched as he strode down the hall like a magnificent creature – maybe a Springbok, or some other beautiful beast in command of its own destiny. His footsteps echoed off the walls and ceiling as he turned at the end of the dimly lit hall and disappeared from sight.

She sat comfortably on the straight-backed bench, surprised at her own ease in the grace of one of the most historic buildings in the country: She, Christie Cole, a schoolteacher from Texas, now Ann Marie Beaudet, a secret agent in the service of her country.

She looked down at her feet; ankles crossed and tucked slightly beneath the bench, very ladylike, and took stock of herself. For the most part, she made good decisions with her life. She, too, was fulfilling her destiny. Briefly, the vision of the dead man lying on the floor of the hotel room flashed through her mind, but she dispelled it with a vigorous shake of her head.

Voices In The Fog

The echo of footsteps roused her from her private thoughts. She looked up to see Williams returning, his strides long and deliberate; his clothes impeccably fitting for the occasion; his graying hair perfectly combed; his stature befitting his place in life.

He spoke softly as he approached her. "They're ready for us." He extended his hand to help her rise. "How're you doing?"

Ann Marie nodded. "I'm ready."

Williams opened the door and stepped aside, allowing her entrance into the semi-darkened room. He followed immediately and closed the door behind him.

She scanned the conference room, estimating it at maybe twenty feet by forty feet; one long conference table filling most of it. The silhouettes of three people appeared at the far end of the table sitting in the lines and shadows of the only illumination in the room. Two dim floor lamps were in opposing corners near the two unoccupied chairs at her end of the table. Williams pulled the chairs out and gestured to her sit in one. He took the other. A commanding male voice, strong but not challenging was the first to speak. "Each of us is profoundly sorry for your experience last evening, Miss Beaudet. Most regrettable." There was extended throat clearing.

She recognized a Cockney note to his voice, no doubt an East Londoner. His was the largest of the three otherwise indistinguishable shapes she saw.

"Still, time is limited. Therefore, let us push on with your findings and your suggestion." He cleared his throat again. "We applaud your investigation. It was quite thorough. In fact, it was exceptional. You accomplished a great deal, and for that we are most grateful."

Voices In The Fog

Ann Marie turned slightly in her chair, once again slipping her feet slightly beneath her seat. She caught herself nodding her head, accepting his accolades.

"Now, if you will excuse my brash comments, I will come directly to the point. Yes, you identified a serious challenge to the American judicial system, but your suggested response begs the question." His dignified voice and manner changed abruptly, angered and disappointed at her. "What in God's name came to you to suggest such a violent response in which you pose the possibility of the Russians and Chinese going to war to save one man? One Justice of the Supreme Court? Would you throw the world in turmoil to save one person? When we accept our responsibilities, don't we also accept the potential risks that accompany that responsibility?"

His questions were rapid fire. She felt her neck and cheeks flush.

Questions? Yes, she expected them. An attack on her personally? No! Why attack her for her suggestions? Why didn't they simply dismiss her ideas and save themselves and her the discomfort of the moment? Why didn't they develop their own solutions? They did doing this for years and had experts tucked away in every corner of Washington and in every corner of the world. She caught herself smiling inwardly. Because they didn't have an answer any better that hers.

Ann Marie removed her purse from her lap, placed it on the floor, and leaned forward with her elbows on the table. She opened her mouth to speak.

"You've not been called upon, Miss Beaudet," A woman's voice, sharp and penetrating as a drill sergeant's command to an anxious recruit in boot camp.

Voices In The Fog

"Before you respond, I suggest you organize your thoughts and comments. The international response you offered to this situation is exceptionally strong, and quite frankly, it is disconcerting that you find it so easy to nudge two or three nations to the brink of war to save one man; albeit a very important and high profile gentleman."

Ann Marie opened her mouth again, but was immediately cut off. It was the first man.

"Young lady, you will have ample opportunity to present your case. I not only suggest, but demand that you take this time to absorb our thoughts and concerns; that when you speak, you present this body with your thinking processes and conclusions. But first, you must learn the lessons of this deadly game in which you have become so deeply enmeshed. You are suggesting we create the pretense of war to save a Supreme Court Justice, but if your charade should fail, then are we not at the point of no return? The beginning of an international conflict with the potential of nuclear holocaust? That sounds extreme. Too extreme."

Ann Marie sat back and accepted the rebuke.

The woman spoke. "Miss Beaudet, how did you arrive at this scenario of pitting our Russian friends against the Chinese? Clearly, the Russians are not a part of the equation in which we find ourselves. Why should you include them in our response?"

Ann Marie detected the third person moving slightly in his chair, preparing himself to challenge her. She braced for the onslaught.

His voice was soft. She leaned forward, tilting her head so as not to miss his questions or comments. "Miss Beaudet. A beautiful name, and an honor to meet you. We seldom have the opportunity to gain the acquaintance of someone who was faced with such a daunting case so early in their career." His words were clear, almost musical.

She lowered her head in acknowledgment of his compliment, then raised it to look at his darkened and anonymous presence. She noticed out of the corner of her eye that Williams scooted back slightly. He was there as her backup, but it was her show.

"Tell me Miss Beaudet," the man asked, "how you arrived at this highly unusual retort to the Chinese and their very scurrilous stab at the American courts."

She listened closely to his words. Clear, distinct, precise. A gentleman, yet a man deeply involved in the mysteries of international intrigue. Suddenly, something caught her attention. Two of the three referred to the situation as "American."

She realized they weren't part of the same organization as Williams and she. They were foreign, yet had a stake in the outcome of the "American" crisis. She remembered Rod's lessons that other countries have similar programs such as the United States' operations. These people were here to obtain a first-hand observation of the American response to the Chinese. Surely, they too, would have a dog in this fight if things went beyond their suggested boundaries.

The thought gave her comfort. She was on the right track with her proposition; otherwise, the foreign interest would not be here. In fact, this meeting would not be taking place.

The soft-spoken gentleman gave a light chuckle. "You have been anxious to speak, so this is your stage." She saw the outline of his extended arm in gesture. "We are anxious to understand how you arrived at this exceptional recommendation. Please."

Voices In The Fog

Once again she leaned forward, exerting her command presence, not cowering to their authority or position. "First of all, we don't know that our American Justice is the only imposter. The implications are much wider. As I am sure all of you know."

She paused a moment, as if gathering her thoughts. "It was in Roswell, at the ranch. We proved the man on the bench was an imposter, and we knew who he was. We knew where our Supreme Court Justice was being held. We knew that we, our government and people, the press, the whole world – were hoodwinked by an imposter. It was so simple it was genius, and they escaped detection for years. To this point, we don't know how they pulled it off, but that is not our immediate concern. Which brought me to focus on undoing the damage they did. First," she held up her right hand, index finger pointed upward, "how do we pull a switch and return Gonzales to the bench?" She pointed the second finger. "Second, how do we handle Duarte, an imposter, and the Chinese? And, third," now another finger joined the first two, "how do we keep the world from knowing our secret? How do we lift the veil of fog and see the faces of the real people who are speaking to us?

"I regress now for a moment, but its important background for my thoughts and suggestions. In high school I was in the drama club; in college I had a double minor of Fine Arts with a specialization in Drama, and in Art History. I love the arts and always have. I enjoy film and imagination. I enjoy the creativity of the arts. That's how it came to me."

She smiled faintly as she thought back on life at El Capitan these last few weeks. "The winter at the ranch was cold. Some days and nights the icy fog settled in on the mountains." She explained her epiphany as she watched the sunrise that fateful morning. "We see things we expect to see. The trees and grass; the cattle, the buzzards, and the mountains. We see things up close and may almost feel them. Things that had been hidden from us at night are clearly visible in the light of day.

"That's how I came to this point. We deal with what our senses tell us, even if it sometimes deludes us with a mirage." She sat back, crossed her legs, adjusted her skirt modestly, and folded her arms across her chest. "Duarte was and is a mirage, but it worked for them for a long time. Now its time for us to create our own mirage to fool them." She paused to take a mint from her purse and slip it into her mouth. "Excuse me, I'm a bit nervous," she said.

"You're fine," the woman responded. "Take your time."

Ann Marie continued. "I thought about some of my classes in college, and it suddenly seemed so simple. Just as simple as their devious game, except we aren't going to take years to put ours in place and we're not going to kidnap anyone. We're going to do it artistically."

She looked over her shoulder at Williams. "Don't we have every world leader, every despot, every dictator in the world digitally recorded? Every vowel; every consonant; every colloquialism? Don't we have a digital library on all of them?" She didn't wait for a response, but turned her attention back to the shadows across the table.

"Yes, we do. We have all the tools we need, and I know we can do it, if not with digitally created persons, at least with digitally created voices. Not replicas, but their own voices. We can turn them against themselves and each other. We can do it just long enough to distract them." She paused to catch her breath. She was on fire and not about to slow down. "We don't need for this to last years; a few days, that all. When it's over, Justice Gonzales goes back to the bench, and no one will be the wiser." She allowed herself a small smile. "Well, practically no one. The world need never know that for at least two years an imposter sat as a Justice of the Supreme Court."

She paused again to take a deep breath, taking the briefest moment to give herself one last opportunity to reconsider what she was about to say. "And Duarte? Well, what has to happen has to happen. As it was said at the ranch, this is war and there are casualties. Part of our job is to minimize them."

"But why all the dramatics? Why get the Chinese and the Russians at each other's throats?" the gentleman asked.

"There must be consequences," the rapidly maturing agent fired back. "If we only slip in and rescue the Judge; do something with Duarte; then things go back to normal, there hasn't been any consequence for their action. They might feel free to try it again." She leaned forward with her finger pointed toward the panel. "We deliver a message. We have a simple little saying back home, 'Don't mess with Texas.' What that message tells people is, we don't want you to throw your trash on the roadside or you'll suffer the consequences. Well, that's what we're telling the Chinese. Don't mess with us, or we can cause you living hell!"

She leaned back in her chair and looked over her shoulder at Williams. She caught him with just the slightest glimmer of a smile.

*****

Ann Marie Beaudet, an agent of multiple talents, walked down the hall; past the mahogany bench, down the long, curving staircases; through the massive doors into the fresh air, the sunlight; the scents of the freshly cut grass and cherry blossoms on the trees. It was good to be alive. She stepped onto the portico and looked back. Williams would join her later. She paused to reflect privately on the passing of this remarkable day: a day like no other in her life.

She gazed out to the heights of the nation's symbols – the Washington Monument, the Lincoln Memorial, beyond the tidal basin to the Jefferson Memorial. In her own little insignificant way, today was her personal memorial. She walked slowly down the steps to the waiting car, its driver standing ready with the door open.

"Back to your hotel, madam?" he asked as she slipped into the back seat.

"No, I think not." She looked up at him and smiled. "I'd like to go to lunch. Can you recommend someplace where a lady can be comfortable alone?"

"Indeed! Blackie's. A pleasant ambiance; excellent food; and, just as they advertise, seamless service." He smiled back at her. "Took my wife there on our anniversary. She loved it, and I think you will, too. Very nice."

Ann Marie leaned back and relaxed for the first time since the horrible episode in her hotel room the previous night. She was barely aware of the drive through the heart of the nation's capitol. When the car pulled to the curb on 22nd Street Northwest, she stepped onto the sidewalk and froze. She was no more than a few minutes walk to *Mi Tios Restaurante*. Just minutes from that place where she first learned the secret, the truth behind the door of deception where Duarte the imposter lurked. Her dream world for the day came to an abrupt end. She was back to reality. She took a deep breath and mumbled to herself. "Screw'em."

Voices In The Fog

The chauffeur opened the restaurant door for her and she stepped inside.

"I'll be across the street," he said as he tipped his cap to her. "I'll see you when you come out. Take your time and enjoy your lunch."

Ann Marie followed the maitre'd to a table tucked into the corner next to the window, comfortably out of the mainstream of tables with small groups of people, yet not too stuffed away so as to be hidden.

He was right, she thought. It was a perfect place.

She whiled away her time. There wasn't any hurry. Williams would find her when he was ready. She knew her appetite returned as she admired the rotisserie-roasted duck, gleaming in the light of the mid-day sun that shone through the window, its lemon ginger glaze and gently darkened skin presented royally. She felt like a queen. Yes, it was a lot for lunch, but what the heck. It was time to allow herself a bit of luxury. She paid the price and deserved it.

After only a few bites, however, she pushed the plate aside. The duck seemed to form a ball in the center of her chest, and no amount of swallowing and sipping water would move it. Her breathing became constricted and her hands trembled. I killed a man last night! How could I possibly be celebrating anything? Suddenly unable to sit there any longer, she groped in her purse for money, threw several bills on the table and hurried out. She stared across the street, looking for the Cadillac. She waved at the astonished driver, who checked his watch, then started the car, drove around the block and stopped a few feet from her. With tears running down her cheeks, she stared out the window as they drove past *Mi Tios,* across the Key Bridge, to her hotel. She had come full circle.

CHAPTER EIGHTEEN

Ann Marie sat Indian-style on her yoga mat and practiced her stretching exercises. She was bare-footed, wearing her old exercise tights and a faded Dallas Cowboys sweat shirt. This was one of her daily obligations to herself – stretch and keep her muscles and joints limber and her mind clear and relaxed. Today, she hoped the yoga would chase away the tendrils of fear, anxiety, and guilt that overwhelmed her, but no such luck. Her mind still felt heavy as if it wanted to close down. Into that mire crept another unpleasant thought. She remembered seeing a recent television exposé on the failure of the so-called finer hotels to test for hygiene. No telling what kind of microbe was crawling around on her yoga mat or her body right now. She shuddered and pushed the thought away. The world was far from perfect. Oh, so far. If people only knew.

She suddenly longed for some kind of contact with Rod. She smiled grimly. Actually, the longing wasn't so sudden. It swirled around in her mind all night, chasing the image of her attacker and the feel of her arm against his neck as she took his life. On some deep level, she understood that a flash of Rod's million-watt smile, a comforting look, anything, would make this okay. She took a deep breath, stubbornly determined to focus on the task at hand. She lay back on the mat and stretched her legs and toes toward the opposite wall as she reached over her head and pointed her fingers, palms up, to the wall behind her. She sucked in her stomach, held it, and counted slowly; one, two, three - -. The jangle of the phone broke her concentration. She rolled over and grabbed the instrument off the nightstand.

Voices In The Fog

"Annie babe." Rod's voice came urgently through the receiver. "I just heard what happened last night. Are you okay?"

She allowed herself to believe he'd somehow sensed the longing she felt. "I'm fine," she said.

Why just the sound of his voice should soothe her, she had no idea, but it did and she wasn't questioning it. She got off the floor and sprawled across the bed, gazing at the ceiling. "Things went wild after you and I talked last night, but it came out okay."

"Are you sure?" His voice was calm, but she detected an undercurrent of anxiety.

She paused and composed her thoughts. "It bothers me. I admit it. But not as much as I was afraid it would, I guess. Maybe it's because he was such a monster." She bit her lip as the man's image swept over her. "Rod, he would have killed me." Her voice quavered.

"Damn. I wish I weren't so far away. I would give anything if there was something I could do to help you get past this."

"Come and hold me. That's what you can do," she thought. Then she spoke softly. "I'll be all right. Don't worry about me."

"I can't help worrying about you. I'd do anything for you, honey. You know that."

Her racing heart stopped her from speaking for a long moment. Finally, she spoke gently, "I know you would."

"Damn!" he said again.

She smiled as she pictured his little boy smile that melted her heart. "Duty calls," she said. "Have you talked to Williams?"

He sighed heavily. "Yes. He said he checked your hotel and then with your chauffeur service and they told him where you went for lunch. Sounds like you were a notch or two above Mickey D's."

No sense mentioning the duck worth a king's ransom she had left on her plate, she thought.

"He's going to catch you sometime this evening, but asked me to touch base with you." Rod gave a soft laugh. "He's figured us out. He knows we have a special feeling for each other."

"Mmm humm. Yeah, I think I could call it a special feeling." Her voice was soft. Almost a whisper. "Did he say anything about how the meeting went?"

"No, but that's all right. I think he would have passed it on to me if it went south. I think you did fine," Rod answered

Ann Marie heaved a sigh of relief. That's what she'd thought, but she couldn't be sure. She grinned into the handset. "I've found a good radio station, and I heard a song I'm going to call our song."

"What is it?"

She gave a soft laugh. "The Jayhawks. All the Right Reasons."

"I know it," Rod replied. "I love it. 'I'm loving you - -.' That's one of the lines. My God, Annie, 'You're my morning star.' That's another one of the lines." He paused. The phone was silent for a moment, then he whispered. "I love you, Ann Marie Beaudet."

"I love you, too, Rod McCarren. I love you with all my heart."

"Come back to the ranch, Sweetheart. I miss you. I want to hold you. I need you."

She rolled over on her stomach and rested on her elbows, her legs and feet bent up behind her. She took a deep breath. "It's been quite a trip. I killed a man, and realized I'm in love." She laughed awkwardly. "Not an everyday trip, that's for damned sure."

"No. For sure, not. Anyhow, Williams will see you tonight," Rod said. "After that, let's play it by ear. We'll see how things go back there, but everything is A-okay here. Just hurry home."

Home. What a beautiful word. Somehow, it didn't mean the HJ ranch. She really had no home anymore. Except wherever Rod McCarren was. That thought stunned her, then she grinned in delight. "As quick as I can."

"I'll keep a light in the window." Rod's voice was so soft it was nearly imperceptible.

"We'll make a team, Mr. McCarren. Quite a team."

*****

Williams and Ann Marie sat in the piano bar and listened to the sounds of the old black gentleman's gentle rhythm on the keys. Candles in the center of each table sent flickers of yellow and orange dancing across the room. Only one other table, with two couples, was occupied.

Williams leaned forward, cupping the candleholder in his hand and playing with the flame as he spoke. "They liked it. Not without some trepidation, but they think it's sufficiently bold on one hand and leaves enough wiggle room on the other."

The light of the flame reflected off his eyes. Gentle eyes, she thought. "So it's a go?"

He sat back, folded his arms across his chest, and crossed his legs as he stretched out. "Not yet. As they say, the devil is in the details. We'll see what and when, or if. There's always a possibility something else will come up."

"What about me? Stay or go home?"

"You did well today," he replied. "You played your cards like a Mississippi gambler. There's no value in waiting here to see what we do. Why don't you get a plane out tomorrow? I'll call you in the morning and get your schedule and let'em know when to pick you up. By the time you get up, you'll have a complete set of new identification cards. For the meantime, you'll travel as Jennifer Lynn Chase."

She nodded. Any name was fine now.

It seemed strange that she was actually homesick for that isolated ranch. Or maybe her desire to return was focused on somebody, not someplace. "What about you? How long before you come back to the ranch?"

He leaned his elbows on the table, looked into the burning candle, and nodded his head. "Don't know. Maybe a few days."

"But there won't be a war? Right? We just put them on edge, and by the time they realize the crap has hit the fan, its over. No war! Right?" she asked urgently.

"That's a hope and a prayer, but no guarantees," Williams responded grimly.

*****

Williams was overdue. It was five days, and still no word from him. She and Rod were appointed by Rucinski to take on one of the more undesirable tasks – removing the shutters, scraping and sanding, then re-painting them to their original eggshell color.

"Can't waste time. Put every minute to good use," he commanded. Of course, he was right. There was no maintenance crew from the base as long as they were there. If work was going to get done, they must do it themselves. Nevertheless, when the last shutter was re-hung, they

294

walked down the drive and turned to take in the results of their handiwork.

"We did pretty damn good," she joked as she extended her hand in an exaggerated motion to shake hands with Rod.

"Yep. Hell, we might have even have found a talent we didn't even know we had," he replied.

They walked slowly back up the drive toward the house in silence. They stepped onto the porch when Ann Marie broke the silence. "He's been gone too long. He should have been back by now."

Rod opened the screen door, but paused and looked back at her. His lips were pursed; his brow furrowed. "Don't second guess him . . . or them. Bide your time. We'll see." He stepped inside and she followed behind.

"Going to get a shower," Rod said as he moved toward the hallway.

"Think I'll get myself something to drink. Will you come out later and have something with me?"

He smiled and nodded. "Yeah, I think you might talk me into it." The door opened and Cowboy came in from the stable. "Howdy, young folks. Saw your work, and reckon you've pretty much paid your room and board for a few more days." He went to the kitchen cabinet and browsed their supply of beverages before selecting a bottle of Jack Daniels. "Get anything for y'all?"

"Not me," Rod replied. "Going to get cleaned up."

The cowboy turned to Ann Marie.

She smiled at him. "You made a tasty Irish Coffee the other night. I could sure take one right now."

"Coming up," he quipped as he reached for the ever-present coffee pot.

Voices In The Fog

Ann Marie sat on the porch and nursed the steamy, frothy Irish coffee he made for her. The Cowboy found one of her weaknesses.

It was nearly dark. She squinted into the fading light in the eastern sky. Something was coming. She could barely see it, but it was there on the horizon. Flying low, skimming the tree tops, following the contours of the land. A helicopter! It came closer, and at a distance behind it, a second one. They were coming directly toward the ranch.

"Oh God, no," she muttered. The cold, clammy fingers of fear stroked her skin. Her muscles weakened like limp rags as the clear, distinct form of the helicopters took shape. She dropped the cup. It shattered on the floor between her feet. The rhythmic chop of the rotor blades sliced into the evening air and became louder and louder. They were coming. A day she never thought could happen was happening, here, and she was in the middle of it. High Jinks was being activated. Like the helicopters, war was on the horizon, moving closer with each passing second. She gasped for breath. Tears ran uncontrollably down her cheeks.

She recognized the choppers from one of her introductory sessions at Millie's - UH60 Blackhawks. Capable of carrying up to a dozen people. Enough to staff the High Jinks for whatever calamity lay ahead of them. How long was it that Rod said they could stay underground? Seven years?

"Oh God," she cried. "God help us."

The first Huey swung around the back of the house – out of sight for a moment, then swooped over the rooftop, blowing grass, dust and gravel from the driveway into her face. Its skids touched lightly for a moment, then settled the bird's weight on the ground.

Voices In The Fog

She covered her face and squinted between her fingers. Williams jumped free from the open door, followed by nearly a dozen men and women she didn't know. He ducked down and led the entourage in a quickstep toward the porch. No sooner did the last occupant climb out the hatch of the helicopter than it tilted forward and eased itself up and out toward the direction from where it came. Ann Marie opened the screen door and stepped aside. Williams grabbed her hand with a strong grip, held it a moment, and went inside. She stood there silently, giving only a polite smile and nod of her head as the others followed.

The second helicopter carried only two men, and they busied themselves unloading briefcases, suitcases, crates, and half a dozen military type sea bags. When the last one was unceremoniously tossed on the heap, the man turned toward the flight crew and waved them off. She watched it go — not as graceful or silent as the scout, but instead, a big, bulky, efficient machine, made for a variety of purposes. War was certainly one of them.

As suddenly as the commotion started, it stopped. Ann Marie stared into the growing darkness when the last helicopter disappeared into the twilight. The chopping sound of its rotors faded into the tranquility of the peaceful countryside.

She went inside where Williams and Cowboy were setting order to the chaos – finding chairs, pulling them into a semi-circle around the fireplace, tossing quick comments back and forth in hushed tones. Rod busied himself being the host, setting out soft drinks and beer; grabbing a few whiskey bottles and ice cubes and putting them on the counter. Ann Marie joined the fray and tossed a couple mesquite logs in the fireplace even though the early days of summer generally precluded a fire for anything but mood. She stoked them into the hot ashes that came to life with small tongues of flames.

Rucinski smiled and nodded approval, then stepped to the front and called everyone to find a seat, and as much as possible, to make themselves comfortable.

Ann Marie quickly swept up her mess on the porch, then stepped around to the back of the room, but not before she took time to get a cold beer and a handful of chips.

"Good evening," Cowboy bellowed out in what she thought was his cafeteria voice as they called it when she taught school. How long had it been? Another lifetime? It all seemed so distant.

People shuffled and scooted. "Excuse me," said one. "Oops, sorry," said another while she tried to extricate her chair leg from between someone else's feet. Quickly though, they came to order. Strangers, but colleagues who come together in a time of un-paralleled crisis.

An awkward silence fell over the gathering. Cowboy stood at the fireplace, a kind and caring sentinel watching over his brood. Finally, he spoke. "My friends, thank you for coming on such short notice. One or two of you have been here before on training sessions, but for others, allow me to introduce myself. I am Doctor Edmund Rucinski, or as Miss Beaudet," he smiled and nodded at her leaning against the wall, "as she refers to me, I am Cowboy Joe. Nevertheless, I am more or less the ranch foreman here, among my other duties. I want to welcome you to your new home. I would be delighted to tell you how long you may expect to be here, but frankly, I have no idea. Obviously, you would not be here if a determination wasn't made that our nation is facing a potential crisis."

He offered a slight smile and sipped from his glass of whiskey. "We are at that stage in which we are duty bound to clarify for you the exact phase of this incident into which we have been thrust. To say the least, it is not pretty. However, the news media hasn't picked up on what's happening, and that is for the good. The fewer people who are aware of the situation, the greater the likelihood that tensions can be appeased without a nuclear disaster. With that said, I must add - -" He paused and again took time to sip a drink while he gathered his thoughts. "There has, in fact, been a Russian missile launch. Fortunately, it occurred in a remote area of the world and the people involved have remained mum on the topic. However, I am jumping to the conclusion, so let me stand aside while Mr. Williams starts at the beginning and brings you up-to-date."

Williams climbed down from a stool near the door and slipped through the crowded chairs to the front of the room. "I, too, have met many of you, but allow me to introduce myself to all of you. It was rather helter-skelter as you were being unloaded from the transport plane and loaded into the helicopters, so I never spoke to some of you. My name is Alfred Williams. This is not my normal duty station. I tend to travel, and to a great extent, live out of a suitcase. I became involved in this matter a number of months ago, so let me take you back to the beginning."

Ann Marie was impressed with the smooth, accurate manner in which he covered her work – the surveillance; getting the fingerprints from the door knob; linking Duarte with the Chinese; *Mi Tios Restaurante* in Georgetown; the ranch near Laredo; Golden Eagle holdings in Laredo; the Panama Canal and Long Beach Shipyard; and, last but not least, the Scout. He covered it in less than thirty minutes, then stopped for a long, cold drink.

"All of which brings us to the here and now." Ann Marie watched as a metamorphosis swept over Williams.

Voices In The Fog

She didn't know whether or not it was noticeable to the others, but she saw it as clear as the morning sun. Calm, cool, in control Alfred Williams now looked like Dr. Strangelove – cold, calculating, and far removed from his usual personable self. Almost robotic, she thought. He was detached from himself, and assumed a whole new personality.

He continued. "Our side has for many years maintained digital recordings of the voices of various world leaders. Not with any particular purpose, but to have them only when and if they were needed. This is one of those times. We have prepared a digital audio recording of the Chairman of the Peoples Republic of China in conversation with the command staff of the Peoples Army, and of course, their navy and police. In the conversation, the Chairman speaks about the weakness of the Russian army. In due course, he arrives at his point. With the Russians in disarray feigning democracy, and the legitimate question about who is or is not in charge of their military, and of more importance, their nuclear stockpile, the only logical solution to bring long-term peace to their frontier is to conduct a preemptive strike. Move quickly. Strike hard and fast! Don't give them time to think about it. In essence, redefine the borders, giving more to the Chinese control and considerably less to the Russians."

He paused for effect and allowed his comments to sink in. "This is more than a simple skirmish. It is nothing short of a major military invasion to take advantage of the Russians' weakness. Now, we come to the last ninety-six hours. Our side delivered the audio recording to the Russian Ambassador. As we suspected, it took them a few hours, but they verified the voices on the tape and were convinced of its accuracy and reliability. As we anticipated, there was a lot of scurrying about and saber rattling. That's exactly what we wanted. They got the attention of the Chinese, who were busy disavowing anything and everything, but to no avail."

Williams stopped to survey the stunned expressions of his listeners, then continued. "In defense, the Chinese started shifting some troops toward the border, all of which further convinced the Russians of the inevitable Chinese invasion. Unfortunately, one of the Russian hotheads, the kind we have come to dread, jumped the gun and went out on his own. A nut named Admiral Omsk, who commands the fleet in the Sea of Okhotsk, hit the button. The dumb shit actually launched his missiles. I don't know whether it's good or bad, but their hardware is so dysfunctional the damned things went off course. We tracked them – actually, two of them — and it appears they never got above three thousand meters in altitude before they swung around from their original course and impacted near Komsomolsk, northeast of Manchuria. To say they had a computer glitch would be a significant understatement. The damned idiot killed dozens, maybe hundreds, of his own people. Of course, the Chinese saw it, and now they are up on a nuclear threshold, ready to hit the Russians with all they've got."

Williams paused for a moment; no one moved or blinked an eye. "We hoped for and anticipated some action on both sides, but not so soon and certainly not this much. Nevertheless, we will go forward with our own plans, all of which brings you here. We are not implementing the full capacity of this site, but have brought you here as a skeleton crew to gear things up and have it ready to be activated at a moment's notice. We cannot stand by while they hit each other and pound one another into oblivion.

We have to recognize that a military force in panic may do anything, which includes the possibility they may try to draw us into their madness. That is why you are here, just in case."

He nodded to Rucinski who returned to the forefront. "While you and your colleagues are in the process of opening the threshold of our safe havens, others are preparing to implement plans to achieve our original goal: return the Justice to his rightful place on the bench of the Supreme Court; and, to secure the Panama Canal and the adjacent air bases once and for all. Naturally, we will also re-institute ourselves in the Long Beach Shipyard.

"Now, I'll go with you to your quarters and help you get yourselves situated. In the meantime, Miss Beaudet, Rod, and Mr. Williams will move forward toward our goal."

*****

Ann Marie made a sandwich for herself and sat near the rapidly cooling fireplace. Rod busied himself shuffling chairs, and in general, putting the room in order. Finally, Williams sat on the edge of the hearth and looked at her. "Ready?"

"Ready as I'll ever be. So, tell me. What's the plan?" Ann Marie asked.

"You'll leave within the hour. A helicopter will take you to Cannon Air Force Base at Clovis. From there you'll go by jet to San Antonio where we've arranged a transfer to another helicopter for the last leg of your flight to the border near Laredo."

He pulled a map from a kitchen drawer and spread it on the counter. He took a few seconds to get his bearings, then pointed to the Texas-Mexico border. "Here. Right about here," he said. "You'll set down pretty much out in the

Voices In The Fog

middle of nowhere in the desert between San Ygnacio and Escobas, Texas. You'll be joined by three Apache Longbow helicopters and another Huey. They're military, but on loan to us and are being flown by non-military personnel. All the aircraft are unmarked, plain olive drab. Each is staffed with some of the best fighters in the world."

He looked at her and gave a confident smile. "They're on our side, and they're damned good at what they do; much like the crew you met at the rest stop. We already have a small ground unit en route there now. They'll be in place by the time you arrive."

He paused and looked deeply into her eyes. "Ann Marie, you're a hell of a good trooper, and I hope this thing goes off without a glitch, but I've got to tell you. Nothing is perfect. Our plan is solid. I'm comfortable with it, and I hope you are, too. As a young man, I was in the infantry. I went to all sorts of command schools, military tactics, guerrilla warfare, everything. But one thing I learned was that when the first shot gets fired, you can pretty much throw away the book. All hell breaks loose. Planning is good. Hell, it's more than that. Its essential, but you never know whose side Lady Luck is on, theirs or ours. It's a throw of the dice. The good guys win a few, but so do the bad guys."

He glanced at Rod and caught his eye.

A quick smile creased the younger man's lips and he nodded his head. "You've got that right, but she'll do fine." He reached over and put his hand on her shoulder. "You'll kick their ass, and you've got the best assault group in the world to take the lead." He nodded his approval again. "Welcome to the ugly world, but this time tomorrow, it'll be over and you'll hold your head high."

Williams moved close to her, so close that she could feel his breath on her face. "There's something else I need to tell you. You told me once that an FBI agent saved your life when your parents were killed."

She nodded, puzzled. Yes, but - - "

"Well, that's partially true. He was FBI for a while, but he disappeared. You know that. You've been trying to find him all these years. Now, no trace of him exists anywhere." He stopped and looked searchingly into her eyes.

"You mean . . .? Is he . . . one of us?" Ann Marie's throat tightened with emotion.

"Yes, he is. In fact . . ." Williams smiled and suddenly she knew.

"It was you! You saved me," she exclaimed.

"I was there, but shortly after that, I became affiliated with - - " he spread his hands. "This. That's why you couldn't find me. But I found you. I've watched you all your life. Now, you're almost like a daughter to me. That's good, and it's bad. I want to protect you, but at the same time, I've got to get out of your way and let you do your job."

Too overcome by emotion to speak, she leaned forward and rested her cheek against his. Williams held her in his arms and gently stroked his fingers through her hair. He put his lips to her ear and whispered, "You've got the right stuff. Just remember the old Marine adage, 'keep your butt down, and watch your flanks.'"

Ann Marie sat up and smiled as tears trickled down her cheeks. "I'll do my best. Maybe, just maybe, you're the dad I never had. Thank you for caring. Now, go ahead and give it to me. We get to Texas - -"

"Yes," he replied. "You should be on the ground at 0200 hours. Take advantage of your flying time and try to get some sleep. Once you get to Texas, lets see, that will be in Zapata County," he remarked as he ran his fingers across the map. "You'll be under the command of Felipe O'Malley, a good Mexican-Irishman. You will move out at 0215 hours. You'll be in a Huey, and the three Apaches and the other Huey will be alongside. However, only one Apache will land with you. Basically, it's a spare in case anything goes wrong. The other two Apaches and the second Huey will continue on. You'll set down, but for only a very short time, about a mile northeast of the ranch house. The first Apache will take out the guardhouse at the gate. Of course, whoever is in there will never know what hit them. The second one will follow the Huey to the house. They'll come in fast and hard. Eight hard-core troops will hit that house like a tornado. The Apache will take out anyone who might try to escape. We'll be watching from here with the Scout and give them any information that may develop, although we don't expect anything but a bunch of folks sleeping. Of course, we'll be in radio contact if anything develops."

Williams stopped and went to the refrigerator. He took time to browse through it until he found an unopened bottle of water. He twisted the cap slowly, taking in her body language.

She was cool, maintaining her demeanor.

He continued, "From the time the Huey sets down until the house is cleared will be just about one minute, maybe a little less. They'll give the all clear, and that's when your chopper will move in. It will take you about two minutes to lift off and get over the ranch house. Assuming all goes as planned, you should be on the ground at the house for no more than two or three minutes, and then you get out of there with the Judge. You'll retrace your flight back to

Clovis, and from there we haven't completely resolved a couple of issues. Nevertheless, by the time you land there, everything will be in order for the next phase."

"What about the others? Mrs. Duarte? What about her?"

Williams shrugged and looked down at his shoes, covered with the dust from the New Mexico earth. "There are casualties in war. What else can I say?"

"And at the restaurant in Georgetown?"

"Casualties, of course."

"Golden Eagle in Laredo?"

"The same. Everything's already in motion. It can't be stopped."

His brow was wet with perspiration when he spoke, "We're taking everything back tonight. It'll all be over before dawn. It's something they started, and they couldn't care less how many people die. They simply don't give a shit. I once heard one of their generals making a presentation, and he gave a hell of a creepy example. He said that if we lined up one soldier and the Chinese lined up one thousand, and if our man killed all of them before they killed him, we would still run out of troops long before them. Hell, they have millions of troops, and to lose a few people tonight means absolutely nothing to them." Williams shook his head. "It means nothing at all. They'll just start somewhere else tomorrow. Life means nothing to them. Maybe they've already started, and we just don't know about it yet."

"So they'll all die tonight? Everyone?"

"All but Mr. Justice Gonzales. That's where you come in. The house will be secured by the time you get there, but have your sidearm ready. Remember, not everything always goes as planned." He wet his lips and continued. "You'll go into the house immediately. I want you - - a woman to get Gonzales. The troops will be wearing their kick-ass outfits and will scare the hell out of everyone. I want him to see you. You need to get your hands on him; let him know he's okay. He's going to be scared shitless."

Williams paused and gazed deeply into her eyes.

"Bring him back in one piece." He turned toward the door, but looked back at Rod. "Why don't you help her get ready?"

"Will do, boss," he replied, then took her hand in his. "C'mon, I'll help you pack a few things."

Ann Marie watched the door close behind Williams, and without a pause pulled Rod to her. Their lips touched lightly. "Hold me. Keep me close. I'm afraid," she whispered as she gazed into his dark eyes.

He kissed her again. "You should be. Fear is what keeps all of us alive in times like this. Plus, you've got something else going for you."

"What's that?"

"Me. I love you too much to let anything happen to you. I'll be looking out for you." He smiled as he took her hand again and led her to her room.

Ann Marie flicked on the light, and just as quickly, he turned it off. He cupped her face in his hands and whispered softly into her ear. "I love you too much to let you go without a real kiss."

She gave a soft laugh, wrapped him in her arms and led him to her bed. "Kiss me," she said as she lay across the bed.

Rod leaned down over her, took her in his arms, and kissed her lips, her ear lobes, then her neck. He touched the button on her blouse, but she put her hand on his.

"Not now, we can't hurry it. I want you as much as you want me, but there isn't time." She kissed his forehead, then rolled out from beneath him and turned on the light. "Like Granny always said, 'business before pleasure.' Can you reach up and get my pack from the top of the closet while I get a few necessities from the drawer?"

Voices In The Fog

CHAPTER NINETEEN

Beaudet tossed her backpack into the helicopter. There wasn't much ceremony about it. She was ready to put things in motion and get it over with for better or worse. She scrambled over the struts and found a seat. The rotor blades began their slow, rhythmic thump-thump-thump while she fastened her shoulder harness and seat belt. She was alone. The pilot and navigator were on the flight deck setting their instruments for the flight to Cannon Air Force Base.

The captain looked over his shoulder at her. "Fifty-four minutes and we'll have you on the ground at Cannon," he shouted.

Nearly an hour alone with her thoughts. The cabin was dark. She closed her eyes. The helicopter lifted slightly, tilted forward and accelerated up and away, free from the bonds of earth; away from Rod, from Williams, from Cowboy Joe; beyond the darkened mountain ridges and the mesquite trees; beyond the mournful wail of the coyotes. The only sound she heard was the steady cadence of the rotors slicing into the night air. The life of Christie Cole was forever changed. Although she tried to focus on what was ahead, her mind was filled with thoughts of Alfred Williams. He was near her all the time. She was right when she told Gran she thought he was her guardian angel. He was there all the time, protecting her. He didn't say as much, but she knew.

A peace she'd never known before came over her. Now, she really had someone. "Two someones." she thought, as Rod's smile flashed through her mind. She wasn't alone anymore.

Voices In The Fog

Good to his word and exactly on time, the captain set the Huey down on the tarmac at Cannon and gracefully settled itself down on to the flair path. A uniformed Air Police Officer slid the door open, made a casual greeting, and quickly escorted her out of the helicopter and into an Air Force staff car that was parked a few yards away. She scooted into the back seat and pulled her backpack in behind her.

With no more than a "Good evening, ma'am," the driver accelerated and drove in silence for the minute or two it took him to get to the far end of the runway. The sedan stopped alongside a jet fighter, its canopies lifted back and open.

"Good evening, Miss Beaudet," a uniformed pilot said when he opened her car door. "I'm Captain Suarez. Welcome to Cannon." He gestured toward the plane. "This is my

T-38. If you'll follow me, I'll help you aboard and get you down to Lackland, chop-chop."

"Thank you, Captain," she responded. She looked over her shoulder at the driver who was busy opening the trunk and pulling something out onto the ground.

"Your flight suit, ma'am," he said. "Pull these on over your clothes and I'll stick your backpack and tennis shoes in the plane. Not much room in there," he joked. "You'll be tight, but it'll be okay for awhile."

She sat on the edge of the car seat, pulled off her shoes, and slipped into the Air Force jump suit and flight boots - - exactly her size, but she wasn't surprised. Why should she be? Everything else the company did was perfect. Why should her clothes size be any different? She buckled the utility belt around her waist and took a quick inventory of its accoutrements: a penlight, the red handled Swiss Army knife, and a first aide kit.

Minutes later she was strapped into the rear seat of the jet. The driver stood on the ladder affixed to the side of the plane and fitted her helmet and oxygen mask over her face and head.

"Just breathe normally," he said with a pat on her head. "You can talk in a regular voice and the Captain can hear you, but for now why don't you hold off on any conversation until you're airborne?"

Ann Marie took his request as a command and settled back against the parachute that was strapped to her back and served as an uncomfortable backrest. She heard the smooth, powerful roar of the twin engines and felt the jet ease forward. At the same time, the twin canopies lowered and locked. It was as if she were in a tomb. She glanced at her watch. Eleven-thirty. They were right on time.

Once again, Ann Marie felt her life changing, never to be the same. The close confines of the cockpit and the reeking smell of jet fuel gave her claustrophobia. She was conscious of listening to the sounds of her own breathing in the face mask. Her heart pounded. Never before and never again, she hoped, would she find herself in a position like this. Closed in, hot, sweat running down her back, terrified of the very thought that she was on her way to deliver the hand of death to people she never met – people who did no personal harm to her.

Christie Cole, the schoolteacher, now the assassin. The one who would deliver up those whose lives would be ended before the sun shone anew on the horizon. A sun that brought a new day and a new life to the world, but not to the ranch. The black hand of the Grim Reaper swept through that desolate and lonesome place, leaving only the shattered remains of those who sought to swathe the world with a veil of fog. She recalled her first conversation with Williams in which she said she wouldn't murder anyone, and he assured her that she would not be required to do it. But, tonight? What about this? She wasn't going to do the killing herself. It wasn't like the monster in her hotel room. Nevertheless, she was a part of it and couldn't escape that plain fact. Tonight, people would die so others could live. All of them at the ranch would be dead within the next couple of hours.

Except, of course, for the Justice of the Supreme Court. The one who would be rescued from his captivity and returned to his rightful place in the heart of the most powerful nation on earth. She could do it, she told herself, and she <u>would</u> do it – all for the service of her country. She heard William's voice ringing in her ears that day at Quantico.

"You will provide a service for the United States of America."

CHAPTER TWENTY

Juan Reynosa Duarte looked forward to indulging himself in his newly discovered hobby of fly-fishing. He learned it in China when he was preparing for his role as Justice Ricardo Huerta Gonzales. It was Justice Gonzales' one true passion, but one that he seldom pursued except once a year when he could get away to Wyoming. For Duarte, this too, had become a passion. His fly fishing vacations gave him the chance to escape from the burden of his onerous service in Washington, D.C.

The U.S. Forest Service maintained an old cabin near Sheridan, Wyoming and provided it free to government officials. Gonzales used it for two weeks every summer, and Duarte had filled in admirably for the Justice. The imposter developed into a fine fisherman, adept at the feel of the rod and the fly. He was especially skilled with judging the water temperature, the hatch of bugs, the appetite of the trout, and most important of all, the presentation of the fly in the exact spot to feed that swimming eating machine, the rainbow trout.

He boarded the morning flight from Ronald Reagan Washington National to Chicago, changed planes to Denver, changed flights again, and was scheduled to land in Sheridan at 3:20 in the afternoon. As was the usual procedure, someone from the U. S. Marshal's Office would pick him up at the airport. They would drive him to the cabin where the driver and one or two other members of the Marshal's Service maintained the grounds and house during his stay.

*****

Voices In The Fog

A handsome black man met him at the baggage carousel. Duarte studied him fixedly. He seemed vaguely familiar, but Duarte couldn't recall having met him before. Then the man smiled and it came to the imposter. He was almost a duplication of Tiger Woods.

"Justice Gonzales, allow me to introduce myself." He showed his credentials to Duarte. "I'm Adolphus Morin. I'll be your driver and look after your needs while you're with us."

"Good afternoon," the imposter replied. They shook hands and lifted the baggage free from the rotating carousel and headed to the driveway.

"I must advise you, sir. I have been warned about your skill with the fly rod. However, it's only fair to tell you that you're going up against one of the best. I learned fly fishing from my grandfather and have been doing it for the last twenty years. When the bosses found out how good I was with a fly rod, they assigned me up here. Yes, sir," he laughed. "Tough duty. Better than traipsing all over the country, which is what I usually do." He flashed another broad smile. "I'm going to show you some of the best places up here to catch the trout of your dreams."

They loaded the suitcases into the Suburban and drove out of the city. Within minutes, they started up the long dirt road toward the mountaintop. Aptly named, Red Grade Road twisted, turned and climbed over the ruts left over from last year's snow and this year's spring rains.

Ever the good host, Morin opened the console and retrieved a bottle of *Tres Generaciones* tequila, Gonzales' favorite.

They glanced at each other and laughed. "It's for you. I'm driving, but you're legal," Morin joked.

Voices In The Fog

With that, Duarte twisted the cork off and took a sip, another, and then a third. "Yes, my good friend," he said. "We're going to have a nice time for the next few days." He smiled to himself and looked out over the valleys below, then continued. "We might even catch a few fish."

"Sir, I need to tell you that the forest has been extra dry this year, so we have a crew up here clearing the underbrush. Fire hazard, you know. They'll be here for a couple more hours today, and probably be back tomorrow. We have to keep the place in good shape just to protect ourselves from a forest fire," Morin said.

"That's fine. I don't mind the noise or the company. From what I'm used to, you could add another dozen people and it still would seem desolate to me," Duarte responded.

They approached the top of the ridge and slowed to make a sharp right turn onto what some referred to as a road, but others called it nothing more than a rut filled, boulder-strewn path. Nevertheless, it had a name, "Mud Coulee." It was on some maps, but not on others. They bounced and crashed for two miles, coming perilously close to hitting trees on one side or falling off the other side. They drove for twenty minutes, but it seemed much longer. Finally, they came out into an open area the size of a football field. At the far end sat the log cabin: plain single story, stone chimney, small front porch, but what a joy to see. For Duarte, it meant two weeks of bliss away from *Mi Tios* and all the other pressures that were cast upon him by his assignment. Here he could taste the tranquility of life as it was meant to be lived. He could sleep, read books, fish to his heart's content, smoke a few cigars, have a drink or two, and in general, gather his sanity that was stretched perilously thin from the tortuous role he volunteered for so long ago.

Duarte saw two big men, lumberjacks, he thought. They came out of the trees on the hill behind the house. Morin stopped in front of the cabin where a stout but attractive middle-aged woman was waiting for them. She opened the door for Duarte.

"Good afternoon, sir. I am Olga Kusindorf and I'll be preparing your meals. Welcome to the Mud Coulee House."

Duarte acknowledged her and climbed out of the Suburban. He reached into the back seat for his travel bag. When he turned his back to Olga, she crashed a powerful judo chop into the back of his neck. He caught his balance for a moment, then fell into the door, cutting a small nick on the side of his head. He staggered and fell to the ground like a limp rag doll.

Without a word, the two men scooped him up and carried him into the house. There was no time to waste. The cuckoo clock on the mantle chimed the hour - - five o'clock. They dumped him on the living room floor. Olga rolled his fingers with ink and pressed the imprints on a standard FBI fingerprint card. The lumberjacks stripped him naked, but took time to go through his pockets and set aside his wallet, airplane ticket, and the change from his pocket.

Duarte began to regain consciousness. His eyes strained to focus.

"Smile for the birdie," Morin said. He began taking digital pictures of the imposter. Not circumcised. When Gonzales had his first physical at Bethesda he was circumcised. Now he wasn't. They rolled him over where they photographed the scar on his back that Ann Marie saw with her MoTracs; definitely something Gonzales never had.

Adolphus stepped back from Duarte who was struggling to sit upright, but could not find his equilibrium.

From the kitchen counter, Olga barked out, "Okay, got it. This definitely is Duarte. I got a quick match on his prints, nine points of comparison and still counting. It sure as hell isn't Gonzales."

She looked at Morin. "Got your man, my friend. Now, I'm out of here. Good luck. Maybe we'll meet again." She left through the back door, heading for her battered, green four-wheel- drive truck that was parked behind the house. The last Morin saw of her was when she was grinding her way up Mud Coulee Road, far away from whatever was going to happen in the cabin.

The lumberjacks lifted Duarte and helped him into the bedroom. The imposter looked panicked. Bare springs. Ropes tied to each corner of the iron bedstead. Electrical wires running to the bed, their alligator clips looking like deadly vipers ready to strike.

In silent teamwork, they laid him spread-eagle on his back. Within seconds, his wrist and ankles were bound tight: the cold bed springs dug into his back and hips.

"Its over, Duarte." Morin pulled a bench alongside the bed. "We have Marisa. We have the ranch. We have Gonzales. All your friends are dead," he lied.

Duarte was startled. "What do you mean? What do you want?" he asked.

"Everything! The truth. We know pretty much the whole story, but it's time for you to start talking."

"There isn't much that I can say. You know it all or I wouldn't be here."

Voices In The Fog

"I can only tell you this much," Morin said. "Start now and tell the truth. It's your only way to get out of this alive. If you try to bullshit us, you see what we can do and we aren't the least bit reluctant to do it."

Duarte tried to swallow, but his mouth was dry. His voice fell to a scratchy whisper. "Water, please?" he asked.

One of the lumberjacks tilted a drink to his lips. Water slurped over the rim onto the springs. "Better be careful," the man said. "If you screw up, we'll give you a charge. It'll be bad enough as it is, but the water will only make it worse."

Duarte looked passively at him. His eyes were vacant; his expression blank. "Why should I talk? You have me. You know what the game is. Why don't you just kill me and get it over with. You know that's what you're going to do."

"Not so," Morin interjected. "We'll put you and Marisa into Federal protection. We'll take care of both of you forever, and that's a promise. Otherwise, why would we have not killed her with the others at the ranch?"

Duarte grimaced in pain. "Somehow, I don't believe you."

"Listen my friend, one way or the other, you'll tell us everything you know. One way, you walk out of here and we hook you back up with Marisa and you live happily ever after as they say in the movies. Or," he nodded to the lumberjack.

In a quick motion, the man clipped an alligator clip to Duarte's big toe. The jolt of electricity shot through him. His lanky, naked body twisted in wild contortions. It was over in an instant. Duarte held his breath but didn't utter a sound.

Voices In The Fog

"Tough little shit, aren't you?" Morin said. "Do you want to talk now or later? You'll talk, and that's a fact. Your call! What do you want to do?" He nodded to the lumberjack. The second jolt of electricity coursed its way through Duarte's body. The lumberjack held it until Morin reached down to the now burnt toe and released the clip.

Duarte gasped. "Okay," he said. He looked at Morin. "Federal protection?"

"Guaranteed. Absolutely." He flashed his bright smile and switched on a tape recorder.

Duarte talked until his voice turned crispy dry. His story was almost exactly as Morin had expected. "Water, please. And how about letting me up? I'm doing everything you asked me to do." Duarte begged.

"Okay," Morin responded. "Let's take a break."

The lumberjacks loosened the ropes and helped the naked Duarte to his feet. He was weak. His knees buckled. Only the quick response of the lumberjack stopped him from falling onto the floor. They escorted him slowly to a wooden chair in the corner and eased him down into it.

"Go ahead," Morin said. "Get your clothes on. You're doing okay. At this pace, we will get you out of here in a couple of hours."

They let Duarte have a soft drink and go to the bathroom after he put his clothes back on. He returned to the living room.

"What now?" he asked. His voice was soft and resigned. He hung his head in defeat.

"Details, my friend. Details. I need to know more about how you went about writing your decisions."

Duarte spent more than an hour describing the techniques they employed. It started in China where he not only had to learn Gonzales' mannerisms, but more important, his writing style. Try as they might, his style, legal theory, philosophy, and logic were nearly impossible to imitate. That was extremely important. Otherwise, he would have been killed because he was useless to them alive. Except that his writing was so hard to replicate, they had to keep him alive. That is where the ranch came in. Keep him hidden. Feed the cases and arguments to him; have him write his thoughts and opinions; take that same material and twist it around to better suit the decision the Chinese wanted. Actually, it was very simple, and they probably turned out their work a little faster that way than if they did it on their own.

"It worked quite well. Of course, I always knew that someone, somewhere, might slip up, but I simply could not worry about that sort of thing. Which brings me to a question for you, if you will permit?"

Morin smiled. "Sure, you've answered enough for now. Your turn. Go ahead."

"What would you do if this became public knowledge? It would shatter the people's trust and faith in their own government. Did you ever think about that?"

"C'mon," Morin replied. "Those are questions for people higher up than me. I think you've done pretty well tonight."

The cuckoo clock on the mantle called out the hour. Midnight.

"We're on a tight schedule and need to get you out of here. By tomorrow afternoon you and your wife will be together. Won't that be nice, considering how long the two of you have been apart? The Feds will have a lot more questions for you, but you'll be fine."

Voices In The Fog

Morin laughed, and Duarte laughed too. Maybe they believed him. "It'll be like a second honeymoon," he replied.

Morin pointed toward the door. "We need to get you to the airport. There's a plane waiting." Morin opened the door and stepped into the crisp night air. Duarte followed. He never saw the wire garrote the lumberjack slipped around his neck from behind and pulled tight. It was a matter of seconds before Juan Reynosa Duarte fell dead on the damp, clammy soil of the Wyoming mountaintop.

They dragged his lifeless body down by the stream to the wood shredder where they cleared the underbrush earlier. Now, it would spew out Duarte's remains. With the professionalism of slaughterhouse butchers, they dismembered his body and fed it into the shredder. The tiny bits of bone and flesh were sprayed into the fast moving stream.

Duarte went fishing.

CHAPTER TWENTY-ONE

The two young couples laughed and appeared to be in high spirits. The clock on the wall at *Mi Tios Restaurante* showed it to be 11:30. Just another thirty minutes to the midnight closing time. Only one other couple was there, and they were finishing their margaritas. In a few minutes, they would be gone.

The first couple was dressed more casually than the second. His red and blue flowered Hawaiian shirt was loose at the waist. His unshaven face was twisted in laughter, apparently at a joke someone told before they came in. His girlfriend was equally causal. A Georgetown T-shirt, dark shorts and tennis shoes. A heavy backpack swung free in her hand, almost dragging the ground. The second couple was more mature, more businesslike in their appearance. His suit looked expensive, but tired and wrinkled like he wore it all day. He loosened his tie and draped his arm around the neck of the woman who was with him. Her protruding, pregnant stomach looked like she was ready to pop. Her maternity dress was bulging, barely able to reach around the broad girth of her stomach. Nevertheless, her youthful face belied the late hour. She, too, was laughing and seemed to be in high spirits.

The waitress, a beautiful Hispanic woman of about thirty-five years, escorted the four to a booth, smiled and placed the menus in front of them. Dark braids cascaded over the shoulders of her white embroidered blouse.

"What will you have to drink?" She was anxious to close and go home, but a customer is a customer and in spite of the lateness, she treated them with courtesy and respect.

322

Voices In The Fog

"Three beers, whatever you have on tap, and a diet coke for her," responded the man in the suit as he gestured toward the pregnant woman. He placed his briefcase on the floor alongside his seat and leaned back, obviously finished with a strenuous day and ready to relax before going home. "What a day. I thought you'd never get those programs back for me. When that damned computer crashed, I saw my whole life flash before my eyes."

"Yeah," quipped the casually dressed man. "But we recovered almost everything, so now we can relax and be cool. Tomorrow we can sleep late and mellow out the whole day. What do you say, want to go sailing on the Potomac?"

The waitress returned with the drinks. She placed them on the table and glanced casually over her shoulder at the couple leaving from the other table.

"Excuse us guys, but when a pregnant lady needs to go potty, you better get out of her way," the pregnant woman said. Both women slid out of the booth and walked toward the restroom door that was adjacent to the swinging doors to the kitchen.

At the same time, the waitress went to the front door and flipped the "OPEN" sign around. They were closed for the evening. She went to the counter, opened the cash register, and began to balance the tickets and cash. A slightly older man came from the kitchen and joined her. A few moments passed before the two women returned from the restroom to their booth.

"Four, total!" said the pregnant woman. "The two at the cash register, and a cook and dishwasher in the kitchen," said the other.

"Now, let's get it on." It was the man in the suit who gave the orders. He lifted his briefcase onto his lap and opened it. He took a .40 caliber semi-automatic from a holster, handed it under the table to the other man and slipped a second one under his belt. Simultaneously, the two women returned to the restroom. The pregnant woman lifted her dress and removed two more semi-automatics that were strapped beneath the padding on her otherwise flat tummy. She checked them both. They were fully loaded. She switched off the safeties. She held one in the creases of her dress, and the second woman placed hers beneath her purse against her side. They stepped out of the restroom and tossed a quick glance at the men who immediately scooted out of the booth and approached the front counter.

"Yes sir, may I - -." The manager never finished the sentence. The silenced weapons emitted only the slightest *Humph, Humph.* Small, bloody holes exploded in the foreheads of the waitress and manager. They fell to the floor without uttering a sound.

The two women swung open the kitchen doors and fired simultaneously. The pregnant one took the cook, a Hispanic man in his forties and wearing a heavily soiled white jacket. Her single bullet hit just above his left ear. The impact knocked him forward over the stove before his lifeless body landed on the floor. A piece of his skull popped and sizzled on the grill.

The second woman shot the dishwasher, another Hispanic man in his late twenties or early thirties. Her bullet hit his left eye as he turned to see who was coming in the kitchen. He uttered something in Spanish, crashed into the counter top and onto the floor, his unseeing eye staring at the ceiling. There was no need for talk. The four assassins went about their jobs with practiced professionalism. The Georgetown T-shirt woman scurried around the floor and picked up the expended brass from the four guns; the "pregnant" one returned to the bathroom, lifted her dress, and removed the padding – a moldable block of plastic explosives. The casually dressed man returned to the booth and removed from the briefcase some wires, a timer, and a detonator. The second man walked into the kitchen and opened a couple of storeroom doors until he found the utility closet.

"Got it!" he barked. Within seconds, the two men attached the explosives to the gas furnace and another one to the water heater.

After she picked up the four brass shells, the T-shirted woman grabbed her backpack and dumped its contents on the floor — two plastic bottles of gasoline. She hurried to the bodies behind the cash register, doused them, ran a trail of gas from their bodies to the kitchen and onto the other two dead men. She spread the remaining drops around the kitchen. Returning to the dining room, she thoroughly doused the whole room with the second bottle of gas. She stuffed the empty containers back into the pack and walked to the door. They were finished. She looked at her watch. Midnight! Exactly.

"Twelve minutes to boom time," said the man in the suit. "Let's move out to our rendezvous point."

They took napkins and walked around the restaurant, wiping any place they might have touched. With a latex-gloved hand, the man in the suit locked the door behind them. Like any other young couples, they walked arm-in-arm and strolled around the corner to their car.

Thirty minutes later their car was parked in the Pentagon parking lot and they were lifting off from the helipad. The Georgetown T-shirt woman sat in the observer's right front seat of the helicopter. A solitary tear streamed down her face as she flipped open her cell phone and punched in a number. "It's done," she said, when she heard Rod McCarren's voice.

Their course took them above the Potomac toward the Key Bridge – directly over the burning building that once housed *Mi Tios Restaurante*. To some, it might have seemed like an overkill, but the message was delivered. Everyone involved in the deception would be dealt with in the harshest way.

*****

Jesse Rodriquez, the president of the Golden State Corporation, finished his last game at the El Caprice Bowling alley. He carried his bag and shoes to the car, unlocked the trunk, and stashed them away until this same time next week when he would get back into league play. The sound of the trunk being slammed shut covered the hushed pop of the gun. A single bullet passed through the back of his head and sent the hulking six foot, two-hundred-pounder crashing into his car where he fell like a sack of garbage to the ground.

The lone assassin turned and walked away. In five minutes, she would be across the bridge into Mexico. In another ten minutes she would be safely ensconced in her apartment high above the lights and noise of Nuevo Laredo. She had done her part, but she couldn't help but be more than a little curious about why? And, who else? What had he, or they, done to receive such retribution? Such was her profession. Little did she know, but only who and when, and, of course, for what amount.

*****

Voices In The Fog

Roldolpho Martinez, the Treasurer of Golden State, sat nude on the edge of his swimming pool. His feet dangled in the water. He kicked them slowly back and forth and watched the tiny ripples expand out across the pool. It was a beautiful evening. His wife and two teenage daughters had gone to New York to see a Broadway play and to shop on Fifth Avenue. Always Fifth Avenue! They had to go there to spend whatever allowance he provided, and it was ample. Shoes, watches, blouses, you name it and they bought it. Of course, they would go to the Today Show and stand in the crowd, hoping to be on television. They had fun, and he had fun giving them the opportunities to do the things his parents were never able to provide for him.

It is said that a person never hears the shot that kills him, and that must be true. Roldolpho's head cracked open from a high velocity gunshot from somewhere on the hillside behind the house. One moment he was alive, reliving pleasant memories about his family. The next, his lifeless body sank to the bottom of the pool, spewing his brains and blood into the crystal clear water.

*****

Willie Lim, the Secretary of the corporation, slept soundly. Darlene, his wife of only three months slept beside him. Willie was curled up in a fetal position with the sheet pulled up, leaving his small, coconut-shaped head protruding from it on the pillow. Darlene lay flat on her back. The sheet covered her feet, but her voluptuous, naked body shone in the reflection of the moon filtering through the window. Her gorgeous body looked down at them from the mirrored ceiling. The dark velvet between her legs; her

327

firm breasts covered with massage oil from their lovemaking.

Like Roldolpho, they heard nothing. The two gunmen stepped to opposite sides of the bed. The man on Darlene's side of the bed leaned forward and placed the muzzle of his gun directly between her breasts. Those beautiful breasts, never again to be suckled by a man.

Total silence except for the gentle breathing of the newlyweds. The assassin on Willie's side of the bed threw a quick glance at his counterpart, then back at the sleeping Willie. He nodded, and they fired. *Humph, Humph.*

Darlene sat up and screamed. The gunman jumped back and laughed. He saw this before. It was strictly a spontaneous, central nervous system reaction. She didn't even realize she was dead. Just as quickly as she sat up, she relaxed and rolled off the bed. Dead! Nevertheless, the assassin fired a second bullet, this one into the back of her head. He stepped back and watched the dark, red blood ooze from the wound and soak her long blond hair, then flow in a steady and gentle manner onto the carpeted floor.

The two men made their way through the house to the back door and into the alley behind the house. They opened the gate as a car made its way toward them, moving at a slow crawl. They opened the passenger side doors and got in without the car coming to a stop. When it reached the end of the alley, the driver turned on the lights and they drove away, blending into the late night traffic across the border.

*****

It was just after midnight when the rental van pulled up to the locked gate at Golden State Distributors. The passenger hopped out, carrying a set of bolt cutters. Seconds later, the gates were pushed open and the truck approached the loading dock. The passenger ran ahead and guided the driver in backing the truck to the loading dock.

The driver pulled a cord that extended into the cab from the back of the truck. The strong, pungent odor of burning fuse instantly filled the cab. Their work was done. The driver bolted out of the truck and joined the passenger, then both jogged toward the gate. A minivan pulled up when they reached the open gate. Someone inside slid the side door open and they climbed in and drove away from Golden State.

Minutes later, they dropped their quarters into the turnstile slot at the international bridge and walked into Mexico. They were nearly across the Rio Grande when they heard the rolling thunder of the one-thousand pound bomb they planted at the loading dock. Everyone on the bridge turned to see the sky brighten in a reddish orange fireball from the industrial park, the former home of Golden State Distributors.

CHAPTER TWENTY-TWO

The T-38 taxied into a hangar and Ann Marie saw a large clock on the wall. Twelve-forty-five. She pulled off the helmet and facemask when the canopies opened. The fresh air was a delight compared to the hot stuffiness of the jet. For the first time in an hour, she felt the slightest bit of tension ease out of her muscles. Maybe, just maybe, she was adjusting to her new role.

In an instant, her body tensed again; her toes and legs cramped; her shoulder ached; her throat went dry, lips cracked. What a horrible thought. She was getting used to the role of a killer. They might be able to use different terminology, but killing is killing, and something she never wanted to get used to doing. Not for any cause. She would never be the same person again.

Simultaneously, she realized her actions were leading to the maintenance and stability of the American government. People would die, but that was the price of freedom. She would survive tonight and go on with her life. She would not look back over her shoulder wondering, "What if?" Her decision was made that day so long ago at the academy. She knew then, and she knew now, that she was a moral person doing what she could to prevent an even greater wrong from occurring. Tonight people would die and her hands would be bloodied, but she was doing all she could do to minimize an ever-greater wrong from happening.

She closed her eyes and took a deep breath, then climbed down the ladder that a ground crewman affixed to the plane.

For the second time tonight, she found herself strapping the seat and shoulder harness in a helicopter. She grew accustomed to the routine. The whirring sound of the engine; the rhythmic whomp-whomp-whomp of the rotor blades; the forward tilt and rocking sensation of the helicopter lifting its skids from the ground; and, finally, the ascent into the dark sky. Away from the base; away from the city lights of San Antonio; into the eerie darkness of the desert; on to a rendezvous with the Grim Reaper in the Mexican desert.

It was less than an hour when the helicopter started its descent into the blackness of the Texas desert. She saw the lights from a truck come on, lighting an open area where they could land. The chopper swung around into the wind. That was the first time she could see the other aircraft. An Apache was following them to the landing zone, but the other Hueys and two Apaches continued on to the south. By the time she landed, the other choppers were out of sight, flying low toward the frontier.

The side hatch slid open. A man in military fatigues spoke. "Ma'am, I'm Felipe O'Malley." His voice was broken English, what she called Spanglish. He continued, "A doctor will be joining you for the rest of the trip. I am the mission *commandante*. I shall be with you for only a short while."

O'Malley jumped into the seat across from her and stuffed his pack beneath his seat. He looked back at the truck to see a person climbing down from the rear cargo area.

Ann Marie saw a small, fragile looking man dart from the truck while the rotors slowed and allowed the dust to settle. He hurtled past the military figure and landed in a heap on the floor.

"Damn, shit, hell," he bellowed. "I hate dust. I have allergies." He looked up at the strikingly attractive woman in her military fatigues and offered a sheepish grin. "I'll be sneezing for the next twenty-four hours."

Ann Marie couldn't help but return the man's infectious smile. "Here, let me help you get buckled up." She grabbed his arm and was surprised how muscular he was. He sat on the seat next to her while a military figure stood outside, leaned in, and pushed what looked to her like a dark medical bag under the seats.

"Hope you don't need it, *senor*, but better safe than sorry." He reached over and shut the hatch.

The helicopters lifted off, south toward Mexico — south to retrieve the Honorable Justice Ricardo Huerta Gonzales.

They rode in silence, each cognizant of the duties they were about to carry out, but also aware that in their world secrecy was the by-word. They did not know each other, and in all likelihood, would never meet again.

Ann Marie was aware of the low altitude they were flying. She peered out the window as they skimmed over the tops of mesquite trees, then she saw the starlight glistening off the murky waters of the Rio Grande River a few feet below them. The chopper bounced in an unexpected wind, and came perilously close to the ground. She caught herself gasping at what she thought surely was going to be her last breath, but the pilot quickly gained control and they continued south, then turned to the southwest.

Minutes later, they landed in an open field. From what little she could see, they were miles from anywhere. Nevertheless, she knew they were almost at their destination. The other helicopters were already there, their engines still running; the rotors turning slowly like giant arms swatting at mosquitoes. No sooner did her Huey and the Apache land than a dozen dark- clad figures jumped out of the first Huey. They hunkered beneath the twirling rotor blades and began an easy jog across the dark desert landscape. They were one mile from the ranch house.

*****

Cowboy Joe and Williams sat at the control panel beneath El Capitan Mountain. It was two-twenty in the morning. They were right on schedule. The Scout hovered at five hundred feet a quarter mile west of the isolated ranch house. Cowboy tilted the camera lens up and refocused to see the gatehouse in the distance. He scanned around counter-clockwise. Far away, he made out the infrared heat patterns of the helicopters. They were on the ground.

The two men sat in silence, each with his private thoughts. They watched the assault group close in on the ranch. They were within a stone's throw of the house when the first Apache lifted off and went to the gatehouse.

With blinding speed, the chopper zoomed directly toward the guardhouse and loosed its rockets and machine guns into the building. The light of the explosions blinded the camera. Moments later, the fire died down. Cowboy and Williams saw the charred remains of the building and the pickup truck that was parked in front of it. Less than three hours ago, two guards relieved the others who went back to the house for the night. Now, they were dead. Just like the four at *Mi Tios*, and the other four in Laredo. The attack group hit the two houses at the precise moment the rockets hit the gatehouse. The assault team came in from three sides. They lobbed flash-bang grenades and high tech hydro-stink bombs through the windows – all of the windows except the one to Gonzales' bedroom.

Voices In The Fog

The flash-bangs were bright and loud, the explosive sound of dynamite. They caused anyone near where they landed to be stunned for a few moments, or possibly deafened for life. The hydro-stink grenades, one of the newest additions to their arsenal, were ultra-putrid stink weapons; so powerfully strong that even the bravest of men would have only two reactions, puke and get away! Between them, the grenades that were thrown through the windows disabled the guards. With any luck at all, the judge might be scared out of his wits, but he would be safe.

The masked assault team entered the houses with programmed exactitude. They walked methodically through the buildings, room-to-room, closet to closet, and their automatic weapons spitting .223 bullets at the rate of seven hundred rounds per minute. It was over in a matter of seconds. Three men and the woman were dead or dying. Only the Honorable Ricardo Huerta Gonzales remained alive – they hoped.

O'Malley opened his pack and pulled out gas masks for each of them. He tossed them across the darkened compartment to Ann Marie and the doctor.

She studied hers for a second and recognized it as the standard mask she and her fellow trainees used at Quantico, a broad polyurethane lens to provide a full 180-degree field of vision; a soft rubber faceplate; and, a dual air canister filter system. She pulled the straps over her hair, and with a gentle tug, fitted the faceplate down with a tight seal to protect her, not from poison gases, but from the nauseous odor of the hydra-stink grenades.

Their helicopter touched down on the north side of the house. The timing was exact. The team entered the house only moments earlier. O'Malley slid the door open while she loosened her harnesses. She caught herself biting her lip and squinting into the horror that filled the night air: the staccato sound of gunfire from inside the house, the muzzle flashes in the otherwise darkened windows. She listened for the sound of screams, but the noise from the Huey and the incessant firing from the assault team drowned out any human sound – if there was any at all. They struck with such blinding speed that the guards were helpless to respond.

O'Malley was on the ground looking back and motioning for her to follow him. She took a deep breath. The swooshing sound of the filter system echoed in her ears. She scooted out of her seat and put her feet on the Mexican soil, a simple political fact that did not escape her.

Ann Marie suddenly was aware of an eerie silence. The gunfire stopped. The helicopter rotors slowed to a soft and gentle hum, not a single human sound emanated from the houses. It was over! Only the slightest stench of the grenades and of the dozens of rounds of expended rounds floated in the night air.

Ann Marie followed in O'Malley's footsteps when he hopped over the patio wall and went to the front door. The sound of her boots crunched on the shards of broken glass and splinters from the shattered doorframe. She followed him into the front room. The only lights were from red laser sights on the gun barrels as the assault team moved through the house. Narrow penetrating beams of bright lights from their helmet lanterns flashed in her eyes as they opened doors and looked behind the furniture. O'Malley flicked on the light switch inside the front door, but nothing happened. They shot out the electrical system.

She freed her flashlight from the loop on her belt, turned it on, and looked around the living room. The couch and chairs were ripped apart by the firepower that was loosened toward the man who apparently was asleep on the couch. His lifeless body slumped from beneath a blanket and hung over the side, his head and shoulders nearly ripped from his torso, blood and tissue lumped in the floor and sprayed over the wall, picture frames blasted and hung askew on the wall beside the fireplace.

The shouted voice of the assault team leader was muffled. *"No esta aqui!"* He came toward them from the hallway, stepping over broken pieces of wallboard and plaster that littered the floor. He moved directly in front of O'Malley. *"Chingale! El senor no esta aqui."*

Ann Marie understood him perfectly. The judge was gone.

O'Malley unsnapped the radio from his lapel with one hand and jerked the walkie-talkie from his belt with the other. He turned abruptly on his heel and went outside with Ann Marie in pursuit. He sat on the edge on the porch and adjusted his radio knobs until he flipped the squelch and got a squelch return, then tossed his gas mask on the ground. He was in contact with Rucinski.

Ann Marie stood over him with her hands on her hips, her eyes piercing through the Plexiglas shield. Sweat poured from her brow, her breath was labored. How could they have lost the judge?

She lifted her mask, then detected the strong odor from the house and put it back down over her face.

"Swamp, this is mosquito. How do you read?" O'Malley said.

Rucinski answered. "Five by five, mosquito. We saw the landing but lost our observations after the first explosions. What is your status?"

"We're searching, but no sign of our target. Did you have anything before we got here?"

"That's negative. Last saw him in his quarters. That was about three hours before you were on scene."

"And nothing else? Nobody came or went? No vehicular movement?" O'Malley asked.

"That's negative. No movement or activity. We're positive he wasn't in the guardhouse. He never went there, and sure didn't tonight." Rucinski's voice was calm and steady. "Checking our notes, he was lights out in his room at 2313 hours and no movement from him after that. We never lost sight of the house or the apartment."

O'Malley looked up at Ann Marie and shrugged. "We'll get him," he said.

She nodded agreement, but felt the sweat run down her back. She was hot and cold at the same time and knew she wasn't sick. Her lips tingled nervously. They were so close. What happened? How could they have lost Gonzales?

Rucinski was back on the radio. "Guards swapped positions at 2345 hours. The female went to her quarters at 2330 hours. Other guards had lights out in the main house at triple zero-five. One was on the couch and one in the back bedroom."

"We account for them," O'Malley replied. "But negative on the target." He got up and snapped the radio onto his belt and spoke into the speaker. "Get back to you in a few minutes."

"*Commandante!*" One of his men shouted as he ran from the apartment at the rear of the property. He pulled his mask off and hung it on his belt. He panted and wiped his brow with the back of his hand. "It's the woman," he pointed. "She's still alive. Do you want to try to talk to her?"

O'Malley brushed past the rifleman and trotted toward the apartment with Ann Marie once again in pursuit. They

337

reached the door where another member of their troop was waiting.

"In there," he pointed. "On the bedroom floor. Looks like she tried to hide under the bed before we got here." He nodded his head. "She's bad, but if you hurry - - "

Ann Marie grabbed O'Malley's arm and pulled him back from the door. "I'll do it," she said as she threw her mask on the ground. She shone her flashlight on the living room furniture that was knocked over, stepped into the hallway, then shoved aside the light fixture that dangled from the ceiling in front of her face. A guard stood at the bedroom door. He pointed with a nod of his head. She stepped past him into the bedroom.

Marisa Duarte lay on the floor, her blood pouring out onto the throw rug where she was gasping for breath. She was halfway on her back and side, twisted from the impact of countless bullets. Her eyes were wide in shock and terror.

Ann Marie knelt beside her. The warmth of the blood soaked her trousers. She held the light into her own face and slipped her other hand under Duarte's head and lifted it slightly. "*Quiere agua?*" she asked. The old lady nodded and touched her lips with her tongue. Ann Marie looked over her shoulder as one of the soldiers unscrewed the lid of his canteen and handed it to her. She tipped it gently to the woman's lips and allowed a few drops to wet her tongue.

Ann Marie looked back and barked an order. "Give me a cloth."

The same soldier pulled his neck scarf loose with a whip of his wrist and handed it to her. She soaked it, then wiped Duarte's face, cleaning the grime from her cheeks and forehead. She leaned down, placing her face directly above the badly wounded woman. *"Donde esta el senor Gonzales?"* she whispered. *"Donde esta?"*

Duarte tried to speak, but choked and faltered. Ann Marie again touched her face with the wet cloth and allowed a few drops of water to wet her parched throat.

"Gracias," the woman said. Her voice cracked.

Ann Marie leaned closer to hear Duarte's nearly imperceptible voice. *"Donde esta el?"* she said.

"Abajo," the woman whispered. *"En la cama."*

O'Malley stood behind the soldier, but leaned past him toward Agent Beaudet. "What did she say?" he inquired.

Ann Marie moved slowly and lowered the woman's head back to the floor, then looked up at O'Malley. "I think he's beneath the bedroom floor or under the bed. I'm not sure, but I think that's what she meant."

She stood up and looked directly at O'Malley. "You've done your job, but he's mine. I'll find him. That's my responsibility." She started out of the bedroom and looked back at Mrs. Duarte lying in a pool of blood. "What about her?"

"That's my job," he replied.

Ann Marie stepped past him and went to the yard, this time with O'Malley following in her footsteps. They went only a half-dozen steps toward the main house when a shot rang out behind them. She froze, then slowly turned to look directly into O'Malley's eyes.

"Don't say a damned thing," he commanded. "You do your job, and we do ours!"

She turned quickly away and walked to the house, her every step an exclamation of her authority and responsibility. She opened the back door to the kitchen where two soldiers stood with their weapons slung over their shoulders. The one closest to her spoke. "We looked everywhere. Closets. Under the kitchen cabinets. In the crawl space above the ceiling. Everywhere, and there's no basement. He's not here."

"Well, we'll just have to look harder," she snapped. "Follow me!" She walked the few steps down the nearly demolished hallway and turned into the judge's bedroom. O'Malley stood beside her as they shone their lights around the room. It was exactly as she saw it when the Scout peered into Gonzales' inner sanctum. The twin bed against the east wall. Its blankets and sheet appeared to have been tossed about as though he was in bed. The sink and toiletries were on the opposite west wall. The desk and chair were in place against the north wall, a chest of drawers next to his desk, the closet door ajar.

"We looked in there," a soldier said when O'Malley shone his light in it. Nevertheless, the commander got on his knees and tapped the floor with his knuckles, starting on one side and working methodically to the other, listening for a hollow echo. There was none.

Taking his lead, two soldiers began moving the furniture to look beneath it, tapping and looking for evidence of a shelter. As they moved the desk, Ann Marie looked at the bed. "Here," she commanded as she took hold of the headboard and began to scoot the bed aside. She grunted. It was heavy, too heavy. The soldiers looked at her, and at the same time, they all came to the same realization. They took hold of the outer edge of the bed frame and lifted. It folded up!

She flicked the beam of her light into the darkened spider hole beneath the floor. The man, curled into a fetal position so he could fit into the cramped space, gazed up at her with bulging, panic filled eyes.

Voices In The Fog

"Mr. Justice Gonzales," she said softly as she leaned down on her knees and reached for his hand with hers, "we're here to take you home."

"Your honor," one of the men said. "You're free." He and O'Malley reached past her and slipped their hands beneath his armpits and lifted the shaking and terrified man from his protective shelter and on to the floor of his bedroom. He wore only a military green T-shirt and boxer shorts. He wrapped his thin arms around himself in a vague gesture of modesty.

"We can find some clothes for you when we get airborne," Ann Marie told him, gently, leading him out of the bedroom of the house that had held him prisoner for so many years. They stepped into the hallway where Gonzales choked, gagged, and threw up. A guard lay dead at their feet, nearly beheaded by the blast of firepower that was loosed on him. The two rescuers glanced at each other, and in the silent communication from those who have worked together before, they lifted Gonzales into a sitting position in their arms. "Close your eyes," one of them said. Gonzales did as directed, and even laid his head back on the man's shoulder and closed out the world of mayhem he was leaving behind. They walked into the fresh air. His rescuers set him on his feet and wiped the sweat from his face with one of their kerchiefs.

"It's over, sir. You're free." One on either side, they held him by his arms and led him to Ann Marie's helicopter. His short legs barely touched the ground as the two men moved hastily to take him from his personal hell and to get themselves out of there before anyone else knew what happened.

"I'm taking you home, sir," she shouted over the whip of wind that rained down on them from the now churning rotor blades. "On behalf of the President of the United States, welcome home."

She climbed into the chopper and helped the two men lift him into the Coleet seat. She hooked his seat belt, looked at him, and smiled. "Welcome back, your honor."

O'Malley stepped to the side of the chopper and reached in to shake her hand. "You did well." The wisp of a smile creased his face. Then he looked at the judge as the doctor wrapped him in a blanket. *"Bienvenido, senor!"* He tipped his cap in a salute and nodded.

Ann Marie last saw him walking toward the shattered remains of the ranch, shaking hands with the shock troops as they walked to the other helicopter.

CHAPTER TWENTY-THREE

Secretary of State Casper Rawlins arrived at the Panamanian Embassy after midnight. Ambassador Rafael Punto-Garza sat at his desk smoking a very good quality Cuban cigar. He watched the trail of smoke waft upward, sweep around the ceiling fan, and dissipate into the ventilation system.

"This is not good news, Mr. Secretary," he said. He turned and nodded to an aide. "A glass of wine, Secretary Rawlins?" he asked. The aide brought a bottle of Cabernet.

"A true joy of the fruit of the vine. Will you join me?" The aide, dressed in a crisp white jacket and tie, uncorked the bottle and poured a taste in a glass for the Ambassador.

"A very special wine." Punto-Garza smiled. "Compliments of my good friends at the French Embassy. Yes, you may pour," he said. He looked at Rawlins, then with great study and care, stubbed out the cigar in an ashtray. His expression belied his thoughts. His lips were pursed; his brow was furrowed.

He looked again at Rawlins, lifted the glass, and spoke. "FromVin du Pays Nantis, an exceptional wine for a truly extraordinary moment. I never trusted those Chinese. They are bastards, you know."

There was a long pause. "So these documents prove the companies who have signed contracts to oversee the management of the canal are nothing more than front organizations for the Chinese government?"

"Absolutely." Rawlins responded.

The ambassador threw a glance at his military attaché. "*Generale*? Your comments?"

"My staff spent yesterday and tonight going over the American documents. We have communicated with our

Intelligence Service, and went to extreme lengths in verifying the accuracy of the American claims, going so far as to use cryptic sources in other governments." He held his ramrod straight stance when he spoke, but sweat dampened his brow.

"Ambassador, we agree with the Americans. The contractors provided false information to obtain the contracts for the canal. Therefore, our President is totally within his legal right to declare the contracts null and void. In fact, it is the opinion not only of my staff and me, but of the governments we used to validate the American allegation. We must not hesitate. We must take immediate control of the canal. Not a minute must pass that we are not aggressively taking back the canal from the Chinese."

Punto-Garza nodded his approval and handed the documents to an aide. "Forward these immediately to *El Presidente*. In the meantime, I will discuss the situation with him over the telephone."

He rose and extended a handshake to the Secretary of State. "Thank you, Mr. Secretary. My country seeks nothing more than good international relations with all people. Nevertheless, we cannot and will not accept the chicanery of the Chinese to take control of this most important waterway. I assure you, and please relay our message to President Summers, that our National Police Force will take control of the Panama Canal and all of the other properties immediately."

Gray dawn broke through the coastal fog when the contingent of U. S. Marshals and Marine Corps Military Police, headed by the Deputy United States Attorney for the Southern District of California, swooped down on the Long Beach Naval Shipyard. With quiet efficiency, they replaced the civilian guards at the gates and took control of the administrative offices that were spread far and wide over the sprawling naval base. Again, the front company for the Chinese was quickly and effectively displaced.

In the time span of less than twelve hours, the Chinese front organization was dismembered. Its parts were thrown to the four winds. They were gone, but not forgotten, and not very likely to return.

As surely as the cold winds swept down from the Taihang Mountain Range into the valleys below, reaching out its icy fingers over the glazed towers of Huixiang City with its fountains and temples, bringing winter's grasp to the provinces below, Lin Nuy would return. Where? When? The answers to those questions would remain for another day.

*****

The U. S. Air Force Boeing 737 lumbered to a stop outside a commercial hangar at the Sheridan, Wyoming airport. It was not all that unusual for military aircraft to be in and out, since so many government officials vacationed in the mountains. There was always someone coming or going. In fact, many townspeople speculated there was a hidden shelter somewhere high in the mountains where there was a secret government hideaway. The early morning arrival did not arouse any unusual excitement. It was just another plane and nothing more. Ann Marie looked at her watch. Six-thirty exactly. She caught a couple hours sleep after they left Lackland Air Force Base in San Antonio, but it was a long, hard night. One that she hoped would never be replicated. The judge was given clean clothes before they left Lackland. He was curled up in his seat, sound asleep. Dr. Bergstein, as she came to know him, gave the judge a sedative after they boarded the plane and he slept the length of the trip.

They wrapped the judge in a warm jacket, pulled a stocking cap down over his head against the bite of the morning chill, and with the help of the flight crew, guided him to the Suburban parked on the tarmac.

Adolphus and Ann Marie silently acknowledged each other before they guided Gonzales' exhausted body into the back seat. He staggered like the town drunk. Nothing could have prepared him for what he went through in the years past, and even less for what he went through last night.

Morin drove while Gonzales and the doctor sat in the back seat. Ann Marie opened the mirror on the sun visor over the passenger's seat and looked at herself. She wasn't surprised at what she saw. Warmed over death. Scraggly hair, no makeup, bags beneath her bloodshot eyes. Never had she looked so mentally and physically wrung out.

The ride down Mud Coulee rousted Gonzales from his slumber. He stretched, yawned, and looked at the surrounding countryside. He glanced at the doctor, then patted her shoulder. His voice was soft. "Thank you from the bottom of my heart. I owe my life to you." He leaned back, lowered his window, and took a deep breath. "I'm alive again."

*****

The morning sun dried the night dew by the time they reached Mud Coulee House. They bounced to a stop in the very same spot where only hours earlier the imposter took the final steps in his infamous journey.

The two lumberjacks opened the door and helped the exhausted judge from the back seat and introduced themselves. The first of the two was the living image of Grizzly Adams. "Good morning, sir," he said. "I'm Tony Morehouse with the Marshal's Service." They shook hands and Tony continued. "We're aware of the difficulty of the situation, but each of us is here to work with you and to help you re-integrate back into society."

He turned to his colleague and spoke, "This is my co-worker, Andy Lone Eagle. He's a member of the White Mountain Apache tribe in Arizona."

"Honored to meet you, your honor." Andy and the Judge shook hands and walked toward the cabin.

A refreshing spark of life zapped through Gonzales. He was safe and on familiar ground. "White Mountain Apache, huh? Been there many times, long ago." He looked at the young Apache and smiled. "Hawley Lake, that's where I used to go fishing. Been there, I suppose?"

"Yes, sir," Andy replied. "We lived in White River. My dad raised some cattle and sheep, so I learned cowboying real early. Hard work. Hey, I can't complain. It paid for my pickup truck and a few dates, so what the hell. But Judge, we're not here to talk about me. We're here to help you get back where you belong."

"I appreciate that, Andy. I will never be able to thank you enough."

Gonzales stopped. He turned slowly and looked at the towering pines, their tops swaying with the light breeze of the warming day. The sky was a crystal clear blue. He sucked in a long deep breath and held it as long as he could.

"Wonderful," he said as he exhaled. A smile swept across his face.

Monarch butterflies swooped and fluttered around a half-dozen or more hummingbird feeders, their golden colors wrapped in delicate threads of black and white. They danced a graceful ultra-light ballet with the hummingbirds that zipped in and out with lightning speed.

"Excuse me, gentlemen," the Judge said. "I want to enjoy the moment. It will never pass this way again. I must immerse myself in it. The years have been long and hard, but I am back. Back to my beloved Wyoming." He laughed and stripped off his hat and coat. He slipped his hands into his pockets and walked a few steps toward the stream. As if on command from a higher being, a rainbow trout broke the surface and snatched a tiny bug into its mouth.

"Oh God, what a sight. Something I thought I would never again experience." He turned to his benefactors. Tears poured from his eyes. He gasped for breath, but struggled to speak. "My friends, I will - -" He stopped, unable to express himself, torn between the joy of the moment and the horror of recent times. He moved to the edge of the water, squatted down and allowed the water to course its way through his fingertips. He splashed it on his face, lightly at first, and then with more vigor. "My God," he exclaimed. "My God, I do not use your name in vain." He stood and looked up beyond the trees into the blue sky. "I use your name in Eucharist. In adoration. My God, my God. You did not forsake me, and I will offer you my everlasting gratitude.

"My friends, shall we?" He walked to the front door. The others followed. A procession of Justice Gonzales, Tony, Ann Marie, Andy, Dr. Bergstein, Grizzly Adams, and Adolphus Morin.

"Just as I remembered it. Do I have the same bedroom?" He glanced at Ann Marie.

Voices In The Fog

"Everything is the same. Exactly as it should be," she responded. She followed Gonzales to his room, opened the closet and commented.

"We did the best we could on pretty short notice. Anyhow, whatever you need that we don't have, I'm sure we can get for you." She opened a second closet. "In here, they stored some fishing gear for you. I'm not into it, but I understand this is quite the rod for the stream out front." She lifted a rod from a rack in the closet and gave it to him.

"My friend," Gonzales said, "what have we here? A one-weight rod? Oh my goodness, young lady. I'm not sure I'm good enough to handle this delicate level of fishing after so many years of living in that damned desert." He hung the rod back on the rack. "Please excuse me, but I do not know your name."

"I'm sorry, sir, for not introducing myself. I just got caught up in all the action of the night. My name is Ann Marie Beaudet, and it has been my job to find you."

"Thank God." Gonzales said fervently.

She stepped to the door, taking a moment to speak. "Mr. Gonzales, we want to begin immediately to help you in your re-integration, but first, why don't you take as much time as you want. The water in the shower is good and hot; the sheets are clean. When you're ready, we'll start to work."

*****

It was only an hour before the squeaky clean and well shaven Judge came out to join his saviors. He had a somber expression on his face.

"First things first," he exclaimed. "Do I cook, or do one of you?"

349

"Whatever you want," Morin responded. He lifted himself from the couch where he napped. "One of my many talents." He walked to the kitchen, looking back at Gonzales.

"Steak, a baked potato, refried beans, and a salad - - with Blue Cheese," Gonzales replied.

"Coming up. What to drink?"

"Right now I would like a glass of milk. And then, if you will excuse me, I'm going fishing." Moments later he was out the door, wading boots over his shoes and pants, snapping on a fishing vest and toting his newly found friend, a one-weight Orvis rod.

Ann Marie pulled up a lawn chair on the front porch and watched. Gonzales took cautious steps into the water, stepping over boulders to mid-stream. He looked back at her, tossed a friendly wave, and turned his attention to the stream. He played out the line, did two or three false casts, and then placed a dry fly up stream from a tree branch that fell into the water on the far side of the stream. She watched as his first cast landed against the rocks in mid-stream. Gonzales immediately hauled it in, played out the line a second time, and presented it perfectly onto the water's surface. The fly was swept up in a seam between the ripples and the smooth water and disappeared into the mouth of a fish. The trout shot free from the water, did a flip, and dove down into the rocks. The fly rod bent over. The line whirled from the reel. Gonzales slipped, but caught his balance on a rock and began hauling in the line. The fish jumped again and did a back flip into the water. Gonzales let some line out and watched his fish shoot back beneath the tree limb. With the touch of the master, he once again began to haul in the line; rod tip elevated; line taut; smooth, easy hauling on the line; never too tight; never too loose. The minutes crawled by, but finally, the rainbow surrendered. Gonzales was careful not to hurt the fish. He eased it into the net and with an expertise he maintained over the years, loosened the barbless hook from the fish's lip.

She watched with sheer joy. The Judge and the trout were almost mystical. Out there in the middle of the stream, a moment of truth was played out. Gonzales held the trout in the water; the cold water flowed over its gills. His soft fingers massaged the big rainbow. It allowed itself to be held captive, if only for this brief period of time. Gonzales slowed the gentle stroking of the fish, and as if exactly on cue, the trout shot free. Back into the depths of the mountain stream. Gonzales smiled.

"Another time, my friend. Another time. But for now, there is nothing like one's freedom."

*****

Gonzales' reputation as a workaholic was an understatement. Nights and days became a blur. He hurried through the mandatory physical and psychological tests, taking an occasional time out for a shower and nap. The bureau shuttled experts on psychological rehabilitation in and out of Mud Coulee, but each left in amazement at Gonzales' resiliency. His survival skills were remarkable. His ability to concentrate and to focus on the issue was unsurpassed. Everything she read about him was true. He possessed an uncanny mind.

Ann Marie debriefed one of the psychologists before he left the mountain.

"Never have I met anyone quite like him," he remarked. "The years of imprisonment did nothing to tarnish his mental or social acuity." He laughed. "Too bad for the bad guys that they had to select one of the most outstanding mental gymnasts in the world. It's fortunate for them that he didn't have them eating out of his hand. In all of my research, I have never heard of a person with such ability to take part not only in social intercourse, but also to have such an extreme level of mental tolerance for problem solving."

He shook his head. "This man is a genius in more ways than one. Oh, but what sorrow I have."

"Why?" she interjected.

"For the simple reason that this great event will go undocumented in scientific journals. What a scholarly paper this would make. It doesn't seem right that this is a story all of us will take to our graves. What a loss," he moaned.

Three days of tests passed before Ann Marie and Morin took their first real opportunity to interview Gonzales. Adolphus poured each of them a soft drink, and they gathered around the kitchen table. She laid out note pads and a tape recorder, then kicked off her shoes and sat on her feet, Indian-style. "Mr. Justice - -"

Gonzales immediately waved her off. "No, not here. Later yes, but for now can we just be friends? Miss Beaudet, Aldolphus and me, Ricardo, if you will," he commanded.

"Very well Mr.- - excuse me, Ricardo," she said. "Please start at the very beginning. How did they kidnap you?"

"A good place to start," he responded. Gonzales sipped his drink and pushed back from the table. They watched him walk to the liquor cabinet. He studied the bottles on the shelf with great intensity. He picked up a bottle of Jack

Daniels, read the label, put it back and took a bottle of Triple Sec. Like the first, he studied it, and then replaced it on the shelf. He finally settled on the big red-labeled Makers Mark.

"This will do," he said. He returned to his chair with an empty glass that he promptly filled to the halfway point. "It is hard." He sipped the whiskey and looked out the window. The butterflies and hummingbirds continued their delicate ballet.

"There are few things I put out of my mind, but I did it for good reason. Never did I expect to face such abject terror. It was so sudden." He stopped and looked at his drink. "May I have some ice?"

Ann Marie brought an ice bucket, and as she dropped two ice cubes into his glass she was aware that he was straining to hold back his tears. His eyes were red and watery. He was strong beyond belief, but that one day, the day they kidnapped him, he reached his breaking point. Today, maybe today, he would do it again.

He took a deep breath. "Where were we? Oh yes. Black Sunday. That's what I called it. Black Sunday! Remember the movie? The apocalypse at the Super Bowl?

"No, I don't think I do," she said.

"I don't either," Morin replied.

"It was my Black Sunday. My personal apocalypse: a day in which I was aware of how my life could be over in a matter of seconds. But, I persevered. I have always been a rather resolute person," he chuckled. "It has been so many years, but let me not get ahead of myself. The beginning - - "

Gonzales spoke until the early hours of the morning. He attended Sunday services at Christ Church and walked home. His usual pattern. Nothing different. Nothing unusual or suspicious. Nothing that is, except the moving crew that was parked along Cameron Street. Moving crews normally do not work on Sundays, but maybe this was an exception. One of the men was holding a box and stepped aside for him. Suddenly, that man and two others grabbed him, threw a padded blanket over him and shoved him into the truck. He lay there for what seemed like hours, bound and gagged in the summer heat. Eventually, he heard voices over the scraping and shoving of furniture being boxed in around him.

"*Vamonos*," he heard.

He felt as if he was suffocating. The truck started moving, and he floated in and out of consciousness from the stifling heat and lack of fresh air. He awakened later, with no idea where he was. He was bound hand and foot, blindfolded, and was on a dirt floor. He heard voices speaking Spanish from another room. At some point, a woman came to him. She helped him eat and drink, but never removed the bonds or the blindfold. He could only guess he was there for at least one if not two days. Too long to be able to maintain his self control, and he urinated on himself several times.

On what he believed was the third day, the woman fed him and then made a grumbled comment to someone else in the room. Gonzales felt the sting of a needle in his arm and immediately felt the drug take effect. He tried to maintain consciousness, but quickly surrendered to the serenity of a deep sleep.

He had no concept of time. When he first was fully conscious of his surroundings, he was lying in his underwear on the bed in the same bedroom from which he was rescued. There, in that house, he stayed as their prisoner. No newspapers. No television. No radio. Minimal intelligent conversation with his captors. Intellectually and mentally, it was a living hell.

Considering he was a prisoner, he was treated humanely. Food, clean sheets every week; a modest supply of utilitarian type clothes – not anything fashionable, but he was clean and neat for the surroundings; an occasional cigar; and, to some extent, he was treated with a modest degree of hospitality. He and his captors became respectful with each other over a period of time, but certainly were not friends. He was free to roam about the house and the immediate grounds, but never strayed more than a hundred yards from the front door.

When court was in session, he lived in front of the word processor they provided for him. He quickly figured out what they were doing and considered the possibility of refusing to write for them, but decided if he refused, his life would be worthless. So, in an effort to out-fox the fox, he invented his own code, hopeful it would somehow escape detection and eventually lead to his freedom. Unfortunately, that was not to be. It was with a heavy heart he eventually abandoned his pathetic code and accepted his status, prayerfully hoping for a brighter future.

An occasional private aircraft landed; there would be what looked like a serious conference between his captors and the people from the plane; sometimes someone from the plane stayed overnight; but, essentially, they came and went. He was always locked in his room or sent to the small house in the backyard. A guard was always with him when he was there, but it generally did not last more than an hour or two. Four times over the years he was directed to the shelter beneath his floor when a plane came in. He never asked, and they offered no explanations – just sometimes he was ordered to lift the bed and slip into his darkened hell on earth.

He inferred over a period of time that the plane was bringing instructions for his "care and feeding" as he referred to it. Nevertheless, he was always struck with a slight anxiety attack when he heard the plane. Even though he developed a certain comfort zone as a prisoner, he recognized that at some point he would lose his value to them. When that happened, there was only one thing they could do: kill him.

Escape? He thought about it, but he had no idea where he was or where he would go. His captors kept referring to the isolation. Too far to walk in the desert. He only knew that at some point, he would be rescued or murdered.

Were there any other prisoners? Not that he knew of, but he picked up bits and pieces of conversations that made him curious over time, but not about anyone or anything specific.

"Keep in mind," Gonzales said. "This is from a muffled word here and there over a period of weeks not long after they kidnapped me."

But, that too passed and his miserable little world continued its daily humdrum life. He never thought about it again. Not until tonight.

"Are there others?" he asked.

Ann Marie took his thin hands in hers and looked directly into his eyes. "We don't know. We hope and pray not, but we know it is a possibility."

The days slipped by too quickly for any of them. So much to cover; so little time to accomplish it. Years of world history had to be crammed into two weeks. They fed him a steady diet of the Internet, a presidential gambling scandal, a judicial challenge to the electoral college, the

Voices In The Fog

Israel and Palestinian situation, Afghanistan, Iraq and Iran, European nationalistic conflicts, tax reductions, corporate scandals, and the unending stream of news and pretend news that flowed from the twenty-four hour news channels.

He continued to amaze his hosts with his surprising ability to understand the issues they presented to him. Conversely, he had a nearly insatiable appetite for more information on the world he lost so long ago.

The days came to an end much too soon for any of them, but in spite of their power and ability, the calendar waits for no one. A few last things to cover. Administrative personnel changes at the court: Personnel Director retired, Data Services Director got married again, Reporter of Decisions recovering from a heart attack, a few new babies in the building custodial staff, a big argument between the news media and the U. S. Marshal about parking privileges, and an unending list of minor arguments and turf battles that afflict every segment of society.

"Enough," Gonzales finally quipped. "At least I know the world is going along as it always did."

"Yes, of course," Ann Marie said. "Look at the clock. If you're lucky, you might get three hours sleep before we get you to the airport." She placed the return tickets on the table in front of him. He looked at them for a moment, then touched them lightly with his fingertips.

"It is true. I'm going home." He sat in silence, staring at the tickets, then tucked them in the breast pocket of his shirt. "I'll be ready."

Morin took his hand and shook it firmly. "Your honor, I'll not be going to the airport with you, so for me, this is good-bye."

Gonzales stood, leaned over, and hugged the young man.

Voices In The Fog

"I will remember you for the rest of my life," he said. The judge turned and went to his room. He paused at the door, looked back at them and nodded.

*****

A golden sunset cast its brilliant glow over the nation's capital. The White House, the Washington Monument, the Memorial Bridge, and beyond the Capital Building, the United States Supreme Court Building at Capital and First Street.

Gonzales stepped off the ramp and was greeted immediately by his long time friend and driver, Winchester Tubfield. They greeted each other with a firm handshake. Gonzales stepped back a half-step and held Tubfield's arms. He looked him up and down, and spoke.

"My friend, what do you say we have some dinner? A steak!"

CHAPTER TWENTY-FOUR

Alfred Williams gathered the staff together in the common room, deep under El Capitan Mountain. It served several purposes: dining room, reading room, lounge, television, ping-pong, and any other cause that suited their desires. Today, though, was one of earnest discussion.

They were an elite cross-section of Americana. Sixteen people, including Ann Marie, Rod, Williams, Gosbeck, Cowboy Joe, and Dr. Hammond. They also included a physician; two physicists; a computer programmer; a Marine sharpshooter, cross-trained as an electrician; a Methodist preacher who also was a licensed nurse; a journeyman plumber and skilled carpenter; a chiropractor and master chef; and a retired newspaper reporter who daily documented the work of the safe site. All were highly respected in the arts and sciences of espionage.

Williams stood at a podium in front of an overhead screen. His casual dress of Levis, hiking boots, and a T-shirt belied the seriousness of his presence.

Williams spoke, "The first phase of our operation was flawless. Now, while we are on the sidelines, our associates are well into the second phase. It is most unfortunate that their operation has encountered a number of obstacles." He nodded to Gosbeck who dimmed the lights and flicked on the overhead projector.

Williams continued. "What you are seeing is a satellite view of the Yellow Sea, an arm of the Pacific Ocean between the Korean Peninsula and China. It's of little value to the United States and most of our allies, but is the home territory of a Chinese Xia class nuclear-powered ballistic missile submarines. Our government does not normally consider it or the Chinese navy as a whole any kind of threat on the high seas. Their submarines are loud, slow, and more of a value to them for morale's sake than a worry for us or our allies. But we believe that, after the recent losses they suffered in the Panama Canal, and the losses of their front organization and the imposter they placed on the Supreme Court, they now understand that the Russian foray was our feint while we carried out the real purpose of our efforts. This brings us to the Yellow Sea."

Williams pointed on the map to the southern tip of Korea. "In the last twenty-four hours, the submarine *Huludao* was detected by our submarines forces on station in the East China Sea. The *Huludao* steamed free of its home port, left the Yellow Sea, and now is swinging east along the thirtieth parallel. Its course appears to be taking it into the North Pacific, directly toward the United States."

A murmur swept through the gathering. Gosbeck switched to another satellite view of the Pacific, then angled the viewpoint up to the Bering Sea and the Aleutian Islands.

Williams continued. "Our intelligence services suggest that if the Chinese intend to retaliate, the *Huludao* will continue north and attempt to remain concealed in the rough seas near the islands and in the ice flow that covers so much of that part of the ocean. What they apparently are not aware of is that our submarines are unmatched in playing Blind Man's Bluff. We can and will stay on their fantail. If it appears they're going to try something, we'll take appropriate action."

He nodded to Gosbeck who brought up a file photo of the *Huludao*, the red star shining brightly against its tall, black sail. Gosbeck glanced back and forth from the overhead to his notes. Perspiration drenched his shirt. Ann

Voices In The Fog

Marie noticed his trembling fingers. His voice was scratchy.

"The *Huludao* - -" he coughed and cleared his throat, then continued, "is powered by a single nuclear reactor; fourteen thousand horse power. It has sixteen JL-2, Sea-to-Land missiles; twenty-one torpedoes; a crew of one-hundred officers and men, and may cruise at 22 knots. It's only the second of two boats of its class. Good news for us; bad news for them; the first one sank in fifteen thousand feet of water on its second cruise, probably the result of structural failure."

Williams again took control of the meeting. Ann Marie noticed the droplets of sweat on his brow.

"We will know within the next one hundred-twenty hours of their intent. If they do as we anticipate, they will move off the Alaskan coast to do one of two things. Launch a nuclear attack is the first possibility. From that distance, they could strike every major city from Kansas City to Seattle and down to San Diego. A second alternative would be to strike some American interest – a navy ship; a commercial fishing fleet; the oil pipeline – something that will get our attention and tell us we can and will be held accountable, yet allow them to remain in the shadows. It is almost a game. They know the Russians maintain a strong fleet in that area, and may try to make it look to us as if it was the Russians who did it. They'll try to turn the tables on us, so to speak. They hope to get us and the Russians going at it."

He paused, his comments being interrupted by the nervous chatter of his audience. He took a long drink of water, giving his charges time to get over their first reactions to the Chinese threat. He tapped his empty glass with his finger, bringing them back to attention.

Voices In The Fog

Williams continued. "Only once before, with the Cuba missile crisis, have we come so close to all-out nuclear war. I caution you to stay focused on your work, not to be distracted by your emotions. This is the moment that each of you has been trained for: the possibility of worldwide nuclear destruction. You will be kept as well informed as I am. I will withhold nothing from you. I assure you, we will not allow the *Huludao* to fire its missiles, but your guess is as good as mine as to how the Chinese hierarchy will respond. Simply stated, we do not know."

Ann Marie allowed her mind to free float. Five days, more of less. War? Seven years inside El Capitan Mountain? Brood mares? Her thoughts turned to her grandmother, then to her eager young students in school, their snotty noses and innocent hearts. How in God's name did this happen? How would it end? Worse yet, would it really be the end of it all?

The group broke off into informal clusters, chattering, gossiping, and worrying aloud. Rod caught her eye and they walked back to the living quarters. She took his hand in hers and held it tightly.

"I'm afraid. Scared out of my wits," she said.

"Join the club. This one is a big mess. We sure as hell had no idea where we were going on this, did we?"

"If it happens, will you stay with me?" She didn't wait for his response before she opened the door to her compartment and stepped inside. The only light was from a small nightlight.

Rod put his arms around her. The sweet scent of her perfume caressed him. He inhaled and held it. Their eyes met for what seemed like forever. He pulled her against him and kissed her. A mere brushing of the lips. She leaned her head on his shoulder and wrapped her arms around his waist.

"Please Rod, I'm so afraid." She looked up and saw his beautiful, reassuring smile.

"Forever," he whispered. "I'll love you forever." They kissed again; his hands massaged her hips, then reached for the buttons of her blouse; her fingers fumbled with his belt buckle. She led him to her bed. He put his lips to her mouth, then to her breasts. Chills ran the length of her body when he tasted her and caressed the whole of her nakedness. Finally, in a near state of exhaustion, she took his love into the depths of her soul.

*****

The Chinese Ambassador to the United Nations played his cards adroitly. It was a misunderstanding of the Russian troop movement. His government accepted the Russian explanation. Each side would withdraw their forces to their previous positions.

Ambassador Jung knew the Americans were behind the whole thing, but his government would deal privately with the Americans. There must not be any open discussion that would bring the covert operations into the forefront.

The Russian Ambassador also offered his explanation. Captain Soyuz Admonovich operated outside of military orders. The missile launch was not authorized. The submarine was re-called to port and the Captain would be tried. If found guilty, he will be executed for crimes against humanity. He slaughtered his own people, and must pay the ultimate price.

*****

Voices In The Fog

On board the *Huludao*, Captain Huang He commanded the boat to a depth of two hundred feet, east-northeast to a position in the turbulent shallow waters near the islands, but beneath the thermal layers of water that hid them from the prying eyes of American anti-submarine aircraft that patrolled the waters off the Alaska coast. While the depth would slow their timing, the current would offset that loss and put them into position within the week.

Captain He understood his orders. The Fleet Admiral himself, Admiral Laio, delivered them in person. The *Huludao* would maintain radio silence.

"Run silent. Run deep," Laio said. "Be wary of the Americans. They will search for you from the sky and from their submarines. The honor and dignity of the Peoples Republic is in your hands. The honor of your ancestors is at stake. You and your crew will be honored for all of history. You will not be forgotten. Redeem our honor, and you will be heroes of the people for generations to come."

The crew talked in only the slightest whisper, aware the Americans would quickly be alerted that their submarine was no longer patrolling the Yellow Sea. They would be hunted like mad dogs, but *Huludao* would prevail. The Americans would taste the bitter poison of defeat. If only in limited fashion, China would enjoy the sweetness of an embarrassing Yankee loss; a loss they would be unable to explain to their President or to the American people.

*****

Somewhat slower than he anticipated, Huang He positioned the submarine within a mile of the Russian submarine *Tomsk* on the ninth day after the Chinese left the safety above the 30th parallel.

The *Tomsk* was on routine patrol in the Gulf of Alaska, east-southeast of Kodiak Island. Their cruise was coming to an end. Only three more days and they would swing about and head for home. They played cat and mouse with the Americans, a not-unusual happening in these waters. Otherwise, a routine and tiresome voyage was almost over. In less than two weeks, the crew would be home with their wives and children. Morale was high. Food was adequate. They surfaced once, and for a few moments the crew went topside and enjoyed the taste and smell of fresh air. It was their best cruise in a long time, but they were ready to head for port.

Their sonar picked up the sound of the screw, but concluded that it was one of the older American boats out to provide relief to the nuclear sub they followed, or were followed by, for the last two weeks. Not much of a game with all that noise. Obviously, the Americans couldn't care less about who knew where they were or what they were doing. If he didn't know better, Captain Kazan thought the loud, grinding single screw was one of the Chinese subs, except they never ventured this far from home. For certain, it was an old U. S. boat.

Like his adversary, Captain Chester Puller of the American sub, USS Sea Wasp, ran silent and deep in the wake behind the *Huludao* as the Americans observed the Chinese sub.

"We have noises," the sonar operator said into his intercom. There was a pause while he adjusted his headset. "Sir, they're opening their tubes, but not toward us."

"What the hell are they doing?" the Executive Officer blurted

Voices In The Fog

"God damn, I think they are going to get the *Tomsk*, those crazy bastards." Puller whispered to his staff.

"*Ataka, ataka!*" the *Tomsk* sonar commander screamed into his microphone. "Their tubes are opening! They're in firing position and range."

"Right full rudder! Dive, dive! Battle stations," Kazan bellowed.

The *Tomsk* swung about, coming to a heading almost directly toward the *Huludao*. They were closing fast. In his headset, Kazan heard a torpedo in the water. One! Two!Three!

"Are they insane?" he asked to no one in particular.

"What the fuck are they doing?" He listened as the three torpedoes sped overhead. They were slow and imprecise. They faded into the dark sea. Moments later, the Russians picked up the booms of the torpedoes crashing into the undersea cliff a few thousand meters north of the submarine.

*****

Puller understood the Chinese game. Sink the Russian sub. It was that easy to understand. Chinese never venture into the North Pacific; only the Americans and the Russians play war games up there. The conclusion was simple. Sink a Russian sub and let the Yanks try to explain it. "Ready torpedoes," he commanded.

"Torpedoes loaded. One thousand-five hundred yards," the Executive Officer said.

"Fire One! Fire Two!" Puller ordered.

The Americans listened as the deadly fish bounded free from the tubes and darted through the icy cold water toward the *Huluado's* slowly spinning screw.

Voices In The Fog

Kazan screamed into his microphone. "Two of them. There are two American subs. One was hiding behind the other." There was a long pause while the Russians listened to the torpedoes hit the water and race toward the *Huludao*.

"They are insane," he whispered to his deck officer. "They'll hit their own people." He pulled off his headset and braced himself against the bulkhead. The first sub, the noisy one, made a hard turn to move out of the way, but it was much too slow.

The noise was deafening. First one, then the second torpedo hit the target.

The Russian and the American crews listened in eerie silence. The *Huludao* exploded, then broke up as it headed toward the bottom of the sea, taking its crew to their dark, cold graves.

Kazan brought his boat back around on a course that would take it toward the other submarine.

"Bastards," Kazan uttered. "They missed us and took out their own people, but I will not give them another chance."

He nodded to his weapons officer. "Fire one," he ordered. They listened for only the briefest moment. The torpedo started out the tube, then sounded like it was frozen in-place.

"What the hell - - ."

The explosion ripped back into the tube. It threw a raging fireball and shrapnel into the torpedo room. Within the first few seconds, the torpedo room crew was dead. Their shredded bodies were cremated instantly. The second explosion of their own torpedoes ripped through the *Tomsk*. Its hull split like a banana and fell into the depths of the ocean.

Voices In The Fog

It was all over in less than a minute. The two submarines and their entire crews were dashed to their graves. The frigid currents carried them to their eternal graves beneath the choppy waters.

CHAPTER TWENTY-FIVE

Two weeks crawled by. The skeleton staff at High Jinks was already tired of looking at one another, and the thought of spending several months underground in these close quarters was starting to wear thin on all of them.

Ann Marie took her tour of duty in the scullery after lunch when Williams came on the public address system.

"Attention. All hands report to the reading room." There was a pause, then he continued. "Good news, everyone. It's over."

She dropped a pan on the floor. It clattered on the cold tile like the bell at the end of a prizefight. She threw her damp apron on the drain board. This was no time for the niceties of life. She would get the hell out of there. She was ready for fresh air and sunlight.

Williams laughed, a deep belly laugh. Chairs were shuffled; people grabbed pillows to sit on; others made room for themselves on counter tops. Rita, the main computer geek, ran down the hall nearly naked. She wrapped a beach towel around her dripping body and bellowed out, "Okay people, I was in the shower, but nothing was going to stop me from getting here."

"My God, I never saw so many people move so fast in my life. But, I don't blame you. We can get out of here and get you back to your homes," Williams said as he paused for a moment. Ann Marie detected the humor of a few moments ago slip away. He was serious.

"We came very close to a major confrontation with the Chinese on one hand and with the Russians on the other. Now, though, tensions are alleviated, and we're calling this exercise over. The President and his staff worked around the clock in meetings and negotiations with the other parties involved, and everyone finally agreed to bury the

hatchet, at least for the time being. The Chinese acknowledged privately to the Russians what happened, and the Russians are more or less accepting the fact that their own torpedo caused the *Tomsk* to explode.
I do not make light of the loss of their boats or of their crews. Those are terrible losses.

"Of course," Williams continued, "we reached our objective without the loss of a single American life. We have returned Gonzales to his place on the bench. You did your jobs well. You did all you were asked to do, and each and every one of you excelled. You have served your country well, and the time has come for me to say, simply, thank you."

*****

With the title of "Case Agent," Ann Marie Beaudet was among the last to leave High Jinks. Her final report was written. She was ready to go. She gave a quick look around the house. It was just like the first night when she arrived. Lived in, but neat and clean.

"Will you do a last walk-through with me?" Cowboy asked. She slipped her hand into his and they walked toward the barn. The golden evening sun slipped behind the dark peak of El Capitan Mountain. The purple shadows of the gathering dusk crawled silently across the high country landscape.

She watched a pair of mourning doves swoop around the top of the barn, then land with the delicacy of ballerinas on the fence rail. She breathed deeply and tasted the sweet taste and scents of the open countryside. Its wild flowers opened their blooms to grasp the last rays of sunlight before they went to sleep.

Voices In The Fog

Cowboy hummed a nameless tune while they rode the elevator down to the seventh floor. The doors opened to reveal the long, sterile hallway in the subdued light of a building shutting down until the "next time."

They carefully inspected each of the rooms to make sure nothing was left behind: Towels were folded and stacked in the laundry room; beds stripped; lavatories cleaned; dishes, pots and pans neatly stacked in the pantry. All was in order! They were ready to close it down.

Ann Marie followed Cowboy up the stairs to the fifth floor and the energy management room. She watched him open the control panel and move the switches and breakers into the "power down" position. She heard the softening hum of the electrical units as they surrendered their power and might and lay quietly like a lion – asleep, but ready to spring back to life at a moment's notice.

The silence roared in her ears. They walked arm-in-arm like father and daughter, each quietly reminiscing in their own minds the thoughts and fears they experienced in the last few weeks.

Back outside, she found Rod putting his and her suitcases in the back of the pickup truck.

"When you get to the airport, just leave the keys under the seat and I'll pick it up later," Williams said.

Ann Marie took one last, wistful look around. The calm, beautiful hills; the wild grasses and flowers; the rolling plains. They belied the truth of El Capitan Mountain.

She stepped toward the truck, then paused to give a hug and kiss to her favorite cowboy and to Williams, her mentor and tower of strength.

"Tell me where you'll be going?" Cowboy asked.

"First things first," Rod responded.

Voices In The Fog

Ann Marie looked at him, and his gorgeous smile filled her heart with love. She put her finger to his lips and hushed him before he answered. She brushed her hair back from her forehead and for the first time in a long time felt totally at peace. "We're going to get married. And then we're going on a honeymoon wherever our hearts desire." She blew a kiss to them as she climbed into the truck. "We understand this type of marriage is similar to a husband and wife on submarine duty - - different subs for sure. We'll have periods we don't see each other, but we'll just have to live with it." She shrugged her shoulders, not in dismay, but in a heartfelt, cheerful mood. "Aren't you gentlemen married?" Her question was directed at Williams, but she already knew her answer from the wedding rings each of them wore.

The elder statesman smiled and nodded his head. "You're going to do fine. Good luck."

"We'll call you in a couple weeks," she promised. "We'll be back, and now anybody who tries to slip that veil of fog over us will have to deal with double trouble."

Rod started the engine and drove slowly down the bumpy dirt road toward the highway. Cowboy and Williams stood silently and watched their good friends and colleagues drive slowly down the hillside. The last rays of sunlight reflected off the back of the truck.

Printed in the United States
128671LV00003B/25/P

9 780978 884390